HAWKE

Billionaire Boys Club

ELLIE MASTERS

JEM Publishing

Editor: Erin Toland

Proofreader: Roxane LeBlanc

Interior Design/Formatting: Ellie Masters

Published in the United States of America

JEM Publishing

ISBN: 978-1-952625-08-4

Created with Vellum

Books by Ellie Masters

The LIGHTER SIDE

Ellie Masters is the lighter side of the Jet & Ellie Masters writing duo! You will find Contemporary Romance, Military Romance, Romantic Suspense, Billionaire Romance, and Rock Star Romance in Ellie's Works.

YOU CAN FIND ELLIE'S BOOKS HERE:

ELLIEMASTERS.COM/BOOKS

Military Romance

Guardian Hostage Rescue Specialists

Rescuing Melissa

*(*Get a FREE copy of Rescuing Melissa

when you join Ellie's Newsletter*)*

Alpha Team

Rescuing Zoe

Rescuing Moira

Rescuing Eve

Rescuing Lily

Rescuing Jinx

Rescuing Maria

Bravo Team

Rescuing Angie

Rescuing Isabelle

Rescuing Carmen

Rescuing Rosalie

Rescuing Kaye

Cara's Protector

Rescuing Barbi

Military Romance

Guardian Personal Protection Specialists

Sybil's Protector

Lyra's Protector

The One I Want Series

(Small Town, Military Heroes)

By Jet & Ellie Masters

EACH BOOK IN THIS SERIES CAN BE READ AS A STANDALONE AND IS ABOUT A DIFFERENT COUPLE WITH AN HEA.

Saving Abby

Saving Ariel

Saving Brie

Saving Cate

Saving Dani

Saving Jen

Rockstar Romance

The Angel Fire Rock Romance Series

EACH BOOK IN THIS SERIES CAN BE READ AS A STANDALONE AND IS ABOUT A DIFFERENT COUPLE WITH AN HEA. IT IS RECOMMENDED THEY ARE READ IN ORDER.

Ashes to New (prequel)

Heart's Insanity (book 1)

Heart's Desire (book 2)

Heart's Collide (book 3)

Hearts Divided (book 4)

Hearts Entwined (book5)

Forest's FALL (book 6)

Hearts The Last Beat (book7)

Contemporary Romance

Firestorm

(KRISTY BROMBERG'S EVERYDAY HEROES WORLD)

Billionaire Romance
Billionaire Boys Club

Hawke

Richard

Brody

Contemporary Romance

Cocky Captain

(VI KEELAND & PENELOPE WARD'S COCKY HERO WORLD)

Romantic Suspense

EACH BOOK IS A STANDALONE NOVEL.

The Starling

~AND~

Science Fiction

Ellie Masters writing as L.A. Warren

Vendel Rising: a Science Fiction Serialized Novel

Grab the First Book in The Guardian Hostage Rescue Specialists Series for Free

https://elliemasters.com/RescuingMelissa

ONE

Quinn

December 21st and my fledgling company, MindScapeVR, is hosting its first official office Christmas event. The party's in full swing. Fifteen minutes late and my timing couldn't be more perfect. Arriving early—hell, even on time—makes my skin crawl, like heebie-jeebies slithering across my arms kind of crawling.

I don't do well in crowds.

Music thumps through the walls. Raucous laughter punctuates the low rumbling of voices. Champagne infuses the air with a rich buttery aroma. The only thing calling to me is the champagne. I have to give it to my team. They certainly know how to party, but we have good reason to do so, given our success, or near success. There's still the matter of securing our venture investment capital.

As quietly as possible, I navigate down the hall, trying not to trip and sprain an ankle in three-inch heels. Whoever invented these torture devices needs to be shot. Not eager to join the party, I stop to breathe in the buttery effervescence of champagne. It grows stronger the closer I get. Eyes closed. Nose lifted. I savor the delicate scent, waiting for the lighter, fruitier taste of apple and pear to penetrate my senses.

The doors to the main lounge bang open, making me jump.

Ted, our lead engineer, drags Shirley, from accounting, into the hall. Arms entwine. Lips lock. Hips grind. They're all over each other. Like all over. She's practically dry humping him as I look on in shock.

I press against the wall and pray they don't see me.

Too engrossed in locking lips, groping hands, and the dry humping going on, my presence goes unnoticed. Ted pulls Shirley down the hall with a husky laugh toward the supply closet, while I give a little sigh.

Their passion gives me pause. I've never felt something like that, and if I'm completely honest, I'm jealous. Scott and I are affectionate, but we don't go at each other like animals. It makes me wonder if there's something broken inside of me.

With them gone, I can no longer delay my entrance.

Nobody notices me when I step into the room, but I'm used to that.

Decked out in silver and gold, pops of shiny red and white draw my eye. The office decorations are modern and garish, nothing like the traditional red and green I prefer, or the homemade decorations which make me think of family, friends, and Christmas.

"Q!" The shout snaps my head up. In the far corner, surrounded by his ever-present orbit of friends and admirers, my boyfriend and business manager, Scott, holds court.

Unlike me, he thrives on social interaction and is always the center of attention. He waves me over but doesn't get up from where his butt perches on the edge of a desk.

I must go to him.

With a sigh, I give a soft smile and wave. Now how to minimize any social entanglements?

Not that I don't like my coworkers. I love them. The issue is me. Awkward doesn't begin to describe me in social situations. I wish it weren't true. I'd love to be more like Scott and have people flock to me. Unfortunately, that's not my gift. I'm a nerd, not a social butterfly.

In addition to the bubbly effervescence, my nose wrinkles at the distinctive, acrid potency of hops.

Scott's favorite drink is beer, which is why there's a keg next to the champagne tower. I hate everything about beer, but not Scott.

He's a dream.

Back to making my way over to Scott. The direct approach is no-go land. Too many conversational landmines lie between me and him. This leaves skirting the edges of the room, which isn't a bad idea. My stomach rumbles, reminding me I, yet again, skipped lunch.

The catering company laid out an impressive spread. I take my time to savor a few of their seasonal offerings. Someone tugs on my arm while I shove a cocktail shrimp in my mouth. I spin around with the shrimp hanging half in, half out, of my mouth.

"Quinn! You made it." My best friend takes my hands and jumps up and down.

I suck the rest of the shrimp into my mouth and smile at Sadie with my mouth full.

Sadie changed for the party, ditching her black pants and form-fitting blouse for a skin-hugging, silver-sequined cocktail dress. Her hair sweeps up in an elegant up-do, and her makeup pops. My best friend is sorority cute, bubbly, and vivacious. She's everything I'm not and the only one in the office who calls me by my real name. I'm Q to everyone else.

She leans in. "Do you think he's going to pop the question tonight?" A little squeal escapes her as she jumps up and down. Her attention shifts to Scott then turns back to me. "I did some snooping."

"Sadie!" I lower my voice and lean in. "You shouldn't have."

"Well…" She glances around and whispers. In addition to being a terrible flirt, Sadie loves secrets, but she's incapable of keeping one. "When I went into his office, I saw a little black box." Another squeal escapes her. "And I may, or may not, have seen tickets to an all-inclusive couple's resort."

"You did?" My heart races, and a tickle of excitement runs through me.

Sadie gives a vigorous nod. "I did. Two tickets to an all-inclusive couple's resort called Euphoria." She gives a little squeak, then a long, breathy sigh. "Oh, I bet he proposes tonight."

I can't help but grin. It's perfect timing really, and I'm all about tying things up with neat little bows.

We should know whether our startup will be funded by the end of the year—less than ten days left. My dream might finally take off. Everything Scott and I have been working for is coming to fruition. Why not merge our private lives at the same time?

My attention shifts to my bare left ring finger, and my imagination goes wild. What kind of ring did he buy? I'm a minimalist. Clean, elegant lines are what I love. Scott is more flamboyant and likes to show off.

"Why are you over here checking out the buffet?" Sadie gives me a little shove. "Go get him."

She comes with me, but not before we fill up on finger foods as we graze down the buffet's length. In the end, Sadie grabs two flutes of champagne.

"Merry Christmas to start." We take a sip, then she lifts her glass again. "To a new year and new beginnings." Her gaze shifts to Scott, and her voice drops to a whisper. "I'm so happy for you." We clink our glasses and take another sip. I navigate the remaining space to my destination with Sadie by my side.

"Make a hole, guys." Scott's booming voice draws attention, and a gap appears in those gathered around him. "My best girl has arrived." His arms spread wide, and he stands to hug me.

I duck my head and smile while avoiding eye contact with those around him. Parties are so not my thing. But when Scott wraps his arms around me, I snuggle in and breathe out any lingering tension. He's my rock, the pillar I lean on for support. When I'm in his arms, the crowd no longer makes my skin crawl. Their eyes are on him and not me.

Sadie stands beside me and shamelessly flirts with the men gathered around us. I'm pretty sure she's slept with most of them. Sadie's gifted in getting around without getting around.

It's her superpower. I'm definitely not like that. Much more discreet, I've never had a one-night-stand and have no desire to do so.

As for Sadie?

She sees it as a challenge to explore all the flavors and varieties of men in the world.

"How are you holding up?" Scott tightens his grip, pulling me deeper into his embrace. He kisses the top of my head. "I'm thrilled you made it."

"I wouldn't miss this." Total lie. I'd rather be upstairs crossing T's, dotting I's, and doing it over again.

"I have something special planned." He squeezes me, and it's as if I'm blanketed in love. I could die right now and be perfectly happy.

"Attention." He raises his hand and shouts.

Everyone quiets and turns toward him. Scott nods to his buddy, Dan, who grins and walks around to the back of the desk.

"All eyes up here." Scott clears his throat and reaches into his pocket. He draws me forward half a step. "As you know, MindScapeVR is on the verge of greatness, and it's all due to Q's brilliant mind and your hard work."

I dip my head and stare at the ground. He's putting me on display, which is far outside my comfort zone.

Dan hops on the desk behind us. I naturally look up. Dan's grin stretches across his face as he dangles mistletoe over our heads.

My eyes widen as Scott gets down on one knee. "You're my best girl, Q. I love you to the moon and back, and I can't think of a better Christmas present than if you would agree to be my wife."

My hands go to my cheeks as he opens a tiny, black velvet box. I can't believe he's doing this here in front of our team, but it makes perfect sense.

"Q..." He looks up at me with love and adoration. "Will you marry me?"

I stare at the most perfect ring I've ever seen. It's flashier than I would like. Instead of a diamond, an emerald glitters in the light. The exact shade of my eyes, it's the one gemstone I absolutely adore.

"We need some kisses under the mistletoe." Dan clears his throat and gives the mistletoe a wiggle.

Scott glances up and grins. "You're keeping me in suspense here, Q. Don't make me wait to kiss you under the mistletoe."

"Yes!" Overwhelmed by his proposal, happy tears spill down my cheeks. My entire body shakes with excitement.

"Then give me your hand and let me put a ring on that finger."

The office erupts in shouts. They cheer as I give him my hand. He slides the ring on, and it's a perfect fit. Then he's on his feet and grabs me. In front of our entire team, he pulls me to him and presses his lips to mine.

It's nothing like Ted and Shirley's passionate kiss, but I'll take it. When I wrap my arms around him, someone shouts, "Get a room!"

Everyone laughs. The kiss ends.

Scott pulls a packet out from his suit pocket and lifts it in the air. "I don't know what the rest of you are doing over Christmas, but I plan to be on the beach with my fiancée." He hands me the packet and smiles. "Ten days in paradise. Just you and me. We leave first thing in the morning."

"You're amazing." I clutch the papers to my chest and lift on tiptoe to kiss him. Dan hops off the desk and runs around, raising the mistletoe over people's heads. Everyone laughs and plays along, kissing under the mistletoe.

"Let me see that rock." Sadie grabs my hand, and the next hour passes in a blur.

My social awkwardness disappears, and I actually have a little bit of fun. I talk more to my coworkers during the party than I have all week. They're excited by the initial testing of our VR technology suite. The initial medical studies show marked improvement of mental functioning in both dementia and Alzheimer's patients. We're going to change the world for the elderly affected with mental decline. It's not just groundbreaking research. It's earth-shattering.

Scott and I drift apart as his friends congratulate him. The women gather around me to fawn over my ring. I float on cloud nine and don't realize when the crowd thins out.

For the first time in my life, I close a party down. Scott, Sadie, and I are the only ones left. He says goodbye to Dan while Sadie pulls the papers out of my grip.

"Ten days, all-inclusive…" Her eyes scan our itinerary. "You know you have to fly to get to Euphoria?"

"Yeah, I'm kind of ignoring that right now."

Sadie knows everything about me, especially my fear of flying. "And?"

"How bad can it be?" I give a little shrug. "Scott will be with me, and I can't live my whole life afraid of flying." If our funding is secured, like I think it will be, I'll have a lot of flying in my future. Although, our VR technology may make even that superfluous. I'm so excited I practically bounce on my toes.

"He's a great catch, I'm so happy for you." Sadie glances over her shoulder to where Scott and Dan say goodbye. A sigh escapes her. "I guess that's one stallion I'll never get a chance to ride."

"Sadie!" A blend of athlete and nerd, Scott lucked out when looks and brains were being passed out.

"Oh, I'm kidding." She gives me a playful shove. "Now, you need to get home and pack." Propping her hands on her hips, she glances around the office. "I'll stay and clean up."

"You're the best." I give her a hug. It's late, and she's right. It'll be midnight by the time I get home. "I'm going to say goodbye to my fiancé." I like the way that rolls off my tongue. I head toward Scott.

"Awesome party, wasn't it?" Scott lifts my hand to his mouth and kisses my engagement ring. "Do you like it?"

"It's the best."

"You excited about our trip?"

"Very much. I'm going home to pack."

"Don't pack too much." He grabs my hips and pulls me to him. "I don't plan on letting you out of the hotel room."

I giggle as he nuzzles my neck, peppering me with kisses until he reaches my mouth. He tastes like beer, but I don't care. I loop my arms over his shoulders and enjoy the soft feel of his lips on mine.

"I'll pick you up just after five. You going to be okay on the plane?"

My fear of flying is no secret. It's a major phobia complete with full-scale meltdowns, but I'll figure something out.

"With you by my side, I'm not afraid of anything." I refuse to allow irrational fear to hold me back. It's time to face my anxiety about flying, and that might not be a bad New Year's resolution: overcome irrational fear of flying.

"I love you, Q. We're going to do great things together." He gives a light slap to my butt. "Now go. I'm already packed." He glances over his shoulder, where Sadie bustles around picking up red cups. "I've got a couple things to wrap up in my office, then I'm headed home."

"I love you too." He kisses me on the nose and leads me to the elevators, where he pushes both the up and down buttons.

My elevator car arrives first. He blows me a kiss as the doors close. My stomach drops as I head down. Enclosed spaces aren't really my thing either.

I make it all the way to my car, only to realize I left my keys on my desk. With a frustrated sigh, I push the up button and head back up.

TWO

Quinn

THE MAIN LIGHTS ARE OUT WHEN I STEP OFF THE ELEVATOR. No surprise. Building maintenance shuts most things off when no one's working. Every third fluorescent light remains on, but they flicker, and that always bugs me.

I can walk these halls blindfolded, but I prefer bright lights. It feels less spooky. When the team heads out to hit the bars, I stay behind, writing code that will one day make us millions. I typically avoid the halls and sprint from my office to the elevator to avoid the flickering lights. My mind conjures zombies wandering the halls, eager to devour human flesh, and I hate everything about zombies.

My office sits at the far end of the hall, right beside Scott's corner office. All the offices are dark, doors closed. Except for the hum of the air handlers, it's quiet, the kind of quiet I find soothing during the day. At night, my mind goes to zombie-land.

I'd be working tonight, except there's no more work to do. Everything's sent, and we're less than two weeks from the new year. Two weeks from finding out if our venture capitalist will fund our project and make all our dreams come true.

Light spills from beneath the crack of Scott's office door. I'll say a quick goodbye before heading home to pack, but first, I retrieve my keys from my desk. Quiet wraps all around me. The carpet muffles my steps. A low moaning makes me jump.

I spin around. My active imagination fills my head with zombies. The sound repeats and comes from behind Scott's door. I cock an ear. There it is again.

I know that sound. It's the sound Scott makes when he's on top of me.

Tiptoeing toward the door, my hand shakes as I grasp the doorknob. A little twist and I pause at the sound of a female voice.

"Oh, yes! Yes! Right there." I know that voice too and release the doorknob as if I've been shot.

"Goddamn, but you're a good fuck." Scott's deep voice rumbles through the door.

I shove a knuckle between my teeth to hold back a sob.

"Harder, baby. Fuck me harder," Sadie cries out.

My heart wedges sideways in my throat.

How could she?

How could he?

I turn. It's instinctual. More of a run and hide kind of girl, I handle conflict poorly. With a lump in my throat, a series of emotions rush through me: shock, anger, indignation.

Shame.

I feel bad for snooping.

Snooping! I hate how I'm always so goddamn apologetic.

How dare they?

The two people in the world I love the most?

I spin back around and grab the door handle. The emerald catches my eye. With my heart pounding like a jackhammer, my hand shakes as I twist off the ring. Blood rushes past my ears, a low roar rages in my veins. I curl my fingers around the damn ring.

"Harder. Goddammit, fuck me harder." Sadie's voice makes me grit my teeth.

"You like it rough, you little bitch?" Raw and hoarse, I barely recognize Scott's voice.

"Yes, Sir!" she screams. "Smack my ass."

"Damn! You're a kinky bitch." A loud crack makes me jump. Sadie's low moan brings tears to my eyes.

Something shifts inside of me. All the love, which filled my heart, pours out in a flood of betrayal, hurt, and misery. I shove the door open and fling the ring at Scott's head. Naked below the waist, his hips thrust forward. Sadie bends over his desk, hands grasping the far side as he fucks her from behind.

"Ow." He raises his hand to the back of his head. When he looks over his shoulder, his face pales. "Q..."

"Don't Q me, you fucking asshole."

He pulls out of Sadie, and she scrambles to pull her dress down.

I point at her. "And you! You—you fucking bitch!" My voice cracks as my fingers curl.

For a moment, I consider launching at the both of them. I want to slap his face and pull her hair, but me and conflict don't get along. This is way outside my comfort zone. A whole body shake rattles through me as I struggle to take a breath. Unable to form any more words, I pivot and rush down the dimly lit hall.

"Shit!" The sound of Scott buckling his pants makes me grit my teeth.

Don't cry.

Don't give them the satisfaction. But hot tears fill my eyes.

I stab at the elevator down button. Jabbing it over and over.

"Come on. Come on." I don't want to face them. I can't.

"Q!" Scott shouts from down the hall. He's coming after me. "It's not what you think."

I spin around and don't give a flying fuck about the tears streaking down my face. "I'm pretty certain it's exactly what I think."

"No." He holds out a hand, begging. "It's the last time."

"Last time? You mean that wasn't the first time? How long have you been fucking my best friend?"

Sadie appears behind him. She struggles to adjust her dress. For some reason, her betrayal cuts deeper than Scott's. It should be the other way around, but it's not. What does that say about my feelings for Scott?

"Quinn, we were just blowing off some steam." Sadie wrings her hands and hovers behind Scott.

"Looks like that's not all you've been blowing, you fucking bitch."

She grabs at Scott's arm. The gesture is natural, practiced, and tells me everything I need to know. They're together.

"Why?" I swipe at my tears. "Why propose to me when you're fucking her behind my back?" I don't understand. "And you? How could you do this to me?" Sadie's betrayal cuts deep.

"Come on, Q, don't overreact." Scott takes a step forward, but I hold up a hand, halting him. "Let's talk this through."

"Talk it through? You're fucking my best friend." My ex-best friend. "There's no talking through this. We're done." I wrap my arms around myself and struggle not to lose my shit. Where's the goddamn elevator? Why is it taking so long? "I want you gone. Both of you. Pack your shit and leave. You're fired. I never want to see either of your faces again."

"You're firing me?" Scott's eyes widen, then an indignant expression replaces the shock on his face.

"Damn straight."

"You can't fire me." His lips twist.

"Yes, I can. You're done here. Pack your things and leave."

His arms cross, and he slowly shakes his head. "That's not happening."

"I want you out of here by morning."

Why is he still standing there?

Sadie won't look at me. She cowers behind him. Her damn hand clutches the curve of his bicep as her eyes shift between me and him. He takes a step forward and she shuffles in lockstep with him.

"There's no way I'm walking away from this," he says. "Not when we're so close."

"It's my idea—"

"But my company."

"Our company." And we're two weeks away from launching,

providing we secure investment capital. We can't afford this shit show, but here we are.

"*My* company." His lip pulls up in a sneer.

I don't like the way he emphasizes 'my,' or the way he broadens his stance. That's what he does when he plays hardball. Never in a million years did I think I would be on the receiving end of that look.

"We're done here."

"No, Q." The corner of his lips curls up. "We're not done. We're going to fix this."

"Then, I quit." I've been working nonstop for the past two years, living and breathing my creation. I can't walk away from it.

"You won't." He sounds sure of himself, but then he knows me. "No way you're walking away. I know you, and you'll be back, right where you belong." He snickers. "Take a few days and think about this, *really think about it.*"

"You proposed. You said you loved me. What the hell?"

"You're a great girl, Q, but not so great in bed. It's not my fault I need to look elsewhere."

"This is my fault?" I press my finger to my breastbone, stunned by his audacity to pin this on me.

His words cut deep and hurt all the more because they're true. We never had the kind of passion I witnessed between him and Sadie, and nothing at all like Ted and Shirley desperately groping each other in the hall.

It's a sobering truth. I suck in bed.

The elevator call bell dings, and the doors slide open.

"You sleep around, and it's my fault?" My voice cracks as I back into the elevator, cheeks heating, tears falling, nose running, and heart breaking—because I believe him. I believe this is all my fault.

He gives a shake of his head. "We make a good team, Q. Give it a few days and you'll realize this is nothing. Why don't you sleep it off, and we'll talk in the morning?"

"Sleep it off?"

"Once you calm down, we'll talk through it." He spreads his arms out wide. "I don't want to lose you. We need you." His sneer turns into that charming smile I fell in love with. But I see something stirring in his eyes.

Fear.

What does he have to fear? He's not the one losing everything.

"There's nothing to talk through." I stab at the button marked L2.

As far as him needing me, that's the only thing he says that makes sense. He can't launch without me. Not to mention, our funding is yet to be secured. If the investors request any changes, Scott *will* need me. I'm the one thing I can take from him. He may not care about me, but he needs my brain.

As the elevator doors close, I roll back my shoulders and look him square in the eyes. "I don't need to sleep anything off. I quit." My entire body shakes. I really suck at confrontation, and I feel as if I've fought a massive battle and lost. Adrenaline surges through my veins, speeding up my heart rate, and making my nerves buzz. My hand shakes and I curl my fingers to keep him from seeing how out of control I really am.

He calls out. "We'll talk this through tomorrow."

Fat chance.

THREE

Quinn

Needless to say, I barely sleep. It's four in the morning when I give up and crawl out of bed. My entire body still shakes from last night. Not to mention my brain won't stop. It's caught on an endless replay of Scott fucking Sadie.

I'm hurt. Angry. Shocked. And more than a little pissed.

If it wouldn't buy jail time, I'd cut Scott's dick off and shove it where the sun doesn't shine.

Bastard.

And the nerve to say it's *my* fault? I'm still working through that.

After I take a long shower, where I cry my eyes out for the hundredth time, I remember the all-inclusive trip Scott planned to Euphoria.

He wants me to think about it? To calm down and slink back to him with my tail tucked between my legs and my dignity shattered beyond repair?

That's not happening.

Since the whole dick-whacking is a no go, I turn to the trip.

Think about it? Clear my head?

I *will* oblige the bastard. The trip is paid for, and while it means flying alone, I'm too angry to bother about my silly fear of certain death in an airplane.

After I dress, I look for the itinerary and check the time. The next few minutes see me racing around my apartment, packing what I hope I'll need for the next ten days. I check into my flight, splurge on a first-class upgrade, and cancel his ticket.

It feels good to take charge of something, even something as small and meaningless as canceling his ticket. Not that I think he'd show up, but it gives me a sense of power and control. Those two things are sorely lacking in life right now.

Before I can think about what I'm doing, and do the reasonable thing, like back out of this hair-brained idea, I call for a car and race to the airport. I'm late, but I have no bag to check, which means I head straight for the line at security.

Goosebumps lift on my arms as I make my way through the line. A tingle of anticipation runs through me, warning me this is a bad idea, as does the certain knowledge I'll soon be sealed inside what practically amounts to a flying coffin.

The urge to turn around overwhelms me, but my bag disappears inside the X-ray scanner, and one of the TSA officers gives me an irritated look when I hesitate outside the full-body scanner.

"Miss, please step inside. Hands over your head."

Feels more like getting arrested than traveling to a dream vacation.

Amid the stares of the passengers queueing up behind me, my feet move. My hands lift over my head. I'm scanned for weapons, explosives, and whatever else it is they're looking for that I don't have.

"Exit now." The TSA officer barks at me as I leave the scanner. He holds up a hand. "Just a moment." His attention shifts to a screen. Before I can back out, he waves me on. An older gentleman steps into the scanner behind me, and I grab my bags off the belt.

You can still turn around. Nothing's stopping you.

Except Scott's hurtful words. *My fault.*

Screw him. It's not my fault, but my inner voice says otherwise. Maybe if I had been wilder and more exciting in bed, I wouldn't be standing here watching white tin-can monstrosities land and take off.

Standing in front of the plate glass windows is not where I need to be, but I need to double-check my gate. Some asshole thought posting the monitors in front of those windows was a goddamn good idea.

Despite running late, I made up time by not checking a bag. All I have are my backpack and a small carry-on. I can't believe I'll be on a plane soon.

Every second, my heart pounds faster. The urge to ditch this act of rebellion grows stronger and stronger. Not that this is really a rebellious act. It's more like giving Scott the proverbial finger. If he wants me to *really think about things*, then I'll do just that. And I'll do it on his dime.

In paradise.

Bastard.

Strangers rush all around me as I tighten my grip on my carry-on. There's no way I'm going to make it through this alone. I need a little help and do a quick google search about anxiety and flying.

Evidently, alcohol helps. As does cold medicine.

One of those sundry stores sits right next to my gate. With fifteen minutes before boarding, I head inside. The books distract me, but I move on to the tiny shelf holding cold and flu medicines. What I want isn't here, but those little bottles of liquor are right next to the checkout counter.

I grab three of the little bottles, not caring what they hold. The long line bothers me. They're going to begin boarding soon. My hope is the first-class ticket will make the flight less terrifying. Maybe I won't feel like I'm crammed into a metal box with three hundred of my newest best friends, aka strangers, as we hurtle toward our death.

We are, after all, counted as 'souls on board.'

That's what they call us. We're automatically counted among the dead from the moment the outer door seals us inside until it opens again on the other side.

I'll be a *soul*, not a person.

With a sigh, I move to the front of the line and spy the cold remedies the cashier keeps behind the counter. Someone is looking out for me.

"Can I have some of that?" I point to the Benadryl.

"Anything else?" The cashier grabs a bottle of Benadryl and places it on the counter.

"Just these." I place down the mystery novel I snagged and three little bottles of booze.

The man behinds me coughs as I flip open my purse to pay. I pull out a credit card. The cashier glances at my card, then flippantly points to the huge sign on the card reader, which says, *'Reader not working. CASH ONLY.'*

"Oh, sorry."

The man behind me shifts in place, getting impatient as I dig through my purse for the one thing I don't have. Cash.

I stand like an idiot. Mouth agape, unable to form words. My cheeks heat with embarrassment.

"Uh, I'm sorry. I don't have cash." I'm not really sure why I keep standing there. With no way to pay, I should leave, but I desperately need that Benadryl if I'm going to make it through this flight. This must be what an addict feels when they can't get their next fix.

"Here." An arm reaches over my shoulder. The man behind me hands over a fifty-dollar bill. "Add this, if you will." He places a bottle of water down on the counter.

Not used to charity from strangers, I'm not sure if I'm more embarrassed for the help than not being able to pay.

He's a little older than me, maybe late twenties, early-thirties, though it's hard to tell because I'm completely captivated by his eyes. They shine like burnished gold and hide secrets I want to uncover. I don't know why that is. It's a very uncharacteristic thought for me to have.

His expression is closed. Guarded. Whatever thoughts swirl in his head, they're locked behind the impenetrable gates of his remarkable eyes.

I itch to pry open his secrets, but there's a warning in his eyes. It tells me doing so is dangerous, and I should fear what I find. Doesn't matter; I'm still undeniably captivated.

His phone alerts with an incoming text. The frown on his face after he reads it somehow makes him appear more handsome than less. More authoritative and striking than his overwhelming presence already suggests. And while he's decked out in a designer suit, tailored to the exquisite perfection of his form, the three days of stubble which peppers his jaw is an imperfection which doesn't match the manicured nails, tailored suit, and expensive watch.

Tiny worry lines edge the corners of his eyes, either from strain, stress, or pain. It doesn't matter, because like the scruff of his beard, that tiny flaw adds more than it takes away.

I can't get beyond the glow in his eyes. If one were to venture close enough, those eyes would pull them in and devour them. But I don't get a chance to feel that pull, because he dismisses both me and the cashier with a curt, "Keep the change."

Before I can thank him, he grabs the bottle of water and marches out of the store. Everything about him screams danger and caution. I'd go after him, but he rushes out without a backward glance. His phone goes to his ear, perhaps answering that text.

Not that it matters. I have a plane to catch.

As for change, our total bill comes to less than twenty dollars. That's one hell of a tip.

The cashier rings up the purchase and hands me the change.

"I think he meant for you to keep it." I try to hand it back.

The man shakes his head. "I can't do that." He bags my things. "Consider it a gift."

"You sure?"

"It'll hold you over until you get to a cash machine." He gives me a soft, understanding smile.

"Is there one that's close?"

"Not really." He rattles off a gate number too far away.

Overhead, the gate attendant for my flight announces pre-boarding.

Evidently, I'm now thirty some odd dollars richer.

"Thanks. I really appreciate it."

With my purchases in hand, I make a quick pit stop in the ladies' restroom. It's there that I open the bottle of cold medicine. The directions are pretty clear, but I double up on the dose. This stuff needs to knock me out; otherwise, I'm not going to make it.

With my entire body a buzzing jangle of nerves, I wait by the gate. They announce boarding for first class, and I squeeze my eyes shut.

Last chance to back out.

I'd leave, except with my eyes shut, all I see is Scott's naked butt and Sadie bent over the desk. I sway a little as the cold medicine takes effect and reaffirm my decision to place my life in the law of probabilities.

The chance of this particular plane going down is astronomical, and I'm betting the pilots aren't interested in dying. That means, technically, it's safe. Right?

Unfortunately, logic doesn't hold a candle to fear. My palms slick with sweat, and the only reason I move forward is because of the pushy lady behind me.

"Move along. Move along." She shoves at me.

Geez, what's the rush? We're boarding in first class.

Nevertheless, her rudeness provides the stimulus I need to get my feet in gear. My ticket is scanned, and I file down the chute to what I hope won't be an untimely death. Inside, I feel like we're all cattle going to slaughter.

My heart pounds so fast it's going to explode if it doesn't slow down. My body barely holds itself together as my grip on my carry-on tightens.

But then I'm there, at the end of the jetway. One step puts me inside the living coffin. I squeeze my eyes shut and ignore the fear edging in on me. One step and I'm on board.

First class does not disappoint. It's spacious, lots of leg room, and dammit if I don't have a window seat. Exactly what I don't need. My lips press together as I consider taking the aisle seat. I'm sure my row partner won't mind? Maybe?

I stow my things overhead, keeping my backpack with the liquor, books, and cold medicine at my feet, and plop into the aisle seat.

Those around me do the same, stowing their gear, as people line up behind us. General boarding has begun. I clamp my seatbelt and draw it tight in preparation for the hurtling into the air part of this trip.

When the flight attendant asks if I want a glass of champagne, I don't hesitate and down it in two long swallows. He doesn't blink when I ask for another, and I slam that one down as well.

My lips feel a bit tingly, as does the tip of my nose. People file past, all in a rush to find their seats. First class fills up with the exception of the seat next to me. I'm thrilled by this. With my people skills, sitting next to a stranger is fraught with all kinds of questions.

Do I say hi?

Do I smile?

What about asking where they're going?

What they do for a living?

If they have a family?

Or what about closing my eyes and pretending they don't exist? That sounds like the best option.

I sway in my seat as the alcohol hits my system. Or maybe that's the cold medicine taking effect? Either way, I'm ready for a nap. Considering I got next to no sleep last night, that sounds perfect.

FOUR

Hawke

A TEXT DEMANDING MY IMMEDIATE RESPONSE POPS ON MY SCREEN. Mother is in her usual imperious mood. The world revolves around her. Nothing else matters.

Doesn't matter what I'm doing at the time. She doesn't tolerate having to wait. I should step out of line, but I'm next up. A frazzled looking woman stands in front of me holding three tiny alcohol bottles in her hand, a book is clutched under her arm, and she stops to ask the register clerk about cold medicines.

With great effort, I school myself to patience. Mother can wait a minute or two.

A minute turns to several when the woman in front of me is unable to pay. She pulls out her credit card, oblivious to the big sign on the card reader that says *Cash Only*.

Instead of waiting for her to sort it out, I pull a fifty from my wallet and pay for us both. I storm out of there without a receipt or change.

Not that I care.

Once I'm free of the store, I find a quiet corner to do battle with my mother.

I hate the way she keeps me under her thumb. One day, I'll be rid of her, but she's tenacious enough to outlive me out of spite. If I don't play by her rules, however, I'll never see a dime of my inheritance. I grit my teeth in frustration and play her little game.

Normally, I would've answered her first text. I waited until the second to tell her I would be with her shortly. Talking to her while standing in line at the airport is grounds for disaster.

I need the space to give her my undivided attention. From her reply, that was not the correct answer. Her third text demanded an immediate response. I slapped down that fifty without a care about change and dutifully answered my summons.

That's what this is. She's not a loving mother reaching out to her son during the holidays. She would never lower herself to that level. Something's wrong, likely some bug up her butt. Most likely, I've disappointed her and she feels a need to remind me how I've failed her expectations.

I find a quiet corner and place myself on a video call. Passengers rush all around me. It's crowded, but no one pays attention to anything except where they're going.

Mother picks up on the first ring, and her pinched expression stares out of the screen full of judgment and disappointment.

"About time, Hawke. You have no respect, keeping me waiting like that."

"Good afternoon, Mother." I greet her with a stiff nod. "I have a plane to catch, so we must make this quick. What's the emergency?"

I'm not against going on the offensive. She twists everything to make it look like I'm the one with an attitude. It's best to attack first rather than respond to whatever it is she intends on throwing at me.

"Well," she says with a huff. "I suppose you needed time to extricate yourself from between whatever pair of legs are the flavor of the week." Her nose pinches with disgust.

"I was not…" My fists curl as I control my temper. She doesn't need to know how close to the truth her words come. I spent last night with two pairs of shapely legs wrapped all around me. Hopefully, I'll do the same tonight, once I reach Euphoria.

"Please, don't pretend you weren't." She always seems to know about my sexual exploits. I don't know how. I'm discreet to a fault.

"What do you need?" I school myself to patience. "What's so important you must interrupt my vacation?"

"So, you're finally admitting it is a vacation." Her gaze sharpens with her derisive tone. "And here you had me convinced you were working. I take it you're headed to your little pet project?"

She hates everything about Euphoria. Listening to her, a person would think Euphoria was a heathen cesspool of STDs, unwilling sex slaves, and a nonstop orgy.

It couldn't be further from the truth. I've created a paradise for couples to immerse themselves in romance. We cater to every fantasy; to either rekindle a couple's love or to allow new lovers to explore their fantasies together for the first time.

Our honeymoon suites sell themselves. That's how strong our word of mouth advertising has become. As for a nonstop orgy, we're not that kind of resort. Everything caters to bringing *couples* together, romantic interludes to satisfy every palate. I operate a classy, high-end exclusive resort, and I won't have her tear it down.

If Mother knew the truth, that I'm a hopeless romantic at heart, she'd string me up by the balls and remind me there's no room in life for love.

"If you're asking, I am going to Euphoria. I finished, and sent, my recommendations yesterday."

"Received and rejected. Were you even thinking when you went through the proposals? Did you read any of them?" Her derisive snort lifts my shoulders to my ears. It takes effort to forcibly relax and endure her verbal dressing down. "I'm not accustomed to such sloppy work, although considering what I have to work with…" She makes a dismissive gesture aimed directly at me.

I'm used to her disappointment. I'll never be enough in her eyes, but I won't cower beneath her ridicule.

Not anymore.

"I gave careful consideration to all the proposals. I read every word. It's in what I sent, and summarized for you." She never reads the reports I diligently pass to her desk, but she pours through every word of my summaries.

A matriarch more than a mother, she's the family tyrant. Her word is law, and the rest of us have no choice but to fall in line. I've been bucking her authority since I was five, trying to separate myself from her power trips and abusive manipulation because deep down I wanted to believe there was more to life than the cold heart of a mother incapable of love.

She sits in the center of her kingdom, a traditional Georgian mansion steeped in the tyranny of the past. Her parlor occupies the majority of the west wing, overlooking her prize-winning rose garden.

Nothing in the room has changed since I was a boy. Not the priceless antiques, the overstated Victorian furniture, or the family portrait of my great-great-great-whatever grandparents.

Mounted beside that monstrosity is a picture of our family; Mother and Father with me lying on the floor and my twin sister cradled in Mother's arms. The only smile in that painting is on the beautiful face of my sister, Cherise.

The only thing which has changed in the room in decades is Mother, herself. She's thinner and more pale than I remember. It may be the lighting of the video call, but to me, she looks old and frail.

Her skin's lost its radiant glow, sagging more than I remember. The lines of her face are more noticeable. Her raven locks, the one feature I inherited from her, are speckled with gray and hang limply around her shoulders. The only thing which remains of the mother I know is the piercing set of her eyes.

That same predatory expression sits on her face now, just like in the painting.

A flood of memories wash over me. Back then, we were happy. We didn't know a few short years separated us from disaster. We didn't know what would happen to my twin sister.

An innocent mistake forever changed her life. My mother will never forgive me for what happened, although she's the one who left two children alone and unsupervised by the pool.

I didn't mean to push Cherise into the water. I don't have any memory of the event, but my mother's blame is something I've endured for a lifetime.

My sister lives with the aftereffects of that fateful day. She survived but went too long without oxygen; her life profoundly affected as a result.

Unlike me, she's happy, blissfully unaware of the horrifying consequences of that one act.

I did that, and Mother never lets me forget it.

Even if I'd only been five at the time.

Even though I'm not the one who left two children alone to grab another bloody mary.

Even though, I'm the one who pulled Cherise from the pool, nearly drowning myself in the process.

If not for me, Cherise would be dead. I saved her. I've always believed Mother wished Cherise had truly drowned instead of survived.

I take a deep breath and remind myself the past can't be rewritten.

"What is it you found so inadequate?" I researched the hell out of each proposal, digging deep into not only the business plans put forth by the eager hopefuls praying for the capital investment of funds to make their dreams a reality, but also by researching their backgrounds and personal lives in addition to their proposals. My work is solid, and Sterling Enterprises will reap the rewards of the solid investment of our venture capital.

"You denied two of the top ten that show the most promise. This is our future, Hawke. How many times do I need to explain the simplest thing? You can't afford to make the wrong decision. Any fool knows the future is in technology. Virtual reality is the next wave, and we need to be riding its crest, not scrambling to keep up. You took…"

"I made a detailed analysis of each proposal. They weren't discarded out of hand."

One of those is a very promising virtual reality start-up, but their proposed business plan lacks development for full implementation. They're onto something extraordinary but without a sound business plan, it's doomed to fail. Of course, I could step in and take over, but I don't have the time for another pet project. Time is money, and my time is infinitely valuable.

My mother gives one of her false smiles, the complete opposite of genuine. Her imperious gaze stares out of the screen. Those hazel eyes of hers shift, flicking downward as if she can't stand the sight of me.

Across the way, they begin boarding for my flight. As a first-class passenger, I should be first to board, but I need to wrap up this call.

I don't know what turned my mother's heart to a frigid block of ice. She's surrounded by wealth and success; success from a generation's long family legacy. When I took the reins of the family business after father's death, her wealth doubled from what it once was, precisely because of the investments I chase.

I'm very good at my job.

It's not my fault she's dead inside. And no matter what she says, my decisions are well-grounded with an eye toward future profitability.

I might be the CEO of Sterling Enterprises, but I answer to the controlling member of our board who happens to be my mother. She never lets me forget I serve her pleasure and not the other way around. My control, what little I have, is merely an illusion.

"Well, I disagree." Her pinched expression tightens. "I want you to invite the authors of all ten proposals to Atlanta the first week of the new year. We'll make our decision then." Her imperious use of *our* makes my skin crawl.

"With all due respect, my recommendations stand. They're well thought out. I've already consulted with the rest of the board…"

"I don't care who you consulted." Her sharp tone cuts deep. "Send the invites. I expect you to attend."

Of course, she does. She wants to lord her power over me.

I brace for a slap in the face. A reminder that my inheritance is not mine. That she can easily ensure I never see a dime of what's owed.

"It's my money," her acidic tone continues, "not yours, maybe never yours if you continue with your insolent tone. We'll invest as I decide. Not you."

"Then why have me look at the proposals at all?"

I hate the way she undermines me. I hate being held under her tyrannical thumb. Someday, I'll be free of her manipulations.

There's enough money in my trust fund that I could walk away. I'd have to work to make it stretch. I don't, not because I'm greedy and crave the money. I stay because I can do so much with the power and reach Sterling Enterprises brings. I'm damn good at what I do.

"Do as you're told." She gives another dismissive wave, but this time punctuates it with a snort. "But that is not why I wanted to speak with you."

"It's not?" There is nothing but business for the two of us to talk about. "I have a plane to catch, so make it quick."

The gate attendant completes pre-boarding and begins boarding the first-class passengers. I should be on the plane sipping champagne by now. Instead, I'm shoved into a corner, speaking with a tyrant.

"It's Cherise." She gives a stiff shake of her head.

"What's wrong with Cherise?" A chill worms down my spine. If anything's happened to Cherise, I won't survive it. "I spoke to her yesterday. She seemed in good spirits. Happy about her orchids." Clueless about the time of year. She has no idea it's Christmas, a time when most families gather together to celebrate familial bonds. Instead, our family scatters to the wind.

Mother does her thing. I run away. And sweet Cherise takes care of her precious orchids.

"Cherise is fine. It's her future I worry about. One which needs to be decided."

I take a deep breath, glad everything is good with my sister.

"And this involves me how?"

Like me, Cherise has a trust fund. Bestowed on us both after our father's death, it provides a modest income. For Cherise, it ensures her medical attendants are well paid. My sister lives a simple life, full of joy and little else, but then she's stuck at the developmental age of a five-year-old.

Mother taps the edge of her desk. The clicking of her manicured nails sends a shiver down my spine. It's all I can do not to look away or fidget beneath her withering gaze.

"You know what it involves." She pins me with a look.

"Is this really the time to bring that back up?" With great difficulty, I hold my temper in check.

"There's never a *good* time. You're dismissive of your obligations."

"Obligations to whom? You?"

She answers with a derisive snort.

"The family name must continue, and that requirement rests on your shoulders. Your sister is incapable, which leaves you."

Me.

The only heir to the Sterling empire.

"We've discussed this." There's no way I'm tying myself to any woman, especially none of the purebred, feeble-minded, vapid socialites Mother's presented in the past.

"You refuse to see reason?"

"I'm not settling down."

I'm not getting married. Not when I can have whomever I want in my bed with the snap of my fingers.

Besides, women are greedy little whores who chase after the best catch they can snag. With Sterling Enterprises sitting on twelve-billion in assets, I'm a pretty fucking good catch.

"That's right. You're still prancing around like a young stud, sticking your dick in anything with two legs, with no care about the family."

"Mother!" Her vulgar language is unexpected and completely out of character. My mother is perfectly poised to a fault.

"Oh, don't be a prick about it. You think I can't say a few choice words. You've really left me with no choice."

"In this, you have no say. It's my life, and I'll live it as I please."

"It's my life, my family, and you'll do as you're told." Her eyes gleam in the way they always do when she has the upper hand and her opponent is, as of yet, unaware of her victory.

Always conniving, my mother is one of the sharpest women I know. She's likely the smartest person I know as well. And she's definitely the most skillful at manipulating others into doing as she says.

I've no idea what she's going to say next, except I won't like it. I hold my tongue and bide my time. She wants a reaction, but I refuse to give her anything. I've done all I can other than tell her to stay the fuck out of my life.

The gate attendant begins general boarding. There's no reason to rush to stand in line now. I'll wait and be one of the last to board, and hopefully conclude this troublesome conversation.

"You're stubborn like your father, but you're smarter than him. He knew not to irritate me with his bullheadedness."

"Is that what you think? I'm being bullheaded?"

"I think you believe your little rebellious project is something I'll ignore. Should I ask how many girls you're planning to fuck? Using my name to satisfy your disgusting cravings."

She's in a mood, that's for sure. I've heard more curse words from her in the past five minutes than in the last two decades.

"That is none of your business."

In an uncharacteristic move, I'm flying solo this trip to Euphoria. With the Christmas holidays, I'd rather spend them alone than with some nameless woman who thinks spreading her legs will open my bank account to an all you can have buffet.

"It is when it affects the family, Hawke, that you force me to step in. You've had your fun. Euphoria is mildly profitable, but ultimately mine."

It's wildly profitable and will never be hers.

"It's not yours. I own Euphoria. It's free and clear of any of entanglements with Sterling Enterprises."

She takes a leisurely sip from a teacup on her desk. The years are catching up to Mother. Her raven hair is nearly gone. Her features sag with the fragilities of age. Her hand shakes, ever so slightly, as she sips her tea.

Despite that, her hawkish gaze remains as piercing as ever and her acidic tone burns like always.

"Let's not bore each other by dancing around the matter. I'll get straight to the point."

The line at my gate is getting shorter, but I still have time.

"Please. This conversation is arduous enough."

I'm not happy with her intruding on my vacation. I plan on spending the holidays at Euphoria, where I can disconnect, forget about Sterling Enterprises, and most importantly, the frigid bitch at its helm.

That's what I consider the perfect Christmas present.

"Then I'll get straight to it. You loathe this family—me in particular—and you flaunt your disgust openly. I want to make it perfectly clear this little rebellion on your part will not continue."

I grit my teeth to avoid arguing. It does no good. Besides, she's completely right, except in one aspect. I hate everything about her, but I love Cherise with every fiber in my soul.

"What is it you want?"

"Is it not obvious? We need an heir." Her eyes gleam in victory, but I see no reason for that. While Mother controls nearly every aspect of my life, she doesn't reign over that particular piece of it.

"I'm not ready to settle down. When I do, it'll be because I've found a woman of my choosing. Is that understood?"

"As clearly as I hope you understand what I have to say. I'm dying, Hawke." She gives a little flap of her hand. "Not that I expect you to care. You'll probably spend the night drinking to your good fortune with the news I'll finally be gone, but it doesn't stop the fact that I am dying."

My mouth gapes. "Excuse me?"

"Pancreatic cancer, and it's advanced. I have very little time left. The doctors say six months at most, maybe less. It's so pedestrian, don't you think, to be taken out by something as common as cancer?" She gives a huff. "Nevertheless, it has forced me to ensure my affairs are in order, which I have done." The look she gives speaks volumes. I'm not coming out of this unscathed.

"Well, I don't know how much you know about medicine, but

it's virtually impossible to provide an heir in less than six months' time."

"Don't be so crude. We're talking about your inheritance, and your sister's as well."

"We each have our trusts after father passed. You can do what you will with the rest of it. I don't want it." *I might lose Sterling Enterprises, but I would be free. It is an exciting prospect.*

"No, I suppose you don't, but Cherise needs it. She needs it very much. Sadly, her trust fund was never as robust as yours. Your father didn't feel a woman needed the means to care for herself. Your sister will be penniless within three years' time."

"Then leave my inheritance to her. I don't want it."

"That would be the easy thing, wouldn't it? But I can't leave my money to a woman who is essentially a child herself. She'll never marry and never conceive. Not that it matters. She does, however, need a guardian."

"I'll always take care of Cherise."

"I know you will. I count on it." *Her words chill me from the inside out.* "But there's the issue of the will."

"Your will? Honestly, I'm not going to play games with you or jump through hoops to take what you're not willing to give. Give it all to Cherise. She deserves it."

"Not my will, you fool!" Her voice snaps across the distance, and I jerk with surprise.

"What are you talking about?"

"If it were up to me, I would give her everything, but it's not… Up to me, that is. Instead, your father buried certain conditions and clauses into his will."

"What are you talking about?"

"It's all yours. He gave everything to his only son. His heir. Which leaves Cherise destitute. Her trust fund will run out, sooner rather than later. With the bills for her medical care…" *There's no need for her to complete that line of thought.*

"You know my feelings for Cherise. I'll do anything for her. If that's what you need, my reassurance, then you have it. I'll see that she lacks for nothing. Her life will be as wonderful and as full as it can be."

And I will shower her with the love and affection you never showed me.

"If only it were that easy. Girls can't continue the family name, and Cherise… Well, she'll never have children. That would be a cruelty."

"Well, I don't want it. Give it to charity. I'm doing well enough with Euphoria to take care of Cherise."

"You have no idea what you're saying. No idea the cost her medical care incurs. I won't have her quality of life degraded because you don't have the means to care for her in the custom she's used to. Not when it's all right here. Just waiting for you to take."

"Then I'll take it. After it passes to me, I'll set up a trust for her care…"

"You don't get it, you silly fool. Don't you think your father thought of all the ways his billions could be broken apart and squandered? How his legacy, his name, would endure? The money will go to you. It will stay with you, and it will pass from you to your son. You're merely the guardian of the estate, like me." She takes another sip of tea with shaky hands. "You'll finally be free of me, but you won't be free of your father's plans for the future of our family. You *will* marry. You *will* provide an heir."

"And if this is not what I want?"

"What you want is inconsequential." She shrugs. "It's all about tradition and heritage. You have the strength of character to carry on the family legacy. You've sure butted heads with me often enough to prove your mettle, and demonstrate your worth. In this, however, you will not prevail. You're a force in the corporate world. You've demonstrated your ability to manage Sterling Enterprises, building its assets and our wealth, and as much as I detest Euphoria—" her eyes flicked up to meet mine, "—you've created something out of nothing. You're a Sterling where it counts, but now it's time to continue the family legacy."

The line for boarding is seriously short. I'll risk missing my flight if I'm not careful.

"I don't see what you can do about that." It's a callous statement considering she told me she's dying. I wish I could summon grief over the thought of losing my mother, but the only emotion I feel is relief. I'll finally be free of her manipulation.

"Obviously, it won't simply be handed over to you. Too much is at risk."

"Ah, and here it is—the hidden hook."

"Don't be vulgar." Her expression pinches, but I see the victorious spark in her eyes. "As I said, the Sterling name must go on. That is the condition of the estate. Consider it my dying wish."

"You're kidding me. You're dying wish is for me to bear a son? A grandson you'll never see?" She flinches at the jab, and I almost feel guilty about it.

"I assure you, this is something you will give me. It's very real I'm told I have six months, maybe more, probably less, but within six months, you will marry. If you remain married long enough to produce a male heir, Sterling Enterprises will be yours. If not…"

"What do you mean? *Will be mine?* It's mine already."

"And that is your first mistake. You thought running the company meant you owned it? I can assure you that is not the case. If you refuse, I'll divest Sterling Enterprises of everything, selling it off piece by piece."

"You'd never do that. You just said Cherise needs that money for her care."

"You're correct. I said exactly that. Like you, she'll be left with nothing."

It hits me like a lightning bolt, the true depravity my mother is capable of, and her determination to leave this life with her clutches firmly attached to my life.

"You fucking bitch."

"Manners Hawke. I've taught you better than that, but then you've always been hotheaded and incapable of holding your temper in check. This is the way it will be. If you don't marry before I'm gone, the Sterling legacy will be sold off to the highest bidder. If you don't produce an heir within the first three years of your marriage, Sterling Enterprises will be ripped apart. You'll lose everything. Although, you'll likely survive. Your little pet project might endure, but you'll lose all your wealth. With that, you condemn your sister to living out her life in some nameless state-run facility. Is that what you want for your sister?"

"You would condemn your own daughter?"

"That choice is in your hands."

"You evil, controlling bitch."

She gives an emphatic eye roll. "Yet again with the vulgarities. Not that it matters to me. I've sent a list of eligible young ladies who are amenable to a short engagement. I suggest you pick one. Your proposal should arrive no later than New Year's Day, and we'll plan a June wedding. It'll be the social event of the season."

"Of course, you have a list." No fucking way am I picking any woman off a list Mother prepared, and as for a proposal by New Year's? She's out of her ever-loving mind.

"It pays to be prepared."

"And I take it my future wife must be one of these overly eager girls?"

"I'm not a monster. You may marry whomever you choose. She must be fertile. You have six months to marry. Less than that, actually. I strongly suggest a proposal by New Year's so we can properly plan the wedding." Her head cocks to the side as she glances at her watch. "Now, I have other things to do. I'll leave you to it."

"I bet you will."

The gate attendant calls out final boarding for my flight.

Mother disconnects without another word.

No, *I love you.*

No, *Merry Christmas.*

As always, my cold-hearted mother gives me nothing remotely associated with love.

And of course, her timing couldn't be more perfect to completely ruin the next ten days. My plans of getting away from everything are now colored by her edict.

Her dying wish?

What a manipulative monster.

I head to the gate moments before they close it. The gate attendant's eyes pop when she sees me and round with interest.

If I didn't want to get on this flight, I'd be planted firmly between her legs in less than five minutes, fucking her brains out.

Instead, I scan my ticket and board the plane. There's still a bit of a line, but soon I'm at my seat.

Except, someone's sitting in it.

FIVE

Quinn

A PRESENCE LOOMS OVER ME. "EXCUSE ME, BUT YOU'RE IN MY seat."

My eyes open and latch onto a molten golden stare. It's the man from the shop.

"Do you mind taking the window seat?" I point beside me. "I'm kind of a nervous flyer."

His heavy gaze sweeps to the window, then returns to me. "First-time flier?"

"More like a terrified-I'm-going-to-die kind of flier." I give a shake of my head. "I know it makes no sense, but I feel like I'm strapped in for my death."

He gives a low, sultry laugh. "I'm sure that's not going to happen. You're really afraid to fly?"

"Terrified barely touches it, but I'm medicating."

"With tiny liquor bottles?"

"Um, yes." My eyes widen because he remembers me. I wiggle in my seat and retrieve the wadded up bills the cashier gave me. "I believe this belongs to you."

He stares at the bills, eyes widening in shock but also edged with a little humor. "Not many people would do that."

"I'm honest to a fault, and thank you, by the way."

The flight attendant comes up behind him. "Sir, we're securing the door. I need you to take your seat."

"Of course." My stranger carries nothing. No briefcase. No luggage. He looks like the kind of person who would carry a briefcase, and I wonder if I should ask what he does for a living.

He's tall, broad-shouldered, and smells delicious, like coffee and chocolate all rolled up in one with a dash of cinnamon and spice sprinkled on top.

He glances at the seat and my legs, which are in the way. Quickly, I unbuckle and start to slide toward the terrifying thin-walled piece of plexiglass that pretends it's a window.

He laughs, a low, sinful sound, and gives a shake of his head. "You really are scared of flying. I promise, that window will not bite you."

"I'm more worried about it cracking and sucking me outside."

He undoes the button of his jacket and holds his tie to his chest. "Let me save you from such a fate." He gestures to the aisle, and I realize he's going to let me keep his seat.

"Thank you."

"Not a problem at all."

As he peels back his suit jacket, the flight attendant takes his coat. My eyes lock to his broad chest, flat abdomen, and the way his belt draws everything together. I'm really looking at the zipper, because it's at eye level, and what shifts behind it. This man is either happy to see me, or is packing something impressive.

"Would you like a glass of champagne?" The flight attendant drapes the jacket over his arm.

"No, thank you. Water will be fine, but she may need some of that champagne."

I should tell him I've downed two glasses. An alcohol buzz swirls in my veins, relaxing me. But I don't. If two glasses are good, a third will be better.

I unbuckle and move into the aisle while he takes the seat beside me. While the first-class accommodations seem to swallow my thin frame, he fills up the seat like it was made just for him.

This may not be such a horrible flight. As for the man beside me, I can use some of the sexy distraction he provides. He puts Scott to shame.

Back in my seat, I tug the seatbelt tight under the watchful eye of my neighbor. The plane gives a quick shudder. I jump and grab at the armrest, which happens to be right where my stranger's hand is resting.

"Sorry." I release his hand and stare down the aisle, anything to keep from looking out that window.

We're moving, rolling back from the gate. The flight attendants are doing the safety thing. Like any of that is going to save my life.

He gives another low chuckle. It's more of a rumble and adjusts his tie. I find myself staring again. Who knew hands could be so damn sexy? Ignoring me, he stares out the window as we taxi to the runway and stop for a few moments.

The engines roar, getting louder as we prepare for departure. My fear escalates with each loud roar. We roll again, turning, lining up with the runway itself.

With one last roar, we blast down the runway, bouncing along like we're moments from crashing. My hand flies out again, grasping for anything.

Something warm and solid holds it. My stranger places his hand on top of mine and gives it a little squeeze.

"Relax. I fly all the time, and so far, I've survived just fine." His attempt at humor is lost on me.

A few moments later, the pilot's calm, confident voice comes over the intercom. He welcomes us on board our flight and tells us all about the weather at our tropical destination.

As the plane climbs smoothly into the sky, I slowly relax until a sharp pain bolts in my ears.

"It's the pressure equalizing." My stranger's grip on my hand eases and I finally open my eyes. "Try yawning or make a chewing motion." He demonstrates. "It'll help to pop the air out."

I do as he says and sure enough a pop sounds and the pain eases.

"Thank you." I glance up at him, into those magical eyes of his.

"No worries. Just sit back, relax, and we'll be there before you know it."

"That's what I'm worried about."

"Why's that?"

"The landing."

Another low, throaty chuckle from him turns my insides to mush. No man deserves to be that sexy.

"Well, don't worry about the landing. I'll hold your hand through that too, if it helps."

Embarrassed doesn't begin to describe my emotional state, but I manage to string together a few words.

"Looks like you saved me again."

"If only things were that easy." He turns away and stares out the window, concluding the speaking portion of our flight.

I polish off the champagne and somehow manage to drift off. If we can nail this landing, I might be able to get through the next ten days. As for what happens next?

I have no clue.

SIX

Hawke

WHAT A DELECTABLE TREAT. THE WOMAN FROM THE STORE IS ON MY flight. Uniquely appealing, she draws my attention. In a rush at the store, I thought nothing of her at first, but then the universe granted me a second look. She's flustered by my presence, but too terrified by the takeoff to let that stop her from grabbing my hand. I find her insanely attractive, and I can't pinpoint why.

As for my attention, she has it now. I'm enraptured and entranced.

Not classically beautiful, or runway gorgeous—my usual go-to types—her stunning, understated beauty stirs my carnal hunger. It makes me want things. Dark things. Filthy things.

And I always get what I want.

I fully embrace my nihilistic desires, satisfying my cravings as I please. Mother considers this a fatal flaw. My cold-hearted mother is one to talk. Where does she think my disinterest in relationships stems from?

You taught your son everything, Mommy Dearest.

My disregard for emotional entanglement is not a flaw. It is, instead, my greatest strength.

Self-absorbed liars, cheats, and whores, women spread their legs at the drop of a hat if it means getting what they want. Mother taught me that. I've spent a lifetime watching everything she does.

And while I may live with a hardened heart, I don't deprive myself the indulgence of female companionship, or the pleasure they provide.

Three rules encapsulate my life and a motto of proceeding with extreme caution serves me well.

As for the rules?

I initiate.

I take.

I'm the one who walks away.

The only one to beat me at my own game is the heartless spinster who raised me.

The rules keep things honest. There's no worrying about feelings, emotions, or a trail of broken hearts littering my past. Every woman I've ever been with, with the exception of one, knows the rules going in.

As for the darling mystery beside me, I've already stripped and fucked her every way imaginable with my mind. She's outmatched, and I'd consider her easy prey, except for the way she looked at me, or rather looked through me. Her initial interest fades. That kind of indifference fascinates me.

There's a story here. It lingers in her breathtaking eyes, which hold a universe of pain and hides in the tumultuous cascade of her long, auburn waves. She makes me itch to discover what caused her so much pain.

I'll uncover the details in time, but that's not what draws me. Sure, there was that initial flare of arousal when she saw me, but it was here and gone in an instant. She's not draping herself over me, trying to figure me out. She's not attempting to entice me in any way.

She's completely unaffected by my presence and that never happens. It makes her an unknown quantity; dangerous, and *that* fascinates me.

Her existence places me in peril because she presents a mystery I must figure out.

That, in and of itself, screams one hell of a bad idea. While my motto of extreme caution tells me to walk away, I fixate on having her.

Taking her.

Making her mine.

What brings you to the tropics, my dear? And how can I turn that to my advantage?

She's the first woman to fall asleep on me. Granted, there's more than a good bit of alcohol flowing through her system, but I'm used to a certain response from women. They're rapt and ravenous for a piece of me. The beauty fitfully sleeping beside me is not.

In the meantime, I appreciate the peace and quiet as she sleeps. Using the onboard Wi-Fi, I dial up my sister and check in on her newest project.

Cherise is eager to show me *everything* about her orchids. A discussion about orchids would normally bore me to tears, but for Cherise, I can't get enough of her exuberance. As the only female on the planet with pure intentions, my defensive walls fall away around her.

My fingers fly over the keys. Normally, I'd speak to her, but the inside of an aircraft isn't the most private place. Many raise an eyebrow at the way I act around Cherise, but I don't give a flying fuck what they think.

Me: Cherise, you around?

Cherise: Hawke!!! Where are you?

Me: On a plane.

Cherise: Oh, so much fun. I want you to take me on a plane ride.

Me: I will.

Cherise: You promise? You're not lying? You know it's bad to lie.

Me: I've never lied to you. And yes, next time I'm home, I'll take you up in the glider. Or, do you want to go in the helicopter?

Cherise: Oh. The glider!!!

I can practically see her hopping up and down. It doesn't take much to get my sister excited.

Me: What are you doing? Are you playing with your orchids?
Cherise: Yes!!! Can I voice?
Me: Yes, but I can't talk back. Tell me all about your lovely orchids and don't leave anything out.

Leaning back, I put an earbud in my ear. Cherise's angelic voice fills my world, and her bright and cheery tone brings a smile to my face. Her childish excitement smooths away my stress. For the next two hours, she tells me everything about her orchids and the time passes quickly.

As for my seat companion, she's out cold. I wave over the flight attendant.

"How many drinks did she have?"

"Two before takeoff." He presses his finger to his chin. "No, wait. Three with the one you got for her."

"Hmm…"

"Is there a problem?"

"No." I give a shake of my head. "She's afraid of flying and may have overdone it a bit. When she wakes, can you be sure to bring her plenty of water?"

A frequent flyer, I'm very aware of the discomfort dehydration brings. Add alcohol to the mix, especially what she imbibed, and she's going to wake up regretting her decision to self-medicate.

"Absolutely."

He leaves me and I continue listening to my sister go on about her orchids, her upcoming show, and which of her favorites she intends to showcase. While I listen, I admire the woman beside me.

Long, auburn hair spills around her shoulders in soft, cascading waves. My fingers itch to slide through the strands and feel their silky texture. Her lids flutter in her sleep and her features relax. Gone are the signs of panic which had her grabbing my hand on takeoff

The vividness of her eyes is something I won't easily forget. They practically glowed and took my breath away.

The electric jolt when she grabbed me came as a surprise. If my body reacts like that to that simple touch, I eagerly await the main event.

But how do I corral my nameless beauty?

I bet she has a soft, feminine name, something that rolls off the tongue and drips with sin. I spend the next few minutes trying out several names, wondering how close I might be.

An hour before our flight ends, she stirs. Her delicate arms reach overhead and she stretches out her legs, curling her toes in a full-body stretch. Her lids flutter, then slowly open. Soft, gentle fingers go to her eyes, where she rubs away the sleep.

Mesmerized by her every movement, I catalogue them and file them away for future masturbatory use. My hand will be busy for weeks to come.

From her pert, rosebud lips, to the tiny upturning of her nose, she's a pretty thing. Her tits are a man's wet dream and I can't wait to feel them in my hands. Not too small. Not too big. They demand my attention and unadulterated exploration with hands, mouth, and more.

She blinks furiously, clearing her eyes, and just when I think she might curl back with a sigh, she bolts upright and tries to stand. The seatbelt cinched across her lap prevents that, tugging her back into her seat.

"Where am I?" Her gaze darts furiously around the cabin. When it lands on the window beside me, her hand flies to her mouth where she bites her knuckles.

"No. No. No." Her agitation increases. "I thought it was a dream." Her chest heaves as she hyperventilates.

"Easy, darling." I place my hand over hers. "You're safe."

"Safe! I'm in a plane." Her head whips back and forth. "Oh my God. Oh my God. Oh my God."

I see her panic build and reach for both her hands. Gently pulling her fist out of her mouth, I shift in my seat to face her.

"Calm down, darling. You're safe."

"Safe! We're all going to die." Her words trail off in an agonized cry.

My grip tightens, letting her know I'm there, but it does nothing to ease her panic. She's truly terrified of flying. Why the fuck is she on this plane?

"What's your name?" Maybe if I use her name, I can get her to listen. To relax.

"Huh?"

"Your name? What's your name?"

"Q."

Maybe my ears are clogged? Such a harsh sounding letter can't possibly be her name.

"Did you just say Q?"

She nods. "Well, it's Quinn, but everyone calls me Q."

Why would anyone butcher her name like that?

"Well, Quinn, my name's Hawke, Hawke Sterling, and I promise we aren't going to die today."

"You do?"

"Well, I certainly don't plan on it." I point to the flight attendant who pays close attention to our exchange. "The flight attendants and pilots don't either. I promise you're safe."

"Hello, Miss Hayes, is there something I can get you?"

The bastard flight attendant needs to back the fuck up. I'm the one taking care of Quinn.

"Can I have something to drink?" She pulls one of her hands free from me and pats her mouth. "My mouth feels like cotton."

Because she downed three drinks, and if I remember correctly, there's a high likelihood she took over the counter cold medicine too. She's going to regret that.

"Yes, what would you like?"

"Water." I clench my teeth. My specific instructions were for him to only bring her water.

She pulls her other hand out of my grip. Jerks it away actually and clasps her hands in her lap. She keeps rubbing at her left hand. The base of her ring finger actually, but there's no sign of a ring. No sign of an indentation of where a ring might go if she wore one.

"No. No water. Something stronger. Do you have any more of that champagne?"

"No, Miss Hayes, but I have red or white wine if you'd like."

"She'll have water." The flight attendant jumps at the low growl in my throat.

Quinn flips the release of her seatbelt and pops to her feet. Her sudden movement takes me by surprise.

"Where's the lavatory?" Her hand goes to her mouth and her eyes widen.

Great. Just great.

The attendant points to the front of the plane where the first-class lavatory sits. Quinn pushes past him and darts to the lavatory. Thankfully, it's open because I'm pretty sure she's in there emptying the contents of her stomach.

With Quinn gone, I unbuckle and bring the full force of my towering presence on the flight attendant. A glance at the tag on his vest tells me his name. I press my finger to his breastbone and push hard enough to get his attention.

"Look, Andy, I told you to only give her water."

"That's not what she asked for." Andy's voice gives a little squeak and I'm pretty sure his balls just drew up a bit.

"I don't care what you think, or why. Get her a damn cup of water and if you bring back alcohol of any kind, I'll personally castrate you. Any questions?"

He shakes his head and retreats to the galley while I head to the lavatory to wait. Quinn didn't seem that steady on her feet.

It doesn't take long before the door opens. Head down, Quinn doesn't see me at first, but I'm a large man and her head pops up. When it does, our eyes lock and something weird happens.

The air between us sizzles. It crackles with electricity.

She brushes her arms, smoothing down the fine hairs which stand on end. I feel it too. Like an electric jolt, something passed through my body.

"Feel better?" I brush the pad of my thumb across her forehead.

"I think so." She wipes at her mouth and her gaze drops.

Placing my hands on her shoulders, I spin her to face down the aisle.

"Let's get you buckled in." The seatbelt sign flickers overhead.

"What's that?" She takes a step back, pressing her tight body against mine. It's all I can do to hold back a groan. That slight contact takes me from flaccid to rock hard in an instant.

Ignoring my discomfort, I walk her back to her seat and stand over her while she buckles in.

"Aren't you going to get in?"

"I need to use the lavatory." And fast.

She gives a tiny nod of her head. Satisfied she's taken care of, I retreat to the only privacy to be found on this plane and take care of a very pressing need.

SEVEN

Hawke

Filled with all manner of filthy thoughts about Quinn, it doesn't take long to ease the ache in my balls. My release takes care of my most pressing issue, but leaves me unfulfilled. I need her. It's weird, this animalistic craving is new. Sure, I've felt an undeniable urge to fuck a woman before, but that was to fulfill a base physical need—to release tension. This woman? I don't want to just fuck her. I want to lay claim to her. Mark her. It's a raw, powerful, primal desire. One I don't understand.

I wash my hands and run my fingers through my hair.

That's a new one.

I've never experienced an instantaneous reaction to a woman's touch, let alone the powerful need to rub one out like that.

When I return to my seat, my fingers curl. Quinn sucks down the last of what looks like wine and shoves something suspiciously like cold medicine into a ratty backpack.

"What's that?" I point to the empty glass.

"What's what?"

"Look, I get you're afraid of flying, but chugging booze and guzzling cold medicine is a recipe for disaster."

She jerks back in her seat and tucks her chin as indignation fills her face. "I think I can make that decision for myself."

"You're right." Her snarky comment draws my anger. "You're a grown woman and if you want to get punch drunk before landing in a foreign country, then far be it for me to get in your way. For the record, it's a piss-poor decision."

"I don't remember asking you." Her eyes flash, sparking with emerald fire.

Her defiance stirs something primitive within me. The need to exert my dominance over her swells, and that's not all that swells. My dick takes notice, growing long and hard within the span of a few heartbeats.

"You didn't. Doesn't mean I'm not right."

Her arms cross with indignation, and her mouth opens and closes as she tries to come back at me. But she can't. She knows I'm right.

Instead of asking her to unbuckle and let me in, I contort my body between the seats and slide into mine. I wouldn't be able to do that in coach.

"Look, I'm just saying a woman traveling on her own needs to be careful."

"Who says I'm traveling alone?"

I cock my head. "Aren't you?"

She squints at me as if deciding whether to be truthful. The moment she gives in, it feels like I've won a major victory.

"I am, but I'm fully capable of taking care of myself."

I glance at her backpack, wondering how much cold medicine she's taken. Is that why she was passed out for practically the entire flight? The intercom pops overhead as Andy speaks to the passengers.

"Our captain has put on the seat belt sign in preparation for landing. Please make sure your tray tables are in their full and upright position…" He drones on with what I've heard hundreds of times.

Quinn, however, listens intently, hanging on every word as if her life depends on it. I snort and turn my attention outside the window. Landings are the most exciting part of flying.

Quinn yawns beside me and sinks deeper into her seat. Her lids droop and she gives a start. A few moments later, a big yawn escapes her and she blinks furiously. The poor thing is going to be passed out again before we hit the ground. That may be the best thing, to be honest. If her reaction to landing is anything like takeoff, I'd rather have her sleep through it.

Which is exactly what she does.

The landing is smooth as silk. I barely feel the wheels touch down before the engine brakes roar, slowing us down. Still no movement out of Quinn. I give her a tiny shove, mindful we're still strangers, but when she doesn't move, I pinch her arm.

Nothing.

Well, shit.

One of the perks of first class is getting to be first off the plane, but Quinn is completely knocked out. We arrive at the gate and everyone surges to their feet. My nudge becomes more forceful. More of a prod. Finally, she stirs.

"Huh?" Her voice slurs and I roll my eyes.

I can't leave her like this.

The outer door opens and those lined up cram forward toward the exit. I give up on getting out of the plane first and work on waking Quinn up. As the passengers file out of the plane, I get her to come around, but now I need to wait for the plane to empty. I slap her hand. Pinch the back of her wrist, and give Andy dirty looks.

Finally, there's no one left but us. Once again, I contort my body and wiggle into the aisle.

"Come on, Quinn. It's time to go."

What the hell am I going to do with her? It's not like I can drop her off someplace.

Fortunately, she's waking up. It's slow, but progress. In the back of my mind, I remember her dragging a rolling carry-on and find it in the bin overhead. I reach down and sling her backpack over my shoulder. Then I lift her out of her seat.

More awake, she rubs at her eyes and sways on her feet. "What's going on?"

"We've landed."

"Landed?"

"Yes. You're back on the ground." I can't wheel her carry-on and take care of her at the same time. After loosening the straps on the backpack, I wear it old school, like a dork, and lift her carry on. With it in hand, I practically carry *her* off the plane as well.

As I pass Andy, my eyes pinch. "Your superiors will hear about this. With no idea who he's dealing with, Andy is in for a rude surprise. The CEO of this airline is a golf buddy of mine and he will hear about this.

With Quinn staggering beside me, I manage to get her up the jet bridge and into the main terminal. But now what?

"Quinn, do you know where you're staying?"

She mumbles something incoherent and I look up and pinch the bridge of my nose in frustration.

"Do you have any bags to claim in baggage claim?"

Her head droops, but it gives a sharp shake. At least I don't have to deal with the fiasco of figuring out which bag is hers. My attention shifts to the small carry-on in my hand. What kind of woman travels with one piece of luggage?

She's not helping me out, leaving no choice but to invade her privacy and look through her backpack. The first thing I want to find is her purse. Everything valuable to a woman resides in her purse. Except Quinn doesn't have one.

I dig through her backpack, looking for anything which might help. I find her passport and ID along with a crumpled piece of paper. I almost toss it, but see print on the inside.

Bingo, but what are the damn odds?

She's staying at my resort.

At least I know where to drop her off. As for the rest of it? I've had my fill of Quinn Hayes. She'll get to the resort in one piece, safe and sound, but the rest of this? I'm not a damn babysitter for a grown woman. She's far more trouble than I'm willing to expend chasing pussy.

Only, that's not what you want.

I ignore the voice in my head, not clear what it thinks I want out of Quinn.

I flag down a worker and get a wheelchair. No way in hell is she making it through customs under her own power. With a grin plastered on my face, I smile to the customs official and tell him my fiancée had too much to drink on the flight. It must not be the first time because he waves me through without blinking.

My driver, Paul, is at the curb by the time I get there. His brow arches when he sees the drunk woman I lift into the limo.

"Don't ask."

"Do I ever?" He holds the door for me to climb in behind Quinn, then shuts me inside.

I can't help but breathe her in. Above the faintest smell of liquor and minty cold medicine, the lightest fragrance of jasmine and rosebuds floods my senses. Another groan escapes my lips because this woman is getting under my skin.

The limo shakes as Paul places her luggage in the trunk, then again when he sits in the driver's seat.

"Your home, Mr. Sterling?"

"No." My plans for the next two weeks included spending time alone at my beach house, but plans are meant to be changed. "Take me to Euphoria. Do me a favor and call ahead. Tell them to prepare my villa."

I thought I could walk away, but the truth is, this woman fascinates me. I need to know more. I plan to take what I want, satisfy this gnawing hunger inside of me, then walk away once I get my fill.

She's semi-conscious through check-in, and I learn a few things. First and foremost, she's booked into one of our honeymoon suites. The booking doesn't come from her, but rather someone named Scott Aiken. Both of them are listed on the reservation.

I study her left hand longer than I should and pull at my jaw while the front desk receptionist, Nalia, checks Quinn into her room.

Not married.

Not engaged.

What's her story?

As an all-inclusive couple's resort, there are several tiers to our suites. Whoever this Scott guy is, he booked the lowest tier. I bump that up because I can.

Not sure why she's traveling alone, I confirm *Scott* is not only not checked in but a note on the reservation says he won't be coming.

Nalia looks up, blushes, and bites her lower lip. She knows who I am and appears overwhelmed to be speaking directly to the owner.

"That's it, Mr. Sterling. I have Miss Hayes checked into her suite and confirmed yours is ready. Is there anything else I can do for you?"

"Call Dr. Conte and have him report to her room?"

"Right away, Mr. Sterling." It's about the tenth time she refers to me by name. A simple 'Sir' will do, but I don't correct her. It's not often I check in at reception. In fact, this might be the very first time.

As far as Miss Quinn Hayes, my decision to bring her straight to the resort, rather than the local hospital, is self-serving. Jack happens to be staying at Euphoria. He's an excellent physician and an old college buddy. If she needs more definitive care, he'll let me know. He'll also be discreet, which serves me well. I'm not interested in news getting out that I brought an incapacitated woman to the resort.

That kind of shit is exactly the fodder my mother eats up. She then turns it against me to serve her purposes to force me into doing shit I don't want to do. Anything to cast her disapproving eye on me is fair game.

The bellhop takes Quinn's bags while I help Quinn to her suite. Her voice slurs and her feet drag, but some of the alcohol and cold medicine is wearing off. I place her on the couch and tip the bellhop, then sit and wait for Jack. No way am I leaving her alone in this state. Although, if she comes around, how am I going to explain all of this?

I may not have thought this through.

It takes about an hour before there's a knock on the door. In that time, I've taken care of the final pieces of a major merger and opened up the latest proposals for my firm's annual venture capital investments—the ones my mother rejected. After my conversation with Mother, I need to review my recommendations.

When I open the door, Jack spreads his arms wide. "Sterling! What the fuck are you doing here?" He wraps me in a man-hug, thumping my back, and flashes his infamous megawatt smile. "Why was I pulled out of the pool and told to come here? I thought you were staying at your house this time around."

"I was, but now I'm not."

"And you need me, why?"

I point to the couch where Quinn begins to stir. "How concerned do I need to be about alcohol and cold medicines?"

"You resorting to drugging the ladies? Lost your magnetic edge?"

My reputation with the ladies borders on legendary. I've never found myself without a date or a satisfying lay. My looks can kill, and if that doesn't work, the size of my bank account seals the deal. I've been featured more times than I care on various world's-most-eligible-bachelor lists. Not that I follow that shit.

"I didn't drug her, asshole."

His hand goes to his chest like he's hurt. "You wound me."

"I wound nothing." I gesture toward Quinn. "She's not even with me."

"Then what the fuck are you doing in her suite?" He glances around and lowers his voice. "And a honeymoon suite to boot. Is there a husband lurking around?"

"Not that I can tell. And as for what I'm doing here, I'm taking care of her."

"Now this promises to be an interesting story." He ambles over to where Quinn rests, kneels down, and takes her pulse. Never without his black doctor bag, he pulls out a stethoscope and listens to her chest. I'm more than a little peeved that he gets to touch her breasts before me. Although, he isn't groping her tits like I want to do. His touch is clinical and professional. "I know what's wrong with her."

"You do?"

"Yes, asshole." He throws my taunt back in my face. "She's

fucking drunk."

"I know she's drunk, but does she need to go to the hospital?"

He shakes his head. "She needs to sleep it off. Do you know what she took? Any chance there are other drugs involved?"

"Doubtful. Three glasses of champagne. At least one glass of wine. And…" I look around for that ratty backpack of hers. "Hang on. Let me find the cold medicine." The backpack is in the bedroom. Yet again, I rifle through her things, and pull out a nearly empty bottle. "Here." I shove the bottle at him.

Jack takes it from me and looks at the label and reads the list of ingredients.

"Looks like she took double or triple the dose. Why the fuck would she do that? Is she sick?"

"I don't think so?" I shrug. "At least, it didn't look like it on the plane."

"Yes!" He stabs a finger toward me. "This is the juicy story I've been waiting for. What did you do to her on the plane?"

"I did nothing."

"You sure about that?"

"Look, I've never taken advantage of a woman and I'm not about to start now. She's afraid of flying. Had one or two or more glasses of champagne, I guess to take the edge off."

Jack nods. "And I bet she googled on how to sleep on a plane. It explains the cold medicine."

"Is it dangerous? Should we be pumping her stomach or something?"

"How long was the flight?"

"About six hours."

"And how long since you landed?"

"Maybe another hour?"

He taps his chin. "Let's assume she had three or four drinks, plus half that bottle of cold medicine. I'd say she'll be okay."

"Is that your professional opinion?"

"It is. She's going to wake up and regret it." He glances around the room. "And she may not have a clear memory of what happened. Are you planning on being here when she wakes?"

"Not really."

He makes a show of the chin tapping thing. "So, you're telling me you took the time to make sure she got off the plane safely. Brought her to Euphoria. Checked her in. Asked me to examine her. And you're walking away?"

"Some things aren't worth the trouble."

"Seems as if you've gone to a great deal of trouble already, but that's cool. I highly recommend someone watches over her. Medically, she's intoxicated, but after nearly seven hours, most of the alcohol is out of her system. The cold medicine will linger for several more hours. She'll be drowsy. Best to put her to bed."

A snort escapes me. "The last thing I'm going to do is put a woman I don't know in bed in a strange place and hang around for her to wake up. That screams all kinds of bad-fucking-idea."

"True, but what are the options?"

I cross my arms over my chest and give him one of my infamous stares.

"Oh, for fuck's sake, Sterling. This is my vacation."

"You'll be compensated for your time."

"And my inconvenience?"

"Name your price."

He mumbles something about rich, entitled bastards always getting what they want. I'd take offense, except he's not wrong about it.

I'm rich. Entitled. And a bastard.

As for always getting what I want? I do.

Which is why I leave Jack with my oddly unnerving flight companion. I'd consider staying, except I don't trust myself. Distance is what I need, because the strange beauty managed to worm her way under my skin. That's not something I tolerate. I don't like not having the upper hand.

Before we meet again, it'll be on my terms, and I'll definitely have the advantage.

I head to the owner's suite and dig up everything there is about Quinn Hayes.

What I find both intrigues and bothers me.

EIGHT

Hawke

"Another whiskey, Mr. Sterling?" Andrew, the bartender, takes my empty glass and wipes away the water ring with a flourish of his towel. He waits for me to look up from the papers spread out in three neat stacks.

"Two fingers, and make it neat this time."

I sit at a bar in the far corner of one of Euphoria's restaurants and enjoy my whiskey. One of many bars, this one is attached to the main dining area. Soft music floats through the air, and cozy, understated lighting adds to the romantic atmosphere. This is a place for love, not a place for a single man to sit alone at the end of the bar.

But I'm here on a mission.

My things were delivered to my villa less than an hour after I arrived with Quinn, brought from my beach house by my staff. Euphoria is a side adventure I started with my best friend Steve Calloway, another rich, entitled, billionaire friend.

Unlike me though, he's not a bastard.

Other than that, we're practically brothers.

Euphoria began as a joke. We bought some land. Formed a LLC. Then built an audacious, over the top, bachelor pad where we basically fucked every girl under the sun. And we wrote the whole thing off as a business expense.

Then we built another for some of our friends to join in on the fun. Then another. And another.

We never intended to take Euphoria commercial, and not once did we envision it would become a successful enterprise. Those initial bachelor pads became the cornerstone of our exclusive honeymoon retreats. The rest of the development followed, taking advantage of tried and true business practices. We took the best of all the couple's resorts we could find around the world and combined them into what Euphoria has become: the best of the best.

This place may be the only thing that is truly mine. All the rest of what I have comes from my mother. With her threats, I'm not likely to see a dime of my inheritance, but if I act the role of dutiful son, bow to her wishes, and scrape the shit off her shoes, she just might give in.

Oh, and there's the whole get married and pop out an heir thing. Mother is officially insane if she thinks that will happen.

There's too much bowing and scraping for my tastes. I constantly buck against her authority and groveling is not my style. Not that it's my fault. She raised me to stand apart and dominate the business world.

The only reason I cave to her demands is because of Cherise.

Irritated by thoughts of my mother, I review the prospectuses on the startups vying for financial backing. If there's one good thing about my mother, she loves supporting new and innovative ideas.

It may be the only trait the two of us share. My recommendations for funding need to be finalized by New Year's Eve. After our conversation earlier today, another look is in order. Yet why does she want them to present in person? We've never done that.

Now, I get to spend ten days in paradise looking over fifty proposals instead of doing something much more interesting.

The one with Quinn's name drives me insane, and for the tenth time, I glance toward the restaurant entrance.

I don't believe in coincidences and my suspicions grow by the second. She wouldn't be the first woman to leverage what she could to secure my good will. Yet again, I tell myself to forget about the auburn beauty with blazing emerald eyes.

Women can't be trusted.

So why am I at the bar waiting for her to come down for dinner?

The woman needs to eat. This is the closest restaurant to her room and by far the most popular. Ergo, she must come here.

Movement at the entrance draws my eye. My good friend Jack arrives with a gorgeous, blonde model draped all over him. I'm curious how things went with Quinn. When he sees me, he gives a chin bump in greeting, then settles his date in a secluded booth. Instead of waiting for a waitress, he comes over to me.

"How's it going?" He throws a fake punch at my midsection. "Where's your girl?"

"I'm flying solo."

"Oh, is that what we're calling it? The cutie in the honeymoon suite is on the down-low?"

"Don't be a jerk." I'm pissed because Jack always sees through my shit. "I'm just having a drink alone."

"While you're waiting for Quinn Hayes? What is it about that woman?"

"Nothing." My attention shifts to the entrance for the fifth time since he arrived.

"No reason to hide it. She cleans up pretty nice by the way."

"You stayed with her?"

"Nah, I got one of the maids to do that, but I went back to check on her. She's nursing a pretty nasty hangover, but otherwise survived."

"How long ago was that?"

"I thought you weren't interested?"

"Shut up."

He grabs the bartender's attention with a flick of two fingers. "Two glasses of champagne."

"Starting the night off with champagne? Who's *your* latest acquisition?"

He turns his attention to his date. "Her name is Emily Harrison, daughter of a shipping mogul and I'm hoping for at least one kind of merger tonight."

"Does he know what you're doing to his daughter?"

"He knows I'm with her, as for what I'm doing to her..." He makes a rude gesture.

Andrew brings my drink, along with Jack's champagne.

Jack grabs the two flutes. "That innocent looking thing is a lioness in bed. I have the scratches to prove it. It's always the ones you don't expect who surprise you the most."

"If you say so. In my experience, I'd watch out. She sees something she wants. When she gets it—game over. How long are you here?" It might be fun to get in a few dives with him, scuba or skydiving. Doesn't matter to me. I need something to destress my life.

"Just a couple days. I have to get her back to her family by Christmas Eve. What about you? How long are you hiding out here?" He knows me too well. The last time I flew home for the holidays was years ago. Now, I fly away from home whenever possible. It keeps things civil between me and my mother.

"I'm here through New Year's, then head back home." I gesture toward the stacks of papers. "It's time for our annual venture capital investment."

He glances at the papers. "Anything interesting? You always get the coolest proposals sent your way."

"A few things stand out." Like Quinn's virtual reality proposal. Such a shame the business plan is a steaming hot mess of ineptitude. Maybe that's why she's stalking me?

"Well, pick one that's really good. Maybe there's someone wanting to build one of those sex robot things?" He jabs me in the ribs. "That could be fun."

"No sex robot in the bunch. Some look promising. Others are just way out there." I crane my neck to check out the woman Jack placed in a booth. "Your date is getting bored. Better hurry up and run back to her before she finds some other rich bastard to take advantage of."

"Your attitude sucks. As for her, she sucks too, but in a really good kind of way. Which is why I don't care what you think. She may or may not be using me, but what do I care? I'm using her too, and it's not like I plan on marrying the girl." With those words, he leaves me to my barstool where there's nothing to do but stew and think.

Is it possible Quinn set me up? She wouldn't be the first. Nor would it be the most extravagant play by a woman dead set on getting what she wants. I've had more than my fair share of wannabes and lionesses dressed in sheep's clothing. In general, I spot them a mile away.

What bothers me is that I didn't spot it in Quinn.

She gives off none of those vibes, which makes me more suspicious rather than less. If she wants to play games, however, I'm up to the task.

It might be fun to string her along, promise her the world, then rip it out from under her feet. I'm bored enough to make it worth the effort, but cautious enough to remind myself of my motto. It's served me well for too many years.

That's when her slender figure draws my eye.

NINE

Hawke

Quinn stops at the entrance and peers inside; her motions are hesitant and unsure. She speaks with the hostess and I roll my shoulders back getting ready to begin our little dance.

Only instead of coming inside, she turns away.

What the fuck?

Now I have to chase her to get the games started. No way is that happening. I refuse to chase after a woman. Which means I'll either spend the rest of my evening alone or do exactly that.

"Dammit." I down my drink in one swallow. Before leaving, I pull the hostess to the side. A glance at her name tag helps. "Mira, the woman who just spoke to you…"

"Yes, Mr. Sterling?"

I don't wear a name tag, but every employee knows me by sight.

"Where is she headed?"

"I'm not sure, sir."

"What did she ask?" Pumping Mira for information might cause problems in the gossip chain, but fuck if I care right now.

"She wanted to know if there were any other places to eat."

"And?"

"I told her the poolside bar was open."

"Thank you." I give her a small token of my gratitude and head off on the hunt.

Maybe the crowd in the restaurant chased her off, or the romantic ambience made her think twice about dining alone. I imagine it might be intimidating for a single woman to eat alone, especially in a place like this. Not that the pool bar is less crowded, but it might be easier to get served and escape to a quiet corner.

I spent six hours beside her on the plane. Most of that engrossed in my work while she slept. Right now, I wish I'd taken the time to get to know her a little better. It might help answer the question of whether I'm being played.

The poolside bar is hopping. Bright lights, loud music, and couples laughing all combine in one raucous mess of sound. The crowd here is younger, drunker, and much more lively than at the restaurant. I can't imagine Quinn preferring this over the restaurant.

It takes questioning all three bartenders before I get anything useful.

"Yes, Mr. Sterling." Juan wipes the bar absentmindedly. "She did come by."

"And?"

"She headed over there." He points across the pool where it's dark and quiet.

"Did she order anything?"

His brows draw together. "She looked at the menu, but then asked for a couple glasses of water and headed over to the grotto."

Everything built at Euphoria is designed with couples in mind to maximize their experience. Our word of mouth advertising is so strong, we barely spend anything to market the resort.

There are places like the first bar I left, with the attached restaurant and its intimate atmosphere. There's the pool bar, a crowded, loud space filled with music, dancing and a general party atmosphere. Then there're places like the other side of the pool where the grotto begins. During the day, it's a quiet refuge for couples needing some alone time. At night, it turns into an intimate retreat with dark, secluded alcoves, perfect for couples to get lost in themselves.

Why she didn't stay at the pool bar confuses me. Now, I need to come up with an excuse to wander over there. Only people don't wander by themselves at our resort.

Beyond the grotto lies the beach. The soft susurration of waves is easily my favorite sound on the planet. Combine that with a gentle breeze blowing off the ocean, the faintest tang of salt in the air, and a dark sky filled with stars, and this place is definitely one of the most romantic places on earth.

Turn around. Don't do it.

The voice of reason tells me this is a bad idea, and I agree with it one hundred percent. Not that I do the smart thing and turn away. Instead, I shove my hands deep in my pockets and set out for the far side of the pool and the grottos beyond.

On the way there, I come up with about half a dozen witty things to say. Different ways of acting surprised that our paths once again cross. Only she's not on any of the loungers on the far side of the pool, or in any of the dark alcoves of the intricate grotto designed for romance.

I run my fingers through my hair with frustration. She's making me do things I never do with a woman. I never chase them, but I'm most definitely on the prowl for her.

Why is she different?

With no sign of her, I resign myself to look for her in the morning. One of the benefits of an all-inclusive resort is our guests stay on resort grounds. Somehow, somewhere, I will run into her.

I should get to bed, but the soft sound of the surf draws me toward the beach. Stopping at the edge of the concrete walk, I roll up my trousers and remove my shoes and socks. After stuffing my socks in my shoes, I put everything inside a locker and step onto the beach.

My toes sink in, curling with pleasure in the soft sand. No longer hot from baking under the sun, it's cool and feels wonderful against the soles of my feet. A full moon shines down on the beach making the sand glisten and the crests of the waves glow. The light breeze coming off the ocean ruffles my hair and I take a moment to simply soak everything in. One deep soul-cleansing breath follows another. I love it here.

While it's quicker to return to my bungalow via the many pathways meandering through the resort, I decide to take the longer way around and walk on the beach. I figure it'll soothe my nerves.

All four of the honeymoon suites open directly onto a private beach. Each one set on a miniature man-made cove. They're private for obvious reasons and are set well apart from the main buildings. Around the point, set even more apart, the two owner's retreats take advantage of a truly private beach. If I could, I would make this my permanent residence, but my mother demands I attend to her back in the States.

One day I'll be free.

I walk to the water's edge. Cold beneath my feet, the wet sand oozes through my toes. The waves lap against the beach, a never-ending movement always in flux, yet always the same.

Hands in my pockets, I stare out into the inky blackness, then tilt my head to take in the full moon. Despite the moonlight, the constellations shine down and I trace out some of my favorites.

Moments like this sustain me. They make me believe I can do anything, be anyone, and live the life I want to live. It frees me from familial obligations and the noose my mother tightens around my neck with each passing year.

Her most recent ultimatum leaves me reeling, so much so that I've shoved it far back into my subconsciousness where I'll deal with it later. Her impending death, on the other hand, makes me feel nothing.

Completely unreasonable, her demands make no sense and jeopardize Cherise's well-being. Not to mention screws me out of my inheritance if I don't comply.

I've got six months, less really. I either cave to her demands, or walk away from my wealth and condemn my twin sister to a state-run group home.

"Oh, it *is* you." The light floral scent of jasmine and rose fills my senses and I turn at the familiar voice.

Quinn Hayes appears like a waif out of the mists. The wind and waves swallow the soft tread of her feet, and a wispy white dress billows around her slender form, revealing more than it hides.

My mouth gapes and I snap it closed before she notices. Between one breath and the next, my cock hardens. It wants her with an irrational hunger. I barely retain control over my own body when she's near. Yet again, that's never happened before.

"Well, if it isn't my terrified seat-mate." I play it aloof and distant, as if I couldn't care if she were there. The opposite is true. Every molecule in my body vibrates with an awareness of her presence. "I told you we would survive." My need to possess her overwhelms all thought and it's a struggle to focus and remain aloof.

She ducks her head, then peeks up at me through her lashes. It's seductive as shit, and on any other woman, I'd call it a well-practiced move designed to lure men in for the killing blow. On her, it's entirely natural and I honestly believe she's clueless about how fucking attractive she is to someone of the opposite sex.

"I guess we did. I..." She glances away to stare out across the ocean. "I owe you an apology and more than a little thank you. Dr. Conte told me what you did. I can't thank you enough for..."

"Taking care of you?" I want to do far more than take care of her. It's a possessive desire I'm struggling to understand.

Her magnetic eyes snap to mine. "I was going to say for not taking advantage of me, but yeah. Thank you for taking care of me. He says I wasn't lucid, something about mixing alcohol with too much cold medicine. I'm thankful. There are too many men who would've taken advantage of the situation."

"It seems you've been hanging out around the wrong men." I desperately try to think about anything other than ripping that dress off her body and taking her right there on the beach. The urge to fuck has never been this strong. She's turning me into a rutting animal.

Fuck. Claim. Take.

"I'm sorry. I didn't mean to imply..." She glances away and her voice drops to a mumble. "I kind of suck at apologies, but when I saw you standing here, then realized who you were, I had to say something. I really am grateful." She glances away and turns her attention back to the surf.

"It's unfortunate a woman needs to be concerned about that at all." I'll kill any man who even thinks to touch her like that. My possessive side rears its beastly head. She's mine. No one else's. "Fortunately, I'm not in the camp who would take advantage."

Except, that's exactly what I want. Not against her will. But most definitely to take advantage of her. I just *want* her. It's an indescribable pull.

"No, I suppose you're not. You're one of the good guys and my hero. I don't know what would've happened to me if you hadn't helped me."

The thoughts running through my head are far from pure and innocent. Good? I laugh at that. The things I want to do to her are far from *good*. They're positively filthy.

The way she looks at me makes my body buzz. My nerves are in a full-on riot. My heart speeds up. My breaths quicken. And my greedy cock is primed and ready. It wants her with an irrational hunger.

It's hard not to stare, and I force myself to look out over the water like she does.

"I'd love to show my gratitude. Buy you a drink? Or dinner?" She turns her attention to me. "Um, that is, if it wouldn't be awkward. I wouldn't want to intrude."

"Intrude?"

"I mean with whoever you're with." She sniffs and forces down a swallow. "I wouldn't want to intrude on your vacation with your wife."

"No wife."

"Fiancée?" The way she glances at her ring finger gives me pause.

"No fiancée."

"Oh." She thinks I'm here with someone.

It's the perfect lead in to figuring out why she's here, what she wants from me, and what kind of game she's playing.

"I'm actually here alone. No wife. No girlfriend. No fiancée. No one."

"Alone?" Her forehead wrinkles.

"Alone, but there's no need to thank me. I wouldn't want your husband, fiancé, or boyfriend—well, you know—I wouldn't want him to get the wrong idea." I'll leave her imagination to fill in that gap.

Her eyes widen, then she nibbles at her lower lip. "I'm actually *not* here with anyone either." She lifts up her left hand and points at her bare ring finger. "This was a gift from my ex. He was my fiancé for all of an hour before he wasn't."

What the fuck did he do to her? My eyes pinch in victory. This is exactly where I want her to be. Time to turn the tables and begin our little game.

"I'm really sorry about that." I shove my hands back in my pockets and make a slight adjustment to ease my straining cock. "We're the only single people in this entire resort. I suppose that means a drink and dinner are in order?" I hold out my hand. "Shall we see what happens?"

It's a risk. If she takes it, I'll take her back to my bungalow, fuck her brains out until I work her out of my system, then I'll walk away.

She takes a long, hard look at my hand. Just when I think she'll reach out, she cups her hands beneath her chin and breaks down with a sob.

Shit.

Well played, Quinn Hayes. Fucking well played.

TEN

Quinn

______

Soul-ripping sobs spill out of me. It's a messy flood of emotion I can't stop. I'm not sure what triggers it. It could be his tenderness, the concern he shows to me, a stranger. I should be sharing this moonlit night with Scott, not this man next to me. Now, I'm crying in front of a stranger.

I'm a pathetic mess.

The soft breeze brings the salty tang of the ocean to my tongue. Or maybe it's from my tears?

The wind is supposed to be refreshing. Instead, I find it terribly suffocating. I'm in paradise, yet my world feels as if it's ended.

How am I going to make it through these next few days? How do I show my face at work? I checked my phone, expecting missed calls and a string of apologies from both Scott and Sadie, but there's nothing. I should've gone home instead of running away to a place I don't belong.

My heart is only now catching up with the loss of both my boyfriend and best friend. What they did was sick and twisted. It's unforgivable, and yet I want to rewind time to before I knew. I'd rather be an oblivious idiot than this tangled mess of emotion.

Whoever said ignorance was bliss is definitely onto something. I don't care what people say, the truth hurts.

"Whoa, are you okay?" A presence shifts beside me. It's him. My sexy stranger; a man who's only seen me at my worst. I'm surprised he's not running for the hills. If he has any sense of self-preservation, he will run and place as much distance between us as possible.

I wipe the tears from my face, embarrassed I broke down in front of him yet again, and struggle to compose myself. In this, I fail miserably.

"I'm sorry." My tears fall in fat drops with a mind all their own. They spill down my cheeks and make me sniffle. I must look a mess.

Waves lap at my feet, pulling the sand out from beneath my heels. My feet slowly sink in and I wish I could do the same. If I disappear, will anyone care?

Scott was my everything. Sadie my best friend. I lost the two people closest to me in one fell swoop. An aching emptiness squeezes my heart and I thump my chest with the palm of my hand. It hurts so damn much.

"Is there anything I can do?" He takes half a step toward me, hand lifted as if to soothe me.

I turn away. I don't need some stranger's comfort. I'll get through this myself. He pauses and thrusts his hands deep into his pockets. I wrap my arms around myself and hold tight.

A hug.

I need a hug, a shoulder to cry on, and someone to tell me I'm worthy of love.

As for my dark and mysterious stranger, I don't want him seeing my tear-streaked cheeks and red-rimmed eyes. I'm bleeding messy emotions all over the place and I'm not comfortable exposing that weakness.

Thankfully, it's dark. Maybe I can hide some of my embarrassment in the darkness.

"You must think I'm a complete mess." I sniffle and resist the urge to wipe my nose.

He cocks his head. "Do you think you're a complete mess?"

"I freak out on the plane. Pass out on booze and cold medicine. Force you to take care of me. And now I break down in front of you. I think that qualifies as a 'certified mess.'" I use air quotes to emphasize my point.

"For the record, you didn't force me to take care of you. You looked like someone who needed help. I'm happy I was able to be there for you." His words roll outward in a soothing rumble. He's blessed with one of those deep, masculine voices. The kind filled with strength and confidence. I bet nothing unnerves this man.

"Well, thank you." In stark contrast, my voice comes out breathy and weak. It's so soft it flutters in the wind, nearly disappearing before being heard. He leans toward me, cocking his head to catch what I say.

"You look like you need to regroup."

That's not what I need. Revenge is what I need, something to show Scott he messed with the wrong woman.

What was Scott's game? Propose? Marry me? And fuck Sadie on the side? How long has it been going on? And why didn't I know?

People aren't my thing, but am I really that blind?

The answer to that is painfully clear. It's a resounding *Yes, you're a flippin' idiot!* I swallow a sob.

"I'm sorry if I ruined your evening." My attention shifts to my stranger. I bet he's the kind who really does care, is a good listener, and doesn't cheat on his girlfriends. He looks like a man who would take care of his woman. I wish I had that.

It doesn't hurt that he's insanely attractive. I catch myself staring for a beat too long, but I can't help myself. The hard angle of his jaw speaks of strength. The warm glow of his eyes radiates concern, tenderness, empathy, and hints at unrestrained passion. I bet he fucks the way Ted fucked Shirley at the party: unrestrained, raw, passionate, one-hundred percent male, driven by base desire.

I've never experienced that all-consuming lust which drags me down to my most base desires. I think too much. But, I bet the man standing before me has. I bet he fucks like an animal and doesn't apologize for it afterward.

His broad shoulders and expansive chest make me think of a

shield. He's the kind of man who would place himself in danger to protect those he loves. The way he stands, feet planted squarely beneath him, brings to mind images of a man who isn't afraid to take charge.

Honestly, I'm projecting a lot on a man I barely know. Although…

I allow my gaze to wander, taking in his attributes one by one. He lent me his strength during takeoff, allowing me to hold his hand. He cautioned me against mixing alcohol and cold medicines, scolding me while looking out for my best interests. While I didn't listen to him, he doesn't seem to hold it against me. When I needed help at the end, he stood up and took control of the situation my bad decision created.

He's the kind of man who doesn't exist in nature, an amalgamation of all things every woman wants.

Which makes me suspicious.

What's he hiding?

What am I missing? My people skills need serious improvement.

"Thank you again for helping me. It means a lot to me." He's shown more kindness than Scott ever did. I turn to leave.

"Don't go." The words sound sincere, although I don't understand why he wants to spend another minute in my presence.

"I've bothered you enough." My steps falter and my brows draw together.

"It really isn't a bother." His magnetic smile unnerves me. It's too genuine and I'm suspicious about pretty much everything right now. If I can't trust myself, how will I ever trust another person ever again? What does this guy—this man—want from me?

Now I don't know whether to stay or go. *This* is exactly the kind of shit I'm not good at. What are the expectations? What's the next appropriate step?

Hell, if I know.

"It looks like you've had a rough day." His head tilts to the side. "Maybe more than one rough day. How about we chill out, enjoy the sound of the waves crashing against the sand, and take a moonlit stroll down the most romantic beach in the world?"

"We?"

He spins in a circle. "Unless you see anyone else around." The deep, throaty sound of his laughter affects me on a gut level. It does weird things, twisting everything up inside and making me want things I can't have. I feel giddy and a tingle of anticipation tickles along my nerves. It would be too easy to fall into that trap, and I do think it's a trap. No way is he interested in me in that way.

He's attractive and looks at me with interest. It's uncomfortable, but exciting as well. Not that I'm going to hop into bed with him.

Why does that cross my mind?

Did I really just think about crawling between the sheets with him?

Yes, you did!

First of all, I seriously doubt he's interested. All I've done is show him exactly how much of a train wreck my life is right now. No sane man would wade into those waters. Second, I'm not the kind of person who bounces from a proposal by one man into the bed of another. The very thought makes me sick to my stomach.

But you want to.

Shut up. I don't need a conversation with my inner self.

"Yeah, I guess it's just you and me." I laugh it off, but my laughter comes out a little forced.

"That's right." He nods as if we've settled something. "Two single people on a beach, going for a stroll."

"In the moonlight?" I cross my arms over my chest. "Sounds more like a place for a couple looking for romance. They should be here, not us."

"Well, *they* are not here, which means you're stuck with me." From the look he gives me, there's more than a little interest in changing our status from strangers to something more. He glances at the full moon. "Unless you have a better idea where we should be?"

I take a long, hard look at him. If he thinks he's getting lucky, he's going to be sorely disappointed.

"Um…" I stammer a bit. "I'm not really looking for that kind of thing."

"What kind of thing?" His comment takes me aback and his lips turn up at the corners. He's waiting for my reaction, like this is a test or something.

Whatever I said amuses him. For some reason, that crooked smile makes him look insanely sexy. He shifts a little, looking out onto the ocean. The light of the moon hits his eyes just right, making them shimmer like burnished gold.

"Um, you know—things."

"Do I?" His smile widens and spreads to his eyes. "As for *things*, are you talking about walking down the beach? Or something else?" His gaze drops to my hand.

As if all you want to do is hold my hand.

"You have the most unusual eyes." Needing a quick change in the topic of our conversation, the comment slips out. I'm not really sure where it came from.

"Do I?" He's having fun with me now, repeating himself. "I might say the same for you. Magnificent comes to mind."

I ignore his comment. Like most things, I don't handle compliments well.

"Your eyes are golden, or burnished copper. Honestly, I've never seen eyes like that before."

"Hmm, and yours are a stunning emerald. Did you know they change color?"

Every time he looks at me, it's with this odd intensity, like he's trying to figure me out. More unnerving, he holds his stare beyond what I'm comfortable with. I'm the first to break eye contact.

"They do?"

"They most certainly do." He glances down at his feet and wiggles his toes in the sand. "They're dark when you think too hard. Light and stormy when you're scared. They shimmer when you're frustrated. Impossibly gorgeous when you reveal your vulnerabilities. And they remind me of a forest when you relax."

He notices my eyes?

"Um—I doubt you've ever seen me relaxed."

"You're right, but I'm looking forward to it." His soft laughter cuts me off and an unusual silence settles between us.

It's the kind of silence that should be awkward between strangers but isn't. It floats on the wind as if perfectly content to shift between us. My attention returns to the surf and the inky black of the water beyond.

"What's your name?" I turn to him. "Did you already tell me? If so, I don't remember. I'm pretty horrible with names."

"Hawke." He thrusts out his hand. "Hawke Sterling, at your service."

Deviant thoughts fill my head with all the ways I'd like to be serviced. Sadie would jump on that. I back away.

ELEVEN

Quinn

"I'M Q." WHEN OUR HANDS CONNECT, A JOLT OF ELECTRICITY shoots up my arm. I'd pull my hand back, but he doesn't let go. Instead of releasing me, like a normal person, he shifts our grip until our palms touch, our fingers lengthen, and then curl as they thread together. The entire time, his eyes lock with mine.

It's a handshake. Kind of. So why is it one of the most erotic things I've ever experienced? All we're doing is holding hands.

Holding.

Not shaking.

"You're far too pretty for anyone to call you Q. It's a harsh nickname for a beautiful woman, too masculine. A man could lose himself in you."

His gaze takes me in from head to toe and back again. He's obvious about it, taking his time to meander the length of my body, while letting me know that's exactly what he's doing. He doesn't linger too long on my breasts or the apex of my thighs, like most men would. It's almost as if everything about me fascinates him and he can't get enough. The entire time, our fingers remain woven together. The pads of his fingers press against my knuckles, and he presses lightly in a soothing, hypnotic rhythm.

I shift my stance and lift my feet out of the hole the waves dig beneath my heels.

Beneath his examination, my shoulders lift toward my ears. I'm torn between feeling uncomfortable and entranced. With effort, I force my shoulders to relax.

"My dad didn't want a frilly girl's name, and I was supposed to be a boy—the fifth boy in the family."

"Fifth?" His eyes widen. "You have four older brothers."

"I have four overly protective older brothers. Anyhow, my dad picked Quinn. He said it would work for a girl or a boy. I kind of got stuck with it. Once I got to high school, I was well into nerd-ville as a computer geek and since I was a Trekkie…"

His eyes widen. "You're nicknamed after a super-race who exists in the continuum of the limitless dimensions of the galaxy; Q from Star Trek?"

"Yeah…" I breathe out slowly, surprised he's that familiar with the character. "I've always hated it. It makes me even more self-conscious about…"

"Being smart?"

"Yeah. Girls aren't supposed to be smart, and they're most definitely not supposed to be smarter than the boys they want to date."

"Why don't you correct people?" He appears unfazed by my comment about being smarter than other boys. Does nothing rock this man? "Smart chicks are beyond hot. They're mesmerizing."

I'm not sure what to make of that comment. Is he talking about me, or smart chicks in the more general sense?

"Have you ever had a nickname?" I can't imagine how someone would shorten Hawke. It's such an unusual name. It makes me think of an established dynasty, like a family name passed down through the generations. "It's impossible to get people to stop using it. They think it's funny and the more I fought it the more it stuck. I'm used to it now."

"You're far too beautiful for your name to be whittled down to a single letter, especially the harshest letter in the English alphabet. I prefer Quinn. It's crisp, elegant, and unexpected. It's a perfect fit for an amazingly beautiful woman. You're stunning." He leans toward me and lowers his voice. We're still holding hands. "To be honest, I've known several Quinn's in my life, none of them were girls. I can honestly say, I never wanted to kiss any of them the way I want to kiss you."

Molten hot, the heat in his eyes warms me up from the inside out. Then it hits.

Kiss me?

Whoa, we jumped way out of my comfort zone. I do what I do best and deflect.

"Wouldn't it be nice if we could pick our own names?" I free my hand with an awkward twist and rub it against my leg.

"Pick our names? How would that work?" He appears unfazed by my sudden retreat.

"You know, like a rite of passage when you hit say—twelve or thirteen?" I snap my fingers. "Or at the end of sixth grade, when you're no longer an elementary school kid. Instead of a sixth-grade graduation, we could have a naming ceremony instead."

"That's—unusual." His head tilts to the side and the corners of his eyes crinkle with amusement. "You're not what I expect, Miss Quinn Hayes. Maybe Q is for quirky instead of smart?"

I bite my lower lip. Chances are one hundred percent, my freaky comments about naming ceremonies make him rethink wanting to kiss me.

"I get that a lot." I rush my words. "Anyway, it was nice seeing you, and thanks again." I rock back on my heels, fully expecting him to take advantage of the out I provide.

"Hold up a second. We're far from done. You intrigue me, Miss Quinn, like a puzzle I can't quite figure out. I'm nowhere near letting you go."

"A puzzle?" Letting go? Holy hotness, what did he just say? Did I imagine that?

"Well, a woman traveling alone is no big thing. I hope you'll forgive me, but I had to look through your backpack to figure out what to do with you. When I saw you had a reservation at this resort, I figured you were meeting up with someone. At the registration desk, they said the other person canceled. Which brings up all kinds of questions—fascinating questions."

Well shit, he's not taking the bait and running. As for his questions, he's going to be disappointed.

"It's a story as old as time." I'm pretty sure I mentioned this to him, but honestly, my memory is foggy. From the beginning of the flight to when I woke up in an unfamiliar bed, my memory is littered with holes. "Boy meets girl. Girl falls in love. Boy proposes. Boy cheats on her, and… Well, here I am."

"So you brought your broken heart to Euphoria?" He scratches his head. "That creates more questions."

"It may not have been my brightest idea." I agree with him. In fact, the longer I'm at Euphoria, I'm sure this is a disaster in progress. "At the time, all I could think about was sticking it to him. You know, using it to get back at him? I figured since he already paid for everything, I would come. I'd have the best time of my life without him. In hindsight, it isn't working out the way I planned, and I kind of feel a little guilty about it."

"Why do you feel guilty?"

I spin toward the resort and place my back to the waves. "It's stealing. Now, I'll have to pay him back and I'm not sure I can do that." My shoulders slump in defeat. I really didn't think this through. Now, I'll be tied to Scott by a debt as well as the company we run together.

"Women use men all the time. Why should this be any different?" His words are not only acidic, they feel like a slap in the face. I spin back toward him, fingers curled into impotent fists.

"Because, I'm. Not. Like. That." I enunciate each word, my anger building. "I don't *use* men, and I definitely don't take advantage of them."

His eyelids pull so far back it looks like his eyes are going to pop out of his head. He holds up a hand. "Whoa, didn't mean to strike a nerve. Just stating what I know."

"Then you've been hanging around the wrong women." I can't help it. Exhaustion pulls at me, mentally and physically. A hole would be a great place right about now. Somewhere I can slip inside and disappear from the world. "Look, I'm sorry. I didn't mean to snap…"

His wide eyes go to the opposite extreme. He stares at me through narrow slits, assessing, appraising, and examining everything about me. It makes me feel like a bug under the microscope.

"You really mean it don't you?" He says it as if he shouldn't believe me, but somehow does.

I'm not sure if I count that as a win.

"Mean what?" I take half a step up the beach, ready to put this night behind me.

"About using men?"

"Damn straight. I've worked too hard to get where I am. I'm not some right-winged feminist, but I stand on my own two feet. I don't need a man to help with that."

"Never said you did."

"No, but you implied I used Scott for his money."

"Actually, I didn't. You said you felt guilty for using his money, or rather coming here when he paid for it. I made a general comment about women, which agreed with what you said."

I want to be pissed at this man, but damn if it's hard to keep my anger boiling. The truth is, I'm tired.

"I think I should go to bed. Alone." Not sure why I added that last part. It just slipped out.

"Can I ask you a question?"

"Sure."

"Why did you come here? If it's not to spend his money to get back at him, then why? Whatever it was, it had to be something, considering your fear of flying."

"Because I wanted to disappear, and if I showed up at home, without Scott, there'd be a gazillion questions."

"A gazillion?" The smirk is back on his face. "That's a pretty big number."

Heat rises to my cheeks. "Yeah, a *gazillion*, but if you knew my brothers, you'd understand."

"They sound like they love you very much. Maybe they can help you through this? Just because you're here, doesn't mean you have to stay. Decisions made in the heat of powerful emotions are seldom good ones."

"And get back on a plane?" My eyes widen and it feels as if the pit of my stomach drops to the center of the earth.

"Unless you plan on swimming back, that's the only way."

"Just kill me now." A low groan escapes me.

His laughter returns, and with it, his eyes shine. I could lose myself in those eyes if I don't watch out.

"Honestly," I blow out my breath, "I was running. I wanted to disappear. And I wanted to get back at him. I'm guilty of that, but now I feel guilty for doing it." I shake my head, not sure if I'm making sense. "This was the only place I had to go. We work together. It's a small startup we're trying to get off the ground. I'm the tech brains. He's the businessman. He proposed at our office Christmas party, in front of everyone. Then cheated on me that same night. I can't go back and face everyone after what he did. Fortunately, the office is closed until the new year. Everyone is off visiting their families."

"I don't get why you didn't go home." The way he looks at me makes me feel like he really cares.

Me? He cares about me? Talk about transference. I'm stupid enough to think a stranger really cares about me.

"Because my family is intense. My brothers wouldn't think twice about murdering Scott once they learn what he did to their little sister. That's not an exaggeration."

"Scott's the ex-fiancé?"

"Yes, the cheating bastard." I mumble the words.

"You know, there's no one here." He gestures down the empty beach. "You don't have to whisper."

I cock my head, confused.

"Go ahead and scream. Gather all that pain and frustration and let it rip."

"Let it rip?"

"You know, let it all loose. Frankly, he's a jerk for doing what he did, and doesn't deserve another moment of your time. All that anger, the pain, the hurt, and heartache…" He gestures toward the ocean. "Let it all out."

"You want me to scream at the ocean?" It's my turn to think he's the weirdo, but I wonder if it wouldn't feel good?

"Sounds like it might help. I'm sorry that douchebag treated you that way. Men can be dicks."

"And sometimes they can be incredibly kind." I smile at him. "Thank you again for helping me."

"You've apologized and thanked me enough. How about we make a pact?"

"A pact?"

"No more apologies. No more *thank yous*. I want you to relax, take a breather, and enjoy time away from that jerk. And while you're here, take advantage of everything Euphoria has to offer. Nobody here knows you. Step away from your life. Indulge a little. Eat. Drink. Sign up for all the activities. Pick one thing each day that challenges you. Let all that negativity disappear from your life. When you go back, you can face him with a new outlook on life, and you'll know you can have the most amazing time without him."

"You make it seem so easy."

"Broken hearts are rough." He glances down the beach. "How about that walk?"

"Actually, I'm going to sit for a little bit, stare at the stars, maybe cry a little bit more, find a shooting star or two and make a wish. Then head to bed. It's been a rough twenty-four hours."

"Mind if I keep you company?"

"You sure about that? I haven't made the best first impression." I really don't want him to go.

"I'll make allowances for your broken heart."

"Surprisingly, it doesn't hurt as much as it should. I guess that should tell me something. I'm more upset at losing my best friend."

"Wait a minute." He looks shocked. "Asshat cheated on you with your best friend?"

"Right after he proposed." I shake my head and hold my hand to my breastbone. It hurts. I'm amazed by how much it actually hurts.

"Shit, that's a low blow." He takes my hand in his. Like before, a shock of electricity shoots up my arm. "You don't deserve that."

"It is what it is." I step back from the waterline and find a place to sit. When he touches me, weird feelings bubble up. I don't know what to make of them.

He follows, watching me closely. I'm going to have sand everywhere, but I don't care. I blow out a breath and lean back to stare at the stars. The light of the moon dims the starlight, but I can still make out my favorite constellations.

Hawke sits down beside me, then lies back. He's close, really close, but doesn't touch me. Instead, the heat of his body leaps across the space between us to sear my skin. The things I want from him aren't civilized. I can't explain it, except I sense he's the one person powerful enough to shut off my brain and make me feel what it means, not to be feminine, but rather a female bending to the desires of the male who claims her. It's so out of the world weird; I dismiss the odd thought.

But my body is buzzing.

TWELVE

Hawke

I can't figure Quinn Hayes out. She's either completely oblivious as to who I am, or incredibly good at playing dumb. I'm smarter than this, but can't help but fall under her spell.

Raw and savage, real pain radiates from her. It slams into me, wave after wave, beating against my defenses until the urge to pull her into my arms and console her becomes unbearable. I can't escape this irrational feeling that she's mine. That means her pain is my pain. I'll bear it for her, if only to ease her trauma. I don't even know her. Where is this coming from?

But that's the thing. I don't comfort women. I use them. Mutual physical gratification. Those are the marching orders. I use them. They use me. I get what I want, and they get what they want.

None of this makes sense. I'm no guardian protector. But I want her to lay her burdens at my feet. I want to soothe her pain and take her burdens from her.

Three times, I reached out. Three times, she turned away.

If I'm her goal, she's playing her game of hard to get too well and risks losing me. I'm not a man who chases women. They come to me. Not that she didn't let me touch her, but she didn't react to the gentle tug I gave when I threaded my fingers with hers.

Instead, she pulled back. Actually, it was more forceful than that. She jerked out of my grip, as if she'd been stung.

Now, we lie beside each other. Less than an inch separates us, yet I'm acutely aware of every movement her body makes. From the way she digs her fingers into the sand beside me, swirling them around and around, to the way her chest rises and falls, I sense all of it.

"I wish the moon wasn't out." Her soft, breathy sigh drifts on the wind.

"Why's that?"

"Because it washes out the stars."

We're alone, on a beach, beneath a moonlit sky. Why the fuck am I lying beside her instead of on top of her where I belong? Why aren't my fingers threading through her auburn waves as I devour her mouth with a kiss? Why am I not buried deep inside of her? We should be naked, or on our way to getting naked, by now.

Instead, we lie side by side, staring up at the moon.

"I used to spend long nights outside staring up at the skies," she says.

I can't see her face, but I feel her smile. This is a happy memory and I hang on her next words.

"I did too. My sister loves it. She taught me all the constellations."

"You know the constellations?"

"Most of them." I point at the sky. "See those three bright stars lined up in a row?"

"That's Scorpio's head." She points at the sky, draws a line down. Her fingers trace the curve of Scorpio's tail. "It's one of my favorite constellations."

I roll to my side, because fuck it, I need to see her face. I prop myself up on my elbow and rest my head on my hand. "I suppose I should've known you'd know the stars, considering you're a Trekkie."

"I used to be a Trekkie, at least until I realized all the laughter and jokes weren't being made in fun, but rather *about* me. I learned early to hide my interests. If it wasn't about dances or the homecoming game, I learned to keep things like that to myself." She squints and a smile tugs at the corners of her lips.

"It's sad how mean kids can be to one another."

"I suppose, but after a while, it didn't matter. It's not like I had a bad experience. High school is difficult for everyone."

"I suppose."

It's not hard for everyone. With my looks, and ample trust fund, I ruled my school. High school was one of the happiest times in my life. I fucked who I wanted. I was the quarterback on our football team. I brought home glory, only to be shown by my mother how none of that mattered.

"Isn't it funny how much high school defines us?" It certainly defined me. "It sticks with us for life,"

"I bet it wasn't rough for you." She shifts away from me. A subtle movement, I'm certain it's deliberate. For a woman trying to worm herself into my good graces, she's doing it all wrong.

"It wasn't that rough if I'm being honest, but that doesn't mean it was easy."

She scoots way back, alarming me for a moment, but I breathe easier when she rolls to her side, mirroring me, and props her head on her hand. She bites her lower lip, it's both seductive and sweet.

"I'm guessing you were in the popular crowd."

"Guilty."

"Lettered in sports." Her eyes narrow. "Baseball or football? Am I close?"

"Hitting it right on the head." Her insight is spot on. It's almost scary. "Both actually."

"Quarterback and homecoming king?"

"Don't forget pitcher for the varsity team. You make it sound bad." I reach between us and draw a hashmark in the sand. "I was prom king as well as homecoming king."

"So, I'm not wrong." She draws an X in the upper left row, middle spot.

I love how she knew exactly what I was doing. It's amazing how in sync we are. It's like she's attuned to my every thought.

"No." I reach out and draw a circle in the middle square.

She places another X, left column, center spot. I stare at our game of tic-tac-toe, not really interested in the outcome. I just want to keep her talking. The sound of her voice draws me in and I hang on every word.

I take my turn, placing an O in the lower corner. Her lips twist.

"I win."

I glance at the game, not seeing it, but when she places an X in the corner opposite my O, I see she's right.

I brush over the sand, erasing the game.

"How about we make this interesting?" I have ulterior motives.

"How's that?"

"Best two out of three?"

"And what does the winner get?" She sounds interested.

"How about winner's choice?"

"I don't understand?"

"If you win, you decide what we do next and I'll have to do it. No backing out. If I win, you do what I want."

"No backing out?" She curled her lower lip. "That sounds dangerous."

"That's what makes it fun. The higher the stakes, the more challenging the game."

"What if it's something I really don't want to do?"

"Like what?"

"Like climbing inside a plane again." Her delicate nose pinches. It's fucking cute as hell.

I can't help but laugh. Here I'm thinking about demanding that kiss I want and she thinks I'll make her get on a plane? She can't be that clueless, but looking into her eyes, I'm beginning to think she really has no idea who I am.

This is going to be so much fun, and not for the reasons I originally thought. It might be possible she's the only woman on the planet who's not interested in taking a piece of me.

"Or jumping out of one."

Her eyes widen and she sucks in a breath.

"Um no. Totally not that. You really want me to die? Climb in a perfectly good airplane only to jump out of it?"

"So, you admit airplanes are *good?*" I laugh as her mouth gapes.

"That's not what I meant."

"I'm pretty sure you'll be safe." She's completely unaware we have a seaplane. It's used for our skydiving adventures, but I'll never ask her to jump out of a plane. Flying is a real fear. I don't agree with it, but I respect her fears.

Actually, that might be fun. I'll save that one for later.

"I'm not okay with *anything*. How about we state the stakes upfront?"

"So you know what you're betting on?"

"Exactly."

"Kind of ruins the surprise." I really want to see her open herself up for a little bit of adventure. I have an irrational need to see her smile and enjoy herself.

"Those are my terms." She draws another tic-tac-toe grid in the sand. Her movements are sure and purposeful.

"Well, since you have me at your mercy…" It's fun to tease her. "I know what mine is going to be."

"What's that?"

I give a shake of my head. "Oh no, these are your rules, that means you go first."

There she goes again, biting her lower lip. "I saw a sign-up for ballroom dancing. I've never done that before and it's not something you can do without a partner."

Ballroom dancing? What an absurd request, and she has no idea I'm quite proficient in all forms of ballroom dancing. It's considered an essential skill according to my mother.

In Mother's world, businesses rise and fall on two battlefields. The first over a game of golf, where the men battle for dominance. According to my mother, the true war is waged on the dance floor, where a real tycoon goes for the jugular and seduces his opponent's wife.

"I think I can handle that." If I lose this silly game, Quinn doesn't realize she's already lost the war. A few spins around the dance floor, she'll be breathless and entranced.

"And if you win?" She turns her amazing eyes toward me.

"Oh, mine is simple, but maybe too much, considering we're strangers."

Her eyes widen, waiting for me to continue. I almost expect her to jump in and say something, anxious about my response.

But she remains deathly quiet.

Quinn is a fucking natural at this game. She waits me out until I'm the one who breaks.

"Don't you want to know?"

"I'm waiting for you to tell me. As long as it doesn't require me getting on a plane, you can ask for the moon and I'd be good with it."

"Remember those are your words, because what I want comes at a terrible cost."

"Oh please, do tell. I'm dying to know." She bats her lashes at me. It's intentionally dramatic.

I reach out and capture her hand, noting the moment her breathing stills. An electrical charge buzzes between us, full of potency and promise. There's no denying our attraction. Not now.

"Easy. I want one kiss."

"You want a kiss?"

"Not just any kiss. I want you wrapped in my arms, our lips pressed together, it begins and ends when I say."

She blinks and there's the slightest hitch in her breathing. The way she licks her lips, almost as if she imagines what kissing me might feel like, tells me she's on board.

"That's… Um." She swallows thickly. "A kiss?"

I nod.

"You want to kiss me?" Her eyes widen and she pulls her hand out from under mine. Shifting in the sand, she drapes an arm over her forehead. "I'm the last person a man like you wants to kiss."

"What do you mean, a man like me?"

She drops her arm and sits up. "I'm a tragic mess. If I've given you the wrong idea, I sincerely apologize, but I'm not looking for something like that."

This doesn't happen to me. Women don't pull away from me.

But she's on her feet, brushing the sand off her hands. Glancing down at me, she sucks in her lower lip.

"Goodnight, Hawke, maybe I'll see you around."

I watch her walk away, stunned by how our evening ends. So much for fucking her brains out. Yet again, she leaves me stiff, engorged, and crazy with lust.

I almost follow her, but I turn away at the last moment. No fucking way will I give chase. Instead, I plod back to my bungalow, strip out of my clothes, and jerk off to thoughts of all the filthy things I want to do with Miss Quinn Hayes. And they are fucking filthy.

THIRTEEN

Quinn

____

So what if I'm a chicken shit?

It's not the first time I've run from something which scares me.

Kissing Hawke scares me, or rather, letting him kiss me. He's not the kind of man who lets a woman kiss him. Oh no, he's the kind of man who dominates and controls. Frankly, that scares the shit out of me, nearly as much, or more, than it excites me. I can't explain it, but I want him to take control. I've never met a man strong enough, confident enough, determined enough, to break through my walls and step up and be a _man._

I'm all for women's liberation. I'm a fucking brilliant scientist, but when it comes to man vs. woman, there's no arguing against basic physiology. One gives. The other takes. And damn if I don't want him to take and stake his claim.

I'm very much afraid of the passion brimming in his eyes. He strikes me as a man who gets what he wants, or takes it outright. But I don't want to be discarded on the other side of all that passion.

All kinds of red flags go up.

First off, why me?

While not on purpose, I've inadvertently done everything humanly possible to be unattractive to someone of the opposite sex.

It's not like I'm trying. This simply isn't my day to shine. I'm supposed to be grieving my heartbreak.

I don't trust Hawke Sterling. Whatever his motives are, they have nothing to do with any attraction toward me. It can't.

I freaked out on the plane. Drank myself under the proverbial table until I was barely conscious. I press my knuckles against my forehead because I distinctly remember puking on the plane. I drag my hand down my face and pull at my chin.

How embarrassing.

What in any of that gives him the hair-brained idea he wants to kiss me?

This is why I don't trust men. None of it adds up. My gut says he's up to something, and my gut never steered me wrong; except with Scott. Hell, my gut wasn't even at the wheel. How wrong did that turn out?

But back to Hawke Sterling. Gah! Even his name inspires images of masculine dominance. It's a powerful name. It holds weight. There's no question of where he stands when it comes to being in charge. He'll allow me just enough to think I'm in charge, before yanking me back to reality.

Not that he would've won that silly bet. Tic-tac-toe might be a kid's game, but I'm pretty good at winning. There was zero chance of losing and having him claim that kiss.

So, here's the million-dollar question.

Why did I run?

I don't know, and, honestly, I don't care.

That's a lie.

I spend all night wondering how Hawke's lips might feel pressed against mine. How he might taste as he plunders my mouth. How it will be fundamentally different from kissing Scott with his weak lips and uninspired kisses.

Would Hawke stop at a kiss? I know the answer to this. He won't. It's ingrained in his basic makeup. He takes, claims, possesses… And holy hell, I want to feel what that might be like.

All damn night, my mind whirls with possibilities.

Not good at reading people, that kiss comment came out of

nowhere. I thought we were sitting on the beach staring at stars and playing a dumb kid's game of tic-tac-toe. At some point, things shifted, and I missed the signs.

He wouldn't ask for a kiss if he wasn't interested? Right?

But if he wanted a kiss, wouldn't he simply take it?

This is why I hate people. Nothing they do makes sense. With Scott, I knew what to expect and where we were headed. He kissed me and we had sex; uninspired sex, but sex nonetheless. At least until I realized Scott was playing a very different game. What does Scott want with me? He's not in love with me. Not if he's fucking Sadie. So, what does he gain by marrying me?

Yet again, I find myself blindsided.

Scott is the reason I ran away from work. He's the reason I'm hiding out in Euphoria instead of spending the holidays at home with my loud and obnoxious family. Scott took something precious when he cheated on me. My ability to trust is irrevocably shattered.

Not that it matters. The truth is I'm not ready to fall into the arms of another man. Not that it would be anything other than a holiday fling, but still.

I'm not that kind of girl.

And why not? He said you could be anything you wanted.

Hawke's words come back to me. He's right about one thing. Nobody here knows me. It might be the perfect time to shed my skin and try out a few things.

I can be whomever I want to be. Whomever? Or is it whoever? Shit, what do I care? It's not like the grammar police are in my head.

With that thought, I drift off to sleep.

In the morning, I wake to an inbox flooded with messages. Only two are from Scott, begging me to call him. There are twenty from Sadie, all full of tears, regrets, and apologies I can't accept.

Irritated by the texts and messages, I flip the downy white comforter off the bed and give a good long stretch. I'm in paradise with absolutely nothing to do all day except be lazy.

But I'm not a lazy person. I'm used to being in motion, and I don't like pity parties. I've already lost one day in paradise to a hangover. Time to see what there is to do at Euphoria.

A quick shower leaves me refreshed, and since I'm in paradise, I slip on a red string bikini, a pair of cheeky short shorts, and a loosely woven crochet top. Yup, I'm strutting my stuff to men who don't give a flying fuck about me. They're here with the love of their lives.

Which means, I'm a stupid peacock on parade.

I take a moment to explore my little retreat. It's beach chic, classy, elegant, and yet casual all at the same time. The bed is large, the pillows fluffy, the bathroom absolutely decadent with a large soaking tub and a shower enclosure more than big enough for two.

An entire wall of windows faces the beach. It's a tiny, secluded cove with a narrow crescent of sparkling sand. It's almost too perfect. Pounding waves break over an outer reef, spraying foam high into the air. I feel their distant thunder vibrating deep in my chest. That outer reef leaves the inner waters of my tiny cove nearly still. They ripple, sending tiny waves lapping at the shore, but are otherwise mirror-smooth.

Seabirds circle overhead looking for their next meal. One tucks its wings and dives under the water. It crests the surface a few seconds later with a tiny wriggling fish in its beak. A few birds strut along the beach, pecking at small crustaceans who hide in the sand. Past all of it, endless swells of water roll inward from an ocean too big to comprehend. I feel incredibly small looking upon all that splendor.

After closer examination, my cove is clearly manmade. There's too much regularity to the arched spits of land. The owners of this resort certainly pulled out all the stops.

I wander the beach for an hour looking for seashells until hunger pains pull me back inside. I could order room service, but like last night, the thought of staying alone in this place makes me feel extremely lonely.

People may confuse me, but I seek them out. Not to socialize with; I'm not interested in intruding on some couple's romantic vacation. I just want to be nearby, so I don't feel so incredibly, achingly alone.

I slip on a pair of sandals and decide food and a little exploration are in order. This takes me on a meandering stroll through immaculately manicured paths and gardens blooming with color. One thing I love about the tropics is they're colorful year-round with all manner of flowering plants.

It's a little funny, but the resort has decorated for the holidays, putting out little holiday scenes, but there's no way to hide that we're in the tropics. Beautiful butterflies flit from bush to bush, drinking nectar from tropical blooms. Tiny tree frogs ribbit, adding their unique sound to the melody. I can almost forget it's Christmas.

As for the resort itself, it's stunning. There's simply no other way to say it. My suite appears to be one of four secluded retreats, but that doesn't mean the rest of the resort isn't over-the-top elegant.

Everything is tied together and yet feels reclusive. There are tons of alcoves and other spaces for couples to find the privacy they crave. I wander past half a dozen couples napping on the grass, sitting at picnic tables, and simply enjoying a timeout from the world.

I envy them but decide it's not going to ruin my experience. It's a gorgeous day with barely a cloud in the deep-blue sky. The sun heats my body, bringing beads of perspiration to my skin, but the constant breeze off the ocean keeps me cool.

It's a perfect day; the perfect day.

I wander by a maze of grottos and find several couples in various stages of physical intimacy. One couple makes me hurry my step. Their soft moans and bodies moving rhythmically in unison leave nothing to the imagination.

The expansive pool welcomes guests to take a soothing dip. Two couples play a game of volleyball, splashing and laughing as they try to score.

I bypass the pool bar and head to the main restaurant. Last night, hunger brought me here, but the romantic atmosphere scared me off. I'm hoping it's a little less daunting in the daylight.

Fortunately, my suspicions are correct. The cozy ambience of last night is replaced by bright sunlight streaming through the windows. Bright and colorful birds fill the air with song and layered over that is the sound of rushing water in a man-made stream which meanders throughout the resort. The air smells fresh, fragrant, and invigorating. It makes me want to be outside, enjoying the tropical climate.

"Miss Hayes." The hostess somehow recognizes me, "How may I help you?"

"Um, table for one?"

"Of course." She picks up a menu and gestures for me to follow. Not one time does she make me feel awkward for requesting a table alone.

She seats me at one of the best tables in the dining room. It's a corner table out of the main flow of traffic. I'll have privacy to enjoy my meal in peace and not feel awkward that I'm alone.

Although, in looking around, it appears I'm not the only one dining alone. An elderly gentleman sits on the far side of the restaurant. He snaps a newspaper and sips his coffee. There's another woman sitting alone, near the middle of the room, with a book in one hand and a mimosa in the other. Her eyes are glued to her book. It must be spicy by the way she keeps nibbling on her lower lip as she reads.

I have nothing but my phone with its unanswered texts and emails clogging up my inbox. I start hitting delete when a man approaches the table. Thinking it's my waiter, I look up with a smile on my face. I quickly discard the smile for a frown when Hawke Sterling pulls out a chair and sits down like he owns the place.

FOURTEEN

Quinn

____

"WHAT ARE YOU DOING?" MY TONE IS CHALLENGING, BUT WAVERS with uncertainty.

"I'm sitting down for brunch." Hawke lifts his hand over his head and beckons with his fingers. Less than thirty-seconds later, my waiter appears. Hawke rattles off an order. "One mimosa. One bloody mary. And bring us a starter of crab claws."

"Right away, Mr. Sterling." Our waiter disappears as I gape at Hawke.

"That's a bit ballsy ordering for me."

"You think that was for you?" His smile is arrestingly gorgeous.

The golden glow of his eyes melts me from the inside out. He's cocky, arrogant, and perfectly at ease. If I thought he was handsome in the moonlight, it's nothing compared to his sultry good looks in the light of day.

"Of course, if you want one of the drinks..." He lets his voice trail off and winks. "I can be persuaded to share."

"You're really going to tell me you're planning on drinking the bloody mary and the mimosa?"

"Am I?" He leans back, all cocksure and tempting.

My decision to run from that kiss comes back to haunt me. What would've been so bad about a little kiss?

Before I can answer, the waiter returns with our drinks. He places the bloody mary in front of Hawke and the mimosa in front of me.

"Your crab claws will be here momentarily." The waiter shifts his attention to me. "Are you ready to order?"

I've yet to look at the menu. Hawke steps up, continuing with his bossy arrogance. It's frustratingly sexy as fuck. "We'll split the seafood tower and if you could bring us each a serving of fresh fruit. I'll take water with my meal and she'll take…" He looks at me, giving me an opportunity to speak for myself.

"I'll have iced tea with lemon, please." It feels like an extravagance to be given the ability to order for myself. His bossiness? It's a hundred times more intoxicating than the mimosa.

The waiter takes our order and leaves us in peace.

"How do you know I'm not allergic to shellfish?" I ask.

"I don't."

"Do you commonly order for your dates without their input?"

"That depends." He leans toward me. "Am I your date?"

"More like an intruder." My tone is supposed to be harsh, but I can't help the smile turning up the corners of my lips. He's impossibly gorgeous, stunning actually, and his take-charge attitude is titillating. Which is weird. I'm usually put off by bossy men who think they know everything. With Hawke, it's not like that.

It's way worse.

He triggers deep-seated fantasies I'm not willing to acknowledge.

"An intruder you're not kicking out." He rests his chin on his hand and gives me a long, appraising look as he dissects everything about me.

At least that's how it feels. Beneath his gaze, I'm exposed as he delves for all my most intimate secrets. Terrified doesn't begin to explain how I feel. I'm not ready for anyone to read me that well.

"An intruder who wouldn't leave if I asked." I counter in the only way I can.

"This is where you're wrong. If you're not interested in sharing a meal with me, just say the word and I'll disappear." He leans back and takes a sip of his drink. "However, if you don't mind a little company, I'm happy to stick around. We are, after all, the only single people in this entire resort."

I've been avoiding the mimosa. Somehow, if I drink from it, I tacitly agree to his presence. But that's the thing, I want his company. I'm utterly, and totally, enthralled with Hawke Sterling.

I take the drink and lift it in a toast. "To a beautiful day in paradise."

"Now, that's something I can get behind." He clinks his glass against mine as the waiter returns with a bed of crab claws arranged on shaved ice.

"Thank you, Julian." Hawke doesn't look at the man's name tag. He either has a really good memory, or is excellent at names. "Can you grab us a second round?"

One of my greatest shortcomings is learning people's names. Hawke seems like a people person, perfectly at ease in the social environment. There's no doubt in my mind he's King of Kings in that department.

I take a sip of my drink, more of a gulp to steady my nerves, and turn my attention to Hawke.

Crab claws are one of my favorite dishes, not that I'm going to let him know it.

"Last night, you learned what brought me here, but I don't know why you're here." My statement is issued in challenge, daring him to fill in the blanks.

I don't know why he's here alone because it never occurred to me to ask. This is how socially inept I am.

"Are you asking why I'm here, or why I'm alone?"

"Does it matter?"

"It most definitely does." He stares at me until I squirm. "You've earned the unique distinction of being the only woman to run from one of my kisses."

"I can't be the first."

The look he gives makes me think that's absolutely the truth. Then I remember what he did tell me.

To hide my discomfort, I nibble on a crab claw. And then another. And another. Finally, the silence stretches too long, and I'm forced to answer.

"I didn't run."

"You sure about that?" His eyes narrow and his brows pinch together. "Because I'm pretty sure sparks were flying as you beat a path away from me."

"I don't know about sparks, but you don't want anything to do with me."

"How can you be so sure?"

"Because I told you why I'm here." I upend my drink and suck it dry. I don't usually guzzle alcohol, but Hawke has a way of getting under my skin. I slam the glass down with more force than I intend. "Why are *you* here?"

"Ah, finally, she has a good question."

"Finally?"

"Yes, it's a rather important question. My answer decides the course of the rest of our time together."

"The rest of our time?"

"Yes." His voice turns low, sultry, and serious. "Why am I here alone?"

"I think that's what I'm asking."

"No, you asked why I'm here. You didn't ask why I'm here alone." He makes a point to emphasize *alone*, then sits back as if waiting on me to do just that.

Ask him.

"Why are you here—alone?"

"Because I don't trust women. Right now, I'm between entanglements."

"Entanglements?" I cock my head. "You make it sound like a bad thing."

"Isn't it?"

"No, it's not. The purest form of love is what happens between two people who love each other. Frankly, it's sad you're here alone."

"How's that?"

"Because you're an attractive man. How is there not a woman attached to you?"

"Maybe you're asking the wrong question."

"You're not making any sense."

"Aren't I?"

I nibble at my lower lip and look at my empty glass. Where the hell is our waiter with the refills Hawke ordered?

"Are you coming off a bad relationship?" My tone is flippant and even I'm annoyed by it.

"No, I'm not, but that's only because I don't allow it to ever get to that point." He fixes me with that mesmerizing gaze. "Do you wonder if you missed any signs with what's-his-name?"

"You mean Scott?"

"Yes, your hour-long fiancé." He leans closer. "Is it possible you missed signs he was a douchebag?"

"Scott is most definitely a douchebag." I can't help but laugh. "Honestly, I'm trying *not* to think about him."

"Well, then it appears you're in luck."

"How's that?"

"Because I'm here, and there's not a single woman on the planet who thinks of another man when they're with me."

What is it about Hawke? That comment sends heat licking up and down my body. Most interesting, and even more concerning, is the aching throb between my legs. It takes incredible willpower not to shift in my seat.

"But I'm not with you." I do what I can to deflect.

"That remains to be seen. You have two weeks at Euphoria, Miss Hayes. It would be a shame spending all that time alone."

"It's actually only a week and a half. Maybe I've given you the wrong impression, but I just got out of a horrible relationship. I'm not looking to jump into another."

"Who said anything about jumping into a relationship?"

"You did."

"No, I suggested spending a little time together. You're the one who turned it sexual."

"I—no I didn't."

"You said relationship. That implies intimacy. Intimacy implies physical contact. Physical contact implies sex. Not that I'd be against a little physical contact." His gaze sweeps my body leaving a blistering trail in its wake.

With one look, he leaves me aching and wanting exactly what's promised in his eyes.

Smoldering?

That's not even close.

It's incendiary.

"That's not what I meant and you know it."

He crosses his arms with a satisfied smirk. I'm pretty sure he knows exactly what that look does to me.

"That's a shame, but the offer stands. Euphoria is a great place to relax, but it's best done with another person. Spend your time with me, Miss Quinn. Let me show you not all men are like Scott."

I bite my lower lip and consider his offer. Every nerve in my body takes notice of the man sitting beside me. He's hot in a nuclear explosive kind of way.

"Perfect." He grins in victory. "We've got one hour before the boat sails."

"I never said…"

"You didn't have to, your body said it all. It's decided. We'll spend the day together. If you aren't having a good time by the time the sun sets, I won't bother you again. However, if you are, we'll enjoy the rest of our time at Euphoria together."

"That's pretty damn ballsy." My words are harsh, but do nothing to put him off. If anything, his smirk turns up in victory.

"There's no point in wasting any more time."

"And why not? Who's to say spending time alone isn't exactly what I want?"

"If you wanted to be alone, you wouldn't have come here for breakfast. You would've had it delivered to your villa. Since you did come here, it's because you crave the company of others, even if they're strangers."

"You seem pretty pleased with yourself."

"I am, but only because I get to spend the day with an incredibly beautiful woman, a woman who ran away from me last night when I mentioned a kiss."

Our waiter arrives with a seafood tower overflowing with lobster, crab, shrimp, and all my favorite things. My attention shifts from Hawke to the food. I can't help it.

He waits for me to take what I want, watching every move I make with his sharp eyes. I fill my plate with shrimp and crab legs, leaving the raw oysters alone. The corner of his mouth tics up.

"Not a fan of oysters?"

My nose crinkles. "Most definitely not. They're slimy and salty. I don't know how anybody eats raw oysters."

He reaches for one, lifts it to his lips, and with his eyes on me, slurps and sucks it down whole. All my attention fixes on his face, his lips, and his fingers. Hell, I even listen to him groan as he swallows the oyster down. The bobbing of his Adam's apple will forever be imprinted on my soul. Never in my life did I think there was anything remotely erotic about the slimy food. Now, I can't stop thinking about it.

Or him.

"Raw oysters are good for you." He pins me down with his golden gaze. "Not only are they rich in zinc, a mineral essential for boosting testosterone production, but they increase dopamine, which is known to increase libido." He reaches for another raw oyster. "You sure you don't want to try one?"

"I'm pretty sure about that." I give a shake of my head.

"Ah, then they are all mine." He licks his fingers. "Now, about our plans for the day."

FIFTEEN

Hawke

A TOUGH NUT TO CRACK, I'M RIGHT ABOUT ONE THING. QUINN Hayes would rather be lonely in the company of others than alone by herself. Who is this captivating woman? Her gaze doesn't waver from my mouth as I enjoy the oysters.

The tiny flick of her lids. The press of her lips. The way her tongue darts out. The woman is interested, but hesitant. She's insanely hot and completely oblivious to her effect on me. It's indecent how much I want her.

What I don't get is why she's not jumping all over my blatant proposition? If she's here to work me over for personal gain, why isn't she taking the opportunity to jump on board and spend time with me? I've given her ample opportunity to take advantage.

I get her hesitation. Coming off a betrayal is never easy, but I'm not against being used as a revenge fuck. It's perfect actually.

No feelings.

Just sex.

The perfect setup.

I can work her out of my system and move on.

Instead, she's making me break all my rules. I'm not happy with that. I should walk away, but my fascination grows with every minute I spend in her company.

By this time, we should be twisting the sheets and fucking each other's brains out. Instead, I'm trying to get her to agree to spend the day with me over bloody marys and mimosas.

Scratch that.

She may not have said yes, but her body broadcasts all the right signals. Once I get her to step outside of her head and let her body lead the way, we'll be good to go.

And what a damn fine body she has. Her crocheted top reveals more than it hides. My mouth salivates, not because of the oysters, but because I can't stop thinking about peeling her out of that string bikini. Her ample breasts beg to be fondled and her nipples demand worshipping with my hands, mouth, and cock. Yes, I said that. I want to fuck her tits.

My goal for today is to get her out of that top. Those shorts need to come off too. Afterwards, I'll work on getting her out of the rest of it during our cruise.

"I hope you enjoy snorkeling." I take a sip of my water and peer at her over the rim of the glass.

She glances at me with a shrimp half in her mouth. When she sucks it in, I hold back a groan.

So fucking sexy.

I want those lips on me. Hell, I want her on her knees with those emerald eyes staring up at me while I fuck her pert little mouth. She stirs dark desires within me, things I normally keep locked down tight.

I wait for her to chew and swallow while amusing myself with fantasies of fucking her face. My hand wraps in her hair, controlling her as I ram between her lips and bump the back of her throat. The heat of her mouth surrounds my cock. The roughness of her tongue licks along my shaft until my entire body explodes.

Images of her on her knees feeds lusty thoughts, spreading her out before me, naked, where I can taste her sweet essence as I eat her pussy. I can't wait for her to scream my name.

Yeah, we're going to have so much fun.

"I love snorkeling." She presses her napkin to her lips, ending my fantasy.

"Good. I signed out a boat for the day and I know the best places on the island." Secluded, private places the staff is not allowed to go.

"How often do you come here?" Her interest excites me. I want to be in the forefront of her thoughts.

"As much as I can."

"And are you always alone?" Her left eyebrow arches. She's not afraid to ask questions. "Or is this unusual for you?"

"This is a first for me. It's a working vacation." I'm here to escape spending the holidays with my mother, but I don't tell Quinn that. My words aren't a total lie. Fifty proposals sit on my desk. One of them belongs to the vixen sitting across from me.

"I find it hard to believe a man like you isn't attached."

"Attached?"

"You know, married, engaged. Off the market?"

"I prefer keeping my options open."

"Meaning, you play the field." I don't like the dismissive tone in her voice. I absolutely play the field. The way she says it makes me sound cheap.

"I wouldn't call it that."

Her head tilts to the side. I'm picking up on her body language. That tells me she thinks I'm full of shit.

"What would you call it?"

"I enjoy women without the entanglements that come from commitment."

"Right…" Her head gives a little jerk, as if my words confirm what she's thinking. "You play the field."

"I find mutually compatible partners who enjoy the time they spend with me."

Her lips press together, as if she's holding back what she wants to say. That makes me want to know what she's thinking even more. I lean forward and cup my chin in my palm.

"You disapprove?" I ask.

"I never said that. How you choose to live your life is none of my business."

"Are you rethinking spending the day with me? Afraid I might take that kiss you denied me last night?" My attention shifts to her mouth and the way her breathing accelerates. She draws her lower lip in, nibbling it with her teeth.

So fucking sexy.

"I didn't say that." She leans back and takes a sip of her drink. "You're right. I don't want to spend all my time alone. A boat ride and snorkeling sounds as good as anything." She makes spending time with me sound like a consolation prize.

Yet again, I tell myself to walk away. Instead, my gaze meanders down her body. The woman rocks her curves and appears completely oblivious to the stares every man in the room gives her as they enjoy their meal.

"There're lots of activities we can do if you prefer something else." I have an extensive list, all of which put us in close physical proximity.

This woman will be mine.

I don't beg. I don't cajole. I never waste a moment of my time convincing someone to spend time with me. So why am I doing just that with Miss Quinn Hayes?

Quinn is right about one thing. I lavish women with pleasure and deliver on the indulgences I promise. I touch, worship, and use them as I decide.

Never the other way around.

When I tire, we part ways. No messy feelings get hurt because they all know the rules.

Time with me comes with an expiration date.

They serve my pleasure. In return, I spoil them with gifts. It's a win-win for all involved.

Clean and simple.

A warm breeze flows through the open windows bringing the fragrant aroma of tropical blooms to our table. Parrots squawk. Tree frogs ribbit. Local squirrels fight over the offerings of nuts and fruit put out by the staff. None of that is accidental. Everything at

Euphoria is designed with esthetics and romance in mind. Quinn may not realize it, but the resort is my greatest weapon.

She nibbles gingerly at her food, picking at a crab leg and pulling the succulent meat delicately out of the spiky shell. Entranced by everything she promises, my mouth waters with anticipation as she lifts the tender meat to her mouth.

I wait, assessing my options, and wonder what it will take to get her to take the next, obvious, step. Of course, I've done my research, delving into her private life without regard for the laws I break.

No physical or mental illness. Health clean. Four older brothers; much older. All working blue-collar jobs in construction. Father and mother alive. Nothing to indicate marital stress.

She's the first in her family to attend college, graduating from Caltech, of all places, with a degree in computer science. She wrote her first computer game in seventh grade. Authored several apps. One sold for pennies when an astute investor realized its worth.

Her current project is groundbreaking, but the business execution is fatally flawed. It would likely have made it to the top five if not for that.

"Snorkeling sounds perfect." Her comment pulls me from my thoughts and I blink, trying to remember what we were talking about. "This place is remarkable. I've never seen water that color of blue. It's majestic. I can't wait to get in it. Snorkeling is one of my favorite things. Do you know if they do any scuba diving?"

The wind kicks up, rustling the palm fronds. It blows through the open windows where it picks up the strands of her hair. She absently reaches up and tucks her hair behind her ear.

"You dive?" This did not show up on my background check.

"I took it for P.E. in college." Her lips twist in the most delicious way. "It was either that or run around on a track."

"Would you prefer to do that?" I prefer snorkeling. It's a surefire way to spend the day admiring her in her bikini, but I'll take anything if it means she's willing to spend the day with me.

"I'd love to, but maybe not today. I want to enjoy the water, snorkel a bit, sunbathe, and go on a cruise."

"Snorkeling it is." I glance at my watch. Not that it matters. The boat's ours for the day with me, the captain, and her, my unwitting captive.

I fold my napkin and place it over my plate. She pushes back and glances out the window, staring at the crystal-blue sky overhead.

"It really is beautiful here." She sighs and pulls at her hair, gathering it at her nape. My fingers itch to run through her long locks, dig my fingers into her silky waves, and capture her mouth while I claim her as my own.

"Yes, it is." Only I'm not talking about Euphoria.

She catches me staring and a blush colors her cheeks a beautiful shade of pink.

"I wasn't keeping track of time, but do we need to get going? I don't want to keep everyone waiting." She releases her hair. It spills over her shoulders and bounces down to the small of her back.

It's cute she thinks there will be others. We're not going on an excursion with a bunch of guests.

"We can leave any time. Are you ready?"

She glances around. "Do I have time to grab sunscreen and my stuff?"

"We have all the time in the world." I have no problem walking her to her villa, and if we never make it to the boat, that's even better.

She glances at me. "Do you need to get your things?"

"No, I have everything I need." I pull out my sunglasses to shield my eyes from the bright sun. "Towels, sunscreen, and lunch are provided. Along with all the gear we need."

"Oh, good. Do I need to tell someone my size for the fins?"

I glance at her feet. "I can message ahead."

Glad she thought of that, I get her shoe size and forward it to the concierge desk. They'll make sure we have everything we need, including the champagne and wine I requested be on board.

Quinn glances at me. She does that thing with her lower lip again. "Look, I just want to be clear about something."

"Really?"

"I appreciate you keeping me company, but like I explained last night, I'm not looking for anything—more right now."

"That's a shame."

Her brows pinch together.

"A shame?"

"Never say never, Quinn Hayes. You've got ten days with nothing to do, no obligations, and no cheating ex to ruin your day. Why not have a little fun and move on?"

"I'm afraid a little fun with you might be a big mistake."

"Like I said, that's a shame. But to ease your mind, how about we make a pact?"

"What kind of pact?"

"I won't initiate, but I will follow through."

"What does that mean?"

"Only that I want you to enjoy yourself. You were dealt a pretty shitty hand with that douchebag. Relax, I won't kiss you…"

"Thank you." She gives a sharp jerk of her head, as if we've settled anything.

"I wasn't finished."

"You're not?"

"Hardly. I won't kiss you, but if you kiss me, I'll finish what you start. You fascinate me. Not to mention, the air crackles when you're close. Consider it a warning."

"How's that?"

"A simple kiss will never be enough."

"Then, I need to make sure I never kiss you."

"I suppose, but there's something you need to know."

"What's that?"

"I always get what I want."

SIXTEEN

Quinn

Cocky and arrogant; two adjectives far too mild when describing Hawke Sterling.

I don't believe him for a second. The man has a one-track mind. That should offend me, but I agree with one thing he says. The air sizzles when we're close. The fine hairs on my arms lift, almost as if they're reaching out, wanting to feel that first jolt of electricity when he touches me.

I shouldn't, but somehow, I agree to his tentative truce.

I consider it a truce because this feels a little like a battleground. Will I fall to his charm? Will I succeed in guarding my heart? Or will he sweep in, take what he wants, and leave nothing but devastation in his wake?

Fine, that might be a *little* overdramatic.

The question I keep asking myself is what's the harm in a little fling?

This is where he's going to get me. His logic. It makes perfect sense and he's not one for commitment. Ten days of pure, unadulterated sex? No strings? We both walk away when this is done? Sounds pretty amazing.

I never have to see him again. It's the perfect opportunity to work Scott out of my system.

There's only one problem. That's not me.

I don't do that kind of thing. I'm a bonder. Using people and walking away feels all kinds of wrong. He's right about one thing. If I want to step out of my comfort zone and do something I would normally never do, this is the perfect place to do it.

I can be whomever I want to be.

I rub at the side of my arm. Goosebumps pebble my skin. He walks beside me, closer than a stranger would walk but not so close that we touch. Not that it matters. Every swing of my arm sends shivers of sensation shooting up my arm.

I feel every inch of him.

We return to my suite in relative silence, enjoying a perfect day. It doesn't take but a minute to grab my sunglasses, hat, and the sunscreen I prefer. Everything else is being provided. It feels a little weird walking around with barely anything, but I guess that's the point.

We take another meandering trail to the main beach area. Shimmering sunlight makes the sand sparkle like a million tiny gems. Seagulls fly overhead, soaring as they hunt their next meal, diving below the majestic turquoise waters to make the kill.

I kick off my sandals at the edge of the walk. Hawke does the same, and we step out onto the beach. Waves crash against the shore, and the birds overhead screech as they call out to one another. The wind blows lightly, easing the tropical heat. And I take a moment to absorb all of it.

Simply majestic.

Warm beneath our feet, the sand gives our feet a gentle massage as we walk down to the cool water. Three boats anchor just beyond the breakwater. Two are large catamarans, perfect for snorkeling tours. One is a schooner; its sails lash tight against the masts. The brochure in my room boasts a sunset dinner cruise, but I have yet to decide if I'm willing to go on that alone.

Although, with the rules of engagement defined between us, I might get Hawke to accompany me. All I need is to resist the romantic pull embedded in everything around me.

There's a fourth boat, a smaller catamaran. Instead of anchoring beyond the breakwaters, the staff ran it aground on the beach. A rope anchors it to the sand, and I wonder if there's a smaller tour going out. It's not big enough to fit more than four, maybe six people.

"A perfect day for a sail and snorkeling." Hawke reaches for my hand, taking it in his. While I should resist, I don't. As long as I don't kiss him, I'm safe.

A sense of calmness washes over me. This really is one of the most peaceful places on the planet.

I glance up at the infinite blue sky full of the sun's warmth and breath in the salty air. Some distance away from the beach, a boat tows a parasail with two people dangling from its canopy.

"Have you ever gone parasailing?" Hawke takes note of the direction of my gaze.

"No, but I've always wanted to try. Is it scary?"

"Are you afraid of heights?"

"No."

"Then it's not scary. It's a lot of fun. Once you get up there, all you hear is the whistling of the wind. It's quiet. We can sign up if you want."

"And if I don't like it?"

"We stop." He gives a little squeeze of my hand. "There're lots of activities we can enjoy together. You up for it?"

"Maybe tomorrow?"

"It's a date." His voice turns husky, low, throaty, hungry. "If you get scared, you can squeeze my hand."

"Let's hope that doesn't happen." A smile fills my face. The last time I squeezed his hand I'd been locked inside a flying tin-can death machine.

"Are you kidding? I'm hoping it does." He gestures toward the small catamaran beached on the shore. "Our chariot awaits."

"We're going on that one?"

"Yes."

"Where's everyone going to fit?"

"It just you and me."

"Just us? I thought it was a snorkeling cruise—like, with other people." A buffer between me and him. Something to keep me safe from that kiss I very much want him to take. Only he won't take it. Not if he's a man of his word. Which means, I must make the first move, and that will never happen.

"It is a snorkeling cruise with just two people." His smirk returns, punctuated with a wink. Bastard smoothly maneuvered me into this.

Well done, Hawke. Well done.

Why am I complaining? I could be here with a cheating bastard. Instead, I have Hawke, and I'm willing to listen with an open heart.

He steps ahead of me to the boat, climbing on board, and offers a hand down. I shield my eyes against the dazzling sand sparkling in the golden sunlight. Light which is nearly the same color as the spark flaring to life in Hawke's remarkable eyes.

There's a certain serenity on the beach. Something about crashing waves, seabirds calling overhead, and the heat of the sun shining down to warm bare skin. The smell of saltwater travels up my nose, flooding my senses with memories of happiness and carefree times. I'm entranced by everything around me, but mostly by the man standing above me, hand lowered, ready for me to climb on board.

One glance out toward the horizon, however, brings different emotions. Something about the vastness of that space stirs agony, pain, regret, and frustration. It pushes out the peace and calm from moments before, reminding me of everything Scott took from me when he cheated. Not only is our personal relationship ruined, but also the business we hoped to build together.

There's no way to move forward as a team after what he did. Which leaves me where? This is the question I need answered.

For now, with the infinite blue sky promising a day full of sunshine and the crystal-clear waters offering relief from the heat, I can forget about Scott and focus on nothing but the present and a man with glowing golden eyes.

I reach for his hand, clasp it, and before I can jump, he hoists me up as if I weigh nothing at all. He pulls me tight against him.

I've yet to see Hawke without a shirt but have a pretty good idea what I'll find when I do. Our bodies momentarily connect, chest to chest, hip to hip, lips inches apart. My body riots with sensation.

Broad-shouldered, his cotton shirt strains against the muscles beneath. Angling down to a trim waist, there's no paunch on Hawke like there is on Scott. Hawke keeps himself fit and I ignore the way his shorts cup his ass. How the muscles of his quads bunch and flex. How incredibly tanned and toned his body is; it's perfection.

He's a lady killer for certain, but I'm too gun shy to step in front of that kind of devastation. I'm practically plastered against him and place my hands on his chest to push away. Hard. Firm. He's chiseled perfection.

"Um, sorry." Why am I apologizing for standing too close when he's the one who lifted me into his arms? A smirk ghosts across his face. Bastard knew exactly what he was doing.

"Take a seat and we'll get going." Hawke points toward the back of the catamaran. Two staff members jog up to the boat. One releases the sand anchor while the other one pushes us out, using the rise of the waves to get us moving. Hawke leaps into action. Clearly, this is not the first time he's done this.

I sit in awe, watching him work, or rather salivate over the rippling muscles as he puts his body to work. We float backward. Hawke engages the engines and we slowly make it over the gentle surf rolling in. Once free of the breakwater, the engine cuts out and Hawke tackles the sails.

We're officially alone.

SEVENTEEN

Quinn

As someone with zero knowledge of how to sail, I do my best to stay out of Hawke's way. Before I know it, wind fills the sail on the main mast and we head along the shoreline. Water rushes along the hull and the boat lifts and falls with the rolling swells.

I lean back, letting the sun kiss my face, then remember to put on sunscreen before I forget and spend the rest of my vacation nursing a sunburn.

Hawke's attention shifts to me as I lift the crochet top over my head. His admiration heats my cheeks and I glance away to cover my unease. Sunscreen in hand, I spread a thin layer over my face, making sure not to miss the tip of my nose or the tops of my ears.

Now that we're in motion, the wind whips at my hair. I gather it into a messy bun and secure it with a hairband. Hawke returns to my side, finishing whatever it was he was doing to the front forward sail. It has a name, I'm certain, but I'm clueless.

"Need help putting that on your back?" He sees more sun than I do, as he has a golden tan to match his golden eyes.

The smart thing to do is to refuse and tell him I can do it myself, but I can't. Since I burn easily, I cave and hand him the sunscreen.

"Thank you."

His attention shifts from the top of my string bikini to my shoulders. He fills his palm with the cool white cream. and places his hands on my shoulders. Instant heat licks up and down my spine.

A shiver lodges at the base of my skull. I try not to move, but a low groan escapes me when his skillful hands go to work.

He's supposed to be putting sunscreen on my shoulders and back. Instead, I'm subjected to the most amazing shoulder and back rub of my life. His deft fingers attack the tight muscles of my neck, digging in until I wince in pain. His fingers press hard until the poor muscles beneath them fatigue and relax.

"Wow."

"You're really tense." His husky voice whispers past my ear. "Take a few breaths and relax."

My shoulders tense when he finds another hard knot. He attacks it with his fingers, digging in.

"It's hard when it hurts."

"Breathe through it. By the time I'm done with you, you're going to be limp and completely relaxed."

There's no doubt about that.

"Don't you need to steer the boat?"

"Don't worry about that. I know what I'm doing."

No arguing with that. He moves from my shoulders to the base of my neck, squirting out more sunscreen to allow his fingers to glide across my skin. His thumbs dig in along my back, and I close my eyes in ecstasy. Slowly, he works his way down my back, until his fingers dip beneath the waistband of my shorts.

"These need to come off." His throaty growl demands a response, and my hands go to the front of my shorts, flicking open the button and lowering the zipper before I fully realize what I'm doing. There's no helping it, not with the thread of command laced in his tone.

I don't think about it as I wriggle out of my shorts and kick them off my legs with my feet. A sharp intake of breath sounds behind me, followed by a low groan.

"Damn, Quinn, you don't make it easy." He doesn't stop his massage.

His hands dip lower, trailing along the top of my string bikini. His fingers sweep around to my hips where he hooks his thumbs under the flimsy thread holding everything together.

My entire body vibrates beneath that touch, long slumbering nerves wake up and desire sweeps through me. My body heats. I lean into his touch, wanting more but knowing only a fine line separates us from something I can't take back.

"I regret our little pact." His voice is a low rumble. "All I can think about is stripping you out of these tiny scraps to take what I need." He presses his lips to the tip of my shoulder. It's not a kiss exactly. It's more like a reverent sigh. "I want to fuck you, Miss Quinn Hayes."

He's not afraid to speak his mind, that's for certain. My entire body stiffens. I'm well aware we're in the middle of nowhere, too far from shore to think about swimming to safety.

I'm his captive.

The thing is—the moment he said he wanted to fuck me, heat licked between my thighs. The needy pulsations are making me squirm. He's not the only one affected.

It's not my fault he looks every bit like the faceless man of my sex dreams. Now, I must face my fantasy, because that fictional man is blessed with not only a face, but a name.

Hawke grips my hips, tight, controlling, desperate for what comes next. He's unlike Scott in every way. No flabby chin. No beer paunch. No weak grip. He's not afraid to tell me he wants to fuck me.

Hawke is flawless, from his sun-kissed skin to the rigid set of his jaw, the molten heat simmering in his eyes brings my fantasies to life. It's like someone reached inside my head, sifted through my fantasies, and wove together every detail I find appealing in a man and created something incredible in Hawke Sterling.

To make things worse, the living embodiment of my dreams wants me. He just said so. He wants to fuck me. I'm almost of a mind to let him do whatever he wants.

I don't mind that at all.

What does that say about me?

If he wants to have his way with me, I won't say no.

I won't resist. He'll have my complete and utter surrender as I cave to his demands and fulfill his fantasies.

It would be nice if he took the burden for whether that happens away from me. But Hawke is a man of his word.

I know that.

He releases me and steps away. Something happens with the sails. The mast, or beam? The long horizontal thing-a-ma-jig, shifts from right to left. Or from starboard to port. Ha, at least I know those terms.

Hawke takes a seat at the tiller, not hiding when he makes an adjustment to his shorts. He's long, engorged, and sporting one hell of an erection. It practically pokes a hole through the fly of his crisp, white shorts.

"Sorry." My shoulders lift to my ears, and I turn away to give him the privacy he needs to fix himself and get as comfortable as possible.

"Don't be." The tone of his voice sharpens. "And, Quinn?"

I spin to look at him, then gasp at the way his fist wraps around the fabric of his shorts.

He grips his cock. "Don't be ashamed of what you do to me. I'm not. I'd have to be dead not to react to you." He releases his cock and shifts his hips away from me. "It doesn't mean I'm going to break my promise, but while I will refrain from kissing you, I can't not get hard around you."

I lick my lips. They're suddenly, incredibly dry and I wish I'd thought to bring Chapstick with me.

"I don't mean to make you uncomfortable."

"I'm not uncomfortable." He flashes me his panty-melting smile. "You're hot and mine for the day. I'm the luckiest man on the planet."

"Not exactly the *luckiest.*" My gaze flicks to his crotch and the tenting of his pants.

"The day's not over, Miss Hayes. You'll cave sooner rather than later. When you do, you know what happens next."

"What's that?"

"After you kiss me, I'm finishing what you start."

"And what if that's not what I want?"

"I strongly suggest you never kiss me." His eyes flash in the sunlight, molten hot, powerful, lusty, and full of promise. He means exactly what he says. "Think very carefully before you do. Kissing me ends only one way and that's with me buried deep inside of you."

Silence descends between us, floating over the promise of his words. My breath hitches as I piece together what that might feel like, our naked bodies moving in unison, him braced over me. Hips moving, thrusting, as we chase our release. Desire blooms within me, coiling in my belly and pulsing in my sex.

Scott never made me feel this way. We had sex. It was good. Nothing earth-shattering, but this longing? The sensations rioting in my body?

This must be what lust feels like.

Delicious.

Decadent.

Maddening.

Frustrating.

I am in deep, deep trouble.

"Awfully cocky, aren't we?" I desperately need to gain the upper hand because mere moments separate me from making a very bad decision and launching myself at him. I sense he's a dominating lover, taking what he wants, and that only makes things worse. Not only does he embody my fantasy man, but I bet he'll deliver on the dark, depraved fantasies I hide from myself. Something along the lines of a captive to a nefarious sea-faring captain comes to mind.

"More like I'm certain of the outcome. You have my word. I won't kiss you first, but it's going to happen. Be prepared for what happens next."

I squeeze my thighs together as that needy ache intensifies. He's right about one thing. My chances of making it through the next two weeks without kissing him are slim to none.

I want everything promised in that panty-melting grin and smoldering eyes.

But I'm not the kind of girl who hops into bed with a stranger. It might be fun in the moment, but as soon as things are done, regret will consume me.

I vow to be incredibly cautious around Hawke. Unless I'm in dire need, my lips will not be pressing against his anytime soon.

EIGHTEEN

Hawke

Fuck me. I'll be sporting a woody all damn day at this rate.

Note to self: DO NOT touch Quinn Hayes unless it's an emergency.

Her buttery smooth skin feels like heaven beneath my hands, and shit if she doesn't react wildly to my touch.

I could hide my erection, but I face it head-on. No way to hide it. Why try? And now, she knows what I want. I'm the one who shackled myself by giving my word. What the fuck was I thinking?

I never accommodate anyone. Why then did I break out the kid gloves for this woman?

Since I don't understand whatever the fuck it is I'm doing, I ignore it. We're here to snorkel and damn if we aren't going to do exactly that. I grab at my crotch again, shifting to a more comfortable position.

Not that it's possible.

Quinn is out of her shorts. Her red string bikini is on full display. She's even more arresting in those tiny scraps of fabric. I swallow my lust and focus on sailing.

We share silence well. I'm not used to that with a woman. She's happy to stretch out, teasing me with her tight, toned body, while I pilot us to our destination. It's a cove I know well on the private side of the island reserved for my exclusive enjoyment only.

The sails come down and I drop an anchor. A little past noon, we have all afternoon to explore the coral reefs below us.

"I need to set a second anchor before we go into the water." I grab my fins and facemask.

"Why?"

"Because if that anchor comes loose, there's no way in hell we'll catch the boat."

We're anchored a couple hundred yards off-shore. It would be a long swim to the beach if the anchor came loose and we lost the boat. I'm a strong swimmer, certain of not only my ability to make it ashore, but my ability to tow her there as well. From the toned muscles in her legs, she may not need my help. Two anchors are sufficient when not leaving a spotter on board. I place a total of three.

When I surface after placing the last anchor, Quinn is ready.

"All secure?" Her bright eyes shimmer with excitement.

"Jump on in."

She puts on her mask and fins, then takes a giant stride off the boat. It's something divers are trained to do and tells me she knows exactly what she's doing.

We spend the next few hours exploring the reefs, diving as deep as our breaths allow, and thoroughly enjoying the day. We break for a late lunch and I open the champagne. Our conversation moves easily, speaking about nothing of importance.

Together, we lie side by side on the netting spanning the twin hulls of the catamaran and watch the clouds roll by, picking out shapes and making up stories. It's amazing how easily I relax in her company.

As for the snorkeling, there's no reason to worry about Quinn. She's confident both on the water and beneath the surface. I can't wait to take her diving and spend time exploring some of my favorite dive sites around the island.

The day passes. I grow more and more comfortable in her

presence, lowering walls I never let down. Well aware of the danger, I can't help but breathe freely in her presence.

With the sun dipping toward the horizon, we call it a day. My intent was to take her on a sunset dinner cruise, but our casual boat ride is far superior and the sun is setting up to put on an amazing display across the sky.

"This has been one of the most relaxing days of my life." Quinn's emerald gaze settles on me, soft and gentle, her face brightens with joy. The wind whips at her hair, drying it as we sail, and I return her smile.

"For me as well."

"Don't you wish you could stay here forever? Wrapped in this bubble of time and never have to go back to the real world?"

"There are times."

Like now.

I'd take this moment and wrap it in forever to spend time with her for the rest of my life. No entrapments. No lies. Just her sweet smile and radiant eyes, which promise more than I'm willing to bear.

"Tell me about your job." She stares off at the horizon, eyes scanning the oranges, yellows, and reds which herald the beginning of our evening light show.

"There's not much to say."

"Oh, come on. I told you about mine, but you've barely said a word about yourself."

She's right about that. My questions began with gentle probing, growing more inquisitive. Despite the euphoria this day brings, and my joy in spending time alone with Quinn, I can't escape the very high probability she's playing me. I've never met a woman who didn't try to take a piece of me, in one way or another.

How can I spin this and answer her question without answering it?

"What do you think I do?"

"You want me to guess?"

"I do. You've spent the day with me and have probably figured out a few things. You must have some guesses. I'm curious, Miss

Hayes, what is it you think a man like me might do to make a living?"

"That is a very dangerous game."

"How so?"

"What if I inadvertently insult you?"

"You'd never do that."

"Okay." An impish grin settles on her face. "I think you won the lottery and are out spending your millions after quitting your job." Her brow arches.

"A pauper turned prince?" My hand flies to my chest as if wounded.

"There's no way you're a pauper."

"And why's that?"

"I come from a blue-collar family. You're different. You come from wealth." She taps her chin. "The question is whether you were born into it, or whether you acquired it yourself."

"What if it's both? Does that alter your opinion of me?"

"Not really." She gives a slight shake of her head. "But it explains a little."

"What's that?"

"Your comments about commitment. Since you're making me guess, I'm going to assume it's more than a little money. I would imagine, for people like you, it's difficult to get to a person's true motives."

"How so?"

"Well, let's go for the obvious first. Here's the most pertinent question. Are your friends your friends because of the money, or because they value your company?" She lifts her first finger in the air. "The same goes for the women. Are they there because they want to date you for you, spend time with you because they're attracted to you, or are they there for the money and the status being associated with you brings?"

"Go on."

"Since you're not fat and ugly…"

"Not sure if that's a compliment or not." Laughter bursts out of me.

"I'm not stroking your ego. You wanted me to guess, so I'm laying it all out. I'm being serious." And she is—being serious.

I'm a puzzle she's unraveling. There's no sense in having fun at my expense, but rather working through her theories. I get the impression this is how she tackles problems at work. Her mind fascinates me.

"You're an attractive man. One of the cool kids in school. Women would flock to you solely based on your looks. For you, though, it's a more complicated question."

"Please, enlighten me."

"We'll lay it all out."

"I'm waiting."

"Women come easily to you. You don't need to put in any effort to get a woman like our fat and ugly man."

"I'm not sure where this comparison is going."

"Hang on... It's not earth-shattering." She lifts her hand up, palm out, telling me to let her finish.

I lean back and grip the wheel. "I'm all ears."

"The fat and ugly man, whether he has, or doesn't have money, will work much harder to find his one true love. He's more selective because he needs to be and he doesn't have a ton of options to wade through. Therefore, it's both easier and harder for him. When he finds his one, the chances are pretty high she loves him for who he is, rather than what he has, whether that's his looks or his money."

"Go on."

"For the popular, esthetically pleasing man," she gestures toward me, "women flock to him. And let's face it, most people are shallow assholes. Men and women. I'm not discriminating. They're out for themselves. If that means status from dating the hot guy, or even better, the status that comes from dating the rich, hot guy, they'll do whatever it takes. This leaves our rich, hot guy with droves of potentials but nobody who's really interested in the man behind the looks—or money. My assumption is this would make a person jaded."

"Jaded?"

"Yes, he'd never know if a girl was there for him, or for what he can offer, and that is a horrible position to be in."

I lift my finger. "Or... It's the perfect position to be in. Why should a man settle for one person when he can have his fill?"

"Because..." Her eyes pinch together like I missed something crucial.

"There's nothing wrong with playing the field." My tone is more defensive than I intend.

"But don't you want to find your one? The person who loves you for yourself. Who would still be with you if you weren't insanely attractive?" She gives a shake of her head. "Life is hard. Things happen. I want someone who will be there for me through better or worse. Whether that worse is sickness or an accident that leaves me crippled or maimed, or when I'm old and wrinkly. Beauty never lasts. Don't you want to know the person you're with will be there with you through the good and the bad?"

"Interesting words coming from a woman engaged to a cheating douchebag." When her lower lip quivers, I realize how insensitive my comment was and how out of line I am in making it. It was a defensive move because she hit every nail on the head.

Hearing her so easily dissect my life hits a nerve. Regardless of my feelings, she doesn't deserve that from me.

"I'm sorry. I didn't mean it like that."

"No. You're right." Her arms cross over her chest and she shifts away from me. "I'm the foolish girl who believes in love and happily-ever-afters. I should be more like you; a person with a hard heart who doesn't give a fuck about other people. Fortunately, I'm not like you. I care about the people I'm with. I don't use them, and if that makes me a chump, I'd rather be a chump than someone who treats people like disposable commodities."

"Quinn..." I place my hand on her shoulder, but she shrugs me off.

"And that is why *I'll* never kiss you. Unlike you, I don't use people." Her comment stings, but what she doesn't say is what hurts the most.

Now I know exactly what she thinks of me.

She puts on her shorts and moves to the front of the boat. She tries to hide the swipe of her thumb across her cheek, but I feel the sting of her tears in my heart. My words weren't meant to hurt, but they cut deep. It's evident in the slump of her shoulders and the way she won't meet my eye.

Way to fuck up a perfect day, asshole.

NINETEEN

Quinn

The rest of the ride back to Euphoria is awkward. Mostly because I'm too caught up pouting over nothing. Hawke reminded me of my broken heart and how blind I'd been with Scott. It's a truth I didn't need shoved in my face.

I pretty much ignore Hawke, and yes, I'm fully aware how immature that makes me.

He's the one who wanted to play that stupid game and have me guess what he does for a living. I warned him, but his arrogance got in the way.

Then my mouth got in the way.

He shot back at me.

And now, we're not speaking.

Way to end what was an otherwise perfect day.

Nevertheless, that dig about Scott was cruel.

Our snorkeling-sailing adventure concludes in stilted silence. Other than water rushing along the twin hulls and the wind snapping the sails, our conversation is virtually nonexistent.

Hawke guides the boat through the surf and several attendants rush up to drag the catamaran past the water's edge. While they loop in a line to a sand anchor, I put on my top beneath Hawke's pensive stare. We may not be speaking, but he says a hell of a lot with those eyes. They're full of regrets and the remnants of our simmering passion.

Talk about throwing cold water on the heat building between us.

"Quinn." He drags his fingers through wind-tossed hair. "I didn't mean to be insensitive." The boat rocks beneath us, rising with an incoming wave, dropping as it recedes. The sun puts on a fiery display, its daily ritual where it relinquishes its supremacy against the darkness.

I'm done with the crying thing. I moved through anger. Now I'm sitting on regret, feeling like an idiot.

"I know."

"Do you forgive me?"

"There's nothing to forgive. I'm the overly sensitive one. Wanting something, and having it, are two completely different things. I consider myself fortunate I discovered the truth before things went any further."

Not sure if I'm talking about Scott, or Hawke, I turn my back to Hawke and jump off the boat. Water splashes on my legs as I look back at him. Tall and as imposing as ever, his expressionless face is unreadable.

He joins me on the sand with a splash. "Did I ruin a chance at dinner?"

I hesitantly look up at him. "I don't know if I'm up for dinner, to be honest. I want to take a shower and... I don't know. Hit the pool? I might grab something from the bar and call it an early night."

He regards me with hooded lids. "At least let me walk you to your villa." The swirls of emotion I see in his eyes makes me gasp. He's not willing to give up, but won't push too hard. I sense he's holding back, moving cautiously with me. If I were any other woman, I'm sure he would've defiled me in the most delicious way several times over by now.

His pull is undeniable, and I answer with a nod. By the time we round the last bend leading to my villa, my emotions settle out. Dinner is back under consideration.

"I'm not upset with you." I place a hand on his arm. It's the first time we've touched in hours.

"You sure about that?"

"Honestly, your comment was a bit harsh, but the person I should be mad at is Scott, not you. You've been incredibly kind, helping me get my mind off the asshole. I appreciate it. If I hadn't met you, I'd probably be weeping in my room, crying on the beach, or drowning my sorrows in too much alcohol. I need to not do that. I'm very thankful for the distraction. And I didn't mean to say the things I did about you. I know very little about you and made broad generalizations. I hope you'll forgive me."

"You're nothing like I expect, Miss Hayes. And you may be giving me more credit than I deserve. I took you out because I want to get in your pants. You make my actions appear much more gallant than they are. I'm waiting for you to cave-in to my charms and give me the kiss I can't stop thinking about. I'm a rather self-serving bastard."

Laughter spills out of me. He's honest and I love that. Not afraid to own up to his needs, I wonder if he doesn't realize the truth.

I've given him every indication I'm not interested in pursuing anything further with him, yet he still took me out. Today is easily one of the best days of my life.

"You very well might be, but for me, you've been nothing but a gentleman. I appreciate that."

"A gentleman? Hmm, I'm not sure if I'd agree with that statement, but then, I am holding back. Have I changed your mind about dinner?"

A soft laugh escapes me, but I cut it off abruptly when a man steps out of the front door of my villa. A man I know entirely too well.

"Scott?" My voice cracks.

"I take it that's the rat bastard?" Hawke practically turns his words into a growl.

"Shit." For whatever reason, I reach for Hawke's hand and give it a hard squeeze. "What do I do?"

"That depends… Do you want to fix things with the asshole or end them forever?"

"End them forever."

Like there's any question what I want.

Scott shields his eyes from the setting sun while the blood in my body grows cold.

Fuck. Fuck. Fuck.

I don't want to see Scott, let alone speak to him. I definitely don't want to be alone with him.

"Let's give him a reason to walk away." Hawke takes my hand and spins me until I face him.

"What…" That's all I have time for before his mouth unexpectedly crashes down on mine.

TWENTY

Quinn

Hawke slams his lips to mine and knocks nearly all the wind from my lungs. I gasp, overwhelmed by the suddenness of the kiss. The powerfulness of his kiss. The exquisite, toe-curling, mind-numbing, intensity of his lips locked to mine.

There's no time to react before his tongue presses against the seam of my lips. I should clamp them shut and deny him access. I should push him away. Instead, I sink into the wave of sensation and ride a surge of adrenaline. In his arms, I fly apart.

The demand behind his passion can't be denied. Harder and harder he claims the kiss he's not supposed to take. His hand drifts to my hip, settling there before pulling me close.

I inhale sharply as I press against his hard chest. His chiseled perfection can't be real, but my fingertips confirm the truth. I splay my hand across his muscles, intending to push him away, but I let my fingers linger where they feel the racing of his heart and the quickening of his breath.

A teasing nibble parts my lips. Our tongues caress, gently at first, cautiously, then more fervently. That's all it takes to lower my defenses. He sweeps me away. Part of me tries to think through this and urge myself to push away.

But I don't.

I don't want to.

My body trembles. Shivers race up and down my spine. Our breaths mingle as my heart flutters inside my chest.

I need to stop this kiss, but I don't.

His hunger heats the simmering lust brewing between us, bringing it to a full boil. That ice in my veins melts beneath the inferno of Hawke's kiss, and warmth spreads throughout my entire body.

Dark and sultry, he tastes a little bit of salt and sea, with something deliciously dark layered on top. I sense he holds back from taking what he wants. I feel his hunger. It's all consuming. Hawke desires far more than a kiss.

Hands move along my body. His fingers dance along the curvature of my spine. They explore the narrowing of my waist and continue onward to meander over the flair of my hips. One moves lower still while the other heads back up to tangle in my hair.

Pressed chest to chest, and hip to hip, our bodies collide in a frisson of passion and desire. His mouth is warm. The caress of his lips is insane, brutal and fierce, yet softer than I imagined. I open my mouth with a low moan.

He takes control.

One hand wraps around my waist as he pulls me tight against him. I loop my arms around his neck, where my fingers move of their own accord, twining through his hair as he towers over me, forcing me to bow beneath him.

His fingers run up and down my spine, spreading devastation in their wake. Coaxing shivers out of my body, making it betray how very much I want this kiss. My body flushes with heat. It travels through my veins, warming me from the inside out with a rush of euphoric bliss. My heart sings with pure joy, a dangerous, irrational emotion.

A breathy sigh escapes my lips, followed by his lusty growl. Our bodies demand more than this simple kiss.

The kiss turns from soft to hard, exploratory to demanding, and urgent to frenzied. His hand slides down from my waist to cup my ass. He pulls me against the hardness of his erection with a deep, throaty groan of desire.

His fingers stab in my hair, pulling, twisting, yanking as he controls my face. He yanks my head back, exposing my neck as he kisses and bites his way down the tender flesh. When he lands on the hollow of my throat, his possessive growl brings an answering mewl from my lips.

"Goddamn, Quinn, you taste like sin."

I roll my hips, grinding against him, wanting something I know I shouldn't. His mouth returns to mine. Our teeth clash. Our tongues tangle.

Behind us, Scott shouts. "What the fuck, Q?"

Hawke lifts his mouth from mine. His breaths tug in and out of his chest while I pant, trying to catch my breath. He leans down, resting his forehead against mine.

I watch as he studies me with silent intensity. The warmth of his breath ghosts across my face, and I close my eyes in anticipation as his soft lips capture mine one last time.

It's over too quickly as he pulls away.

"Now, do I take the lead? Or will you?" Hawke takes a deep breath then looks toward Scott.

"You kiss like a madman." I pant so hard my lips tingle from hyperventilation.

"I kiss like I fuck, but answer the question. I'm happy to put this asshat in his place, but that's your call."

I wipe at the stray wisps of my hair, which catch in my mouth. My tingling lips pulse with the echoes of that kiss. That needy throb within me demands relief.

But my head is still in charge.

"I've got this." I take a step back and press my fingers to my lips. They're bruised and taste of Hawke. Already, I want more. Instead, I turn around and face Scott.

Hawke reaches for my shaky hand and takes it in his, providing the support I need. I want to race inside, drag him with me, as we divest ourselves of the annoyance of our clothing and finish that kiss with the movement of our bodies skin on skin in a more horizontal plane.

I want to know what it feels like to be made love to with the fire and passion Hawke gave to that kiss. It's also clear I won't survive the encounter.

I'm not like Hawke. I don't do casual sex. Yet, I'm considering it, all the while knowing it's a horrible idea.

Scott marches up to me, eyes stormy, hands clenched, face full of fury. His eyes shift to take in Hawke, slide away, and then move back to me. I understand the hesitation. Hawke is a formidable force and towers over Scott.

"What are you doing here?" I prop one hand on my hip. The other remains shackled in Hawke's grip. He's not letting me go. Somehow, I know this, and while that little bit of male possessiveness normally puts me off, it does something else entirely with Hawke. I crave his touch and blossom beneath his protection.

"What am I doing here?" Scott's voice rises in pitch. It cracks. He clears his throat. "I might ask the same thing. Who the fuck is this?" He gestures to Hawke. "She's engaged to me, asshole."

Hawke laughs and pulls me against his chest. "Then why am I the one who had my tongue shoved down her throat? Doesn't look like she belongs to you anymore."

I try to look like I agree with Hawke.

Inside, it's a completely different matter. Memories of Scott flood my mind, the late nights, the whispered conversations, the talk about the future and our love. We were great together, and I miss it. I miss being a couple. A couple with dreams of creating something wonderful.

But he slept with Sadie.

I glance over Scott's shoulder, pretending to look inside the open doorway. "Where's Sadie? Did you bring her with you? Or, are you done fucking my best friend?"

She's not your best friend anymore.

Shut up, I know that.

"That wasn't what it looked like." He runs his hand through his hair. "It was the last time. I swear."

"The last time?" My voice shakes and I hate that it does. Scott confirms a truth I've been trying to avoid. I like to think it was only that one time, rather than an ongoing thing.

Hawke pulls me back against his chest and wraps and arm around my waist. His support is welcome. This should be something I can deal with on my own, but I'm not as strong as I'd like to think. My entire world, as I knew it, fell apart the night of our office Christmas party. All the truths I believed became lies I couldn't ignore.

"That implies it wasn't the first time." My voice breaks and I clear my throat, trying to inject strength into my outrage. It doesn't work. My words come out slow and shaky. "How long? How long were you fucking my best friend?"

"Shit, Q, not like it matters. You're the one I want, the one I want to spend the rest of my life with." He speaks to me, but his attention keeps shifting to the imposing presence of Hawke standing behind me. "Let me make it up to you. Come inside. We'll talk."

"She's with me." Hawke's voice rumbles over my head, full of possession and implied threat. His hand tightens around my waist. "And she's made herself very clear."

Scott draws away, eyes widening. I give him credit, he doesn't run, but he takes two steps back before coming to a halt and growing a backbone. His focus shifts away from Hawke; turns back to me.

"Look, I get you want to hurt me, Q, but this isn't you. You're not the revenge fuck kind of girl. We have history. That means something. And our company? What about that?"

"What about it?" After seeing Scott again, one thing becomes crystal clear. I never want to work with him again. Although, can I walk away from our dream? My creation? Can I turn my back on years of work?

"Look, buddy." Hawke's deep voice sends a shudder down my spine. "She doesn't want you here. I suggest you take the hint and leave."

Aggressive anger flashes in Scott's eyes. "I know Q. You mean nothing to her. She's using you to get back at me."

"I think you're done here." Hawke's comment comes as two men in white shorts and matching polo shirts arrive.

"Mr. Sterling?"

Hawke points to Scott. "Please see this gentleman off the premises."

I crane my neck to look at Hawke. When did he call for help? And why are those men speaking to him as if he owns this place?

"Sir, if you'll come with us." One of the men approaches Scott.

"See that he's escorted off the premises and never steps foot here again."

"Yes, Mr. Sterling." The men bracket Scott and make it clear he can walk out on his own or be dragged out kicking and screaming.

Scott's face turns beet red and his attention shifts to me. "You'll be back, Q, and when you come back you'll regret this." Anger threads through his tone, a sense of indignation that I dare to tell him no.

The sinking sensation in the pit of my stomach makes me want to puke, but I hold in my fear as Scott shakes off the grip of the men and storms out of my life.

With him gone, all my hopes and dreams disappear. There's no way we're salvaging our working relationship, let alone anything personal.

I've lost everything.

I collapse against Hawke and close my eyes. I'm not sure how long we stand there, except the fiery reds and oranges of the sunset are gone. The deep purples and blues of the night replace them as twilight blankets the earth. Soon, the moon will rise and the stars will come out of hiding. They'll spill across the sky and shine as my future fades away.

My hand goes to my belly. My fingers shake. I want to puke. It all hits me at once, what I lost.

"Are you going to be okay?" Hawke places his hand over mine.

"No, I'm not okay."

"I'm sorry about that."

"Don't be. It's not your fault." I swipe at my nose, sniffing away the tears.

He has nothing to do with Scott, but I'm thankful that I don't have to go through this alone. I step away from Hawke, breaking the connection of our bodies.

"Do you want to come inside and have that drink?"

His head slants down and his gaze cuts to the open door of my villa. "I don't think so. Come, let's head to the bar. We'll grab something there."

"I don't want to be around other people right now."

"I get that, but inviting me inside is too dangerous. We need to talk about that kiss."

The kiss he wasn't supposed to take.

The kiss I still feel on my lips.

A kiss that will forever be imprinted on my soul.

"You want to talk about it?" I want to finish what we started and work Scott out of my system for good. I thought he was going to finish it. Isn't that what he said?

Only if you kissed him, idiot.

"I'm afraid we must."

TWENTY-ONE

Hawke

A MAN IS NOTHING WITHOUT HIS WORD, AND I BROKE MINE.

Granted, I gave it in jest, fully expecting to win Quinn over with my charm. Our snorkeling cruise hit every mark in the playbook and I've always had a hundred percent success rate.

Except, Quinn Hayes isn't like any woman I've ever come across.

At least we settle one issue. Her asshat ex-fiancé is no longer in the picture. With him out of the way, I have free rein to do as I please. Or, rather, I should have.

Instead, I fucked things up. Not that I would take back stealing that kiss for anything in the world. I think I found Nirvana. As for hot? Explosive comes to mind. I'm still reeling from the aftershocks.

She tasted so damn sweet, like an ambrosia, which tickled my senses and promised decadent pleasures to come.

Once again, I'm rock hard and unfulfilled. My body responds like a teenager, constantly aching and weeping for more of sexy Quinn Hayes. Any other woman would've been in and out of my bed ten times by now, and I'd be walking away.

So what's different about her?

I glance down, fully aware of the tears spilling down her cheeks.

Her tiny sniffles aren't supposed to be things I hear, but come on. Each one of them thuds against my heart creating a jarring dissonance within me.

As for Asshat Scott, my men escort him off the premises, and he's permanently banned, which leaves me alone with Quinn until we ring in the new year.

"Can I ask you something?" She glances up, eyes shimmering.

"Anything."

"You're not a regular guest, are you?"

"Is that what you want to ask right now?"

"Not really, but I'm not ready to talk about—the other thing."

Right, the other thing. She means that scorching kiss. The heat still licks along my nerves and gathers in my balls, ready to explode.

That *other* thing.

A kiss which detonated my senses.

I feel her in every pore. Every cell in my body vibrates with the need for her, a raging hunger I can't quench.

You went back on your word.

I *never* go back on my word.

Quinn has me breaking every damn rule.

"I suppose that's fair, but we need to talk about it."

"I know." She ducks her head, unable to look me in the eye. I'd give a million dollars to know what thoughts are swirling in her head right now.

When we round the bend, the grotto comes into view. Low lighting built into the pavers illuminates our way. We stroll without purpose, passing secluded alcoves occupied by couples enjoying a romantic interlude.

I want Quinn in one of those. Tucked back into the shadows, I'd strip her down to nothing and drive her wild with need as we fuck. It's the only way to wring this excess energy from my body.

That's all I need. One good fuck to get her out of my head.

"You're correct. I'm not a regular guest."

"Do you work here?"

"Hardly." I can't help but scoff at that mental image.

"Do you…" Her voice drops as she struggles to piece together her words. I'm not interested in forcing her into a guessing game.

"I'm part owner of the resort." The majority stakeholder by default.

"Oh." Her voice is so soft. She extricates her hand from mine and scrubs the tears off her cheeks.

"Does that change anything?" I force her to face me. "Because I hope not."

Her shrug is noncommittal, but it matters. I see it in the slump of her shoulders and in the way she's unable to meet my gaze. I stoop down, forcing her to look at me.

"It shouldn't matter, Quinn."

Her fingers lift and press against her lips—Lips still swollen from my kiss.

Mine.

A kiss that shattered the foundations of my world. A kiss that continues to spark beneath my skin. A kiss that keeps me in a state of perpetual hardness when I'm around her.

Well, that last bit isn't because of the kiss. I've ached for her from the moment we met on the plane.

"It doesn't." Her soft voice whispers in my ears with the lie it carries.

Used to women taking advantage of me for my money, and the status their association with me brings, no matter how brief, my first thought is not to believe her. But I sense she doesn't care about it. In fact, I get the feeling it turns her off. I'm not accustomed to a woman who sees my wealth as a negative. To be honest, my ego is a bit bruised.

She continues toward the pool bar. If I'm not careful, this is where I'll lose her. As I'm unaccustomed to losing anything, it's time to double down. I take note of the way she presses her fingers to her lips and suppress a low growl. I want her with a possessiveness I've never felt before.

Unfortunately, the next bend takes us out of the meandering maze of the grottos and dumps us beside the pool. The night is young, which means the sparkling waters of the pool are empty.

Couples who spent the day sunbathing are back in their rooms getting ready for dinner and the evening festivities.

The evening festivities… An idea comes to mind.

Quinn heads to the nearly empty bar and props her elbows on the rich wood. The bartender comes over. Before she can order, I step up.

"A bottle of champagne."

"Yes, Mr. Sterling."

She looks at me over her shoulder. "I thought it was just a thing they did here."

"What's that?"

"The name thing."

"What do you mean?"

"I thought they called everyone by name, but I guess they all know who you are." There she goes again with the dismissive shrug.

"Actually, it's something we pride ourselves on. Every guest is treated like royalty. Every wish fulfilled. Knowing the guests on sight is a requirement of the staff."

"How do they do it?" She gives a shake of her head like she thinks I'm full of shit.

"It's not hard."

"Are you kidding me? There are people on my team—people I've worked with for years—that I couldn't tell you their name if it was tattooed on their forehead. I can remember a face, but names? It's not possible."

"There are tricks that help."

"Really."

"Yes, really." I can't help but smile. My perfect Miss Quinn Hayes is flawed. "Every morning, they're provided a list of new arrivals. We created an app that turns it into a game. The staff get rewards for their success on the app. Like a matching game." It's more complicated than that, but she's smart. She'll get it.

"That's a really cool idea." Her eyes brighten. "I need that in my life."

"It was my business partner's idea. I wish I could take the credit. I'm excellent with names. Perfect scores earned by our staff give them certain incentives. There are competitions between different groups. Everyone enjoys it."

"That's really cool how you did that."

Our conversation turns more relaxed, back the way it should be. The tightness in her eyes eases. Her shoulders relax. Even her smile makes a resurgence. I couldn't have asked for a better way to cut through the tension swirling between us.

"Let's sit away from the bar." There's no easy way to have an intimate conversation by the bar. Not to mention, my staff doesn't need to be privy to my personal affairs.

We settle down on a pair of chaise loungers. Justin, our bartender, comes over with two flutes and a bottle of champagne. The next few minutes are spent with Quinn watching him uncork the champagne and me dissecting her every move.

Where is her head at?

I've come to realize she's a thinker, not a feeler like me. Emotions guide me through life. If something resonates within me, I go for it. If not I back away. I don't need facts to make a decision.

My polar opposite in many ways, she approaches life with logic, thinking her way through every situation.

After Justin leaves us, I lift my glass for a toast. "To us."

She's a bit hesitant but follows my toast. "To us?" Her brows pinch and her delectable lips twist with thought.

I know what she's thinking, but I need to put our insane attraction on the back burner for a minute or two. She's not ready to accept the inevitability of our union. With time, I'll get her there.

"Tell me about Scott."

"I'd rather not."

"Considering what happened back there…" I leave off the kiss. "I'd like to know more. The two of you were involved. He proposed. I know what happened next. But tell me about your business venture." I cock my head and watch the wheels turn in her head.

"I suppose it's a bit complicated now."

Very careful with how much I reveal, I remind myself I'm not supposed to know much about her startup company.

"I thought maybe we could spend the rest of tonight getting to know each other better. You know a little more about me. I'm a rich, entitled bastard who happens to own Euphoria. Most of what you said on the boat hit things pretty much on the head."

She winces. "I'm sorry about that overgeneralization."

"Don't be. Sometimes it's helpful to see yourself through a different lens. Now, here's what I know about you. You come from a big family, four older, overly protective brothers, blue-collar, I think those are the words you used. I sense strong family bonds."

"All true."

"But you chose to come here instead of heading home for the holidays because you didn't want them to…. What was it you said?"

"Murder Scott." She huffs a laugh. "Not sure if that's what I said, but it's pretty much the truth."

"You're lucky to have that. Mother? Father?"

"Yes, to both, and very much in love. They're your stereotypical high school sweethearts. They started dating in high school, went to prom together senior year. He was a senior; she was a freshman. It was scandalous, and of course, he knocked her up."

I can't help but laugh. "You're kidding?"

"Not at all. Mom dropped out. Had my brother. Dad finished high school, enlisted in the Army. Served six years. In that time, Mom popped out Gideon, Brett, Ian, and Steven. Dad started his construction business. Mom got her GED and went to work for Dad as his office assistant and accountant. They're still wildly in love."

"I feel like I'm reading a trashy romance novel."

"You wouldn't be far off. They hit it hard and heavy, and they're still incredibly affectionate. Nobody thought they'd last. But Dad stepped up, did what he needed to support Mom; their family grew. Not that it was easy. They were on food stamps. Shopped at the thrift stores. Everyone got hand-me-downs. When Daddy felt he had his feet under him, he got out of the Army, started his business, and the rest is history."

"Then you came along. How many years separate you from your brothers?"

"Steven is twelve years older than me. Gideon is eighteen years older. I really am the baby. Kind of a surprise pregnancy."

"Wow. So, the youngest and only girl. The only one to graduate college?" I'm not entirely certain if she's told me this. I'm confusing what I read in her dossier with what she's shared.

"I did. Caltech, actually."

"Wow, you're like a super nerd."

"I told you I was."

"You're a very cute nerd." Her glass is empty. I swallow down the rest of my drink and refill our glasses. "Then what happened?" I want to get to how she and Scott got together and their startup.

"I majored in computer science. Dabbled in apps. I actually sold my very first app in high school."

"Really?"

"Yeah, I got taken."

I wondered if she knew her worth.

"I'm sorry."

"It was a learning experience." She shrugs like it's water under the bridge. I'm going to have some people look into that. I swear, nothing keeps this girl down.

"Then what?"

"Got my degree and got this wild idea stuck in my head."

"Really? Tell me about it."

"Oh, you don't want to hear about my work."

"I want to know about everything. You fascinate me." The strange thing is, it's the truth.

"Do I now?" Her eyes pinch as she gives me a look like I'm full of shit. "Tell me something."

"Anything."

"Am I anything like the women you date?"

"I don't date, but we've been over that."

"That's right. You fuck."

"I'm very honest about it. You say it like it's a bad thing. Honestly, the expression of pure, unadulterated lust can be quite freeing."

"I don't know about that." Her arms cross. It's a dangerous sign. "We're wired differently."

"You disapprove?"

"I just don't get it. You're an attractive man, interesting, and fun to be around. Why have you closed yourself off to something more than base, physical release? There's more to love than sex, and I think that's the part you're missing out on."

"I disagree. First off, sex is fun, and I indulge myself. Why not take advantage of what's freely offered? Second, there are too many who see me, my wealth, and my status as stepping stones to what they want. I learned very early what my worth was to others and what they wanted from me. I figure if they're willing to take from me, then I'll take what I want from them."

"Don't you ever want more?"

She says it as if there is more to be had. Sadly, I know the truth.

"I'm content. Why are you afraid of sex?"

"I'm not afraid of sex." Her tone turns defensive. I hit a nerve, more like a landmine from the way her body language closes off. But truth is revealed in her eyes. She's wary, cautious, and untrusting of men.

Of me.

Shit.

Suddenly, I realize something incredible. My little vixen is clueless how potent her sexuality can be to a man. What did Asshat Scott do to mess with her head? Why is she so repressed?

She wasn't repressed in my arms. She fucking melted when I held her. My chest puffs out because I'm a pretentious prick, preening over my ability to make women swoon—to make *her* swoon.

We've yet to discuss that kiss. The one I took without permission.

"Poor choice of words." I hold my hand to my chest and give a slight bow. "My apologies."

She was a hot and fiery vixen in my arms. I bet I saw more passion in that one kiss than Scott ever saw in the years they dated.

Fucking putz. He has no idea what he fucked up.

"Hawke, you deserve better from life." Her fingers lift to her lips, brushing them softly. "You have wealth and power. I don't know what you do for a living, but you're more than the sum of your bank account. I hope, someday, you find the right woman who sees the real you. Who falls madly, and desperately, in love with *you*. When that happens, you'll understand what 'more' means, and why everything that came before was achingly empty."

I'm entranced by everything she says. The way she keeps touching her lips reminds me how they felt against my mouth. I imagine how they'll feel wrapped around my cock and hold back a groan.

Her breathy moans awakened the slumbering beast inside of me. I'm desperate to lay claim to her body, but I'm willing to wait for the right moment.

"Achingly empty?" My brow lifts. "I don't feel empty."

"Maybe those were my poor choice in words."

"Well…" I place my glass down and fix her with a stare. "Now that we've sufficiently danced around the issue, it's time to actually dance."

TWENTY-TWO

Quinn

"Dance?" What the hell does Hawke mean? I'd ask, but I'm pretty sure my expression says it all. "I don't dance."

He extends his hand to me. I take it, cautiously, and he lifts me to my feet. I stumble forward, into him, and place my hand over his chest. The steady lub-dub of his heart beats beneath my palm. I swear the man is unflappable, always in complete control.

As for myself?

I'm a fucking mess. I still taste him. I still feel his lips on mine. My entire body buzzes with memories of that kiss, confused about pretty much everything.

"You and I are going to dance." He gives a wink. "Then, we'll talk about that kiss."

"Um…" I glance around the pool area. "There's nobody dancing."

"Not here silly."

"Then where?"

"Do you know how to tango?"

"No."

"Salsa?" His eyes narrow wickedly.

I sense he's up to something.

"No."

"Dirty dancing? The kind your mother would never allow and your brothers would kill me for if they knew I danced with you like that?"

"I have two left feet and the rhythm of a white chick. I'm better off standing on the sidelines. Trust me. You do not want to dance with me."

"I'd never let you sit on the sidelines." His voice turns husky. It's hot as fuck. Not to mention his golden eyes practically glow with all manner of dirty thoughts.

I'm not sure how to answer. Not that I have a choice. Before I know it, he leads me through the expansive gardens.

"You're going to learn how to dance like a goddess." Not only does he sound sure of himself, the rat bastard is positively smug about it.

"Um, two left feet. Did you miss that part?"

"Your feet don't need to move. Don't worry, I'll show you everything you need to know." His wink is a devastating force of nature. I practically swoon.

He brings me to a pavilion where a handful of couples gather. Two staff are present, a man and a woman. The man's dressed in the resort's signature white shorts and matching white polo shirt. She's dressed in a flowing white diaphanous gown, which makes me think of clouds billowing in the wind. Each one of her dainty steps is a sensual testament to the beauty of the human body.

"Mr. Sterling, it's so good to have you joining us." She comes over to greet us.

"Thank you, Lisette."

While he's good with people and names, I'm glad for the name tag pinned to her top.

"I think you'll be very pleased with tonight's lesson." Her smile is bright. Her makeup is practically nonexistent. She's gorgeous. And she gives me a knowing wink.

What does she know that I do not?

"This is Quinn." He introduces me. "She claims to have two left feet and is better left on the sidelines." I give his teasing tone my best stink eye. A deep booming laugh is his response.

Lisette takes my hands in hers. "You have nothing to worry about, Miss Hayes. I've taught people with three left feet to dance and they've all left very satisfied. Besides, you have an amazing partner. Mr. Sterling is an accomplished dancer."

"Really?" My eyes gravitate back to Hawke's imposing presence.

"Just wait and see." He pulls me out of Lisette's grip and tugs me tight to his side. "We're going to make magic tonight."

Magic? I don't think we define *magic* the same way.

Lisette's partner claps his hands to get everyone's attention. Everybody quiets and turns toward him.

"Gather 'round. We're getting ready to start." Lisette glides up beside him, whispers something into his ear. His attention shifts to me and I'm taken in with one sweep of his gaze. "How many people have seen the movie Dirty Dancing?"

Most of the couples in this crowd are older, in their forties and young fifties. Nearly every hand goes up. Mine does too, but only because it's my mother's favorite movie. I spent many Saturday nights watching it with her. She would tell me how salacious the movie was when she was a girl and how her parents wouldn't let her watch it.

I think she liked it because it reminded her of my dad. He was the older, more experienced boy, a senior in high school, and she was the young girl, a naive freshman, just blooming into a beautiful woman. I'm sure there's more to their relationship than I want to know. After all, he did knock her up on prom night.

The corner of Hawke's mouth turns up in a smirk. He tugs me tight against his body.

"You ready for a little dirty dancing?"

"You ready for me to step on your toes?"

This is when I would normally excuse myself, too embarrassed by my lack of rhythm to have fun. I'm not the kind of person who lets myself go. I'm rigid and focused. This is the kind of wild and crazy shit I don't do.

But somehow, I find myself in the middle of the dance floor

with Hawke's hand wrapped around my waist. His fingers splay across the small of my back. He gives a little kick to my right foot.

"Widen your stance a bit, Miss Hayes." His voice simmers with passion, lust, and other dark thoughts.

"Why?"

"So I can step between your legs, silly."

Lisette and her partner, whose name is Brian, stand on a slightly raised podium. It allows us, their students, to see them and for them to see us. Brian demonstrates how he wants the men to hold the women; how it allows the man to *lead*.

Hawke follows with no hesitation. He's got the moves down.

"Now, ladies—" Lisette's crystal-clear voice rings overhead. "You need to let him in. You're going to be riding his leg. This isn't called dirty dancing for nothing. We're going to be doing a lot of bumping and grinding, and you can't grind if his leg isn't bumping between your thighs."

Nervous giggles surround us as everyone loosens up. My cheeks heat because there's no way I'm going to grind on Hawke's leg. Except he pulls me to him and forces his leg between my thighs. He presses tight, right against my sex.

Mortified doesn't begin to describe my current state, but then Brian starts the music and we all move. Well, everyone but me. I stand like a statue, terrified to move.

Lissette and Brian encourage us and walk us through three basic moves. Hawke is right about one thing. My two left feet have nothing to worry about. They aren't involved in what we're doing. As for the rest of my body?

I'm stiff as a board while Hawke oozes raw, potent sex appeal. His entire body is one fluid movement, a pulsating wave that begins with his head, rolls through his shoulders, and undulates somewhere between his waist, hips, and knees. Honestly, I didn't know the human body could move like that.

Lisette and Brian demonstrate those three moves again, combining them. One's a slow sway back and forth. Beginner stuff. The next is more of a grind. That one makes me blush. Hawke's grip tightens. His husky laugh has me looking anywhere but at him.

The last one, kind of a mixture of the first two, is sexy, sinuous, and looks a lot like fucking.

Our instructors demonstrate one last time, then separate. They hop off their podium to circulate between the couples. Brian shows the men how to lead, and Lisette shows the women how to follow.

Like a scene right out of the movie, I find myself sandwiched between Lisette and Hawke as she comes up behind me. Her fingers press lightly on my hips and she shows me how to meet and match the undulations of Hawke's body.

Holy hell, the man can move. I'm stiff and gangly, more than awkward, and just want it all to stop. But there's no stopping the force which is Hawke Sterling when he sets his mind to something.

"That's it, Miss Hayes." Lisette brings me back to the moment, forcing me to crawl out of my introverted shell. "Let your hands hang down. We'll get to those in a bit. For now, feel the music wash through you. Focus on the beat. Shift to the left. Shift to the right. That's it. Left. Right…" Her voice soothes and guides me. All the while, Hawke keeps his hands on my waist, applying slight pressure, which accentuates the push and pull of Lisette's hands. "Keep your feet in place. Move only your hips and your knees." She stays with me for a moment.

The first bit is awkward. My entire body locks up, but she's phenomenal at her job. Hawke is simply Hawke. He echoes Lisette's words without overpowering her instruction.

Her fingers guide one hip forward, the other back. Once I get a hang of that, she shows me how to roll my hips forward and back. Like a figure eight, or something like that.

Hawke says nothing. I think he does that on purpose because the moment I relax, he clears his throat. My hips move up and down, forward and back. I may not be a total loser at this dancing thing. Just don't ask me to move my feet. Lisette moves on to the next couple, which leaves Hawke and me alone.

My arms dangle. Normally, I'd feel self-conscious about that, except they seem perfectly capable of swaying to the low, sultry beat on their own. It's hypnotic and sensual as hell. The music rolls out of the speakers and settles into my body, one pulsating wave after the next.

The song is sexy, filthy, absolutely dirty. It carries a wanton, lustful sound—a wild, carnal beat which demands an answer.

"Your body was made for this, luv. You're fucking intoxicating." Hawke leans in. His low breaths heat the skin of my neck and raise the fine hairs on my arms.

I'm not sure if I agree with him, but something is happening. Not worried about how I look, who might be watching, or who might laugh at me, I surrender to the beat and follow Hawke's sultry lead.

There's no thinking. Only feeling.

And I feel like a fucking goddess.

Sexy.

Sexual.

Powerful.

Hawke grabs my wrist. He moves it to his shoulder, placing it precisely where he wants it. He takes my other hand and lifts it too. Now, my arms dangle over his shoulders while my hips move with his. I'm getting that part down. He leads, adding in his shoulders, showing my body how to move with him.

I've never danced like this before. With his leg wedged between my legs, my pussy rubs up against him. A cascade of sensation ricochets through my body. Nerves on fire. Senses overloaded. I'm coming apart in his arms.

There's no cautious touching going on down there. Our bodies are in close, physical contact, in the middle of a dance floor with several other couples who are similarly grinding and bumping, and practically humping.

I've fallen into a different world, an erotic realm where the rules are different. Inhibitions aren't allowed. My brain steps back to let my body lead.

It's magical, sensual, maddening, and freeing. The normal stiffness of my body disappears. Hawke leads. I follow. He commands my body to let go. To move. To simply exist in the moment.

I can do, and be, anything I want. No repercussions. No consequences. No regrets.

I feel like I can fly.

And I'm getting more turned on by the second. My blood heats with each breath. That steady throb between my legs turns nearly unbearable. My entire body coils with tension, and I know it won't take much to explode. I'm a little more than slightly aroused. My body aches for Hawke.

That might be the only reason I don't run for the hills. Goddamn, but he's sexy. I'm not sure what to fear the most. Hawke dirty talking me, or Hawke not speaking, but saying everything with the sway of his hips, the pulse of his breath, and the heat building between us.

"See…" His husky voice makes me shiver. "You're not so bad at this."

Our foreheads touch. Our breaths meld. Our bodies sway in unison. My sex throbs with each intoxicating rub against his leg, and I grind against him, shamelessly seeking more friction. More heat. More everything as my core tightens and pleasure builds.

He's hard. Every now and again, the rocking of his hips hits in just the right way that I can't help but feel the stiff length of him pressing against me.

Good to know I'm not the only one affected.

"You're a good teacher." I barely recognize my voice. Low and sultry, I sound drunk on lust. Each press of his thigh against my sex makes me want to climb his body. Wrap my legs around his hips and damn the consequences.

And why the fuck not? What do you have to lose? One night of passion?

I can't argue with myself.

Why let my brain lead when my body clearly says yes? Will I ever have another opportunity like this? Sex, freely offered, by a man who's basically every woman's wet dream. No strings. No regrets. Nothing but one night of inhibitions falling away. I'll never have to see him again.

It sounds perfect.

He holds me close. My nipples tighten each time they brush

against his chest. My entire body buzzes with the need for more. It tells my brain to shut the fuck up, and for once in my life, take a chance.

"About that kiss…" The low, sultry tones of his voice barely register. "I shouldn't have taken it, but that asshole needed to know what he lost."

I place my finger over Hawke's lips. "I don't want to talk about Scott."

"I gave you my word…"

"About that…" I take in a deep breath and go for it, knowing full well what will happen next. My hands wrap around his neck. I lift on tiptoe. And I kiss Hawke Sterling.

His entire body stills. The music thumps around us, but the world ceases to exist. He pulls me tight, leaning into the kiss.

Taking it over.

One hand presses against the small of my back. The other lifts to tangle in my hair. Shivers race up and down my spine.

I've never done anything like this before. I've never taken the initiative, although I'm not really leading anything here. Hawke is a dominant man who isn't content to follow, but he is a man of his word.

That kiss? The one we've literally danced around since it happened, gets filed away as unavoidable. I couldn't ask for a more effective way to toss Scott out of my life with his tail tucked between his legs.

But this is my time.

My choice.

My kiss.

"Fuck, Quinn." Hawke pulls away and rests his forehead against mine. "You shouldn't have done that."

"Why? You said if I kissed you…" I peek up at him through my lashes and press my lips together. I taste him. Dark, exotic, primal, and all male, I know exactly what I'm doing.

"I damn well know what I said." The swirls of emotion simmering in his eyes make me gasp. Lust, desire, hunger, and need all mix together. Before I can think about what I've done, he yanks me back to him and covers my mouth with his. Hungry, possessive, and demanding, our lips crush together.

I'm not sure when he lifts me off my feet, except he carries me off the dance floor. My legs wrap around his hips. They know exactly what to do. The way his mouth molds to mine is magic. The velvety press of his lips is soft, loving, and insane.

I open my mouth with a low moan.

All I feel is heat; a raging inferno lights my brain on fire. That warmth spreads down my neck, tightens my nipples, and surges through my body where it gathers with a needy throb between my legs.

If the world ends right now, I wouldn't care. His kisses are something beyond what I've ever experienced. If I'm not careful, I'll become an addict, but I remind myself this is only for one night.

It has to be. I won't be able to face him in the morning. But that's okay. I'll take this one night. In the morning, I'll pack my bags, swallow my fear, and book a flight home. I miss my family.

And after this, I'll have to walk away.

Lust and desire twist inside of me, a force of nature impossible to resist. One night of shedding my identity, loosening the tight hold I keep on my emotions. All I need is one night with Hawke.

We become a grappling mess of limbs. Or at least I do. He holds me in his strong grip as I climb his body. Not really sure where we're headed, all I care about is getting there fast. Ripping off my clothes. And finally feeling what it means to be truly fucked by a man pushed beyond restraint.

A shudder ripples through my body.

Suddenly, we stop.

"Last chance." Husky and low, his voice vibrates with passion. "I told you what would happen if you kissed me. I'm going to fuck you. You get one chance to stop this. I'm not a gentle lover, Quinn. I'm going to fuck you and take what I need. Is this what you really want?"

No way am I stopping this.

Not a gentle lover? It takes less than a millisecond to make my decision. My entire life, I've played things safe. I've thought through every permutation. Weighed the consequences. Compared risks against benefits.

For once in my life, I don't want that burden. I want to give up that right and simply experience one blissful night with a man driven mad with lust.

My legs tighten around his hips. My ankles cross one another. Between us, his erection strains in his pants.

"Don't stop."

"Fuuuck." He buries his face in the soft hollow of my throat. Wire-tight, I feel his restraint snap.

"Hawke?"

"Yes?"

I never ask for what I need. I've never told a man what I wanted. I've never allowed myself that freedom.

Never.

And I'm a bit hesitant as it is. But I swallow back my fear, my hesitation, all those things—barriers—which keep me locked inside my head.

"I don't want gentle."

I want wild, unrestrained, carnal, lust-fueled fucking from a man I know can give me that and more.

"Thank fuck for that." His rumbly laughter is both terrifying and exciting. I have a feeling tonight is going to be like nothing I've ever experienced before, as long as I can keep my mind out of it.

That'll be the trick.

His growl is the last thing I hear before he heads into one of the grottos and carries me to the back of a secluded cave.

His wire-tight control slips and falls apart to reveal a snarling beast. One that nips and bites and takes and claims. As if in answer, something snaps within me too.

TWENTY-THREE

Hawke

Something happened when Quinn kissed me.

My brain lit on fire.

All thought, except one, fizzled in my head.

I need to fuck, and rut, and mount her until I claim every piece of her soul.

I'm not talking about a simple fuck-and-done. An exchange of mutual pleasure and that's it. I want to imprint myself on her soul. Lay claim to her body. Erase any evidence of those who came before me. One asshole in particular.

In short, I want to make her mine.

I can't bear one more minute without her, like she's some drug I can't get enough of. I've become an addict who needs an instant fix. I'm so strung out; my lungs strain to pull in enough oxygen. There doesn't seem to be enough air to breathe in the humid mix of salt and sea.

There never is around Quinn.

From our first meeting at the airport, to our time spent on the plane, she keeps me breathless with my need for her.

Her kiss is my salvation, but I recognize it as my torment as well.

I'll take her tonight, and every day until our time here comes to an end.

But then what?

The barrage of emotion slamming against my heart is nonstop, and if I'm not careful, she'll lodge herself in where no woman has before.

Salvation and torment all rolled into one.

I'm truly fucked.

The universe is sending a message, but fuck if I care. All that matters is Quinn. I yank her to me, grabbing the back of her neck, and cover her mouth with mine.

She made a mistake in giving me free rein to do as I please. Our lips crush together and we connect in a tangle of limbs. My grip on her neck tightens, asserting dominance. Her breathy moans fill with her surrender. There's no way she'll control what comes next, and I have a sinking suspicion that's exactly what she wants. Miss Quinn Hayes doesn't want to be in control. That she surrenders that part of herself to me is the most potent aphrodisiac in the world.

Her fingers twine in the hair at my nape, coaxing shivers down my spine. I need her out of these clothes. My dick is about ready to explode. Not that I'll rush this. I plan on fucking her now and on through morning. This is only the first taste of what I'll take.

Our kiss ignites the primal desire within us both. I feel it in her soft sighs and the tiny whimpers she can't control. It's present in the surrender she yields. We're connecting on the most basic level a man and woman can connect, but we've yet to complete the final act.

My lips brush against hers, not innocently. Not like a tease, but hot, fiery, demanding, and certain of the outcome.

The temperature of the water is warm. The air heated. Mist drifts all around us, cloaking us in a shroud of privacy.

Our clothes are no longer dry, but damp from the misty air. I yank at her ankles, releasing their grip, and force her to her feet. She gives a little mewl of frustration as our lips separate, but then I crash us against the uneven wall of the grotto.

My hands go to the hem of her shirt, and I yank it out from her shorts. She follows, mimicking my actions, and draws mine over my head. I would do the same to her, but would probably rip the fabric in my haste. I'm not so far gone that I forget about the walk back to my private villa. I plan to fuck her beneath the stars and listen to her screams through dawn.

She's right there with me, panting and biting her lower lip, as she tugs her top over her head. We fumble a bit, too excited to extricate her arms from the wet fabric, but we finally get her free.

A shy smile curves her lips and she looks up at me with her molten, emerald gaze. Her eyes brim with excitement. Her skin flushes with arousal. She wants this, but more than that, I sense this kind of passion is new for her.

It fucking turns me on even more, as if that's possible. I love that I bring her to this state of frenzied need. And yes, it strokes my ego.

Although, I want her to stroke something else. My cock is so engorged its head peeks out from the tops of my shorts.

Water falls all around us. The grottos are a mixture of hot tub and showers with cascading waterfalls, and steamy mist injected into the air. Faux rock surrounds us, colored in muted greens and blues to emulate the real thing. A traction enhancing surface covers the uneven floor, for obvious reasons. We're in an alcove tucked behind a waterfall. The rush of water covers the sounds of our lovemaking, sounds which shall soon escalate to cries of passion.

Quinn slips out of her bikini top and attacks me, pressing her lips against mine as my hands find the curve of her breasts. I finally get to explore her body as a lover instead of a sex-starved man held at arm's length.

If I'm not careful, however, I'll lose myself to my lust. Which is why I forcibly slow things down and indulge in the sensation of her breasts filling my hands.

Soft and pillowy, her tits pull a groan from my core. My cock gives a nod. It's eager to quench its thirst and plunge into her wet heat. Quinn's nipples tighten into hard pebbles.

My dick jerks when I roll her nipples between my thumb and forefinger. The hitching of her breath is a fucking drug. I gently squeeze the tight nubs, but that's not enough. I need more.

I increase the pressure until she gasps and lifts up on her toes.

Bending down, I growl into her ear. It's the only warning I'll give. "You still sure about not being gentle? Because this is only a taste of what's to come."

Her panting breath rushes past my ear. Beyond capacity to form words, she answers with a nod. I pull back, so I can see her, and confirm her consent before I forge forward.

She draws her lower lip between her teeth, biting gently, and sucks in a deep breath. I tighten the vise on her nipples, watching her body hitch in pain. Her eyes close, wincing as I press tighter, but then they fly open when I release my hold.

"Holy fuck, Hawke—that's…" She's unable to finish whatever it is because I claim her mouth as mine. I do let up, but only because I'm a pretentious prick.

"You liked that?" My question is more for my amusement than needing her reassurance. I sense she's never experienced the kind of sexual aggression I bring to the table.

"Yes." She's fucking drunk on sensation and her breathy response fuels the fire.

I flick open the top button of her shorts and slide the zipper down. She's going to drive me insane with that whole lip-biting thing, but that's okay. Revenge will taste so fucking sweet.

I lower her shorts over the flare of her hips and hook my fingers beneath her bikini bottoms. No need to draw this out. Her clothes are wet and they stick to her skin, but my need is greater than that small bit of resistance. Another yank and her bikini slides over her ass. I lower them further to reveal a neatly trimmed patch of hair and the glistening folds of her sex.

She steps out of her shorts, then goes still when I grip her hips and bury my face between her legs. I get the distinct impression she's never been with a man who took the time to see to her pleasure before his own.

Yet another reason to hate Asshat Scott. By the end of tonight, she'll know her worth and what to expect from a lover.

I intend to make her come apart. And come. And come again.

A deep inhale and her unique musk floods my senses. Ambrosia of the gods, I can't wait to taste her. She squirms a bit, but I hold her in place, letting her know she's mine to control and not the other way around.

My tongue darts out and licks the tip of her clit. She gasps and her entire body shudders. She's fucking close and I've yet to really begin. What Scott doesn't know is that selfish pricks miss out on all the fun. The best part of sex isn't the plunge-and-go orgasm. It's in taking your partner to new heights of sensation. In making her come apart in your hands and fly over and over again.

I won't be satisfied until she's had at least one orgasm before I take her. Two would be better. And by the time the sun rises, we'll be working our way to double digits. From her responsiveness to my touch, I'm pretty certain we'll hit that number, or come remarkably close.

With that goal in mind, I dive right in and lick along the seam of her sex. She gives a little screech and her hands fly to my head where her fingers dig into my hair. They twist and grab, pulling at the roots while I lick her through and past her first soul-sundering orgasm. Her throat opens and she screams my name.

Fucking hell! My name on her lips practically makes me come right there.

She practically rips my hair out by the roots. Her thighs quiver and her body shakes. I have to hold her through it because I'm afraid she'll actually fall over.

Slowly, the wave courses through her. The shaking in her legs eases. Her breaths deepen as she recovers. I stand, supporting her the entire time, and take her in my arms where she weeps with pleasure.

Or at least that's what I think. Those must be tears of joy. If not, I've royally fucked up.

TWENTY-FOUR

Quinn

WHAT THE HELL JUST HAPPENED?

My entire world exploded. Bright lights. Shooting stars. Light followed by blissful nothingness.

Little death? I think that's what people say an orgasm should feel like: *le petit morte.*

I never knew it could feel like *that.*

I've never experienced that kind of earth-shattering, toe-curling, breath-taking, mind-altering, whole-body experience before. My nerves are still firing erratically as if they're not sure what happened either.

Hawke holds me. Strong arms wrap around me. If not for him, I'd be passed out on the ground.

And I'm crying.

Soft sobs spill from my lips. Tears leak from my eyes. I'm a blubbering, blissfully sedated mess.

Why?

I don't know.

Maybe, because I never knew sex could be like that. I didn't know it could *feel* like that.

I'm still catching my breath. My heart's given up the chase. My pulse galloped away and it's going to be some time before I come down from this high.

It's as if I've been robbed of orgasms my entire life. Scott was a thief, giving me only the bare minimum to keep me interested. I thought the orgasms he gave me were normal.

A light tingling.

A bit of tightness.

A flush of pleasure, featherlight, tickling between my legs.

Who knew an orgasm could be so much more? So intense?

"Are you okay?" Hawke rubs my back and soothes me with the liquid silk of his voice.

Sometimes, his voice is like that, smooth, silky, reassuring. Other times, his voice turns harsh and raspy. When he's turned on, rumbles surface from somewhere deep within him.

"I'm sorry. That was…" I brush the wet hair from my face and try to finish my thought. What am I trying to say? "Intense."

That word is far from adequate. In fact, it's wholly inadequate, but it's the best I can do considering my brain turned to mush after that orgasm. Those neurons aren't firing. They're incapable of piecing together a coherent thought.

My body still echoes with the aftershocks of that orgasm. Little flashes of pleasure zing along overstimulated nerve endings.

Slowly, the ability to think returns to me.

His low chuckle rumbles through my chest.

"We've barely begun, luv. If you think that was intense, wait until I get inside of you."

Oh, I need him inside of me. If he can do that with his tongue, what is he capable of with that straining, jutting erection standing rigidly at attention at the apex of his thighs?

Shit!

He's yet to get off. I know Scott's frustration when sex takes too long. He's all about getting in and getting out. Like sex is a job, or an itch he needs to scratch. Something to relieve the tension of his day, and nothing more.

My fingers dig into Hawke's shoulders. I hate that my thoughts turn to Scott when I'm in his arms. But comparisons are inevitable.

My sexual history is rather limited. To be honest, I'm not that impressed with sex. It's more of a chore than anything else—except whatever just happened.

That was no chore.

It was amazing. So amazing, that I want more. I *crave* more. There's a hunger, a need, boiling up inside of me, which demands Hawke's cock.

Emboldened by all these new sensations, I do something I've never done before.

I ask for more.

"If that was the appetizer, I'm ready for the main event." I bite at my lower lip, unsure how the next part of this goes.

Am I supposed to lay down and spread my legs?

Somehow, I don't think Hawke is big on the whole missionary position. He seems more of an adventurous lover.

Unfortunately, that position, and doggy style, are the only two I know.

There's about an inch or two of water covering the ground. Tiny protrusions in the fake rock make the floor sticky. I'm not keen on lying down. Nor am I happy about getting on all fours. I want to watch him, not endure the whole thing like I did with Scott.

His finger traces along the line of my jaw and he sweeps a wet strand of my hair off my face.

"What are you thinking?"

I glance up at him, eyes wide, as my mind spins. No way in hell am I telling him I was thinking about Scott.

Instead, I let my hand trace down the dips and valleys of his chest. He's all sinew and stacked muscle. I saw a little of it while we snorkeled earlier today, but now I get to touch.

A low groan vibrates in the back of his throat as my fingers dip over the well-defined muscles of his abs.

"I like the direction you're headed." His rumbly words resonate with unspent lust and flicker with amusement.

"Do you…" I glance down, and my hand hesitates.

"Do I, what?" Mischief glimmers in his eyes. "Do I want your hand on me, fisting me to release? Or maybe it's that pretty little mouth of yours I desire. Lips wrapping around my cock as I thrust inside and knock around your tonsils for a bit? Maybe, I want it all? Your hands on my balls, your lips wrapped around my cock, and your tongue licking along my shaft."

Holy fuck, the man doesn't mince words.

"To be honest, I want to see you on your knees. It's a bit of a power trip to stand over a woman while she pleasures me. There's just something about a woman on her knees, the submission of it, that gets me off."

Heat licks between my legs as his rumbly voice grows harsher, coarser, more forceful and demanding. It's enough to drop me to my knees.

"Um…" My hand presses against his belly, fingers barely touching the incredible grooves which angle down to where his very erect cock weeps for me.

He grips my wrist and takes control. "The answer is most definitely yes to all of that. I want to put you on your knees and fuck that mouth." He forces my hand to the root of his cock. "I want to feel your hand on me, fisting me, fucking me."

My fingers move of their own accord and wrap around the base of his erection. His eyes close and his head tips back.

"Fuck, your hand feels so damn good."

He doesn't release my hand. Instead, he moves his along his thick shaft, taking mine with it. His grip tightens as we move, showing me how he likes to be handled.

I dip down, getting ready to go to my knees. I've never had a man eat me out like that before. Those aren't even words I use. *Eat me out.* But I do know one thing kind of demands the other.

Of course, I had boyfriends who tried and bungled the whole thing. More frustrating than anything else, I usually couldn't wait to yank them off and get to the fucking so we could finish and get on with our night.

That is not what goes through my mind with Hawke.

First, he surprised me by going to his knees. I barely registered what was happening before the heat of his mouth turned me into a quivering fool.

Instant orgasm.

Like lighting a fuse, or setting off a bomb, my body detonated.

Or so I thought.

That lick of his tongue sent me spiraling into oblivion.

I've never come that fast.

I've never come that hard.

I've never had the world disappear as I flew free.

If he wants me on my knees, I'm not only willing to repay the favor, but I'm willing to assume the role he's hinting at. Me serving him. Him commanding me. Unlike all the other men with whom I wanted to rush through it to get to the end, I never want this night to end.

I need more.

I want more.

And I'm going to take it.

But first, I'll repay the favor he graciously bestowed on me.

The pace of his hand quickens. This must be how he masturbates: hard, fast, and frenzied.

But when I try to lower to my knees, he gives a sharp shake of his head.

"As much as I want you on your knees, if you put your mouth on me, I won't last." He glances around until he finds his shorts. Releasing me, he steps away to dig in the pockets, searching for something.

A shiny foil pack.

In my lust-crazed brain, I forgot about needing protection. Honestly, I'd take the risk.

He rips open the wrapper and smoothly slides the condom over his shaft.

We're going to fuck.

My insides clench in anticipation. But how? And where? Surely, he doesn't mean to take me here?

A quick glance around reveals I can see nothing outside our secluded retreat. That means no one can see inside. I don't remember much of the mad dash in here, except we somehow managed to step through a waterfall and curve around the walls to reach the very back of this place.

Well, not the very back of the grotto. We stand in a little open area. Water splashes all around us. Tiny jets inject heated mist into the air. Maybe it's steam? I don't know.

But tucked in the corner is a bubbling hot tub with steam rising off the warm, frothy water. The floor runs right into the hot tub as if it were specially molded to gradually descend into the pool.

Hawke takes my hand and leads me into the water. We stop waist deep and his hands run up my arms. His eyes gaze deeply into mine, dipping down to admire my breasts more often than not.

His golden eyes are molten pools of desire. He sweeps his hand down my arm and back up my side, where he fondles my breast. His eyes narrow as he grips my nipple.

My eyes widen because I remember the pain when he pinched them. Pain that should have sent me running, but instead set up a deep throbbing between my legs. Never have I experienced anything like that.

"Come." He commands me and leads me by my breast. Specifically, by the grip he has on my poor nipple.

I don't dare hesitate, because—pain. And holy hell, the way he commands me to follow? I don't understand why that's turning me on as much, or more, than his grip on my poor tortured nipple.

Although, I'm not against seeing what might happen. I have a strong sense Hawke knows how to make sex fun. Like deliciously dirty and downright filthy, but in the best way possible.

He heads to the far wall, where the designers of this little escape molded in a depression that looks a lot like a seat. My gaze meanders over the rock walls and I'm pretty sure that's what it's supposed to be.

We spin around and he backs me up to the seat. It rests just above the water's edge. Water laps onto it, keeping the surface warm. But it's not slick. Like the floor, tiny nubs provide traction to keep me from slipping.

"Come." He lifts me by the hips and deposits me on the seat.

My arms naturally go to his shoulders, to support me. To touch him. I can't get enough of his muscular physique. He leans in until our lips are kissably close.

"Open your legs, luv. It's time to get properly fucked. I'd take my time and make you come again, but I honestly can't wait to sink into your wet heat. I need inside of you now."

I completely agree and spread my legs.

It's weird.

I always feel self-conscious about this kind of stuff, hiding my body, trying to rush to the finish line. I prefer sex in the dark. There's no darkness here.

Yes, the lighting is subdued, but I don't have to squint to see every bit of Hawke's devastating physique. Especially, his cock: long, thick, with ropey veins along the shaft. A thick, bulbous head, it's painfully engorged with blood. He's hard for me.

Hawke doesn't rush anything. He could shove right on in. Instead, he leans in for a kiss.

An utterly unforgettable kiss.

Our lips mold together and slide against each other. He nips at my lower lip, light at first, then eliciting a flicker of pain. I draw back, but instead of a hiss, a low moan escapes me.

How is that? Why is that? What the fuck is he doing to me?

Sensations that should make me recoil are instead intense, erotic, and mind-numbingly insane.

I let my hands run freely across the expanse of his back. He leans in. Our bodies move and writhe together like two sinuous souls wrapping around each other.

If I thought it felt like we were fucking on the dance floor with all that bumping and grinding, it's nothing compared to this. He reaches between us. Cups my breast. Plays with my nipple. And, basically, turns me into a quivering mess.

"I'm going to fuck your tits, luv. Right after I fuck your mouth." He grabs my lower lip between his teeth and gives a slight tug. "But first…"

That familiar sensation coils in my core, a flush of pleasure, a needy throb, that tightening which only needs the right touch to explode.

I jump when he presses a finger to my sex, then cry out when he shoves a finger inside. He does something with his thumb, pressing the sensitive bundle of nerves of my clit while stroking me from the inside.

He hits *something* inside me and my entire body detonates with an orgasm I knew was coming but didn't think was anywhere that close.

As my legs clamp around his hips and my head tilts back with the primal cries ripping out of me, the flare of his cock presses against my entrance. With my orgasm still surging within me, he thrusts inside. His hands move to my hips, my butt, and he grabs hold.

I'm still coming from my second orgasm when he buries himself inside of me. No gentle easing in. He takes me with one powerful thrust until he's buried to the root.

A pinch of pain passes through me. It's brief, barely noticeable, as my climax ebbs.

"Fuuuck…" His raspy moan sounds like a man who's found heaven. "You're fucking tight. So hot. So slick. So fucking perfect." His hand flies up to grasp the back of my neck and he forcibly kisses me.

Raw. Urgent. It's feral and uncontrolled.

I can't catch my breath. My body is recovering, sliding down the opposite side of yet another powerful orgasm.

That downward fall is interrupted when Hawke pulls out and slams forward.

If I thought he could move those hips on the dance floor, that is nothing compared to the way they gyrate as he fucks.

The man is an animal when he finally surrenders to his lust. He takes me hard, and true to his word, there's nothing gentle about his punishing thrusts.

That gentle downslide of my orgasm gets hijacked by the sensation of him filling my pussy, by the slow glide of his cock outward, and the hard thrust inward.

His breaths pulse in and out as his breathing deepens. For now, he's still in control.

As for me?

Heat coils in my core with each glide of his cock, each punishing thrust. I've never come from penetrative sex. I've never felt the slightest tremor of arousal.

With Hawke, I'm a different animal. He drags me up another impossible cliff, and I fly right over the edge, sailing into oblivion with my third orgasm of the night.

I come in waves until my voice is hoarse. He milks more pleasure from my body until I can't take any more.

And that's when he truly begins.

He fucks me senseless in the grotto until my legs shake so hard that I can barely stand. He spins me around and takes me from behind. He hoists me up and fucks me against the wall. I go down to my knees and kneel for him while he mounts me from behind. There's no denying who's in control while he manhandles me as he wishes. I surrender fully to his authority, happy to simply let this happen. I've never let go like this. I never knew *this* kind of thing existed. With Hawke, I don't think. I merely react to everything he does to me.

I scream and cry as he wrings one orgasm after the other from my body until I'm utterly spent.

We laugh as we try to drag our wet clothes over our bodies and give up, falling with exhaustion into the bubbling waters of the tiny pool.

Tangled in each other's arms, we kiss. We make love again.

And my heart breaks.

This isn't real. It's a fantasy. One I'll never forget, but there's no running from the truth.

I don't belong in his life and he doesn't belong in mine.

I'd like to think otherwise, but that's me. I'm a thinker. Logical to a fault, I know how this ends. While I try to keep my heart out of all of this, it's not possible.

He'll move on, while I'll muddle my way through, holding onto memories of Christmas in paradise and the man I had to leave behind.

Only, we're not there yet.

It's still tonight. Or maybe early in the morning of the next day.

Either way, it's too late to make arrangements to leave.

When we come up for air, I'll call the airline and change my ticket. I miss my family, my obnoxious brothers who never fail to bring a smile to my face. I miss my mom and daddy too.

I should spend the holidays with them, rather than alone, even if it's in paradise.

I'll tell them about Scott, and they'll think the tears I shed are for him. I'll be the only one who knows the truth.

I knew the stakes going in. No strings. Just fun. I thought I could separate my feelings and live in the moment. Or some such crap like that.

I gave my heart to a man with raven hair and golden eyes, a man who not only doesn't love me, but never will.

I'm the one who took a chance.

I don't blame Hawke. He never lied to me or led me to think a future waited for us beyond these few days.

It was a mistake. I know that now, but I don't regret one second of what we shared.

I already think about us in past tense, even as he pulls me into his arms and kisses me until I can't breathe.

TWENTY-FIVE

Hawke

Something's off with Quinn. The moment I tie her to me is the moment she drifts away.

It makes no sense.

We fucked like rabbits in the grotto, then laughed all the way back to my villa where we had sex on the deck beneath the stars. We slept out there too. The warm, humid air and the lulling sound of the surf were too intoxicating to resist.

I pulled the mattress from my bed while she carried the sheets and pillows. We snuggled. We fucked one last time. Then sleep pulled us under. I plan on fucking her the moment I wake, but she's not in bed.

It takes a moment to find her. My first thought is that's she's inside, using the facilities, but there's no sign of her in there.

This sinking feeling in my gut is not the usual reaction I have after a night of sensational sex. To be honest, I'm usually the one who pulls away.

Then I see her on the beach, staring out at the turquoise waters. The wind blows her hair out behind her and golden highlights glint in the sun. The bottom of my tee-shirt billows around her legs.

I have to say she looks fucking sexy in my shirt. It helps that it's somewhat see-through. I see every inch of her long, toned legs. My mouth waters, eager for another taste. I'll never get enough of her.

She looks deep in thought and I struggle with staying where I am, admiring her from afar. I should pull her back to bed. My cock stirs, giving a little twitch. Fucker got a workout last night—made me proud—it can't get enough of her pussy and her mouth.

Fuck, when she took me in her mouth last night, my balls drew up and my eyes rolled into the back of my head. The woman knows how to suck cock. Not what I expected, given her hesitation at the start.

Not that my ego needs any stroking, but I have a feeling I rocked her world. She's never had a lover like me, a lover who saw to her needs above his own. I can tell in the way she came apart in my hands and came on my cock and my face—over and over and over again.

I lost count of the number of orgasms I wrung from her body.

Which makes me wonder what she's doing on the beach instead of riding my cock. No way are we done exploring this thing between us.

Not that we can fuck all day. A man has limits.

My lips press together as my brain kicks in. We need another day like yesterday. Time to connect and get to know each other better. I enjoyed the snorkeling trip, but there are so many other things we can do.

Before I go to her, I call the front desk and arrange a few activities for the day. My thoughts are to keep us active and together as much as possible. We'll steal a moment here and there, naturally, but I don't want her to think I only want one thing.

With plans for the day settled, I pull on my shorts and go to meet her.

She doesn't notice me at first. I take the time to admire the soft curves of her body before I surprise her with a hug from behind.

"Good morning, gorgeous." I nuzzle against her, placing one soft kiss in the hollow of her neck.

"Good morning." Her hands go to mine, and she leans into me. "It's beautiful here. Hard to remember it's almost Christmas."

We've got two days before Christmas and I have some thoughts about how to make it a fun day for us both.

"Have you ever had Christmas in paradise before?"

"Never." She gives a little squeeze of my hands.

I sense tension in her body. We need to fix that.

"Last night was fun." I feather a line of kisses along her neck. It's a ticklish spot for her, one of many wonderful discoveries made last night.

She squirms in my grip but doesn't pull away.

"Stop that!" she lightly teases.

"Never." I reach up to cup her breast and let my thumb drag across her nipple. She responds instantly with a low sigh. Her nipple draws tight and I give it a teasing flick. "I like when you squirm."

"I'm at your mercy."

She's much more submissive than I ever would've thought, something I plan on taking advantage of as much as possible. It's not play or pretend with her, she gets off when I take the lead.

I extricate my other hand from her grip and reach down to cup her mound. Her breathy sigh is a cock tease. I'm instantly hard, something she knows because her ass presses against my groin.

More nibbles along her neck feed my hunger. So fucking responsive. I rub her clit over the fabric of my tee-shirt, then say fuck it and lift the shirt until she's bare to me. One finger slips between her folds. She's fucking dripping for me.

"Damn, but I can't get enough of you." I work her to a frenzy with my fingers and thumb. I know what she likes and what it takes to get her off. She's moaning in seconds, shamelessly grinding to get off.

Suddenly her body tenses with her climax. I hold her against me and let her ride my fingers through it. Once she stills, she spins in my arms and wraps her arms around my neck. Lifting on tiptoe, she kisses me.

Her kisses are nothing like mine. Soft, tentative, and unsure, she's hesitant to initiate. Normally, I take over, but I let her set the pace, perfectly content to enjoy the pillowy-light licks and nibbles she gives.

Her hand reaches down between us, cupping my erection through my shorts.

"What are we going to do about this?"

"Whatever the hell you want." My cock gives an enthusiastic jerk. I could order her to her knees, be powerful and forceful; she'd like that. Quinn responds fantastically when I order her around, but dominating her isn't something I press too hard. We're still too knew to each other and I fear crossing a line and making a fatal mistake. Sex is all about give and take. For now, I keep things light.

"I've never had sex on the beach before..." Her hand glides down with a little twist, then pulls up to the crown. She teases me there, rubbing under the flare of my cock where it's most sensitive, until I can no longer hold back a groan.

"Sex on the beach isn't as glamorous as it sounds. The sand is gritty and gets in places it shouldn't." I'd love to throw her on her back, or put her on her knees and mount her from behind. Unlike her, I've had sex on the beach and it never ended well.

We have a few options. One involves her mouth. The other requires a little more vigorous activity on my part. The only problem is I don't have a condom in these shorts.

In an uncharacteristic move, she takes the initiative from me, going to her knees. She looks up at me, eyes simmering with an unreadable emotion. She's waiting for me to take the next step.

I remember from last night how she responds when I take over. My girl likes things rough. Rougher than I imagined, which brings up all kinds of possibilities for our future.

One thing women don't quite understand, even if they respond to it unconsciously, is that men are base creatures in our core makeup. We all want the same thing.

While we admire powerful, independent women—those who are proud and well-poised—we tell them lies when we say we value their independence when it comes to sex.

The truth is far different. Submission fuels our lust. Our very nature demands it. When a woman submits, she gives us the right to unleash the snarling beast within. It gives us permission to release our restraint and be the brutal assholes who take what they want.

She doesn't realize what she's doing, at least not on a conscious level.

But I do.

Her surrender is the most powerful turn on in the world.

"Fuck, do you have any idea what that does to me?"

Does she know taking control flips a switch inside me?

A low groan escapes me when she leans forward and lightly kisses the tip of my cock. Her action is reverent, as if asking permission, or waiting for me to take control. She doesn't take me in her mouth. Instead, she turns those eyes on me, the ones that beg for those things she's not able to openly accept.

If we had all the time in the world, this is something we'd have time to explore. But we don't.

My hand goes to her head and I take a grip of her hair. I'm not beyond taking what I need. With a press of my lips, my jaw locks as I force her onto my cock.

The rest is a blur as I rut and fuck and come down her throat. My toes curl. The arch of my foot cramps as I come. It hurts like a motherfucker, but I'm too far gone with lust and the pleasure rushing through me from the force of my orgasm to care.

She sits back on her heels, looking pleased. Ignoring the cramp in my foot, I comb back her hair, sweeping it off her face. I tap her upper lip.

"I think I'm an addict. I can't get enough of this mouth."

Her expression brightens beneath my praise. I could seriously keep her here all day long, fucking each other's brains out, but we need to eat.

And honestly, I'm more entranced than ever before. Any other woman, I wouldn't think twice about spending the rest of the week doing nothing but fucking. Quinn, however, piques my curiosity.

I need to know her better.

Crouching down to her level, I ignore the spasm in my foot. Tiny aftershocks from my orgasm flood my system as I gaze into her eyes.

"You're something quite unexpected, Miss Quinn Hayes."

She nibbles on her lower lip. It's my new, instant turn on. However, my dick is happily spent, satiated for the moment.

"As are you." She gives a little shake of her head. "Last night was…" Her gaze takes on a faraway look as her mind pieces together the rest of that thought.

I'm learning little things about her with each passing hour. I know her ticklish spots. Her erogenous zones are firmly imprinted in my mind. I know other things, things she's unaware of, like her inherent submissiveness during sex.

I'm well aware last night was an eye-opening experience for her, which makes me sad. It's sad to think this amazing woman, this sexual creature, never truly had a chance to open up and embrace her sexuality until last night. That goes on the long list of reasons why I hate Scott, as well as any other lovers she's taken in her life. We haven't talked about our pasts, but I have a feeling she's had very few lovers.

"Last night was perfect. You were perfect. You are perfect." I can't praise her perfection enough. "I enjoyed every second of last night." I lean forward to kiss her. A gentle kiss meant to connect rather than arouse. "Are you hungry?"

Her hand covers her belly and she gives a nod.

"I thought to order room service, but if you're up for a little adventure, there's something else we can do."

"Something else?"

"How are you around horses?"

"Um…" She bites at her lower lip. "Not familiar with them, but willing to try? I rode a couple of times as a girl. You know, state fair kinds of things. We were in a corral and walked in circles. I didn't fall off."

I can't help but laugh. "I think you'll be okay. These horses are easygoing and used to new riders. I was thinking we'd take them for a walk on the trails. It's one of the resort's most popular activities. It ends on the beach and the horses wade in the water."

"It sounds fun. I should probably head back to my place and get something to wear."

A grin fills my face. Our clothes are a bit of a mess after last night.

"Give me a second to change, then I'll walk you there."

We head back inside where I change and grab a small backpack full of bug spray and sunscreen. We hold hands all the way to her villa. I love how her small hand fits inside mine. That's another thing that's new. I never hold hands. I'll drape my arm around my dates. Hold them tight to me around the waist. I'll lend the crook of my arm, but never have I ever held hands with a woman.

I've spent many Christmas holidays here, hiding from my mother, and realize how it must feel for someone not used to the tropical climate this time of year.

We try to dress the place up. Festive red and green lights illuminate the palm trees at night, but they're there most of the year. The gardeners have fun, hanging large ornaments from the palm fronds. There's a tiny Christmas village set up outside the main dining room. Stick reindeer stand in the many gardens. We try to bring the Christmas spirit to paradise, but it's hard to compete with the tropical climate.

Lunch is a success. Quinn shows no hesitation with the horses. Two other couples join us for our horseback riding adventure. I typically don't indulge in the sponsored activities, preferring to spend my time isolated in my villa where either work consumes me, or the flavor of the week satisfies my sexual cravings.

It's nice to ignore work and relax. With Quinn by my side, that's exactly what I do.

We mount up on our horses and our guides take us through a lush canopy. Dense foliage crowds the trail. Birds flutter overhead, chirping and singing to one another. I breathe in the floral aromas of tropical flowers mixed in with the musk of the horse beneath me and the loamy soil underneath its hooves.

We wander for a bit until the thick vegetation parts before us and reveals the glistening expanse of a pristine private beach. We have fun here, letting the horses lead. They canter and dance, eager to spend time outside of their stalls.

Our guide takes us to the water's edge where the horses prance in the ripples left by the waves lapping the shore. He leads us into the water and the horses happily follow. I sense this is their favorite part of the trail. They head out until the water laps at their bellies. Snorting and shaking their manes.

My feet trail in the water and my heart warms at the excitement filling Quinn's face. She's positively radiant. If I could, I'd bottle this moment and keep it with me forever.

We get off the horses to enjoy lunch on the beach. The staff puts out an amazing spread. Each couple gets a blanket, and while we could separate, the six of us have bonded during the ride. We pull the blankets close and enjoy a meal together as we talk about everything and nothing. Quinn leans against me; holds my hand. She's in constant contact, and it feels—*good*. Perfect, actually.

But then my mother intrudes.

Her short, concise text demands an immediate response. Not answering isn't possible. She knows I'm at Euphoria and why. I'm fortunate she agrees with me. She's no more interested in wasting her holidays with her son than I am spending it with my mother.

Nevertheless, I must answer.

After our ride, I have us scheduled for parasailing, and I plan a romantic sunset dinner cruise with dancing afterward. I want to get Quinn back out on the dance floor where I can hold her in my arms.

"This is simply perfect." Quinn sighs with contentment in my arms.

"You're perfect." Her smile brings a flush of warmth to my body. I trace the outline of her jaw, and run the pad of my finger across her lips. She sucks my finger into her mouth. The swirling of her tongue sends heat rushing to my groin.

"I planned on parasailing after this, but I just received a text I must answer."

"That's okay."

"It's a business call." Family business but business nonetheless.

She places her hand on my knee. "Really, don't worry about it. We've got all day. If you need a minute or two, or even a couple hours, I could use a nap." As if to emphasize her point, she yawns. "Sorry."

Our guide gathers us together and we set off down the beach, heading back to the main area of the resort. It's been a beautiful day. I'm loath to leave Quinn alone, but I need to see what my mother needs.

For her to contact me is never a good sign.

TWENTY-SIX

Quinn

There's a problem with perfect days, perfect escapes, and a man who adds that final, crucial layer of perfection to the most perfect getaway.

Like all things, this must end. It kills me when I leave Hawke so he can take care of that business call. I tell him I'm headed back to my villa for a much-needed nap.

But it's a lie.

Instead, I head to the main desk and speak with the concierge.

"May I help you, Miss Hayes?" A beautiful girl named Iris beams the brightest smile at me. It's as if she exists for only one purpose, and that's to please me.

"I hope so." I twist my fingers. My nerves are at an all-time high.

This is wrong. This is wrong.

"I need to change my return flight."

Don't do it.

"Of course. Will you be extending your stay with us then?"

"Sadly, no. I need to leave tomorrow."

My mind is made up. It's not often I ignore my inner voice, but I seem to be doing it a lot lately—responding with emotions instead of logical thought.

Iris' eyes widen with alarm. She covers quickly and ducks her head. The blue glow of the monitor shines in her eyes. She speaks without looking at me, all her concentration on that monitor.

"Has everything been satisfactory?" Her gaze flicks up to meet mine then dodges back down.

"Yes, it's been amazing. The staff is incredible. I've never felt so pampered in my life."

Or so well fucked, but she doesn't need to know that little bit.

"I see. If there's anything we can do to improve, please let us know."

"There's nothing. I just had a change in plans." More like a change in heart. Or a realization. "I'm trying to make it home for Christmas."

I miss my family. My obnoxious brothers will be happy to have me home. I can't *not* tell them about this change in plans, but I want to keep my arrival a surprise for Mother and Daddy. A visit to the gift shop is in order. I'll need something for presents.

"Oh, yes, of course, let's see if we can make that happen." Her fingers fly quickly over the keys.

Presents for my brothers are easy. All they need are tee-shirts and ball caps. Mom deserves something fancier. There's a small collection of jewelry I spied in the gift shop, which should do fine. Daddy will be the tough one.

"Do you have your return flight confirmation code?" Iris glances up at me, all sweet smiles and gracious eyes.

I pull up the information on my phone.

My stomach does a little flip and I press my hand to my belly. I survived the flight out here, I can damn well survive the flight home. Only this time, I won't mix alcohol and cough medicine.

And you won't have a handsome stranger sitting next to you either.

I know exactly what I leave behind, but that's the thing.

Hawke isn't mine.

Her fingers continue their mad dance across the keyboard.

"There's a flight leaving tomorrow at noon. It doesn't get in until eleven at night. Will that be okay?"

I press my lips together thinking about that. My hope had been to get home earlier in the day. That way I could spend Christmas Eve with my family and go to church with them in the evening. Christmas Eve services are a big deal for my parents.

"Is there anything earlier?"

"I'm afraid not, unless you want to leave today, and there's a significant charge to change the ticket." She looks at me with regret. "It's an additional three hundred dollars."

Ouch.

"I knew there would be a rebooking fee, but damn that's steep."

"I'm sorry."

Not really keen on leaving today, I consider my options. Truthfully, I'm not ready to leave Hawke. I need one more night.

One selfish night in paradise.

I could stay through New Year's and investigate my fascination with Hawke. Truly look at it from all angles. Weigh the pros and cons of letting whatever we have continue. See if there's any future with my enigmatic new flame.

But there's not. I'm not fooling myself.

The resort offers plenty of amenities I've yet to explore. It would be fun to enjoy everything Euphoria offers with someone else. There's really not a compelling reason to leave. Except, the circumstances that brought me here no longer apply.

My intention had been to get away from Scott and nurse my broken heart in paradise. I anticipated days of moping around, licking my wounds, and bemoaning my fate.

I figured paradise would make me forget it's the Christmas season; a time typically spent with family, friends, and new fiancés.

Euphoria tries to be festive. They decorate with tiny touches of the holidays, but what they can't hide are the turquoise waters, the endless skies, and foliage, which is always in bloom. They can't hide the flocks of parrots roosting in the trees, brightly colored birds that call and sing to one another. They can't hide the rustling of the palm fronds as they're tickled by the ocean breeze. They can't hide the sparkling sand and warm waters, which welcome weary travelers and wash away their fatigue.

I wish I could stay.

Then why don't you?

Because.

I sound petulant even to myself.

Yesterday, when I faced down Scott, I found strength I didn't think I had. Granted, Hawke started this craziness with a kiss.

A kiss he stole.

The kiss I'll never forget.

A kiss that released me from any feelings I still harbored for Scott. All the anger and hatred I had for Scott evaporated once I realized we shared a pale reflection of what true love could be like.

Not that I'm in love with Hawke. It's more like an insane sexual attraction, a biological urge I never imagined could exist.

I now understand what lust feels like.

It's more than simple desire. It's an all-consuming sexual awakening.

Truthfully, I'm not done with Hawke Sterling. Whatever this is, it's one hell of a ride. I'm crazy walking away from it, but I'm also a realist and practical to a fault.

My father always told me I was a thinker, not a feeler. It's why he named me Quinn, a name that took a long time to embrace. Too many said it was a boy's name, but whenever I ran home with tears in my eyes from the taunts and teases of my classmates, he'd crouch down and hold me at arm's length.

"Your name is drawn from your Gaelic roots. It represents wisdom and intelligence, baby girl. Be proud of your name. Wear it well. You're a thinker. One of the greatest minds of the century."

He isn't wrong about that.

I approach life weighing the facts. I never act impulsively. Except when I'm around a raven-haired man with golden eyes. The things he makes me feel drown out all thought. With him, I become something else, but I'm not ignoring the facts.

Hawke is a player. Women are commodities, things to be used

and discarded. I'm not so infatuated that I can't read between the lines.

Hell, he told me there's no reason to attach himself to one woman. Unfortunately, I see his point. I'm nothing more than a dalliance to him, much as he is the nidus of my sexual awakening.

He's a catch—the catch that can never be caught—and we're having a good time together, but that's all this is.

We're stealing time.

Time that comes with a countdown timer and expiration date.

As for Scott, I'm still angry. I'm furious with Sadie for betraying me. Mostly though, my eyes are finally open. My heart is laid bare. It hurts, but I'll heal. I see that now.

Scott was comfortable and familiar, but he never invoked the sexual cravings I feel with Hawke.

When I'm with Hawke, the air crackles. Sparks race along my skin. Heat flows in my veins. These are things I can't ignore, and I have to believe I'll find it again.

Speaking of things that can't be ignored. I love the way Hawke takes control during sex. That's probably the most powerful aphrodisiac in the world: a man who knows what he wants and isn't afraid to take it.

I feel different. More aware? More in tune with what I want and willing to try out new things.

What the hell am I going to do about Hawke?

You're going to run away.

Our time together will end. I know this. I feel it. And I need to be the one who walks away. I don't think I can handle being discarded again.

The ability to control our end is crucial right now, and the longer I spend with Hawke, the more likely it is that I'll fall in love with him.

That can't happen.

I don't have the strength to mend two broken hearts.

"Miss Hayes?" Iris clears her throat and I give a little shake of my head.

"I'm sorry. I was thinking about something else."

That something else is a man with a cock who knows how to use it.

"I found another flight on a different airline. It's under five hundred, but it leaves early in the morning. You'll be in Atlanta by noon. There's another one that leaves this evening and will get you in by six in the morning. They're about the same price."

"Really?"

"Of course, there's no refund on your current ticket, but I can book one of the other flights if you'd like. The other option is to pay the rebooking fee on your original flight…"

"And get in late Christmas Eve?"

"Yes."

Hawke mentioned a sunset cruise. I may be running away from this crazy thing happening between us, but I'm not ready to completely turn my back on it.

Not yet.

I feel like a putz because I'll be leaving him on Christmas Eve. Although, he doesn't seem that enamored with the holidays.

"I'll take the one that gets me in at noon. How early is early?"

"The flight leaves at five. We can have a shuttle available to take you to the airport at four."

"Don't I need more time?"

She shakes her head. "Our airport isn't that big. Trust me, an hour is plenty of time to get checked in and past security."

Then all I have to do is worry about my fear of flying. Maybe I can sleep through the flight?

"I'll take it. Thank you so much for looking around for other options."

"It's no problem, Miss Hayes. It's important to be around the ones you love during the holidays. I'm happy I could assist you. Now, is there anything else I can do for you?"

"No. Thank you very much."

She works her concierge magic, and I walk away five hundred dollars lighter but weighed down by my conscience.

Do I tell Hawke about my change in plans?

You'd be a heel if you didn't.

I know.

That would be something Scott would do.

With another couple hours before I need to meet back up with Hawke, I head to the gift shop where I buy four tee-shirts and four baseball hats. I get a tennis hat for my mother along with a set of pearl earrings and a matching necklace. This leaves me one gift short, but I'm out of time.

I race back to my villa and change. It's a dinner sunset cruise. I'm not sure if that involves any swimming. Fortunately, I have the perfect little black dress.

It's at once casual and sultry chic. Instead of a bra and panties, I slip on a black string bikini. This way, I'm ready, no matter if we're playing it casual or classy.

There's no reason to fuss with my hair. I sweep it into an elegant updo. If the cruise is more casual, I can put it into a ponytail on the spot. With a few minutes to spare, I take the time to pack my suitcase. Since I didn't bring much, it doesn't take long. I throw everything inside, leaving out a pair of pants and loose-fitting shirt for the flight. I leave the suitcase open. When I get back tonight, all I'll have to do is pack my dress.

And won't that be the trick? How will I extricate myself from Hawke's bed in time to make my flight?

Good thing, I'm thinking ahead and pack my bags.

Not eager to be late, I take one last look in the mirror and square off my shoulders.

"You can do this, Q."

The pep talk does me little good.

A knock on the door draws me up short. I'm not expecting anyone.

When I open the door, I can't help but smile. Hawke's roguish smile is in full force. He's simply irresistible.

"You ready for tonight?" His gaze flicks over my shoulder and his brows draw tight. "Going somewhere, Miss Hayes?"

I spin around and curse my need to always be over-prepared.

"Um, about that…"

TWENTY-SEVEN

Hawke

She packed her bags?

It hits me like a load of bricks. This will be the first time a woman walks out on me. My stare fixes on the suitcase as anger builds within me. I initiate. I take. I'm always the one who walks away. Quinn breaks all my rules.

"I thought we were having fun?" I grind out each syllable as my anger builds. "You're running away?"

"We are." Her eyes round, not with surprise, but an innocence that is as fake as a white Christmas tree. "Having fun that is. We are having fun."

"Then explain that." I step around her and head to the bed. Sure enough, her suitcase is packed. A change of clothes sits on the bed, a forethought for the morning when she leaves. At least that's what it looks like.

"I'm leaving tomorrow." Her fingers twist in knots and her head dips.

"Tomorrow? On Christmas Eve?"

"Yes."

"I thought you were here through New Year's?" When did she decide to leave me?

"I changed my plans."

More like she's plagued with a sudden change of heart.

"Were you going to tell me? Or was I supposed to find out tomorrow after you left?" This is low. She's walking out on me.

"I was going to tell you."

"When? After dinner? After you fucked me? When exactly were you going to tell me?"

"Don't be crass."

"Why not? You had me going."

"What do you mean by that?"

"You really had me going, but you're not so innocent, are you, Miss Hayes? You got exactly what you were looking for."

"I don't know what you're talking about, but that's not what this is."

"Then explain what *this* is, because it looks like you're running away from me."

"Come on, Hawke. I'm leaving a few days early and it's not as if…"

"Not as if what?" Anger surges through me. I'm barely keeping my temper in check. "You say I'm the fuck-them-and-leave-them kind of guy, but it looks like I don't hold a candle to you."

"That's unfair."

"Is it? You got what you came for and now you're leaving." She better not be running back to that douchebag, Scott. Not after I held her in my arms.

"You make it sound ugly."

"Enlighten me, because it sounds like once you got what you wanted, you're turning your back…"

"Got what I wanted? What are you talking about?" Her brows knit together, then her expression changes to shock and indignation. "Don't you dare cheapen what happened between us. As far as getting what I wanted, that's a low blow, even for you."

"You used me."

She fucked me and used me.

"No, I didn't. And for the record, that's exactly what you do with the women you date." She holds up an imperious finger.

"Correction. You don't date. You fuck and then you leave. Why are we even talking about this? Isn't this exactly what you want? You said it often enough. We're the only single people here. Why not hook up and fuck? And that's it. There was never a future beyond Euphoria. I'm just ending things sooner rather than later to spend the holidays with my family. So why are you pissed?"

I'm far too smart to answer that question. She hit every major point on the head. I school myself to patience. One deep breath in and out and I'm back in control.

"Perhaps you're right. Maybe this was nothing more than two adults fucking and having fun; fuck buddies, but you still should've told me."

"Fucking and having fun?" Her voice cracks. "Is that all it was to you?"

"Your words, not mine."

"No, they absolutely *are* your words. I would never say that to someone I care about. I'd never cheapen what we shared. Until now, it was one of the most intense nights of my life. As for fuck buddies, I guess you'll be fucking yourself after I'm gone. As far as telling you about my decision to leave, I didn't decide until after lunch. This is the first time I'm seeing you. It's not like I hid anything from you."

"Then why?"

"Because I miss my brothers and my parents. This place, as amazing as it is, only reminds me of what I'm missing by not being home. The holidays are for family. The only reason I came here was because I was afraid to tell them what happened with Scott. After he left yesterday, I've had a lot of deep soul-searching going on in my head. I've never had a night like last night. I didn't think something like that could exist. You opened my eyes to what's been missing in my life. But as much as I enjoyed it, you've made it clear from the beginning that we came with an expiration date. There's an *end* to us. You're just pissed because you aren't the one walking away. Or have I got that wrong?" Her eyes flash emerald fire. She's a feisty one, with no problems telling me exactly what she thinks.

I should be pissed. I should turn around and leave, but I stand and let every word hit me where it hurts the most.

At least she's honest.

"Are you done?"

"Yes." She gives a sharp shake of her head to emphasize her point.

"I apologize for my insensitive choice of words. You're much more to me than a fuck buddy. Please forgive me."

Her eyes shimmer with unshed tears. I put those there.

Me, my arrogance, and my bruised ego are at fault.

"As for leaving? You're right. I'm not so arrogant that I won't admit I would've rather been the one to say goodbye. Despite what you think, and what I said, we're connecting. I know you feel it. I'm disappointed, not pissed, that we won't have the opportunity to explore it more. As for going our separate ways, I'm not sure I want that."

"You don't?"

"Does it matter? We won't have the chance to find out. I wish we had a chance to discuss it, but I won't stand in your way from leaving." I've never been this open, this vulnerable, with a woman before. I'm eagerly handing her all the ammunition she needs to dig into my chest and rip my heart out. I definitely won't beg for her to stay. That's a line I refuse to cross.

She gives me a long, hard look as if weighing every word. I can't tell if she believes me or thinks I'm full of shit. What I do know is whatever this crazy attraction is, it's over. She closed that door and there's no way in hell I'm chasing her down.

What I will do is forget her. After all, there're plenty of willing women out there vying for their chance to have a piece of me. Unfortunately, Quinn is the only woman who succeeded in stealing the one thing I've never surrendered.

She carries a piece of my heart.

I take one last look at the open carry-on. Like a Band-Aid, it's best to rip it off quick. There's no use in pursuing whatever this was any further.

"Have a safe flight, Miss Hayes."

Without waiting for an answer, I spin on my heels and walk out of her life.

TWENTY-EIGHT

Quinn

I'm not sure how long I stand there, mouth agape, heart hammering, tears falling down my cheeks. Why does Hawke's departure hurt a thousand times worse than Scott's infidelity?

I press a hand to my chest as if that can help the ripping and shredding going on in my heart. Watching his slow stroll away from my villa feels like my world is ending.

Overly dramatic?

Yes, I know.

I'm stunned by how much it hurts. I'm not ready to see him go. We had the entire evening ahead of us, an evening where I planned on talking to him about why I wanted to leave early.

Why I *needed* to leave.

Or at least tell him the lie I'm trying to force myself to believe.

The truth is more complicated. One of my greatest weaknesses is that I fall hard and fast. I may be a thinker, and not a feeler, but even I lose control when my emotions take the wheel.

I see the signs.

I'm falling for Hawke.

Hard.

Give me the full ten days, and I'd be hopelessly in love with him.

And then what?

Will that heartache hurt any less than the devastating loss I feel now? I know the answer to that. It will be far worse.

Not wanting to risk running into him on the resort grounds, I order room service and spend the evening alone. I walk along the beach and watch an amazing sunset. I look for shooting stars, but find none to make a wish on. I swim in the warm, tropical waters until my fingers wrinkle. Only then do I drag myself inside and take a long shower.

My last night in paradise is spent horribly alone. In a fit, I go to bed early, but I get very little sleep. All my dreams are filled with Hawke Sterling and his dominating commands while he fucks me.

My alarm goes off at three thirty in the morning. I catch the shuttle to the airport and find myself staring at the departure gate with rampant terror flowing through my veins.

There's no alcohol to dull my senses. No cold medicine to put me out of my misery. If I'm going to do this, I do it on my own.

It doesn't help when my pulse gallops wildly. My chest constricts as I fight off hyperventilation. My pep talk consists of the facts. I survived the flight out here, I'll survive the flight home. Only this time, I don't have the luxury of first-class accommodations. I'm crammed in the back of the plane.

And there's nothing logical about my fear.

Passengers file into the jetway while I fight off a full-blown panic attack. Finally, the gate attendant calls final boarding. She checks her screen and her eyes pinch in confusion. When she looks up, she notices me standing in the empty waiting area.

"Miss? Are you on this flight?"

I give a tight nod, too nervous to speak.

"You need to board. We're closing the gate."

Her words provide the impetus I need to take a step forward. That leads to another step. Before I realize what I'm doing, my shaky hand holds out my boarding pass. She scans it. I jump at the tiny beep, which confirms my place on this flight.

She gives me another weird look, then gestures to the door

leading to the plane. "Please, Miss Hayes, we need to close the gate."

An empty jetway stretches before me. All other passengers are on board. I walk into the suffocating emptiness and slowly make it to the end. All that's left is that final committed step.

The flight attendant beams a wide smile at me as I step onto the plane. She welcomes me onto the flying coffin with a death grin. I don't understand what she's so damn happy about when I'm the one marching to my death.

Last time I was on a plane, I only had to walk a few steps to get to my seat in first class. This time, I'm way at the back. The flight is nearly full. A few passengers stand in the aisle as they put their carry-ons into the bins over their head. They hold me up while I wait patiently for them to take their seats.

I make it to the back of the plane, stow my single carry-on into the overhead bin, and slip into the aisle seat. At least I got that right. No getting sucked out of the window for me. My backpack goes at my feet, but there's no soothing alcohol hidden inside of it.

I'm on my own. My gut tells me to get up and run. Race down the aisle to the safety of the concourse. My head tells me to stop being silly.

I'm a hysterical mess barely holding on.

But I do hold on.

There's no other choice. I already checked out of Euphoria and there's no going back.

There's an older gentleman sitting by the window and an empty middle seat between us. He gives a soft smile as I take my seat. Other than that, he doesn't engage me in conversation. Considering my pathetic small-talk skills, I'm fine with that.

My hands shake as I buckle in. No going back now.

I squeeze my eyes shut on takeoff and don't open them until we touch down in Atlanta, nearly six hours later.

I send a quick text to my brothers letting them know my change in plans. Steven, youngest of the brothers, but older than me by twelve years, immediately calls my phone.

"I can't believe you're here, little Quinney." His deep baritone rumbles through the phone and brings a smile to my face.

"Just landed."

"Do you need a ride? I'm not far." Steven works as a welder for the family construction business. He's probably coming off work.

"I was going to call a car. I don't want to bother you."

"No bother. If you don't mind waiting, I can save you the fare."

"That would be great." I learned a long time ago to let my brothers take care of me. They're strong, obstinate, pricks when they want to be, but I'm their baby sister, and they can't help but spoil me rotten.

"Cool. I want to be the first to hear the big news." I hear the smile in his voice, but my stomach clenches with his words. "Although, I'm kind of surprised y'all chose to spend Christmas with the family. Thought maybe you'd spend it alone someplace romantic." If only he knew, but that comment is my fault. I may have hinted about expecting a proposal this Christmas.

"Yeah, please tell Ian, Brett, and Gideon to keep their traps shut. I really want this to be a surprise."

"Oh, Mother and Daddy will be surprised."

It may sound strange for a grown man to call his father daddy, but we're an old southern family. We never did Mom or Mommy. It was always *Mother*, and our father has always been *Daddy*. People look at me sideways at work. They don't get the regional custom.

"Well, don't ruin it. Okay?" I send a group text to my brothers telling them not to spoil the surprise. I don't trust them. Steven gives a low laugh when the text comes through on his end.

"Geez, message received and acknowledged. You guys staying at Mother and Daddy's, or do you want to crash at my place?" He thinks he's picking up two people. "I've got my truck. You better not have like a gazillion bags. The two of you will need to both sit up front with me on the bench seat."

Right, the two of us. I guess we're going to get to that juicy bit of gossip sooner rather than later. Gideon is going to be pissed he's not the first to know.

"I was planning on staying with Mother and Daddy, if that's okay."

We all gather there for the holidays, and I honestly feel there'll be fewer questions there. My brothers are vicious interrogators. I wasn't kidding when I told Hawke they'd try and rip Scott's head off.

Hawke.

A stabbing pain brings me to a halt and I hold back a sob.

"Everything okay, Quinney?" Steven has a nearly sixth sense about me. It's uncanny, but I'm not about to go into all of that on the phone.

"Yeah, I'm really looking forward to seeing you."

"Me too, baby girl. Me too." There's a pause on his end. "Where am I picking you up?"

I tell him where to find me and hang up. I've got a few minutes to get myself together before the interrogation begins.

A little while later, his old pickup truck rounds the bend. He's had the same truck since high school, lovingly keeping it running, although it's seen better days. It's on its second engine and pushing over three hundred thousand miles, all told. He pulls up to the curb and hops out to help me with my bags. His piercing gaze takes me in, a head-to-toe assessment, which ends in a pissed-off expression.

"What the fuck did he do?" Steven wraps me in his arms, giving me one of the best bear hugs on the planet.

"I don't really want to talk about it."

"Oh, we're going to talk about it." His protective instincts are already engaged.

"How about we not?"

He cocks his head. "You know that's not going to happen. Now, spill." He grabs my carry-on and tosses it in the back seat, then he opens the passenger side door for me to climb in. Or rather *up*. His truck is lifted and it's a bit of a jump to get in.

I buckle up and he climbs in the driver's seat. His eyes pinch and he gives a sharp nod. "We're going to Dale's."

"I don't want to go to Dale's. Are they even open on Christmas Eve?"

The local mom and pop ice-cream parlor, Dale's, is where my brothers took me every time someone made me cry or broke my heart when I was growing up. I have nothing but fond memories of Dale's.

"It's not up to you." He sends word to our brothers. There's no doubt they'll all drop whatever they're doing to gather around me. My friends complained about their brothers growing up. I never did. They've always had my back, defending me against the evil in the world.

When we pull up outside Dale's less than half an hour later, Ian and Brett are already there. They lean against their Harleys—arms crossed, scowls fixed on their faces, ready for battle. I take in a deep breath and prepare for the interrogation. Gideon arrives on his Harley last. He pulls in beside Ian and Brett, yanks off his helmet, and turns his scowl to me. The eldest of the Hayes brothers, he's the leader of our little pack.

His arms stretch wide when he sees me. "Come home, baby girl."

I practically run into his embrace. I may be twenty-five, but I'll always be his baby girl. And Brett's. And Ian's. And Steven's. They're my fiercest protectors.

Gideon practically swallows me in his embrace. He tenderly kisses the crown of my head. Then he passes me to Brett and Ian until I've been thoroughly hugged. Gideon then leads us all inside, heading toward the back booth I practically grew up in.

They took me for ice cream every Sunday after church without fail. I started out riding behind Gideon's bicycle, then progressed to the back of his motorcycle when he learned to ride. We have a lot of really good memories in this booth.

As always, I scoot in to the middle of the U-shaped booth. Steven slides in on one side. Ian takes the other side. Brett and Gideon, as the older siblings, bracket us in. My brothers say nothing as Gideon waves the pretty waitress over. He orders for us all, our usual, five sodas and one family-sized banana split. After the waitress leaves, he turns to me.

"What did that bastard do to you?"

I wither beneath my brother's intense stare. He doesn't tolerate anyone fucking with his baby sister, but I'm not getting out of this booth until all my brothers are satisfied.

"I'll tell you, but you have to promise not to do anything."

"You know that's not going to happen." Brett huffs a laugh as he leans back and takes me in. "What did that douchebag do?"

My heart gives a little squeeze. That's the word Hawke uses. I miss him terribly. Tears well up in my eyes. All around me, my brothers growl their anger as I wipe my tears.

"If you promise not to kill anyone, I'll spill." I hold out my hand, pinky finger extended. The one thing my brothers never go back on is their word.

They all look at my little pinky finger like it's a snake ready to bite them, but I don't cave. I will get their promise.

Steven is the first to hook his pinky with mine. "Promise, but I don't like it."

Ian waits for Steven to release my pinky before hooking his with mine. "Promise, no killing."

I wait for Brett and Gideon. When neither of them moves, I clear my throat.

"Brett, you have to promise."

"I won't kill anyone, but he might find life a little more challenging." It's the best I'm going to get out of him.

"Gideon, you have to pinky swear." I look at big, burly Gideon and wait for him to grudgingly accept my terms.

"That shit is for kids."

"I don't care." I pull back my hand and cross my arms over my chest and stare him down. To anyone watching us, I must look ridiculous. Gideon is not only the eldest, but he's the biggest of the Hayes men. His muscles are stacked with muscles, but then he used to be a bouncer and is still a fanatic with his weight training.

"Look at Quinney all grow'd up, like she can intimidate me." He huffs, but I see the moment he caves. Leaning across the table, he holds out his massive hand and extends his pinky. "I won't kill him, but I agree with Ian. Doesn't mean we won't fuck him up."

"Well, I don't want that either."

There's no way Scott is coming out of this unscathed. There are a few things my brothers don't tolerate in life. The first is when a man forces himself on a woman. The second is when a man cheats on one.

Scott is doomed.

Knowing this, I slowly hook my pinky around Gideon's finger.

"Pinky swear?" He will say the words. Gideon's a mischievous fucker and he's damn good at finding loopholes.

"Fine." He rolls his eyes and gives a huff. "I pinky swear."

Our waitress returns with our drinks. She takes in my brothers, jaw working soundlessly as her eyes dart around the table. I know exactly what she's thinking. My brothers aren't just good looking. With their blazing green eyes, the same shade as mine, and golden complexions, they are fucking arresting.

She manages to deliver our drinks. Ignores me. Don't know why that is, clearly, I'm their sister. Same hair. Same eyes. I'm like less than a zero threat when it comes to her options.

"They're all available." I speak up. "Give me a little extra chocolate sauce and I'll hook you up with one of them."

Her eyes widen.

"Little Quinney." Ian's voice deepens to a sultry rumble, "We don't need your help getting dates."

Brett gives a low chuckle.

Our waitress runs from the table. I punch Ian in the arm.

"You do because you keep running them off. How is it that none of you are married yet, or seeing anyone?" I let my gaze wander around the table, stopping on each brother in turn. "Not even a steady girl for any of you?"

Gideon gives a shrug. "We're not here to talk about our love lives." I wither beneath his penetrating gaze. "Now spill. We all did the pinky swear thing. What did that fucker do to you?"

I blow out my breath. I really hoped the ice cream sundae would make an appearance before I had to spill my guts, but that is not to be the case. I stall for time and take a sip of my soda while staring defiantly back at Gideon.

He gives a little shake of his head and glances at Steven. Without words, Steven reaches for my soda and yanks it away.

"You get that back when you tell us what happened." Gideon sits back with a satisfied smirk plastered on his face. He also turns his head, craning it to watch our pretty waitress. I have a feeling her evening plans are going to suddenly change.

"There's not much to tell."

"Considering we expected a ring on your finger and there's obviously nothing there…" His low growl is like a rumble of thunder.

"Well, I got the ring…" I flash my most innocent expression at him.

"Spill it, baby girl." Ian pokes me in the ribs, making me jump.

I spill. All the horrid details come out. The party. The proposal. Scott fucking Sadie.

"Damn." Brett covers his mouth and drags his hand down his face. "Sadie?"

"Yeah. It kind of sucked."

"Kind of?" Gideon's murderous scowl softens. "Quinney girl, I'm really sorry about that. What can we do?"

"Well, not murdering Scott is a step in the right direction." I really haven't thought much further than that. "Promise you let me tell Mother and Daddy."

"Promise." Gideon speaks for everyone. My other brothers nod in agreement. "How does this impact your job? Aren't you waiting on some funds? You're going to have to work with him."

"Honestly, I haven't thought that far ahead."

Brett's brows draw together. He's the silent one of the bunch. Incredibly smart, he's a talented woodworker. He works as a carpenter for the family business, but his artistry is greater than that. One day, I'm going to get him to pursue his carvings in earnest. The man simply has too much talent to waste.

He slowly taps on the table, then turns his thoughtful expression on me. "If your party was on the twenty-first and it's now Christmas Eve, where the hell have you been hiding out?"

I practically choke with his comment. All my brothers turn their attention to me while I squirm and figure out how best to lie.

Fortunately, our waitress returns with a massive banana split. It's filled with twelve scoops of ice-cream, several bananas, drizzled with chocolate sauce and caramel, and topped with whipped cream and five cherries. Our waitress puts down a silver dish with extra chocolate sauce and slides it across the table to me.

I gotcha sister.

My brothers stare at her retreating backside, mouths agape, and eyes practically bugging out of their heads.

"Shit, if I thought it was that easy…" Ian gives a little drumroll on the tabletop. "It's settled. Quinney is my official wingman." He grabs a spoon and takes a scoop of the whipped cream and shoves it in his mouth.

Gideon stares at the waitress and gives a slow shake of his head. "Well, I'm out. The three of you can arm wrestle for that."

"You're out?" My voice rises with interest. "Why's that? Are you seeing someone?"

Steven gives a huff. "Gideon is seeing nobody but his own damn stubbornness."

"What does that mean?" I look between my brothers, glad to have the conversation turn away from me.

"It means nothing." Gideon picks up a spoon and digs in. "Don't think you're getting out of answering Brett's question. Where have you been, baby girl?"

TWENTY-NINE

Hawke

THREE DAYS.

That's how long it took for Quinn to worm her way into my heart and cut a hole in it.

A huge-fucking-gaping hole.

It's my fault. I'm the one who let her in.

All my rules?

Ignored.

Every throbbing pang?

Mine to bear.

If I hadn't walked in on her, would she have told me?

Or did she intend to sneak away and leave without an explanation?

When did I become the pussy who cared what a woman thought about me?

Not that it matters. I left before she could tender her excuses. I turned around.

I walked away.

Anger thundered in my veins. Rage pumped through my muscles. Seething fury pulsed within each painful breath. For three days I ached for her before deciding to do something about it.

She got under my skin. It's a sin I can't let go unpunished. All I can think about is throttling her delicate neck. She will pay. It's a visceral need surging within me. The need to take. To claim. To make her hurt for walking out on me.

I'll hurt her as much as she hurt me. The only question is how.

My bruised ego demands retribution. It wants a piece of her, something to chew and spit away. Like I can discard the emotions she etched in my heart.

I wish I never met Miss Quinn Hayes.

I slam my fist against my chest, pounding away the pain her departure leaves. Roiling anger simmers in the background as I mull over where I went wrong. What signs did I miss? When the fuck did I lose control?

I'm the one who walks away.

Always me.

For the third time in as many days, my stormy stride brings me to the concierge desk. I could call, but this requires discretion. The information already belongs to me. No one will deny my right. However, rumors among the staff aren't something I can avoid. There will be talk.

Fuck if I care.

A glance inside reveals no guests in the vicinity. The clerk on duty is Iris, a young girl filling the empty hours of her summer with an idyllic summer job. In the fall, she'll return to the rigors of her education, learning how to run an enterprise such as this. She shows great promise.

But for now, she's nothing other than a receptionist presiding over a concierge's desk.

Her delicate fingers tap over the keyboard and the blue glow of the monitor reflects off her eyes. She looks up at my entrance and a smile fills her face. I ignore the blush coloring her cheeks.

"Mr. Sterling, how may I help you?" A sweet smile fills her face and her eyes take one long sweep of my physique. If I wanted her, all it would take is the crook of my finger. Almost, I consider it, but a hasty fuck won't satisfy what I'm craving.

Only one woman can do that.

I suppress the low growl in my throat and flash one of my devastating smiles. It's one that never fails to make a woman blush, or loosen her tongue. For now, I'm only interested in what Iris can tell me, not what she can do for me. Nothing will ease this ache.

"Do you remember a guest named Quinn Hayes?"

"Yes, sir." Her eyes brighten with the memory. "She had to cut her visit with us short."

"Did you handle the arrangements?"

"Yes, sir. I helped her rebook her flight. I wish I could've saved her more money, but she insisted on flying out on the twenty-fourth."

"No doubt the holidays called her back." I rub at the back of my neck. "Can you tell me where you booked her flight?"

Iris gives only the tiniest flicker of surprise before bending her head to the task.

One of the benefits of owning this place is there's seldom a request I make that is questioned by the staff.

"It was a straight flight into Atlanta." She glances up with a smile.

"I see."

Quinn's dossier sits on my desk. I know far more than I should about my holiday fling.

Fling? Is that what I'm calling this? Because I've never before been this obsessed about a *fling*.

My mistake.

"I suppose that makes sense. I need to change my reservations." I pull out my phone and call up my fight information.

"Of course, Mr. Sterling. When do you need to leave?"

"As soon as possible."

Quinn flew home for the holidays, but she doesn't live in Atlanta. It may be too late as it is. Christmas came and went with very little fanfare in the tropics.

Iris changes my reservation.

Less than four hours later, I'm on my way home. That brings all kinds of unpleasant sensations swirling in my gut, but I'm not here to see my family.

My driver picks me up, asks where I want to go, and I pause. I could storm Quinn's family home, burst in like a jilted lover, but there would be questions.

I don't answer questions.

What the hell am I doing?

Instead of having the driver take me to Quinn, I tell him the address of my sister's group home. It's been a few months since I visited Cherise. Hopefully, my surprise visit will bring a smile to her face.

A short walk takes me to the front desk where I check in. The pretty receptionist behind the counter blushes furiously as she logs me into the visitor book.

"How long will you be staying, Mr. Sterling? Dinner is at six. If you'd like, we can set a seat for you."

I shouldn't, but it's barely half-past four. There's no way I'm getting out of here in less than two hours.

"Please. That would be wonderful. Can you tell me where Cherise might be?"

"Yes, sir." She consults her computer and pulls up my sister's daily schedule. "She's out back with the gardeners."

No doubt fawning over her prize orchids.

"Thank you."

"Do you need help finding the way?"

"No, I know it well."

It's been nearly a decade that I've been coming here.

Mother put Cherise into this home a few months shy of our eighteenth birthday. It was right after I graduated from high school and the end of an era.

The first few years afterward were difficult for me. I hated this place with seething resentment for Mother. She abandoned Cherise to a group home.

Slowly, as the years passed, I understood how much Cherise loves her life here. She's surrounded by friends who don't see her disability as a liability.

The staff are wonderful, encouraging her interests. Cherise may be simpleminded, but she's living a good life. Some might call it a perfect life because she's immune to the realities the rest of us bear.

The lies and disappointment which litter my life. The mother who abandoned her. The brother who tries, but fails. I want to be her hero, the one who makes her life the most perfect it can be.

But that's not what I am.

I fail Cherise each and every day, falling short of the hero she needs. I can't fix her. I can't go back in time and reverse the damage I caused. All I can do is visit when I'm able and let her go. Let her enjoy a life I don't understand.

This place brings Cherise a great deal of happiness.

I wish I was half as content with my lot as Cherise is with hers.

As for the orchids?

My sister's mind may have been stolen from her, but she's a savant when it comes to cultivating orchids. Her passion for the delicate blooms is something I don't understand, although I've come to accept it over the years.

My purposeful stride takes me through the long corridors to the back of the estate. I cross a wide covered porch and take the steps two at a time, heading toward the greenhouse I commissioned five years ago specifically for Cherise's orchids.

A young man sees me. His hand goes high overhead and he gives a vigorous wave. "Hi, Mr. Sterling." He doesn't get up, too engrossed with the beautiful woman sitting beside him.

"Hi, Freddy! How's it hanging?"

"To the left!" His smile spreads across his entire face.

I taught him that, although his sister will never forgive me. Evidently, Freddy shared his joke with his sister's mother-in-law who happens to be the Queen of England. But that's a story for a different day.

I don't interrupt them and continue toward my destination. My mother's threat remains ever-present on my mind. She'll take all of this away from Cherise to spite me.

That won't happen.

One way or another, I'll see to my sister's welfare, and it won't be from some false wedding to one of the approved names on Mother's list.

Honestly, my mother can go fuck that list. No way in hell will I give her the satisfaction. In fact, I'll find a way to support my sister without my mother's interference. She may be my sister's guardian, but everything comes with an expiration date. I'm more than willing to wait out my mother's life.

I rap lightly on the door of the greenhouse but don't wait for an answer before heading inside. Made entirely of glass, the heat and humidity jump a notch. I tug on the collar of my suit.

Intricate wrought-iron scrollwork provides the architectural framework for the glass wall. I commissioned the artistic iron myself. Built into the framework, sprays of wrought iron roses, irises, and orchids are everywhere.

A beautiful, young woman with a flowing mane of the darkest, midnight-black looks up with tawny hazel eyes. Cherise and I share many things. Our hair ties us together as siblings, but it's our golden eyes that set us apart.

She's simply the most stunning creature on earth. I wish life treated her differently. Cherise will never know true love. She'll never have a family, children who will frustrate her, complete her, and make her life whole.

I stole that from her. Me and the innocent mistake of a five-year-old boy.

It takes a second before her mind processes what her eyes see. In that brief moment, while I wait for her to recognize me, intense grief washes through me. I did that. I caused the damage, which left her irreparably impaired.

But the moment passes. I take a breath and her eyes widen with recognition. Cherise beams her brightest smile and shouts with glee.

"Hawke!"

My sister climbs to her feet and races over to me. She stops midway, looks confused, turns around, then glances down at the black and royal purple orchid clasped in her hands. I watch her mind as it toils to piece together her thoughts. It struggles to process the most basic information, working ten times slower than normal.

Not that it matters to Cherise. She's blissfully unaware when it comes to her handicap.

I wish the same were true for me.

She spins around and raises the orchid. Confusion fills her face. The orchid lowers. Then comprehension takes root.

"Look what I made!"

Cherise races into my embrace. I narrowly save the poor bloom from getting crushed, plucking it from her fingers, as she throws her arms around my neck and hugs me tight.

"My dearest, Cherise, how are you doing?"

She clutches me. Hard. Then releases me. Her brows tug together, intense thoughts storming through her mind.

"You're not supposed to be here."

"No. I'm not, but I wanted to surprise you."

I wanted to storm in on Quinn and demand answers for why she left me, but I'll take a surprise visit with my sister any day.

"Are you staying for the show?" Her eyes brighten with hope.

"Show?" I bring her orchid to my nose and take a deep breath.

Most orchids have very little to no scent, relying on shape and color to attract insects and birds for pollination. Some are very fragrant with scents that defy description. This one smells of coconut and the sea; two of my sister's favorite scents. Two of my favorite scents.

"I smell the ocean." I pull the black orchid away and look at it with amazement. "Did you do that?"

She nods furiously. "It's right, isn't it?" She looks to me for affirmation.

"It's heavenly. Show me everything."

I take in the rows and rows of flowering orchids. There must be over a hundred. Nearly every pot presents a bloom for my inspection. Some hold half a dozen sprays of tiny, delicate flowers. Some are a single stem with a solitary bloom the size of my palm.

With the limitless joy of a child's mind, trapped in a thirty-year-old body, we spend the next hour looking at every orchid in her collection. Her face radiates joy as she takes me around by the hand.

I'm treated to a riot of color, from the palest white to the deepest black, and every hue in between. My senses are flooded with familiar fragrances of raspberry, lilacs, citrus, and smells I'm unable to place.

Cherise tests me, proffering blooms with no scent at all to see if I'm indeed telling her the truth about how much I love her flowers. She hands me one with an impish grin. I don't want to, but I play along fully knowing this is going to be one with an obnoxious scent.

The taste of rotten meat floods my senses. I barely hold back from retching. She claps her hands together, pleased with her prank, as my eyes water.

"It's stinky!" Her bright eyes prohibit any reaction except an answering smile.

"Come here." I tug her into my embrace and rub playfully at the top of her head. "You got me."

"I did! You always fall for it."

It's true. Every damn time because it brings her such joy.

A knock on the door turns our heads.

"Miss Cherise, it's dinnertime." One of the employees gently reminds her about dinner. "Mr. Sterling, will you be joining us."

"Yes, and can you please ask Mrs. Sampson if I could have a word with her after dinner?"

"Of course." He gives a slight nod and holds the door, waiting for us to head to dinner.

"Oh, goody!" Cherise jumps up and down again, clapping with joy. My visit today will be the highlight of her month.

One of the things I love about this place is how rigidly they adhere to their routines. Most of the residents have some degree of mental handicap, like my sister. Some are patients with Down's Syndrome. Others, like Freddy, are on the spectrum. Sweet souls who thrive in a safe harbor, secluded from those who would torment them with taunts of being different, instead of special.

We spend dinner with her friends. Freddy and his sister, Rowan, join us and we're regaled with Freddy's first trip out of the country and his newest, best buddy, the Crown Prince Richard.

After dinner, Cherise leaves me for social hour with the rest of the residents. I watch her leave, with a smile on my face and my heart full and warm with her love. I pivot and march toward the administrative offices and my meeting with Mrs. Sampson. I need to find out how much it costs to keep Cherise here. How much power does my mother wield?

Then I get an idea for how to arrange a meeting with Quinn.

THIRTY

Hawke

THE CHIME OF THE ANTIQUE GRANDFATHER CLOCK RIPPLES THROUGH the air. The first deep gong pierces the air as I step through the doorway of my childhood home. I brace for a flood of bad memories. When I was a kid, that clock ruled my world. Mother was punctual to a fault and demanded the same from everyone else. My life revolved around the metallic clicking of the gears and the deep booming gongs of the clock.

I hate that clock.

To be a moment late equated to an egregious sin, discipline followed by any number of painful punishments. Breakfast was set at precisely six. Get to the table after the last gong, and no food would be served until lunch at high noon. Again, twelve long gongs determined whether I ate or starved. Not that I ever really starved, but explain that to a six-year-old with an empty belly why he can't eat the food on his plate.

It was one more way Mother kept me under her thumb, and a way to show favor to my sister. Mother never let me forget that I was at fault for poor Cherise. My sister didn't live and breathe by the ticking of that damned clock, but I did. It wasn't until many years later that I understood how she used Cherise to punish me. My mother made the rules. We lived by them, and I couldn't fault Cherise for my mother's brutality.

I tell myself I'm over the fear licking up and down my spine as the sound of those deep gongs vibrate through the air, but that is a lie. I'll never get over the terror that clock held over my life for so many years.

Eleven more strikes will announce high noon. I have that long to traverse the prominent southern home and make my way to the dining room in the east wing where I'm to join Mother for lunch. I slow my stride and admire the paintings of long-deceased relations. I use this time to brace myself against whatever recriminations Mother will use in her attack. A headache builds behind my eyes and I rub at my temples. I'm not up for verbal warfare with my mother.

I'm tired and a little hungover. I've been licking my wounds every night since Quinn left. The visit to my sister buoyed my spirits, for a moment. There is a way out from under Mother's thumb, but it's risky. Honestly, I'm not sure I'll follow through. The upside is getting out from the demands Mother places on me. The downside is condemning Cherise to overcrowded living facilities where her spirit will wither and die. Mother has me exactly where she wants me, which means I remain her obedient and dutiful son. That includes answering her summons for lunch.

The clock counts down the seconds, and I hurry my step. I could arrive late and irritate my mother, but I decide against it.

I've been stewing over what to do about Quinn. My anger stirs again, heating me up from the inside out. I want her to hurt the way she hurt me.

By the ache in my arm from doing the five-knuckle-hustle, every morning and each night, my body would disagree. I ache for Quinn. We never really had a chance to get started. Needy, lustful thoughts fill my mind all day and through each of the lonely nights. I only had Quinn in my bed for one night. We spent it under the stars, making love all the way through dawn. One night, and I can't stop thinking about her.

Making love?

When did I go from fucking women to making love?

I know the answer to that. I just don't want to acknowledge what it means. I don't do relationships. They're nothing more than traps.

Bruce, Mother's butler, snaps to attention as I approach the entry to the dining room. He takes in a deep breath to formally introduce my arrival.

"Madame Sterling, Master Hawke has arrived." He announces my presence as if we're fucking royalty at court.

I can't wait to be free of the power and manipulation of the Sterling Matriarch. That it comes only after her death should bother me, but I'm eager to be relieved of the burdens she places on me. The last gong of the clock sounds through the house as I take my seat.

"Good afternoon, Mother."

"Good afternoon." Her pinched expression says it's anything but good. She picks up her napkin and flicks it open. The moment she places it in her lap, Bruce is on the move. He serves the first course while Mother and I sit in stony silence. "Thank you for coming."

I had no choice in the matter, so remain silent. She brought me here for a reason, and I'll wait her out. The first course is removed, and salads are placed before us. We eat on the finest china, drink from priceless crystal, and wipe our mouths with only the best silk napkins.

It's a tedious bore.

When the main course is served, Mother cracks.

"You visited Sissy?"

I hate that nickname. She spent my childhood trying to force me to use it. I stubbornly refused.

"Yes, I visited *Cherise*."

Her eyes tighten, and her mouth pinches.

"And how is your sister?"

"She's well. You should take the time to visit her." According to the staff, it's been well over half a year since my mother made the trek out to Cherise's group home.

Mother doesn't take the bait. She takes a sip of water and flaps her hand until poor Bruce comes running. Pointing imperiously at her nearly full water glass, she demands he refill it.

Nothing in the dining room has changed since I was a boy. Nor has the service. We ate on fine china and drank from crystal glasses ever since I can remember. I learned quickly to be exceedingly careful not to break a plate or shatter a glass. Perfection in her son, and impeccable table manners, were an expectation. A flood of memories wash over me. A young boy crying over another cracked glass. Desperate tears of a child who never understood why his mother hated him. She treated Cherise like a princess and me as a monster.

My mother says nothing about visiting Cherise. My comment is summarily dismissed.

"Tomorrow is New Year's Eve." She states the obvious without completing her thought. I play along.

"Yes, it is." She wants me to dig for information, but I sit back and wipe my chin. I wave Bruce away when he tries to refill my half-empty glass.

"And will you grace us with your presence?" Her mouth twists as if she's tasted something sour.

"That depends. Does anything I have to say matter, or have you already made up my mind for me?" I'm the tie-breaking vote on the board. Not that the vote isn't always unanimous and perfectly aligned with Mother's wishes. Sometimes, I vote against her just to be irritating, not that it matters. She's got the board wrapped around her finger. I do it out of spite.

Time. All I have to do is wait. I'd be a better son if she'd been a better mother. I'm not proud of this.

"I expect you at the office at seven sharp. The first proposal begins at eight."

"Why do I need to be there an hour early?" It's been difficult getting out of bed early lately. I'm *preoccupied* with thoughts of Quinn after I wake. "You have my notes."

I went over all fifty proposals a second time and came up with the same ten potentials. MindScapeVR remains in the top ten, but will lose out due to a fragmented, and ultimately doomed, business plan. We provide capital, not handholding.

In addition, since I have intimate knowledge about the fiasco brewing between MindScapeVR's CEO and Creative Head, I should amend my list and place them at the bottom. The only reason I don't is because Mother will ask questions I don't want to answer. There's no way I'm telling her how I know about MindScapeVR's pending implosion.

Mother snaps her fingers, and Bruce rushes in to clear our plates. No sooner is the table cleared than he brings in a set of files. Mother is old school and refuses to go digital. She forces us to print everything and place them into folders like we're back in the seventies.

She flips through the stack. "You have great insight, son, but lack the tenacity for this job. I want to show you the difference between being passable at your job and being great."

I brace for a verbal dressing down. She's getting ready to rake me over the coals, highlighting my presumed ineptitudes. Amazing how she ignores the success Sterling Enterprises enjoys because of my leadership. I took a billion-dollar organization and tripled our portfolio in the last five years. It's why Sterling Venture Capital Inc. exists today.

"PharmB is a promising company. They're in FDA trials of their latest drug and are requesting research capital to explore an orphan drug for neuromuscular disorders. We will fund them."

"Fine." I agree with that. PharmB is quite promising, and their researchers are topnotch.

She flips through the top five proposals and tells me why SVC Inc. will fund their venture capital requests. There's nothing new or unexpected in her final decisions. I shift in my seat, wondering why I'm even here.

"This one…" She picks up a folder with MindScapeVR prominently scrawled over the outside of the manila folder. "You say the idea has merit, but the business plan is flawed. I agree with that."

"Are we going to sit here while you go over all the proposals only to tell me you agree with the report I sent over last month?"

"No." She gives a sharp shake of her head. "I'm going to show you the difference between making a bad investment versus seeing potential and taking advantage of greatness."

There's an odd stirring in my gut. I don't like the predatory gleam in her eyes. She lifts MindScapeVR's proposal and tosses it at me.

"We can invest ten million," she says. "And watch our investment go down the drain, or we can buy out the intellectual property and invest in it ourselves. We'll make hundreds of millions off this idea, but not if we leave it in the hands of MindScapeVR. Tomorrow, you'll buy them out."

"Me?"

"You'll offer five million. It's more than generous, and after reviewing their finances, they're starving for any cash. They're lucky I'm willing to part with that much. It's a generous offer, and you'll use some of that Sterling charm to close the deal."

"Generous? It's highway robbery." I can't help the anger rising within me. My mother wants to steal Quinn's idea and pay pennies on the dollar. I agree with my mother about the potential value of Quinn's idea, but Mother isn't thinking big enough. In the proper hands, we could be looking at billions.

We, meaning Quinn. A greedy company took advantage of her when she was young, stealing her creative brilliance to make millions while paying her less than ten thousand for the rights to her app. I won't do that to her again. It's not right. Not fair. And certainly not generous.

Quinn could be looking at billions. MindScapeVR's adaptive learning process is her creation. Her hard work. I offer an alternative.

"We'll give them the ten million, but stipulate Sterling Enterprises run the business." It's been done before, and there's no way Scott is going to be involved. Not after what he did to my girl. Generally, SVC Inc. remains a silent partner, taking in a percentage of the revenue on the startups we fund, but our parent company

Sterling Enterprises could step in and manage the project. We have the resources. "There's no reason to buy out their intellectual property rights." I stand firm and oppose my mother's plans.

Quinn would be forever locked out of her creation if Mother gets her way. No matter my feelings regarding Quinn, this isn't the kind of revenge I want. Actually, the more I think about it, I don't want to do anything which will hurt Quinn. I come to a very sobering conclusion.

I have feelings for Miss Quinn Hayes, and there's no way in hell Mother is going to take MindScapeVR away from Quinn. I won't allow it.

"The papers are already drawn up. You'll make the offer tomorrow when they present their idea to the board."

"No, Mother. I won't."

"Yes, you will, and one more thing." She tosses another folder in my direction and points her bony finger at it. "Tomorrow is New Year's Eve. You will choose your bride by midnight, or I will choose for you."

"You can't force a marriage on me." I scoot back in my chair, indignation rising. I don't bother opening the folder. I know what I'll see. Hopeful socialites, looking to improve their status by bartering their bodies to get their hands on me, not to mention the Sterling fortune. "That's not how this works."

She continues to jab her finger in the air. "There are ten to choose from, picked with meticulous care to meet your particular tastes. All fertile."

"Fertile?" I laugh at the word.

"I ensured they were tested."

"Wait a second, you tested these women?"

"Yes."

"Let me get this straight." I can't believe the gall of my mother. "You tested them?"

"Of course, it was part of the selection process."

"What did you do, send out a general bulletin soliciting a wife for me?"

"You make it sound crass. Each of those young ladies comes

from a respectable family. Their pedigrees are superior. Any will make for a favorable merger. What you decide to do with your *wife* is of no concern to me, but you will fulfill your obligation to produce an heir. Your wife, will, of course, be bound by a fidelity clause for the first three years of your marriage to ensure the product of conception is a Sterling. Paternity testing is a requirement. After that, you can do what you want with your wife, except divorce."

"You have some nerve, shackling me for life to a stranger. Using me as a stud to produce your heir. You've thought of everything, Mother Dearest, except for one thing." She wants to lock me into a loveless marriage and set the terms of my marriage bed. "I'm surprised you haven't slapped a fidelity clause on me as well, making sure I don't inadvertently spread my seed."

"Men's urges are impossible to control. I know better than to —*restrict*—you like that." Her mouth twists on the words. "No bastard can claim the Sterling fortune. You'll announce your engagement tomorrow night. I suggest you take a long hard look at that portfolio."

"You control many things in my life, Mother, but you can't have that." I slap my napkin down on the table and stand. "That's ridiculous, even for you." I pick up the portfolio of potential Sterling wives and fling it across the table. Glossy 8x10's of beautiful women fly through the air.

She doesn't even flinch at my outburst. Instead, she shakes her head and clicks her tongue. It's a look I know entirely too well.

I'm immediately transported to the past when I was a sad little boy denied any compassion by a mother without the capacity to love. My gut twists, and I press my palm to my chest. I'm thirty years old and it still hurts as much as it did back then.

Her gaze settles on the photos and accompanying dossiers. "Choose wisely, Son, and make your announcement tomorrow night."

"And if I don't? You can force me to marry, but you most certainly can't force me to fuck any of these women."

Her eyes flare at my vulgarity. Mother abhors swearing in any form, and I used the most offensive curse word. It takes her a minute to respond, and I take great pleasure in watching her compose herself. For a moment, I think she'll lob a return shot at me, but she doesn't. She collects herself and launches an attack I don't see coming. In cold, calculated words, she reasserts who's in charge.

"If you don't announce your engagement tomorrow night, then I have made arrangements for Sissy to be re-homed."

"You wouldn't dare." My plans for Cherise will take time. More time than I have in the next twenty-four hours. "You may not love me, but you care deeply for your daughter. That's an empty threat, Mother."

"Appearances are deceiving, and when have you ever known me to make an *empty* threat? I know all about your visit with Sissy and your conversation with management that followed. You will do as you're told." She snaps her fingers and Bruce comes running. He gathers all the papers and photos, placing them neatly back inside the folder. With his hand shaking, he holds the folder with its dossiers and pedigreed hopefuls out to me. "You have until tomorrow night."

"And if I refuse?"

"Sissy will be moved to a place where you'll never find her."

It shouldn't surprise me Mother knows about my plans for Cherise, but I'm taken completely by surprise that she would use Cherise against me.

"You wouldn't dare."

"It's already done. Do as your told and Sissy will return from her brief adventure. Refuse, and you'll never see your sister again."

"You fucking bitch." I grab the folder out of Bruce's hand and storm out of my mother's home. The first thing I do is call Cherise. When there's no answer, I call Mrs. Sampson. It takes but a moment to confirm the truth. Mother checked Cherise out of the home for a 'family' vacation.

Not that I should be surprised. Mother never bluffs.

THIRTY-ONE

Quinn

Christmas with my family is everything I hoped it would be. Gone are the garish silver and gold decorations from my office party. So too are ocean breezes, tropical palms, and the whispers of a man capable of breaking my heart. I tell myself to be strong. That I made the right choice.

My heart wouldn't survive a loss that profound.

As I sit in my mother's home, surrounded by the pungent aroma of pine, cinnamon, and spice, the deep greens and warm reds of Mother's homemade decorations fill every nook and cranny with cozy, festive, holiday cheer.

I've never felt this bereft and hollow inside, mourning the loss of a lover I turned away from.

My brothers stalk around me, grumbling about *that damn pinky swear.* They believe my sour mood stems from heartache over my loss of Scott. Little do they know the true reason my heart bleeds.

Mother and Daddy listen as I tell them the news. They surround me with love, support my grief, and cheer me toward a brighter future and a better year to come. They don't seem that upset, which brings up all manner of questions. I sense great relief on their part.

Did everyone but me dislike Scott? What did they see that I did not?

Not that it matters now. Scott is out of my life.

Almost. There's still something that ties us together. My dream keeps me moving forward. I can't give it up.

With my brothers hanging around me, shooting the shit and bragging about their tall tales, I log into my email account with my breath held tight. I expect to see the same flurry of desperate emails from Scott as the texts he sent before I blocked his number. Actually, I blocked both Scott and Sadie, sparing me from wading through the dozens of text messages they kept sending. Sadie's sounded more and more desperate while Scott's became more demanding and angry.

The flood of emails brings a hitch to my breath. Most are from Scott. I scan them quickly then give up. A quick sort groups them all together. I select them all and delete everything with one press of a button. I do the same with Sadie's emails.

Then I dive in and begin the task of recovering from nearly a week away from my inbox. I see one from Ted, my lead engineer, marked URGENT and open it to read the body of his email.

SUBJECT: URGENT

Q! Where are U? Please respond the moment you get this. Urgent meeting planned for Friday, Dec 31st. SVC Inc. demands meeting of MindScapeVR project team for **IN PERSON** presentation. I'll be traveling to Atlanta on the 30th. Meeting is at two. **CALL ME!**

MY GUT CLENCHES. THIS IS BIG. LIKE HUGE. THERE'S NO REASON for SVC Inc. to demand an in-person presentation if they aren't seriously considering funding our project.

And I almost missed it.

My fingers tremble as I pull up Tom's number. He answers on the first ring.

"Q! Where the hell are you? Did you get my email?"

"Yes, I did. What's going on?"

"You'd better get your ass to Atlanta by car, train, plane, or hell a boat if you can." He continues on in a rush, telling me all about the short notice presentation. "They practically demanded it."

Fortunately, I'm already in Atlanta. No need to hop in a car, ride a train, or attempt fate on a plane.

"Really?"

"Yes. Scott has been trying to get a hold of you. When he couldn't…"

"I blocked him."

"You what?"

My brothers give me side-eyes, listening in to my conversation. They're well aware I've told no one at work about Scott and Sadie.

Gideon locks his jaw, suppressing a low growl, while Steven supports me with a nod, encouraging me to spill the beans. He wants everyone to know what a douchebag Scott is, hoping they'll support me over him. That's going to be problematic if we begin drawing lines in the sand and picking sides. It's the best way to destroy us before we even begin.

"I blocked Scott." I give in to Steven's silent support and tell Tom what happened.

"That makes no sense." Tom's surprise is not unexpected. "How could he do that to you?"

I clench my phone as I try not to cry. "I don't even know if I still work there."

"What do you mean? Of course, you do."

"I think I quit."

"Look, I'm really sorry about what happened between you two, but I spoke to Scott yesterday. He's the one who asked me to email you. I guess it makes a little more sense now. We need you. He can't do this without you."

It's true. I'm the brains of the operation. Scott is merely the business manager.

"Tell me where and when and I'll be there." I'll leave Scott in a lurch all damn day, but I won't do that to my team. Whatever happened between us needs to stay between us. I have a lot of great programmers who need this project to launch their careers.

If we're funded.

If we're successful.

I can't deny them that.

Honestly, there's no reason I can't be professional. Except for the ache in my heart. Scott's betrayal cuts deep.

When I hang up, Gideon is by my side. He folds me against his massive frame and strokes his fingers through my hair. He knows how difficult it was to hold it together through that call.

"It'll get easier." His rumbly murmur almost makes me believe he's right.

"Will it?"

"With time." Gideon releases me. "So, what was that all about?"

I tell them about the meeting tomorrow.

"Why is that unusual?" Brett, who watched me through the entire phone conversation, leans forward. "Does something like that not happen?"

I understand his confusion. In construction, things are different. They often present their projects in person, submitting bids, and defending them. It's simply not the same when trying to woo millions out of a venture capitalist. I'm sure there are many deals made at bars, on the golf course, and many other places, but that's after an initial introduction. MindScapeVR is brand new, with no contacts. No visibility. We've cast a wide net, selling our idea to anyone who might listen, and this is the only bite we've received.

We're beggars and well aware of our position.

Maybe next time, when we're a success, we won't be sitting at the far end of an electronic submission. Until then, we play the game and know our place.

"Not for SVC Inc. They have a strict online proposal submission process. I didn't think they asked contenders in to pitch projects in person. I imagine they must get hundreds of proposals every year."

"This must be a good sign then." Brett takes a sip of his beer. "You must be a top contender."

"I hope so." I sit back down and rub my hands together. "At least if I don't fuck things up because of Scott."

"You know…" Gideon sits on the floor in front of me. He grabs the nearly half-empty tub of popcorn into his lap. "Scott won't be a problem."

"Easy for you to say."

"Easy because we'll make certain of it." His tone takes on a dangerous edge.

"What does that mean?"

"Only that you're not going to face him alone." He flashes a cheeky grin, but there's no humor in his expression. Gideon shoves a kernel of popcorn into his mouth. "You're going to have us."

"Us?"

"Yes—us." He gestures to my brothers.

"Oh, no. You *aren't* coming." I shove him, but he doesn't budge.

"Yes, we are." Ian joins Gideon with the madness.

"This isn't exactly—your speed." How do I tell them, without being too insulting, that their blue-collar world doesn't fit into the glass and steel offices of SVC Inc.?

"Don't worry, little sis." Brett jabs Ian in the ribs. "We clean up pretty well."

"I don't doubt that for a second, but this is a suit and tie kind of event."

"You're not facing douchebag without backup." Gideon makes it a pronouncement, like his word is law, but I'm not done fighting him on this.

"I appreciate it. I really do, but I have to face him sooner or later. I won't always have the four of you around to fight my battles. I've got this."

"I know you do." Gideon makes it seem as if he's relenting, but his next words bring a groan to my lips. "But you'll face him tomorrow with our support." He tosses popcorn at Steven. "Time to get off the game. We need to make sure we look pretty for Quinney's little thing tomorrow."

"My *little thing* is a really, really big deal. Please don't ruin it for me." Whining is my last resort. I hope it's enough.

"We'd never…" Gideon reassures.

I nearly pump my fist in victory, but lay in for the kill. "How am I going to explain why you're there?"

"They'll want to know you have investors." He points to Ian, Brett, and Steven in turn. "We're your investors."

"What?" This is not what I expect.

I've never asked my family for money, and I'm not about to do that now. "I can't pass you off as investors. I'm a horrible liar."

Gideon climbs to his full six-foot-plus towering height. "Don't waste your breath arguing. We talked about it yesterday and agree. You've got something pretty amazing and Hayes Construction has a little extra cash we need to invest. We believe in you."

"I really appreciate it, but…" There's no way their tiny contribution will make any difference. From the hard glint in his eyes, I'm not going to win this argument with my brothers. Not when they all gang up on me. "Fine. I give up. We have to be there no later than two. Earlier is better. I won't be late on this. And all of you have to wear a suit and tie."

"We know how to dress, baby girl." Steven rolls his eyes at me. "Not our first rodeo."

I get it. Our father owns Hayes Construction, but my brothers are full partners in the family-run business. They're doing well, but I'm not happy about tying up any of their capital.

We spend the rest of the day together, playing video games, watching movies, and eating Mother's amazing leftovers. I pull her aside, hoping to enlist her aid in keeping my brothers out of my hair, but I lose the battle in the end. They got to her first.

Noon the next day, they're waiting for me downstairs. Used to seeing my brothers in faded blue jeans, work boots, and wearing the brightly colored green Hayes Construction tee-shirts, I'm struck dumb when I see them in suits and ties.

"Damn, you clean up nice." I stop midway down the stairs to take in the sight of my four brothers in their dark suits, clean, pressed shirts, and matching green ties that display the Hayes company logo in small letters throughout.

"Told ya." Ian spreads his arms out wide and gives me a little spin. "We clean up really good."

Mother stands beside them, beaming at her boys; men who fill out a suit as if they were born to wear one.

"And why are you all still single?" My gaze sweeps the four of them and I shake my head. I don't get why they aren't already married and bouncing babies on their knees.

We climb into the family SUV. I get squished in the middle seat in the back because I'm the girl and the only one who fits there. Gideon is at the helm. Ian is our navigator. Steven supports me on my left, and Brett keeps a hand on my leg, just above my kneecap. His firm touch reminds me I can tackle anything with them at my back.

I just hope that holds true when I have to face Scott again.

Tom sent over the slides we're using for our presentation. Scott will give it. Standing up in front of a boardroom full of suits is outside my comfort zone. Reluctantly, I unblock Scott's number, but only so I can tell him we're going to be late. We run into a patch of construction that eats up all the extra time I built into our drive.

We head into the heart of Atlanta and weave between skyscrapers of steel and glass. Before long, we head into an underground parking garage where I receive my tenth pep talk of the day.

My brothers are overly proud of their little sister. They may not understand anything about the code I write, but they get the practical applications of what I do. After talking with them this morning about my virtual reality applications, they already have my mind spinning with ways to adapt it to meet the needs of companies like Hayes Construction. I'm actually a little embarrassed I didn't think of it myself.

We file into an elevator, which takes us to the twentieth floor and dumps us out into a classically understated reception area. Tom is there, pacing back and forth. He turns when we exit and gives a relieved sigh.

"I didn't think you'd make it." He glances at his watch while I avoid looking at the clock over the receptionist's desk. It's a minute until two.

"Sorry, traffic delays."

Movement in the corner draws my eye. Scott presses out the wrinkles in his suit. He's arrestingly gorgeous, and my heart pinches as he takes a step toward me. I'm not ready for this, but then Gideon places his hand against the small of my back, pushing me forward.

"Q?" Scott glances at my brothers. "Why are they here?"

"Why do you think?" Gideon's response is a growl.

"We're here for moral support, and as investors, we're here to support our sister in any way we can." Brett steps in front of Scott, forming a barrier between me and the man who broke my heart.

"Gentlemen…" The receptionist interrupts the male posturing. She comes around from behind her desk and with a sweep of her arm ushers us to follow. "They're ready to see you. Please, if you'll follow me."

With Scott's aborted attempt to speak with me, we all file in to fight for the funding our project desperately needs. Scott is first in line, followed by Tom. Brett continues his job as a shield, walking in front of me as he blocks Scott from getting too close. Steven and Ian flank me, and Gideon takes up the rear.

I'm surrounded by Hayes men, protected and sheltered from the evils of the world.

We march into a boardroom as a united front. A long glass table awaits us. Eight men and one woman sit to the right. I pull up short when the man sitting at the head slowly rises to his feet.

Hawke Sterling's heated glare drills into me. Full of molten fury, his golden eyes simmer on the verge of boiling over.

I can endure Scott's presence, but Hawke knots my stomach in an endless falling loop of regret and false promises. With a hard gulp, I swallow down my unease, because there's something to fear in this room. My jilted lover holds my future in his hands, and I'm standing beside my ex-fiancé. I'd like to think Hawke won't hold that over my head, but I'm here with Scott after walking out on Hawke.

I'm screwed.

With a hard shake of my head, I try, and fail, to grab a hold of the emotions racing through me. My pulse careens into a hard gallop. My heart labors to keep up. All the while, I desperately school my features into something devoid of all the emotions rattling around inside my head.

I ache for Hawke. God, I've missed him. I want to push past my brothers and leap into Hawke's arms, wrap my body around him, and let the rest of the world disappear as our lips lock and our hearts meld.

He sends my heart into a dizzying spiral, wishing and wanting things it can't have. I feel him. I feel our connection vibrating in the space between us. But the hard set of his jaw gives me pause. Those eyes of his are full of anger, and judgment. I'm pretty sure he's not happy to see me.

Gideon closes the distance behind me. His strong hand presses firmly against my back, urging me to continue toward the empty row of seats along the left-hand side of the table.

Hawke stands at the head. His commanding presence owns the room and makes my knees wobble. Power rests firmly upon his shoulders and he wears it as a comfortable companion. Muscles bounce on his stony jaw, locked in battle over which of us will break the suffocating silence first.

An older woman, with the same mane of black hair, but speckled with gray, and the same tawny eyes, sits to his right. Her piercing gaze sweeps past Scott, Tom, and my brothers, to fix on me. There they twitch before flicking back to Hawke, only to return to me. A sublime smile creeps across her face.

I wait for a break in Hawke's expression, needing a smile to soften his eyes, but he greets me only with stony indifference and waves toward the empty seats.

"Please, take a seat so we may begin." Tightly controlled, I melt beneath his command. There's just something about Hawke that demands my obedience. I thought it was just during sex, but there's more to it.

I surrender any will I may have, wanting only to run into Hawke's arms. To feel his strength. To lay all my worries at his feet. But my breath catches and flutters in my throat, where it's strangled into silence.

Ian grabs my elbow, urging me forward. With Gideon at my back and Ian to my side, I make it to the third chair. I won't sit. Not until Hawke acknowledges me.

But then Scott opens his mouth.

THIRTY-TWO

Quinn

"It's you." Scott's face reddens with indignation. "You were at Euphoria." He stabs an accusatory finger toward me. "Kissing my fiancée. What the fuck is this?"

I cringe with Scott's outburst. He lobs a grenade in the room, opening his mouth before thinking, obliterating our chances before we begin.

Why can't he keep his mouth shut?

Because he's an arrogant prick; A hotheaded asshole you once thought you were in love with.

Well, I definitely know how to pick losers.

My fingers dig into the supple leather of the back of the chair while the only other woman in the room straightens with indignation.

"I will kindly invite you to watch your language in my presence, son." Her haughty tone sends a shiver down my spine. I initially dismissed the frail woman, but with a flick of her fingers, two men move away from the walls. My gaze shifts to Hawke who grits his teeth. No doubt he's holding his tongue. He may be leading this meeting, but that woman is the one in charge.

And he hates it.

I blink in surprise, not having noticed the men along the wall.

Hawke holds up his hand and the men hover, looking between him and the woman who I assume is his mother. They share too many characteristics for that not to be the case.

"What this is, Mr. Aiken, is you blowing the deal of a lifetime." Hawke's eyes narrow and his chiseled jaw hardens. "You will apologize to my mother."

Scott's mouth works, but no sound comes out. Hawke simply shakes his head. "I think it's decided then." He sounds disappointed, but then he turns his furious gaze to me.

What does he want with that stormy gaze? One outburst and our future lies in ruin. Scott killed us before we had a chance to plead our case. I don't know whether to run with our tails tucked between our legs or to defend our case.

"Hawke?" His mother pins me with her eyes. I feel like a tiny field mouse before the hawk strikes. My heart seizes in my chest, waiting for the fatal snatch into oblivion. "You know this woman?" Her tone is dismissive and unsurprised.

"Yes, Mother, I do." Hawke's jaw clenches. Tension winds through his entire body. Any moment and his restraint will snap. I feel this intuitively. "We met at Euphoria."

"Was that before or after you tabled their request?" Her acidic words drip with venom. Not to wound us, but rather to embarrass her son.

"After." His long fingers press against the glass tabletop. "They're here on your request, not mine. I'm sure you remember that correctly."

"There's nothing wrong with my memory, Hawke." I flinch at the cutting words his mother uses, but Hawke doesn't flinch. He absorbs it without any reaction. "This is certainly more interesting than I thought it would be." This woman enjoys playing with her prey. It's clear in the calculated cruelty she wields and in how she speaks down to everyone in the room.

Why does Hawke tolerate it?

"This…" Hawke grinds the words from between clenched teeth.

"It's what you wanted. To see if MindScapeVR would accept your conditions."

"Conditions?" I can't help it. I blurt out the word, stepping into a landmine of conversation. "What do you mean by conditions?"

Hawke's focus swivels back to me. "Your company's proposal, Miss Hayes, has merit, but lacks significantly in the execution of its business plan. My mother invited you here to listen to your pitch and to offer an alternative. She's interested in seeing whether you would accept our terms."

She's interested. Not we. I sense a rift between Hawke and his mother, but have no basis to understand it. He and I didn't share much in the short time we had together. Or rather, I realize I shared a great deal, while he managed to say very little about himself. Although for a man who fucks and never dates, I understand why. My regrets over leaving him make less and less sense.

While I made the right decision, I can't help but whither beneath his gaze. It's full of the betrayal I put at his feet when I left him. My heart trips a little, missing a beat. We should be summarily dismissed after Scott's outburst, but we're still standing.

"What terms?"

Hawke's gaze sweeps past Tom and lands on my brothers. "And who are you?" His eyes pinch. "The invitation was for three."

"And yet here we are." Gideon places a hand on my shoulder. "Quinney, I take it you're *familiar* with this person?" I hear his protective tone and cringe. For the past three days, he and my brothers tried to get me to tell them where I spent my time after Scott's infidelity broke our incredibly brief engagement.

So far, I avoided supplying that little bit of information. It's not theirs, but rather my closely guarded secret. For three days, I knew true happiness, then I walked away. I wanted to keep that sliver of happiness to myself, something I cherish above everything else.

Now everyone knows, and it's not my little secret anymore. The hardest thing I've ever had to do was walk away from Hawke Sterling. I was falling for him, too hard and too fast, even knowing he's the kind of man who fucked and never entered into a relationship.

What I wanted with him was much more. I cut and ran.

"She slept with him at Euphoria." Scott's face turns a nasty shade of purple as he spits around his words. His attention shifts to Hawke. "Why are we here?"

Why is Scott acting as if he's the injured party?

My stomach ties its final knot and plummets off a cliff. My dream is dead. Dead because of Scott's assholery, not to mention my brother's overprotective nonsense. Oh, and then there's Hawke and the little bit of history we share.

"I'm sorry, Mr. Sterling. It seems we've wasted your time." I'd stay and fight, but there's no recovering from this. I release my death grip on the leather chair. "Mrs. Sterling, I apologize for my associate's vulgarity. Gentlemen, my apologies for wasting your time." I give a nod to the other men in the room and push back from the chair. If we're going to get kicked out, I'd rather at least start heading toward the door. They won't have as far to kick us that way.

"Miss Hayes…" The scratchy voice of Hawke's mother pulls my ears to my shoulders. "Stay." When she takes to her feet, the men sitting rise as one. "Mr. Aiken and Mr…" Her brow arches as she takes in Tom.

Tom's face is the palest shade of white, caught in a situation he never could've imagined finding himself in.

"Tom Sparks." He supplies his name and takes to his feet, following the lead of the other men. Scott is the only man still sitting.

"Mr. Sparks, follow Mr. Lewis and his associates to the library. We'll collect you momentarily." Her request carries the force of an order.

Tom swallows thickly. His gaze bounces to me, questions swirling in their depths. I should play it cool, like I know what's happening, but I give up with a shrug.

"You might as well." I wave him out, and he follows the other men out of the room, leaving Scott, Hawke, Mrs. Sterling, and my obnoxious, overly protective brothers to measure the weight of our stares with one another. I believe the men are measuring dick lengths while Mrs. Sterling laughs silently to herself. Male posturing can be amusing, but not now.

"And who are they?" Mrs. Sterling lifts a gnarled knuckle toward my brothers.

"Representatives of Hayes Construction," Gideon proudly answers.

"Ah…" She dismisses Gideon out of hand, but he's not one to allow anyone to minimize him.

"We're investors, so if you're not offering capital, what's on the table? We have a vested interest in how this plays out."

"Gideon," I practically hiss as I place my hand on his arm, "don't antagonize her."

"Well, isn't that cute. Miss Hayes has her family investing in her little project." Her derisive snort curls my fingers into fists, but I force myself to relax. She watches me, not Gideon, and I'm very well aware what that means.

"Mother…" Hawke barely suppresses a growl.

My attention shifts to his protective instincts. Defending me over his mother? It's not what I expect.

"Oh, come on, surely you think it's adorable too?" She pivots toward her son, back ramrod straight and eyes cruelly set. "I'm curious as to your connection with Miss Hayes and why this is the first I'm hearing of it?" Her acidic gaze burns into Hawke.

"This is not the time…" A low warning tone threads through Hawke's words.

"Seems like it's exactly the time, when one of your torrid affairs affects our business." Her long fingernails click on the glass tabletop. "I suppose I understand now why you rejected their proposal."

What's this? My stomach does all kinds of swooping looping maneuvers, making me clutch the back of the chair or risk falling over.

"I rejected it before…" Hawke clears his throat and locks stares with his mother as she lifts an imperious finger and cuts him off.

"Before you slept with her? Is that what you're going to say?" She shakes her head with disappointment.

"Before I met her." His eyes pinch. "Do not test me."

I'm getting wicked bad vibes between Hawke and his mother. It's feral and rotten.

"Never could keep it in your pants." Her derisive snort curls my fingers. I want to gouge her eyes out for speaking to Hawke like that.

Mrs. Sterling turns her attention to me. "Hawke toys with his playthings, Miss Hayes, but tires of them all too quickly. I doubt you lasted more than one night. If you thought to insert yourself into his bed to receive preferential terms, your efforts came to naught. As for you, Mr. Aiken, while this project has some degree of merit, the business plan behind it is bungled beyond repair. It's true. My son wanted to drop the project altogether. You're here at my behest, but I must say after your vulgar use of profanity, I won't do business with you at all. You just cost your associate," she makes a dismissive wave in my general direction, "millions." She sneers as she says the words while I stagger.

Millions?

All color drains from Scott's face as she dresses him down.

"And as cute as it is to see a girl supported by her brothers, a woman doesn't need men to protect her interests. That alone is reason to dismiss this project altogether. I can't bear weak women."

I'm about ready to fly across the conference table and claw her eyes out.

"I'm not weak." Finally, my voice finds itself. I can't get beyond that question. "You say Hawke, um Mr. Sterling, rejected our proposal, then claim you're the one who asked us to come. You see merit in what we bring to the table. A shrewd business woman wouldn't dismiss that. Or did you bring me here to humiliate me? Or maybe your son?"

"You give me far too much credit, my dear. This is the first I'm hearing about your little dalliance with my son." Her focus swivels back to Hawke. "No surprise, this was at Euphoria. Again—terribly disappointing, but not unexpected. My son, Miss Hayes, likes to play with his toys. You may not have known who he was, but I'm certain he knew exactly who he invited into his bed."

I roll my shoulders back, hating the way she speaks to me and my brothers, but more than anything, I despise the way she dresses down her son in public. Hawke doesn't deserve that.

"Mrs. Sterling, you can degrade those who work for you until the cows come home, but I refuse to stand here and have you talk to me like a child, or worse—one of your son's disposable flings. What happened between us, is frankly none of your concern. As for MindScapeVR, it's a solid investment. Spectacular in fact. We've tested it in aged-care facilities, and it shows remarkable progress in slowing, halting, and even reversing the signs of dementia. I did that. My *team* accomplished that. My virtual reality simulation brings adaptive mental challenges to those individuals. You may want nothing to do with investing in my company, but others will. And when you see them profiting off something you walked away from, you'll regret not getting in on the ground floor. Good day." Ready to march out of the room, Gideon's words halt me in my tracks.

"Not to mention the applications it has in construction." Gideon's steady baritone rolls right through the tense silence. "That's why we're putting five million of our own capital into Quinn's project." Something happens to my heart. I clutch my chest, waiting for it to beat again. Gideon places his hand on my shoulder and gives a firm squeeze, telling me to hold myself together.

Five million?

We've never discussed the family investing in my project. I would never put them in the position where they had to refuse me. Five million is half of what we need to get started.

Half.

Surely, I can scrounge up the other five million elsewhere?

It's a surprise how well I keep it together, but the wheels in my head spin like a hamster in a hamster wheel. We're not dead in the water as I feared.

"Thank you for your time, but MindScapeVR is no longer interested in any capital investment from SVC Inc." I hate leaving. It feels like I'm walking out on Hawke for the second time. All I want is to run to him and fold into his embrace, but he's not sending any signals I'd be welcome in his arms.

In fact, he stands ramrod stiff. The muscles of his jaw clench as his astute gaze pins me in place. I don't know what he's thinking, but the smoldering looks and the heat which licked between us, is still there, stronger than ever before. I know I'm not imagining it.

It doesn't help one bit that I walked away from him. From us. This feels incredibly final.

Gideon releases me, which allows me to complete my dramatic exit. I storm out while Scott remains sitting, struck dumb by our conversation.

With my brothers at my back, I exit the room, leaving ten million in venture capital investment on the floor. We head past the library where Tom sits in conference with the rest of Mrs. Sterling's team.

"We're leaving." I wave him out.

"Leaving?" Tom stands, surprise scrawls all across his face. "But?" He gives the suits in the room another quick look, then stands and joins me in the hall. "Where's Scott?"

"Who cares. He ruined this for us."

That may not be entirely fair. My illicit affair with Mrs. Sterling's son ruined things as much as Scott not keeping a lid on his foul mouth. We stand at the elevator, waiting for it to take us back down to the garage.

"What was that?" I turn to my brothers and crane my neck

"What was what?" Gideon can't help the idiotic grin on his face. "Did we forget to tell you?"

"There's no way Hayes Construction is putting five million into a VR startup, but I appreciate the support."

"Damn thing's taking forever." Brett stabs at the elevator call button.

Steven and Ian remain suspiciously quiet, rocking back on their heels and exchanging smug expressions. My gaze darts between them, jumps to Brett, and finally lands on Gideon.

"You made it all up." I expect him to give in and admit he was posturing the whole time.

The elevator arrives and the doors hiss open. Tom keeps looking between me and my brothers.

"What happened back there? I'm assuming we didn't get the funding."

"Well, maybe not the ten million you wanted, but you have half." Gideon steps into the elevator and crosses his arms. We all pile in behind him. "I made none of it up, sis."

"What do you mean, we got half?" Confusion spins in Tom's eyes. "They gave us five million? That's not enough for what we need." He scratches his head. "I guess there are a few other options out there. We can canvas for smaller investors. It means more hands in the pot. More opinions…" His voice trails off in thought.

Poor Tom. He's trying to figure it all out.

"Gideon was just posturing back there." I still don't believe him. "Hayes Construction doesn't have that kind of capital to risk on a startup."

The elevator doors begin to close, but then Scott jogs up and shoves his arm between the closing doors.

"Well, look who it is." I roll my eyes. "You really screwed the pooch on that one Scott. Did it ever occur to you to keep your damn mouth shut?"

"Did you know who he was when you fucked him?" Scott points an accusatory finger at me.

"Whoa." Ian reaches out, grabs Scott's finger, and gives it a hefty twist.

Scott cries out and jerks his hand free. He backs down as Steven, Brett, and Gideon puff out their chests. The testosterone level in this cramped elevator escalates a thousand-fold.

"You probably don't want to speak to our sister like that," Ian says. "Especially after you fucked her best friend. I think who she sleeps with is no longer your concern."

Tom glances at me, his eyes widening.

"Not that your question deserves an answer." I feel a need to explain. Not to Scott, but rather to my lead engineer and maybe my brothers. Tom doesn't deserve any of this. "I didn't know who Hawke was when we met. As for the rest, it's none of your business.

You lost the right to it being your business when you fucked Sadie after proposing to me. And as for the rest of this, I'm not sure what they thought about the business plan, except they were willing to back us with some kind of contingency surrounding that. As far as I see it, you're no longer a part of this project."

"I own the company."

"Correct. You're right about that, but after you threw that in my face, I looked up our charter documents. The company is yours, but the IP rights are mine." I'm nearly certain this is true. Honestly, I'm bluffing my way through this. I never really read our company's articles of incorporation, trusting it all to Scott's capable hands.

But he slips. The shocked expression on his face tells me I nailed it on the head. Damn, but that feels amazing. I may not have the funds to push forward with my project, but it's still mine. As for losing the venture capital, Tom and I will figure something out.

Not Scott.

"Does this mean he's no longer my boss?" Tom's gaze bounces between us.

"Only if you quit." I shrug. "But I'm pretty sure I'm going to need a lead engineer. It's up to you if you want to jump ship." I leave it unsaid that I'll be making the same offer to all our employees.

Well, all but Sadie.

"You wouldn't do that." Scott's mouth opens and closes as he struggles to add more to whatever it is he wants to say. Fortunately, we're spared whatever it is as the elevator doors open.

Gideon rushes me out of the elevator, putting distance between me and Scott.

"Give me a call when you get home. We'll talk." I give a little wave to Tom.

"Will do." Tom makes a beeline away from Scott who remains sputtering where we leave him.

"Damn, I didn't think this would be that entertaining." Brett huffs a laugh. "I'm glad we decided to come with you today. Little sister's got some spunk in her. Well done, Quinney."

Although I didn't ask for it, I appreciate their support. However,

I agree with Mrs. Sterling on one little bit. I shouldn't cower behind the protection of my brothers. I'm twenty-five, a grown woman, and no longer their baby sister.

"Did that really just happen?" I rub my hand down my face and squeeze my eyes shut. Now that we're no longer in that conference room, all that adrenaline racing through my body has nowhere to go. My entire body shakes. Fine tremors settle in my hands, making my fingers move on their own.

My eyes open and I take a deep breath, only to find Hawke casually leaning against our SUV.

Dressed in his tailored suit, he commands an impressive presence. He's as tall as my muscular brothers, but his body isn't hewn from hard physical labor like theirs. Not that it matters. There's a certain gravitas about him, and he doesn't back down before the united front my brothers present. His stormy gaze takes in my brothers, and he takes a step forward, advancing rather than retreating.

My knees wobble beneath his stony expression. Muscles bounce in the clenching of his jaw. It begins as a twitching at the corners, then breaks across his face into a massive shit-eating grin. His smile, while arrestingly gorgeous, confuses the hell out of me.

"Miss Hayes, I want to kiss you." The look in his eyes says that's not all he wants.

"You're not touching one hair on her head." Gideon steps in front of me.

"How did you get down here before us?" I glance around Gideon's blocky frame. We left Hawke in the conference room with his mother.

"Executive elevator." He hitches his thumb over his shoulder. "It's an express to the garage, very private." Straight nose and strong jaw, his face is an expressionless void. At least until that smile reaches his eyes, fanning their golden glow into a lusty flame.

The desire brimming in his eyes stops me in my tracks. Slowly, I take a moment to reacquaint myself with his hardened features and his expressive face with its sun-kissed glow. His infectious smile widens and deepens the crinkles at the corners of his golden eyes. Breathtaking is too weak of an adjective to describe him.

But beneath the smile, turbulent emotions simmer on the verge of boiling over. My palms slick with nervous perspiration, forcing me to rub them against my skirt. It's been less than a week since we saw each other, but it feels like a lifetime. I miss him. My body aches for him. Our chemistry is hard at work, electrifying the air between us.

"You left my mother speechless, and I have to say it's the first time that's happened. I don't think anyone's ever had the balls to storm out on her. You're fearless, and damn, I've missed you." He spreads out his arms, urging me into his embrace. "Don't make me beg, Quinn. You belong right here." He thumps on his chest and holds his arms outstretched.

My brother's protective shield, however, remains firmly in place. They have questions about Hawke and what he wants with their baby sister.

THIRTY-THREE

Hawke

QUINN DIDN'T LIE ABOUT HER BROTHERS. THEY SHIELD AND PROTECT her from what they see as a threat. Which I am. I have every intention of taking her and making her mine. They know I've had my hands on their baby sister, and it pisses them off. That hatred simmering in their eyes is real.

When they don't budge, I weigh my options. Pushing could lead to a more physical confrontation. The odds are stacked against me, but I don't run from a challenge.

With Quinn hovering behind the largest of her brothers, I take a step forward. Not back. There's no running from this. No backing down. A quick flick with my fingers, and my jacket button comes undone. I take it off, fold it in half, and drape it over the SUV. Slowly, with my eyes on Quinn the entire time, I unfasten my cuffs and methodically roll up my sleeves. I'm making a statement, not afraid of this confrontation turning physical.

"You can stand aside, or not. Either way, I'm taking Quinn." For the first time, I acknowledge Gideon. "Your sister belongs to me now." And I'm stepping up to the plate.

Gideon's chest puffs out, then he reaches for Quinn. He pushes her solidly behind him, and fixes me with a glare. "I'd like to see you try." He cocks his head toward his brothers, who form a Hayes brothers' protective wall.

I tilt my head side to side, loosening up.

"Quinn, don't make me repeat myself." I will have her by my side, then we're going to have a nice long talk. The moment she peeks around her brother's shoulder, I beam in victory, but there goes Gideon again.

Shifting and blocking my view.

Keeping her from me.

Not keen on a fight with her brothers, I will if it comes down to it. I firm my stance, refusing to back down. My attention latches onto Quinn.

"What's it going to be, Miss Hayes? You want a brawl or…?" I spread my arms out again. Not as wide, but certainly conveying my intentions.

She peeks out from behind her eldest brother.

"Why didn't you tell me you're the CEO of SVC Inc.? What were you trying to prove?" Accusation hangs heavy in her voice.

"Technically, I'm the CEO of Sterling Enterprises. I thought you knew the whole time. You wouldn't be the first woman who used me to get what she wanted." The corner of my mouth ticks up, and I promptly erase that flicker of amusement.

"I had no idea, but you did. You knew the whole time."

"I did."

"I never used you, Hawke. What we had…"

"Have." I correct her and take another step toward the Hayes Brother Blockade. I'm not kidding about taking her. It's only been a few days, but it feels like an eternity to me. I've had a lot of time to think things through.

"Have?" She sounds confused. "We don't have anything anymore."

This conversation wanders into dangerous territory. Time to reel her back in. Back to me.

"Imagine my surprise when I realized you didn't know who I was, that you weren't using me to get what you wanted. What we *have* is real, and you're not going to walk away from me again. Now, come out from behind your brothers where we can talk like civilized humans." Not sure how wise it is to issue commands in front of her brothers; I'm taking a risk, but I know how she responds to me when I do. I want her to remember what it was like in my bed. The flush in her cheeks tells me she does.

"Was any of it real?" Her whisper is so low, I have to lean forward to hear her. "Were you stringing me along because you thought I was using you?"

"Is that really the question you want to ask right now?" We need to get to that but now's not the time. "Did it feel like I was using you? And need I remind you that you walked out on me?"

"Answer her!" Gideon practically shouts, but I ignore him.

"I'll answer all *her* questions—" I pointedly ignore Gideon, "but not while you hide behind your brothers."

"What do we have to talk about?" She glances back to the elevator, and I know what she's thinking. SVC Inc. isn't investing in her company. Unless she finds the capital she needs, her dream will never get off the ground. Fortunately, I have a solution.

"Us for starters."

"There's no us."

"You ran before we could work that out. I'm here to rectify that error. As for the other bit, I have some thoughts about MindScapeVR." I lift my chin toward her brothers. "Are you really investing five million into her company?"

"We are." Gideon's reply is not only nearly instantaneous but filled with pride.

"I think that's wise. I have a question about douchebag Scott."

No mistaking Gideon's snicker. He may turn into my biggest ally if I play things right.

"You left Euphoria because of some of the things I said when we first met. Things that are no longer true. I'm chasing you, something I've never done for any woman before. That alone shows you the truth of what we have. As for MindScapeVR, there are a few things I need to know. Specifically, who owns the IP? Your project wasn't deselected based on the merits of the creative content, but rather the business proposal attached to it. We can build something incredible together, but I need to know who owns the IP."

"We?" Her emerald gaze shimmers with a veil of unshed tears.

"Me and you. Your brothers see how it can be applied to their business. I have a few ideas myself, and I bring the one thing you're lacking."

"What's that?"

"A solid business plan, along with strategic and operational expertise. You've barely scraped the surface. It's time to dream big."

"You speak as if it's easy."

"Are you in a position to walk away from MindScapeVR? Do you own the intellectual property rights or does douchebag?"

"I do."

"Good." I take a step forward. Then another. Her brothers crowd closer. "Call off the hounds, Quinn. You know what comes next." I could push harder, but I risk losing her forever if I do. Her pride will have her digging in her heels. I'm hoping she feels the air crackling between us because I damn sure feel it. I won't say it out loud, not in front of her brothers, but this ends only one way. Me buried deep within her as she cries out my name.

I take in a deep breath and hold it, counting to five. When I reach five, I'll walk away.

My count barely passes three when she squeezes between her brothers and slips free. They don't move, continuing to support her from behind.

"What do you mean by me and you? Your mother made it very clear we weren't getting a penny of SVC Inc. venture capital."

"And you won't, but that's on Scott's head. Mother wants to buy you out and have you sell the idea to us. She was going to offer five million for the IP rights."

"Five million?" Quinn sways on her feet. Her brother, Gideon, reaches out to support her.

As much as they stand between me and my girl, I respect his protectiveness toward his sister. He's really going to hate me when I tell him to step aside.

Quinn is mine.

"Quinney." Gideon places his arm around her shoulders. "I'm so sorry. You just lost…"

"Quinn lost nothing." I interrupt him. "It was a shit deal. Your idea is worth tens of millions, probably ten times more than that." I never considered the applications Gideon mentioned in other industries. This could very well become a billion-dollar idea. I want to give her the chance to change the world.

Her eyes widen with my comment. It's a part of the meeting we never got to because the whole thing derailed before it ever began. But there's hope.

"I'll put the rest up myself. There may be a few others who want to get in on the ground floor."

My buddies, Jack and Steve, will want to invest. Between the three of us, we can come up with the entire ten million. To be honest, I'd rather have full control, but I'm not in a position to fund her dreams entirely by myself. As for her brothers, and the investment of Hayes Construction, I have a few concerns.

"You want to invest in me?" She does the worst possible thing she can do and nibbles on her bottom lip. I suppress a groan with great difficulty.

"Your idea has the potential to become what they often refer to as a singularity event. There're a lot of VR applications out there, but none with the adaptive learning you bring to the table. I don't understand all of it, but I see enough of what your brothers saw to know there are wide-reaching implications. Honestly, you were ripped off with that first app you sold. I don't want that to happen again. I want to invest in our future."

I realize that's exactly what I want.

"Our future?"

"If you want me to beg, I'll beg, but you'll pay for that later." I don't have to tell her how I'll make her pay. The way her eyes widen tell me she knows exactly what I mean, and she's doing that lip-biting thing again. I shift my attention to her brothers. They don't scare me. "The four of you are done here." I gesture toward the car. "Quinn and I have something to discuss." Something that doesn't involve clothes.

Gideon doesn't look like he's ready to surrender his sister into a stranger's arms, but I don't worry about him. Quinn edges around her brothers. Her gaze flicks from me back to them.

"Um, guys…" She stares at the ground. "I'm good."

"You sure?" Gideon looks at Quinn.

"Yeah." She ducks her head. "I am."

"If you hurt her…" Gideon shifts his attention to me.

"I won't."

"You better not." He gives a jerk of his chin to her brothers. "What do I tell Mother and Daddy? I take it you won't be home for dinner."

"She won't be home for breakfast either." I can't help it, but Gideon needs to understand I mean what I said. Quinn is mine. Her cheeks turn bright pink. I love how she refuses to look her brothers in the eye. She knows I plan to fuck her, and that her brothers probably figured that part out already.

Nothing more is said. Each of her brothers gives her a hug as I step away from their vehicle and grab my suit jacket. Four doors open, and four doors shut. I wait patiently for the engine to crank over. As they drive off, Gideon gestures, telling me he'll be watching me.

As soon as they turn the corner, I close the distance before Quinn can move. My arms fold around her delicate shoulders and I pull her to me. Electricity rushes along my nerves with the same crackling charge as the first time we touched. I want to kiss her, but there's no way I'll be able to stop with a kiss.

"God, I've missed you. I need you. I've missed your touch." I gently bite down on her earlobe. "Let's get out of here." Preferably someplace private where we can divest ourselves of our clothes.

"Is it true?" She tilts her head to look at me. "Everything you said?"

"It is. How entangled are you with Scott? We can set a legal team on it."

"I'm fairly certain the IP remains mine, but we should be certain."

We.

I like the sound of that.

"I need to be inside of you, Miss Hayes. I've missed you terribly." The need to reconnect with her in the most intimate of ways pounds in my veins. I'm aching and hard for her, desperate to feel her wet heat wrap around my cock.

"I've missed you too, and I'm sorry."

"For what?"

"For leaving, I guess. For not telling you. For not explaining why." She tilts her head back. Tears shimmer in her eyes. "I can't do this if it's just a fling. I'm not wired that way. If that's all I am to you, now's the time to stand aside. I'm a bonder. I won't survive the heartbreak when you walk away."

"All I've thought about is you. At first, I wanted to strangle you. I wanted to get back at you for walking out on me. I've never felt that before, and it's not because you're the only woman who's ever walked out on me. I've gone crazy these past few days, and I finally figured out why."

"Why?"

"Because you make me feel things I've never felt before. I can't promise forever, but I want to try. As for the way you left me, we can discuss an appropriate punishment later, preferably with a whole lot less clothing between us." Her eyes widen, and her breath hitches. The pulse in her neck jumps. I give a low chuckle and press the tip of my finger on her pert nose. "That excites you, doesn't it?" I think it's more than that, but first things first.

She nibbles at her lower lip and loops her arms around my neck. Rising up on tiptoe, she presses a featherlight kiss against my lips. A low groan escapes me as I yank her hot body against mine. She draws back, breaking our connection, and stares up at me.

"If you don't fuck me right now, Hawke Sterling, I'm going to scream."

"Oh, I definitely plan on making you scream." I drag her to the executive elevator and swipe my card key. The moment the doors open, I shove her inside and press her against the wall. I claim her mouth, hungry, needful, and determined. The moment the elevator starts to rise, I hit the emergency override, and we come to a bone-jarring stop.

She looks up at me, shocked, then her attention drifts to the controls where my palm rests over the emergency stop. She scans the ceiling, and I give a low snicker as I unbuckle my belt and slide it out of the belt loops.

"No security cameras in here, luv. Now, give me your hands." She does as I command. Her breathing quickens as I wrap my belt around her wrists, cinching it down tight. I spin her around, facing away from me, and place her hands high over her head. "Your punishment is that I'm going to take from you, and you can't touch me. At least with your hands. You can use your mouth to make it up to me later." I grip her wrists, emphasizing my point. "Don't you dare move those hands."

"Or what?"

"If you want to test me, go ahead. You're a smart girl. I'm sure you can figure it out, but right now, I'm taking what's mine." I slide my palm over her ass and give a light swat. We'll get to the heavier stuff later. I free my cock and wrap a hand around my shaft. A low moan slips from my lips.

"This is going to be fast and ugly, Quinn. I need to…"

She twists her neck. Her gaze is hooded with desire.

"I'm yours, Hawke, do with me as you please."

"Fuck, Quinn, do you really mean that?"

"Any way you need me." She licks her lips. "Just please, don't make me wait. I need to feel you inside of me."

I slide her skirt up and yank her panties to the side. I finger her for a moment, checking to see if she's wet. Quinn's more than ready. She's fucking dripping. No need to waste another second. I plunge into her, sinking all the way in. A sigh escapes her, and a low groan rumbles out of my chest as her pussy wraps all around me.

"I don't know if I can be gentle." I don't want to hurt her. More importantly, I want this to be good for her.

"I like when you're rough." Her husky words make my cock jerk.

That's all she needs to say.

My hips move, and I fuck my girl like I'm a goddamn animal until she screams my name and her pussy convulses around my cock. I follow her over the edge, too fucking eager to make this last. I don't come with Quinn Hayes. No, it's far more than that. She makes me fucking *hurtle* over the edge.

She likes hard, rough fucking. Which is perfectly fine by me.

As for whether she believes me, I didn't lie when I said she was mine.

THIRTY-FOUR

Quinn

HAWKE PULLS OUT WHILE MY ENTIRE BODY STILL QUAKES. HARD AND rough? *Yes, please.* Any day. Any time, as long as it's him. He smacks my ass, hard, lifting me up on my toes. I give a screech as his teeth graze my earlobe.

"That's for walking out on me." He reaches back, and his hand cracks down on my ass again. "And that's because you make me hard. I'm constantly hard for you." He soothes the sting in my ass cheek as I give a low moan. "You like that?"

I give a barely perceptible nod.

"You like when I'm rough, or when I smack your ass?"

I close my eyes and hold back a whimper. My skirt is hiked up, revealing my bare ass. He rubs light circles around the burning sting. My answer comes in the form of shoving my ass out where I rub it against the bulge of his spent cock.

"Answer me." His sharp command pulls a whimper from my throat.

"I like everything you do."

"Duly noted. And, Quinn?"

"Yes?" Breathy and excited, I need more. The quick orgasm, while powerful, isn't enough.

"I'm going to fuck you all the way into the new year. We've got less than eight hours left, and when we get to the other side, do you know what happens?"

"No." I squirm as his palm glides against my ass.

"You start the new year as mine." The low growl in his throat makes my pussy throb. The way he says *mine* makes me believe he means it. "How does that make you feel, knowing you're mine?"

"Hot."

Desperately hot.

He jerks me back against him, and his teeth scrape along the skin of my neck.

"There are things we need to discuss, but they'll wait for the new year." He reaches between my legs and slips his fingers under the cotton edge of my panties. He dips his fingertips between my damp folds, still sensitive from the rough fuck moments ago. Hawke toys lightly until my breath comes in short gasps and takes his time driving me crazy.

He presses with the pads of his fingers, one by one, until he finds the perfect spot to drive me wild. Once there, his fingers move in a punishing rhythm that quickly makes my legs shake and drives all thought out of my mind. Hawke definitely knows how to play my body.

I groan and press my face against the wall. My hands, still tied by his belt, push against the wall as I arch back, needing more stimulation before I go out of my ever-loving mind.

"Keep your hands where they are, luv. Drop them and all this stops." His command weakens my knees, and it's all I can do to remain upright. Fortunately, the brace of his body behind me lends some support. Meanwhile, his fingers continue to work my clit with expert precision as he rubs in slow, delicious circles.

I've missed his sensuous touch.

"Goddammit, you're shaking." His reverent words are full of awe. "You're shaking for me, aren't you, luv?" His mouth hovers near my ear, and the heat of his breath drives me insane. "It's been a long few days without this pussy to keep me occupied."

His words do something inside of me. I melt for him as he gives me exactly what I need. His fingers on my clit continue their maddening rhythm. The pad of his thumb presses against the sensitive tissue. I'm almost there.

"I'm going to have you in every way. When I say you're mine, you need to know what that means." His fingers slide down and tickle my soaking-wet entrance. "But not now." A growl emanates from his throat, low and needy.

"Ummmm." The things he's doing with his fingers drive the ability to speak right out of my head. I'm reduced to my most base desires. Complete sentences are beyond me. Simple words are too difficult to speak.

He leans against me, letting me feel he's long and engorged again. He's ready for me. Two fingers slip inside me and slowly glide in and out while his other hand moves faster and harder over my clit.

A low, needy moan escapes me.

He takes me right to the edge, then pulls away, denying my release. Just by the slightest adjustment of the cadence of his fingers, I'm totally at his mercy. Slower. Faster. Then he slows everything down again as I cry out in frustration. So fucking close.

He knows this. He's intentionally punishing me.

"Hawke…" I whimper because, while I'll do whatever he says, he's got me going and I need to come. "Please fuck me, or let me come." I want his dick. I need to feel his strength and power as he takes me. As he lays claim to me like he promises.

There's a low chuckle behind my ear. "I'm going to leave you needy and wanting, make you suffer like I've suffered these past few days. I'm going to deny your release." The hot, wet tip of his tongue traces along the edge of my ear. "As punishment." He dips his head forward and lets out a sigh. "Fuck, Quinn, you have no idea what you do to me."

With those words, he removes his fingers—all of them—and leaves me gasping at the aching emptiness he leaves behind. I suck in a breath as he reaches for my wrists and undoes the belt securing them in place.

Before I know what's happening, he smooths my skirt back down over my hips and spins me around. I blink and gape. When I try to speak, he places his finger on my lower lip.

"For making me ache for you."

"Hawke…"

He gives a shake of his head. "This is me controlling what happens between us. If you have a problem with that, I'll drop it. We'll fuck like rabbits. I'll give you the orgasms you desperately want. Otherwise…" He gives me a hard stare, and I sense this is a critical moment. "You hand over control. You give me the authority to see to our mutual pleasure, and I'll fulfill your wildest fantasies."

A rush of pleasure flows through me. He's not kidding around. I don't know why I find that sexy as hell, but I do. I really do.

"What's it going to be, Miss Quinn Hayes? You want to take that orgasm now? Or wait until I decide to give it to you?"

He's not backing down, forcing me to choose. I can have all the sex I want, or I can put my faith in him and allow him to lead us as he chooses.

"I need an answer." Leaning forward, he presses his forehead against mine.

"I hate you a little bit right now." I adjust my skirt and smooth out the wrinkles. I'm hotter now than when he had his hands on me. My insides clench and throb as he waits. "But okay." I can't believe I'm agreeing to this, but the way my pussy throbs with the thought of him dominating me makes me want to take a chance.

"Okay?"

I give a nod.

"To which part?"

Dammit, he's going to make me say it.

"I'll wait." I close my eyes and seal my fate.

"It'll be worth it, Quinn. Trust me, when I finally give you that orgasm, you'll know you made the right choice." His low, throaty chuckle will be my undoing. "As for right now, I have business to conclude upstairs."

I stare at his cock, which is no longer spent, but heavy again with his arousal. When I lick my lips, a hiss escapes him. Our little conversation about control affects him as much as it affects me.

The idea of being in charge is intoxicating. Maybe I can work this to my advantage. "If you fuck me, it'll relieve some of that tension."

"Oh, didn't I mention?"

"Mention what?"

"I'm not denying myself any orgasms. That's part of the punishment." He points to the floor. "On your knees and open that pretty mouth of yours."

I stare at him, knowing if I do this, I accept the shifting of power between us, but the thing is—his dominance is sexy as hell. I'll forgo one orgasm because I know he's capable of delivering on his promise. Hawke Sterling may control what happens next, but he's a generous lover and likes making me come. I go to my knees, accepting his terms.

"You're fucking beautiful like this. Do you know what it does to me? Your eyes all big and wide. Your lips waiting to take my cock." Desire drips from his lips. He grabs his cock, fisting it with a low moan. "Open your mouth."

I do as I'm told, and he feeds me his cock one slow inch at a time. I savor the taste of him, the feel as he fills my mouth. He pulls out, then slowly slides back in with a shuddering breath.

"Look at me while you suck my cock. Watch what you do to me."

I moan, sucking him as he pushes further inside. In and out, he takes his time, slowly fucking my mouth. I can't get enough of the expressions on his face as his desire builds and he slowly loses control. He reaches down and cups my cheek.

"I'm getting close." His body clenches. "Fuck, I'm going to lose it."

I still, obsessed over watching him take his pleasure. There's something insanely riveting about the raw desire etched in his chiseled face. He wants me to watch him come undone, and I do exactly that.

I watch the hitch in his breathing. The way he draws his lower lip in as his pleasure builds. I see the muscles of his abdomen tighten, then ripple as the first waves of his orgasm hit him. I watch him tremble as he comes. The whole time, his golden eyes lock onto mine.

"You're fucking incredible." He pulls me up and holds me tight. He takes my jaw and kisses me, long and languid, reverent even. No words are spoken for the longest time.

Desire coils in my belly, a pang of pleasure so strong that I moan.

"Hawke, are you really going to make me wait?"

"Absolutely." His grin is panty-melting hot, and I realize he's serious about being in control.

"And while you're concluding your business for the day, what am I supposed to do?"

"Ache for me." He presses a button on the control panel, and we're in motion again. As we climb the floors, he puts himself back together, even sliding the belt back through the loops of his pants. He gives another one of his smirks and leans down to whisper in my ear. "One more thing, no touching what's mine." He gives a squeeze of my ass before ushering me out of the elevator.

With his hand on the small of my back, he escorts me through a maze of hallways until finally winding up at a large corner office. A receptionist sits at a desk outside.

"Jenny, Miss Hayes will wait for me in my office. Please see to it if she needs anything."

"Of course, Mr. Sterling." Jenny's focus shifts to me. In one look, she takes in everything and understands what I am. "If you need anything, Miss Hayes, please let me know."

Hawke opens the door to a jaw-dropping gorgeous corner office and gives a grand flourish. "Please, make yourself comfortable."

The low, needy ache between my legs is not letting up, and I bite my lower lip with frustration.

"How long will you be gone?"

"We finish at four thirty. After that, I'll be back. We'll fool around a bit..." His eyes spark with mischief. "Then it's dinner. More fooling around. Drinks. More..."

I laugh. "I get it. More fooling around."

"At least once an hour until we ring in the new year."

"Once an hour?" I cross my arms and give him a look. "Yet you're leaving me alone for two hours. What am I to do?"

He shows me how to work the large-screen TV and hooks me into his streaming channels.

"I expect you to wait for me. I promise; it'll be worth it."

I don't doubt him at all. With a kiss, he excuses himself and promises to be back soon. I settle into one of the plush couches, determined to make the time pass quickly, and pull up a book to read on my phone.

An hour passes, and I get up to stretch, moving to look out over the city through the floor-to-ceiling plate glass windows. The view is spectacular. I rub at my arms and close my eyes. Tonight will bring the end to a tumultuous year. MindScapeVR might finally see itself launched into the world. With my brothers' backing and Hawke funding the rest, I can't believe there may actually be a light at the end of the tunnel. As for Hawke, I sense a change in him. I'm hopeful we have a future together, something which promises to be more permanent. It's too early to head down that path, but he definitely is interested in getting to know me better.

The door creaks behind me, and I twirl with a smile on my face. If Hawke's back…

His mother stands in the doorway; her hawkish gaze rakes me from head to toe.

"I heard you returned." She sounds less than enthused. "You're not his usual type. Word of advice, don't get too used to being around. My son tends to be a little flighty when it comes to women. Enjoy it while it lasts, darling, eventually he'll tire of you."

"I think he'll be the judge of that." The woman terrifies me. There's something wrong with her, like she's rotten all the way to her core.

"Right. He most definitely will. You've known him for a handful of days, whereas I've known him his entire life. We'll see which one of us is right in the end."

I glance over her shoulder, hoping Hawke will be back soon. She holds a folder in her hands and taps it against her thigh.

"My son is not for you." She says it as if it's a royal decree, like her word matters. "Here." She thrusts the manila folder at me.

"What's that?"

"An offer. One you'll be foolish to refuse."

"I think I'll pass." There's something about this woman I don't trust.

"Five million is a lot to turn your back on."

This is the offer Hawke mentioned. My back bristles with indignation.

"I'm sorry, but I'm not interested."

Her eyes narrow. "I see he's told you. What exactly do you think you're going to do? Scrounge up what you need on your own?"

"I believe in my idea and my company." I don't tell her that Hawke promised to put up what we need, or that he's agreed to help our launch. I sense this isn't something he wants shared.

"Well, don't think for a minute you'll get your hands on Sterling money, or my son."

"That's really none of your concern."

"As he's my son, it's very much my concern, not that it'll matter after tonight."

"And what does that mean?"

"Hasn't he told you?" She cocks her head, and a predatory gleam shines in her eyes. "I suppose not. Whatever it is you think you have with him, he's only stringing you along. My son is announcing his engagement tonight. I wonder if he told you that while you were on your knees."

She points to the large-screen television. No, she's not pointing. There's a remote in her hand. "There's nothing that happens in this building I don't know about." It's a video of Hawke and me in the elevator, of me going to my knees. I watch in horror as Hawke stares down at me while I take him in my mouth. "I have a feeling that could be quite damaging for a company launch."

"Why do you hate him so much?"

"Hate is a vulgar word." She points to the recording. "Leave, and this recording will be erased. Stay and…"

"Mother!" Hawke's shout fills the room. He gives one look at the video then turns to his mother. His eyes widen with fury. The expression on his face is murderous, and I shrink back from it. Only his anger is not directed at me.

"Miss Hayes and I were just having a conversation." She dismisses him.

"This doesn't look like a conversation."

"I'm simply explaining a few things, like your engagement announcement. Miss Hayes, remove yourself from my building and stay away from my son."

"I'll do no such thing." I roll my shoulders back. It's the hardest thing I've had to do in a very long time, but I won't let this woman talk down to me.

"Oh, I think you will." Her thin lips spread into a serene smile. She pulls out her phone and lifts it to her ear. "Sissy?"

Hawke lunges for the phone and rips it out of his mother's hand.

"Cherise? Cherise, where are you?" He clutches desperately at the phone while a triumphant expression fills his mother's face. He stares at the phone, and it's clear no one's on the other end.

"I wonder what Miss Hayes will think when she realizes her true worth." His mother crooks her fingers demanding Hawke return her phone. He slaps it into her palm with a murderous expression.

"Mother, you're despicable."

"Hawke, what's going on?" A bad feeling stirs in my gut.

"My terms," she says with a sneer. "Cut ties with this blue-blooded hussy, and Cherise is yours. Refuse me and—well, I don't need to specify what will happen, do I?"

The color drains from his face, defeat pulls at his expression, and his shoulders slump. Hawke runs his fingers through his hair, and then he turns around, placing his back to me.

"I'm sorry, Quinn. I'm so sorry. You need to leave."

The victorious gleam in his mother's eyes makes me swallow what I want to say. Whoever Cherise is, Hawke chooses her over me. I suppose I really am just an easy fuck, something to pass the time.

I don't stick around. If he's not going to fight for me, then why should I fight for him? I grab my purse and leave without saying goodbye. Outside his office, two burly security guards fall in step behind me. They follow me to the elevators, push the down button, then crowd inside the elevator with me when it arrives. One of them jabs the button for the lobby, and we descend in complete silence. They walk me to the door and hold it open as I exit the building.

I hold it in for the time it takes me to walk one city block. By then, my brothers have turned around. They pick me up and say nothing as I squeeze in between Brett and Ian in the back seat. No words are spoken as they bracket me inside the back booth at Dale's Ice-cream Parlor. We devour the family-sized banana split in silence.

My brothers bolster me through it all. Instead of taking me to our parents, they drop me off with Steven at his house. The moment I cross over the threshold, the tears fall.

It takes two weeks for them to stop.

THIRTY-FIVE

Hawke

I NEVER REALLY UNDERSTOOD TRUE HATRED UNTIL THE MOMENT Mother forces me to choose between the only two women I've ever loved. My plans for Cherise will take time, time I don't have. Not when Mother forces me to make an impossible choice on the spot.

Not two hours earlier, I promised Quinn's brothers I would never hurt her. Yet here I am, breaking Quinn's heart. She didn't even say goodbye.

Now, she's gone.

"Good riddance." Mother wipes her hands as if she's brushing Quinn out of my life for good.

"Why?" I run a hand through my hair, stunned by what happened. "You didn't need to run her off. I love her."

"That's what I was afraid of."

"You want me to marry." I point at the door, knowing I should never reveal vulnerability to my mother. My happiness is her greatest weapon, and she's an expert at taking it away. "That's the woman I want to marry." Hell, I can't believe those words came out of my mouth, but they have the weight of truth to them. Whatever this thing is with Quinn, my future is nothing without her in it.

"That little blue-collar hussy is not fit to be a Sterling." She gives a dismissive snort. "You've known her for all of what? A few days? Be thankful I allowed you the dalliance at all. Now, as for marriage, it's been settled."

"Settled?" The floor shifts under my feet. I feel like I need to reach out to steady myself, but I refuse to show Mother she's got my undivided attention. "What the fuck does *settled* mean?"

"I finalized everything yesterday."

"Finalized?" It's like I'm in an alternate dimension where my life is not mine to control. She's a master manipulator, but she's never done something like this. I want to throttle her bony throat. If I get too close, I will. The anger seething inside of me is going to boil over any minute. And each minute takes Quinn farther away.

I need to be going after her, explaining what's going on, not standing here being lectured by a monster. Mother's using Cherise to blackmail me into doing what she wants.

"How can you finalize anything without my input?" I stare at her, while barely holding my temper. My fingers curl, movement she catches. Her gaze cuts to my fists and she shakes her head.

"Not to be crass, but men tend to think with their dicks instead of their heads. Or let anger rule their actions. I've arranged for you to marry Candace Yarbrough—"

"No." Heat fills my face. "I will not marry that conniving bitch. She's been trying to get her hooks into me since high school."

Candace was my first mistake. We dated in high school. As loose as they come, she fucked anyone with a sizable bank account who offered the slightest chance for her to climb the social ladder. She set her ambitious sights on me, and I fell for it, hook, line, and sinker. She was the first to show me the lengths a woman would go to if it meant landing me as her prize.

Cue prom night and the pregnancy scare which followed. Candace tried to rush an engagement before the baby started showing. I dug in my heels and demanded proof the kid was mine. Turns out, there was no kid, just a crazy bitch who nearly cost me everything. Needless to say, Mother was not pleased with the whole situation.

As for my mistake, it wasn't taking Candace to prom. Nor was it the whole fake-baby thing which followed. Candace is good in bed, kinky as fuck, and the perfect thing to scratch an itch whenever I felt the need. My mistake is that I continued to fuck Candace as it suits me, and she suits—suited—me well for many years. Several times each year, generally when I found myself between entanglements with other women, I called her up and we fucked each other senseless.

That's my biggest mistake.

"Why Candace? Out of your eligible socialites, why her?"

"Why not? The Yarbrough's are a respectable family. You and Candace seem to get together with some frequency." Her sneer tells me she knows exactly what Candace and I do when we're together. "Besides, Tom Yarbrough is offering a sizable donation to my favorite charity."

"He's paying to have me take his daughter off his hands?"

"Don't be crass."

"Candace and I get together to fuck, Mother. She fucks a lot of men. I mean as little to her as she does to me. I have no doubt her father is willing to pay to unload his daughter. I'm more than a little surprised you'd attach her to the Sterling name."

"Times are much more forgiving than when I was young. You're a playboy, always with some nameless woman hanging from your arm—filling your bed_yet it doesn't stain your reputation. She's a young woman not afraid to embrace her sexuality. You've both been playing the field, but it's time to settle down."

"So, you've already thought about the lies we'll tell?" I can't believe my mother's gall.

"Candace is eager to start a family. Once word of my illness gets out, people will understand how eager you are to provide me a grandson before I die. It's a good match."

It's a total shit show. The lump in my throat only grows heavier. I know my mother. I know what she's capable of, but I'm not ready to give in to her demands.

"She's eager to get her hands on our money. That alone makes her ineligible."

Maybe if I can buy some time, I'll have a chance to fix things with Quinn to the point where she might consider rushing into marriage with me. The only problem is Quinn is a thinker. She doesn't rush into anything. Not like me. When I know, I know. My gut never steers me wrong, and it's telling me Quinn is the woman I'm meant to spend my life with.

"There will be a prenup, of course. It's been decided and signed. Once she provides a male heir—"

"I don't even want to know what you've put into the provisions of the prenup." Knowing Mother, there are clauses in there which specify minimum copulation frequencies. "When did you have time to barter away your son's happiness? Seems like you should be the one up on stage proposing instead of me. Hell, you don't need me there at all."

Not to mention I need to go after Quinn and explain what happened.

"There are certain things *you're* needed for, and you'll perform your duties as required. Those are specified in the prenup." And that confirms exactly what I suspected. Marital coital frequency is written in like a line number to ensure this grandson she won't live to see.

"Like a thoroughbred stud?"

"If that's how you want to see it. At least we know it won't be a hardship. Candace assures me you're an excellent lover."

"You discussed my sex life with her? Is there any part of my life which is my own?"

"Of course, you can always refuse, but doing that has certain repercussions."

And now we get down to the heart of the matter.

"Where's Cherise?"

"Safe and out of your reach until I'm satisfied you're holding up your end of the arrangement."

"You'll be dead before any kid is born. That's not good enough. And how will you know if I am? Holding up my end as it were?"

I hate using her illness as a weapon, but her last act in this world is to consign me to a loveless marriage with a woman I barely tolerate. Mother doesn't even flinch. Her cold eyes stare at me, unblinking, and hard as stone.

"Part of the prenup are certain status updates."

"Really? I'm to report when I've fucked my wife?"

"I wouldn't consider burdening you with that. Her reports will, of course, include information about ovulation and likelihood of conception."

"You're out of your ever-loving mind."

After Quinn, the idea of touching any other woman is enough to make me sick. My dick shrivels thinking about having to touch Candace Yarbrough.

"I'm thorough. And you can dislike it as much as you want, but you forced this on yourself. If you'd only done as I asked…"

"Your demands are insane. You wanted me to comb through your list of eligible bachelorettes and pick one like a goddamn Christmas present. The thing is, we don't do Christmas."

"That doesn't change anything. And since I knew you would react like a child, I've made sure you will follow through."

"Where's Cherise?"

"Sissy is in good hands. I gave you the option to do as you're told. You ran off to Euphoria and hooked up with a nameless nobody instead of choosing your wife. Now, I've settled things. You will marry Candace."

"I don't love her. How about that?"

"And yet, the two of you are compatible. You make a good match. People will accept it."

"They'll accept it because Candace runs at the mouth."

This is where my mistake really shines. The constant on again-off again hookups gives the illusion there's more going on between me and Candace than there is. Candace, being a gold-digging bitch, fans those rumors into something more than they are. She tells anyone who'll listen how progressive she is, that we've *agreed* to see other people, and that she's *letting* me sow my wild oats until I'm ready to settle down.

With her.

As my wife.

"Compatible?" My fists clench. "We fuck, Mother." She twitches at the vulgar word. "That's as far as any compatibility goes. I'm not marrying her, and that's final."

As soon as I can get out of this room, I'm going to find Quinn. Not sure where her thoughts are about the two of us, I'm hoping I can fix this mess and convince her Mother is the crazy one, not me.

Quinn will forgive me. At least, once I explain what's happening.

I hope.

"Where's Cherise?" I know how to protect Cherise from Mother, but it's going to take time, money, and lawyers.

"Cherise is comfortable and safe." Her lips press into a hard line, telling me that's all she'll say.

"I swear to God, if you do anything to hurt her…" I leave unsaid what I'll do. Cherise is my one fatal weakness. I'll do anything to keep her safe and make her happy. It's why Mother uses Cherise to bend me to her will.

"I'm dying, Hawke. No need to spout off vulgar threats about killing me. This is what's going to happen." Her eyes sharpen and glitter like knives. "Tonight, you'll attend the New Year's Gala with Candace on your arm. Rumors are already circulating about a big announcement. Right before midnight, you'll take the stage, find something witty to say, and propose."

"Not going to happen. There's no way you can make me do this."

"You'll not only do it, but you'll tell everyone how excited you are. So much so, that you can't wait for a proper engagement. Instead of a June wedding, you'll marry on the first day of Spring. A nice March wedding will kick off the social season. You'll perform your duties, consummate the marriage, and…"

"You're insane."

"You'll never see Sissy again if you don't. Her guardianship will not pass to you until you fulfill the requirements of your father's will. Bear a son for the Sterling name and Cherise will be returned to you. Fail to do so, and she'll be gone to you forever."

"You can't do that. I'll find her, and—"

"You won't find her." A sublime smile creeps across her face. "As for Miss Hayes, don't contact her again. You're an engaged man. If you do, you'll never see your sister again."

"What do you have against her?"

"Other than the complete lack of breeding, social status, and money? Everything." Mother gives an unladylike snort. "She's beneath you. When I'm gone, you're the face of Sterling Enterprises and everything that comes with it. Fail to produce an heir and Sterling Enterprises gets sold off piece by piece. You have three years."

Fucking bitch.

I've never hated being a Sterling more than I do in this moment, but until I can sort a few things out, I'm bound to play along. I do it for Cherise.

As for Quinn, I pray she'll forgive me.

That night, I ring in the new year with Candace Yarbrough hanging from my arm and a five-carat ring sparkling on her finger. Mother makes the announcement, not me. All I do is play along like the dutiful son. I give Candace an uninspired kiss under a moldy spray of mistletoe and swallow the bile rising in my throat. Candace gives me a strange look, but the excitement of landing the heir to the Sterling fortune makes up for my lackluster performance.

Mother's terms for giving Cherise back to me include locking me in this loveless marriage. The wedding will be in three short months. I did get Mother to relent on one small thing. After the vows, Cherise will be returned to me.

There's something about hatred. It sparks creativity and ingenuity. Although it kills me, I make no effort to contact Quinn. Until Cherise is taken care of, I won't tempt fate.

The engagement makes international news as one of the world's most eligible bachelors is taken off the market. Meanwhile, I fulfill a promise and unravel the chains my mother binds me in, looking for the loophole which will set me free.

THIRTY-SIX

Quinn

Six more weeks pass, and I lick my wounds. News of Hawke Sterling's engagement to Candace Yarbrough splashed all across the news on New Year's Day. I keep kicking myself for being such a fool, and for believing a word out of his mouth. I tried to call him once, only to find his number blocked.

I get the message and try to move on with my life.

As for MindScapeVR, it's the only thing that gets me out of bed every day. I need to come up with five million in venture capital if I'm going to make my dream come true.

Tom and I pour over a stack of potential investors while I fight off a wave of nausea. My stomach's been more sensitive lately. As for now, something I ate doesn't agree with me. I blame it on the lox and cream cheese bagel I ate on my way to the office. My stomach is staging a full-on revolt. Wave after wave of nausea slams into me, nothing too terrible to make me puke, but it's enough to stop me in my tracks.

"You sure you want to look at these?" Tom arches a brow. "You look a little green."

"It's nothing." I swallow down the queasiness. "I tried out the new bagel place down the street and got bad lox."

"Bad lox?" He gives a goofy grin. "Bad lox for you!"

I ignore his silly pun.

"Bad luck for them. Do you think I should call and let them know?" The wave of nausea passes. I hope it stays away this time.

"You should. Maybe other customers got sick too. Not good for opening day." He shuffles through the stack of mail, his keen eyes sweeping the addresses for what we hope will be new investors. "These came today." He adds three new envelopes to the stack in front of me.

"Okay, once we're done with this." I pick up one of the new letters off the stack. "That's odd."

"What?"

"No stamp." I lift the envelope and show him the face without the postage on it.

"You going to open it?" Since he seems unconcerned by the lack of postage, I let it go.

"Hand me the letter opener."

He hands over the letter opener, and I open it with a clean slice. The heavy paper inside feels expensive. Far more fancy than the cheap, bulk paper we get by on, but then we're very mindful of our expenses. Unfolding the letter, I scan the contents, expecting another rejection, but my eyes pop.

"What's wrong?" Tom looks on with concern.

"A firm called Conte Investments wants to invest a million in MindScapeVR. I don't remember contacting them. Did You?" The name sounds vaguely familiar, but I can't seem to place it.

"Could've. They all kind of blend together."

Scott's completely out of the picture, as is Hawke. A sharp pain stabs at my chest when I think of Hawke. The only good thing that came after the fiasco on New Year's Eve is the IP rights are in fact mine.

Rather than being a royal dick, Scott allowed me to keep the name of the company and bowed out with more grace than I thought possible. He could've fought me on it, but I think he truly is remorseful. We parted amicably.

As for Hawke, it's been radio silence. No calls. No emails. No nothing. I don't know who Cherise is, but she was enough for him to do a complete 180 as far as we're concerned. I thought Cherise was his new fiancée, but that's Candace, similar name, but different person.

I try not to think about him. It's too painful. Fortunately, MindScapeVR keeps me plenty occupied. I've been putting in 12- and 14-hour days for over a month and a half, and will probably continue to do so.

Keeping the name MindScapeVR was a parting gift from Scott. It allows us to continue forward in our attempts to secure funding without a complete rebrand. Scott didn't have to give me that. He could've been an ass about it, but he did. And I'm thankful.

"Only four million more to go." Tom places Conte Investments into a very small pile of papers. We've scrounged other investors, one thousand here, five thousand there. But it's a drop in the bucket considering what our startup costs will be.

I hate not getting excited by the million dollars Conte Investments brings to the table. It's more than we had yesterday, but still not enough.

I take the next letter off the stack, and my eyes bulge when I read the contents. My entire arm trembles as I hand the letter to Tom.

"What's this?" He clutches it to his chest. "One-point-five million? Who's Calloway Inc.?"

The entire month of January has been nothing but non-stop rejections. Tom and I are at our wits' end and are beyond desperate.

"Two and a half million in investment capital in the same day's mail? What are the odds?" I grab the letter out of Tom's hand and read it again. Sure enough, Calloway Inc. wants to invest 1.5 million in our company.

Since Scott's departure, Tom's stepped up to help me with the business end of things. We're both engineers, and there's much about the business world that is way over our heads. I feel like we've been drinking from a firehose, trying to learn the ins and outs of the corporate world without drowning. Honestly, we're barely treading water. Soon, we'll hire a business manager. For now, we're doing the best we can.

Tom grabs the next letter off the stack and slides the opener through it. He pulls out a thick sheaf of papers, and his brows draw together. His eyes scan left to right as he speed reads to get to the important stuff.

"Holy shit." His eyes widen.

"What?"

"Four million." A smile brightens his entire expression. "Holy fuck, Q, we have six and a half million. Plus the five from Hayes Construction..." He drops the papers and jumps to his feet. Grabbing my hands, he pulls me from my seat to twirl me around the room in an excited whirl.

"You better not be shitting me." I grab at his arms.

"Look for yourself." The papers sprawl all over the floor.

"I will, what else did it say? That's a lot of paper."

"I don't know. I stopped reading when I got to the four million part."

I stoop down to grab the papers. The movement does something to trigger my nausea. I brace my hand on the table and cover my mouth with the other.

"Hey, this is weird." Tom ignores my distress and reaches across the desk. "None of these have postage on them. How'd they get in our mail?"

There's a soft knock on our door, which I ignore. I'm more than a little nauseous. I swallow, hoping that'll make things pass, but saliva pools in my mouth. My stomach clenches, and I stand, ready to make a run for the bathroom. When I straighten, my gaze lands on a set of golden eyes.

"Hawke?" That's all I get out before I grab a trashcan to empty the contents of my stomach. I retch and retch and retch. Hands gather my hair and draw it away from my face as I puke out the remnants of bad lox and bagels.

"Not exactly the reception I was expecting, Miss Hayes." Hawke's liquid-smooth voice rolls over me. It's like melted chocolate, drizzling ooey-gooey goodness everywhere. Fuck, if he isn't more attractive than I remember. Although, I've really tried to put him out of my mind.

"What are you doing here?" I wipe the spittle from my mouth and lean back. The last time I saw him, he gave me his back and told me to go. He did that right after promising me I was more than a fling. I think he got confused, because even flings are given more respect than he showed me.

"We need to talk."

"We don't need to…" I bend forward again, retching violently. No way can there be anything left in my stomach, but evidently, I'm wrong. A foul stench rises from the poor waste bin. It makes me want to throw up again.

"Can I get you some water?" Tom hovers behind me.

"Yes, please." I feel like shit. This is more than simple food poisoning. Actually, I've felt a little off for the past few days. I attribute it to stress. MindScapeVR is running out of time.

Hawke finger combs the hair back from my face and gathers it together at my nape. I shake my head violently, freeing myself from his touch. The last time he gripped my hair, he'd been buried balls deep inside my mouth as I gave him one of the best orgasms of his life.

Two hours later, he told me to leave.

"We have nothing to discuss." I gather my hair at the back of my neck and ride another wave of nausea. This time, it passes, relieving me from getting up close and comfortable with the poor trashcan.

"Maybe *we* don't, but I hope you'll give *me* a chance to explain."

I whip around to look at him, fixing the harshest glare I can manage, and give a sharp shake of my head. "You made things perfectly clear. I'm sorry, but there really is nothing to discuss."

"Not even five million?" He glances at the top of the table. "Or rather, six and a half million?"

"How do you…" Tom hands me a glass of water.

"Thank you." I take a sip and stumble to my feet, ignoring Hawke's attempts to help me stand. I jerk away because I don't know what'll happen when he touches me. I'm afraid I'll feel that *zing* of electricity shooting up my arm.

As far as my feelings go, they're twisted and confused. It's been eight weeks, and I miss Hawke more today than yesterday, and the day before that. Each day, rather than dulling the terrible ache, only increases the pain I feel with him gone. I miss him terribly.

When he forced me to leave, he ripped out a piece of my soul. I haven't been whole since. And now, he's back. Why?

"I gave you my word," he says with a sigh. "I'd get you the capital you need. I brought the letters earlier. You weren't here, so I put them in the mailbox. I tried to leave, but I couldn't. I needed to see you."

"I don't understand." He's speaking, but the words aren't connecting in my head.

"I spoke with my friends who offered to help. You know one of them. Remember Jack Conte? The doctor who took care of you?"

"I do?" I shake my head, too weary to make sense of what Hawke's saying. I can't even figure out why he's here. "I feel like I could use him about now."

"Are you okay?" The tenderness of his words isn't forced. He seems genuinely happy to see me, despite my current state, which I don't understand. There's none of that murderous fury or that soul-shattering defeat like when his mother mentioned *Cherise*.

"Just bad lox." I wobble on my feet and take another sip of the water Tom gave me. He hovers just out of reach, eyes wide as he looks at Hawke. Tom knows everything about Hawke. I speak about little else. Tom's been a good friend listening to my nonsense.

The acidic tang of vomit coats my mouth. "I'm going to the bathroom to brush my teeth." This sour taste is gross. Not to mention, I need a moment alone before I can face the heady intoxication Hawke's sudden, and unannounced, arrival brings.

THIRTY-SEVEN

Hawke

"How long has she been sick?" I turn to Quinn's lead engineer, demanding an answer.

He hesitates before answering. "She's fine. Just had bad lox this morning."

"You sure it's the lox?" I itch to go to her, but sense she needs a moment. Hell, I need a moment. Coming unannounced was a risk. I didn't know what kind of reception I'd receive.

The puking part is an unexpected twist and was not on the list of potential possibilities.

There's simply something about Quinn I can't escape. In the two months since I last saw her, she's all I can think about.

Two months. I can't believe it's been nearly two months. All day, every day, Quinn has been on my mind. During the day, I wonder what she's doing. At night the fantasies return, each one filthier than the last. My balls ache for her. My dick weeps for her. As for me, I simply ache to hold her in my arms.

I miss my girl.

Instead of Quinn, I'm saddled with Candace, a royal bitch who's getting worse by the day. Demanding and insufferable, she's determined to get into my bed. None of her little tricks does anything for me. Fondling my crotch has me lashing out. I left bruises on her wrist the last time she tried. She believes if she can get me hard, she'll cement her place by my side. It won't. I don't want her anywhere near me, but she clings to Mother's damn agreement.

When she tried using her toe to stimulate me during a charity dinner, I practically spit out my drink and left her there alone for the rest of the night. When she later slipped into my bed, naked, I stormed out of my penthouse in nothing but boxers.

I spent the first of many nights at Jack Conte's place. Turns out, Mother gave Candace the keys and codes to my penthouse.

I haven't had sex in two months. If it's not going to be with Quinn, I'm not interested.

For the few nights after Candace chased me out of my penthouse, I stayed with Jack. He's excited about MindScapeVR and what it can do for his medical practice. A phone call to Steve Calloway and we're excited by the entertainment possibilities. With Quinn's adaptive learning capability, there's no limit to what we can do in the virtual world. Steve's already thinking about a new resort venture, one catering to the gaming community. I'm right there with him. Between the three of us, there's more than enough to launch MindScapeVR into the future.

All I need now is to get Quinn on board.

First, I have to explain myself and hope I haven't completely ruined what we had.

All I'm waiting on is a phone call, which will tell me the hundreds of thousands I've sunk into finding Cherise are worth it. Jack's the one who hooked me up with Guardian Hostage Rescue Specialists. My needs are a little outside their typical wheelhouse, but we worked something out. Cherise isn't technically a hostage, but she is missing to me.

Mother turned over guardianship to a trust. I've been systematically building my legal case to tear all that down. But I can't do anything until I know Cherise is safe. If that means I have to kidnap her, or pay someone to do it for me, so be it. I consider Cherise to be a hostage in need of rescuing.

Any minute and I'll get the call. It's risky coming here before knowing Cherise is in safe hands, but I can't spend one more minute away from Quinn.

I knock softly on the bathroom door.

"Hey there. Do you think we could talk?" Fingers crossed she says yes.

"There's really nothing to talk about." She tries to hide a soft sob, but I feel it. I feel it all the way in my soul. I hurt her.

"I have a few things I need to tell you." I place my palm on the door and lean my forehead against it.

"You don't need to tell me anything."

The door opens, and I nearly fall into her. I brace myself on the door jamb as she stands inches from my face. Her light floral scent floods my senses. She overwhelms me, and all I can do is stare as my heart races.

She looks up at me with her gorgeous eyes and gives a long, slow blink. Red-rimmed, she's been crying. When I reach out to cup her cheek, she draws back.

"Please, don't."

"I just want to touch you."

"I don't want you to touch me."

"Why?"

"You know why." She takes in a deep breath and presses her lips together. "Do you mind?" She gestures for me to stand aside. I do, and she marches right past me.

Numbly, I follow her to the table stacked with papers and the three envelopes I placed in her mail earlier. Quinn gathers up the papers, the envelopes, and shoves them out at me as she sniffs away her tears. Glassy-eyed, new tears are building.

I hate that I'm the cause of any of her pain. When I don't take the stack of papers, she gives them a little flick.

"Take them."

"Why?"

"I don't want it." She closes the distance between us and smashes the envelopes and papers against my chest. Her eyes close, and two lonely tears track down her cheeks. I catch the papers as she steps away.

"I'm not taking these back, if that's what you're trying to do. That money is for MindScapeVR."

"I don't think we should be in business together."

Behind her, all the color drains out of Tom's face. I glance over her shoulder and get his attention. "Tom, do you mind?" I hold out the mess of papers to him. Tom takes the papers off my hands and shuffles them back into some semblance of order. "Do you mind if I have a word alone with Quinn?"

He looks to Quinn, who surprises the hell out of me by giving him the okay. She could kick me out. I deserve it. Hell knows I deserve it, but I've done the best I can.

As soon as Tom leaves, Quinn grabs at her stomach again.

"Do I need to take you to the hospital?" I'm concerned.

"Thanks, but it's nothing. It usually passes in just a little bit." She retreats to a gently worn sofa that's seen better days and lies down. Her arm immediately goes over her face. "What do you want? Why are you here?"

My phone vibrates with an incoming text,a text which brings a smile to my face. Nothing's stopping me now.

"I want to talk about Cherise, and why I had to tell you to go."

It's hard holding back my excitement. My sister is in the custody of Guardian HRS. She's safe and will remain that way. I'm officially her legal guardian. Celebration will happen later. Right now, I need to reclaim the other half of my soul.

Quinn peeks at me from under her arm. "You mean Candace?"

"Well yeah, I guess her too." There's no place for me to sit, seeing how Quinn takes up the entire couch. I yank one of the chairs away from the table and drag it over.

"Congratulations."

"Huh?"

"On your engagement?"

"About that." I blow out a frustrated breath and drag my hand down my face. "Look, do you mind moving your arm. It feels weird talking to you like this."

"I'm not really interested in talking to you at all." But she drops her arm. "You know, I thought what Scott did to me was the worst thing imaginable, but you really took the cake. What you did is far worse."

"I need you to let me explain, then I'll beg."

"Beg?"

"For forgiveness. A second chance. Hell, I'm ready to grovel. What I did when I told you to leave is unforgivable. I need to tell you why."

"There is no *why* that will make any difference, Hawke. You turned your back to me and told me to leave. I've never felt so used and abandoned. You did more than hurt me. You destroyed me."

"I know, and I'm sorry, but I had no choice. Please, let me explain. I didn't have a chance to do that at the time. You deserved an explanation right then. An explanation I didn't give because my mother…"

"Your mother is a piece of work. I've seen people with cold hearts, but she puts an iceberg to shame." Her brows pinch together. "I'm sorry. I shouldn't say that about your mother."

"No, you pretty much hit the nail on the head. My mother is a cold-hearted bitch." Her eyes widen. She shifts position on the couch, turning toward me. Her sparkling gaze warms me up from the inside out. "I've missed you." I can't help it. I reach for her, but Quinn shifts away.

"You don't have the right to miss me." She sniffles again.

"I want to show you something." I pull up my phone and pop open the picture from the text I just got.

"I'm not interested."

"Please, it's a picture of my twin sister, Cherise. She's the reason I…" I rub at my face, getting tongue-tied. I'm usually much more sure of myself. Quinn, however, makes me nervous. She's probably the only person on the planet with the ability to destroy me.

Like you destroyed her.

I lean back, defeated by Quinn's unwillingness to talk to me. Not that I blame her.

"Twin sister?" She peeks up at me.

"Yes, Cherise is my twin. It's a long story, but my cold-hearted mother is a good place to start. Can you please sit and let me explain why I did what I did?"

"I get dizzy when I sit. I'm listening."

"I hope you don't have anywhere to be. It's kind of a long story."

"I have time." She cracks an eye and looks up at me.

"I don't really know where to start."

"The beginning is usually the best place."

"That might take a while. I wish we had more time together before everything fell apart. I have a lot to explain."

"You'd better hurry up. I'll probably be puking again in about ten minutes."

"Well, the beginning—I guess that begins when I was five. You see, there was an accident…" I settle back in my chair and tell Quinn all the horrible details about the accident, which took Cherise from me. I relive all the years of mother doting on Cherise while punishing me. Through it all, Quinn remains silent. When I get to the part about Mother taking Cherise and hiding her from me, Quinn's breath hitches. She knows before I tell her and swings her legs around on the couch. Tears fall freely down her cheeks, and she lets them fall.

"How could someone be that cruel?"

"That's a question I've asked my entire life." I reach out, and this time she gives me her hand. I hold her hand with reverence, stunned and relieved. I scoot around to sit beside her but wind up shifting her onto my lap. "I've missed you so much."

"Why didn't you try to contact me?" Quinn lays her cheek against my chest and places her palm over the beating of my heart. "I thought you threw me away, and then when the engagement announcement came about Candace, I thought that was why."

"I can see how that may be confusing. Cherise is not Candace. I want you to meet my sister. She's amazing."

"It sounds like you love her very much."

"I love you very much."

"You what?"

"Yeah." I give a soft laugh. "That kind of slipped out before I had a chance to stop it, but I've known for a while now."

"So, do you mean it, or not?" She scoots off my lap. Her hands rub at her upper arms.

"Not that I expect you to believe me, but I love you very much. Each day without you in my life is a living death."

"Living death?" She laughs. "You need to work on your metaphors."

"Well, I'm kind of winging it here. I love you. Not having you around hurts, physically, emotionally, spiritually, and I don't really understand it. We only spent a few days together, but I see you in my life."

She twists around and folds her legs beneath her. It places space between us, but I'll take it. She's not kicking me out. "Tell me again why you had to tell me to leave."

Over the next hour, I tell her everything. From Mother's threats, the conditions of my father's will, to Cherise's love of orchids. Tom never returns. He's a smart guy. I'll have to tell him thanks later.

"It feels good." I draw her tight against my chest.

"What does?"

"Talking." I kiss her forehead. "We never really talked much. I feel like we skipped a lot of important steps." The urge to tell her my thoughts about our future overwhelms me, but I say nothing.

"I like it too." She places her hand on my arm. "I've missed you."

"Can you forgive me for putting you through hell? I know it doesn't matter why. What I did to you was wrong. I want to make it up to you, and I want you in my life. I meant what I said."

"Which part?"

"All of it, but especially the part where I love you." I draw her into my lap again and wrap my arms around her. "Please say you forgive me."

"I forgive you, but I'm not so sure it's going to be easy to forget. I feel really lost right now. My trust in men is really shot."

"Then I'll make it up to you, if you'll let me."

"I'd like that, but I think you're going to have a much harder time with my brothers." Her answer isn't exactly what I'm hoping for, but I'll take it.

"I'll find a way to convince them."

"Good luck." She snuggles against me and closes her eyes. "I miss this." A heavy sigh escapes her, and her body relaxes.

My work is cut out for me. Somehow, I need to convince Quinn I mean what I say. One idea comes to mind, but it's risky. I say nothing else and simply enjoy the simple act of holding the woman I love in my arms.

THIRTY-EIGHT

Quinn

THE SLOW, STEADY BEAT OF HAWKE'S HEART LULLS ME TO SLEEP. I'M not really sure when I fell asleep, or how long he held me while I did, except I wake to the press of his warm lips to my forehead.

"Quinn, I need you to get up."

"Huh?" I rub at sleepy eyes.

"Hey, sleepy head." The rich tones of his voice send shivers down my spine. His simple existence is enough to light all my senses on fire.

"How long was I out?"

"Long enough to make my legs go to sleep, and I kind of need to take a pi—um, use the restroom."

"Sorry." I slip off his lap and stretch while he massages his legs.

"I still feel like I'm dreaming." His husky laugh sends a tremor down my spine. Memories of his voice telling me to do certain, other things, brings a steady throb to other parts of my body. Our connection feels tenuous, with all the shit that's happened, but it's still there.

Unbreakable.

"Bathroom is the first door on the left." I glance outside and give a start. "What time is it?"

"Late enough for me to take you to dinner." He rubs the back of his neck. "That is, if you'll let me."

"I'd like that very much." I fold my knees to my chest. "Hawke?"

"Yeah?"

"When I said I forgive you, I mean it. The not forgetting part isn't meant to make things awkward. I don't want any weirdness between us. It's just that it's going to take time to process. I have a lot of anger I've been dealing with. I just need time to sort through it."

"I'll give you all the time you need. This isn't exactly the way I thought things would be between us." He gets up and heads for the restroom, which leaves me to consider what I want to happen next.

I don't want things to be awkward. I'd really like for things to go back to the way they were. The question in my head is how do I do that? He wants to take me to dinner, which is great, but we're still kind of in a weird place.

My mind thinks back to the last day we were together. The pain and heartbreak when he told me to leave hurts. That's not something I want to focus on. I'd rather rewind time to just before that shitstorm happened. He told me come New Year's I would be his.

I wasn't.

Do I want to be?

This is the most important question.

No, that's not true. The question is whether I believe him. Do I trust him?

Most definitely.

Which means—I have a decision to make. Knowing how we work best, I'm going to close my eyes and jump right into the deep end. But first, I lock the outer door to the office.

Knowing what I'm about to do makes me feel a little nauseous. Not sick to my stomach, but rather nervous as all fuck. The toilet flushes, and the water in the sink runs. If I'm really going to do this, it's now or never.

I move to the center of the room and wait. My stomach flutters like crazy as my nerves run wild. My heart is kind of in freeform panic. My hands shake, and I feel a little unsteady. The door opens, and I take in a deep breath. Then another.

Hawke pauses at the edge of the room.

"Quinn?" His brows draw together as he looks at me.

"Do you remember what you said to me in the elevator? Before everything went to shit?"

"I said a lot of things to you in the elevator."

"You said you couldn't promise a forever…"

"But I wanted to try." He runs his hands through his hair. "I remember that very much."

"Do you remember what I said?"

"You said a lot of things." The timbre of his voice changes, getting deeper and coarser by the second. He stays right where he is, yet I feel every bit of him lick my skin. "What thing in particular are you thinking about?"

"You said that I was yours."

"I remember that." His breath hitches, and those golden eyes of his simmer with lust. "Is this recap of our elevator fuck going somewhere, or is this just a way to punish me for pushing you away?"

"I'm not punishing you, but simply wondering if you meant it."

"Love, I meant every word. Things just got fucked up."

"Then let's un-fuck them."

"Un-fuck?" His smoldering gaze sweeps my body, and I'm well aware of the thin shirt I'm wearing.

"You told me that I was yours."

"I did."

"Then you told me you were taking what's yours."

"I did." He rubs the back of his neck again. "Where are you going with this?"

"Well, I'm yours, which means…"

"Quinn…" Raw and aroused, he growls my name.

"I want to go back to that elevator and reset everything from there."

"Reset?"

"Yes, ignore everything that came after. If I'm yours, then take me. Fast and hard, or slow and sweet, whatever way you need me. I don't want to suffer through an awkward dinner. If I'm yours, prove it. Take me."

"Fuck. You sure this is what you want?"

I pull my shirt over my head. Slide my pants over my hips and kick them off my feet. I strip for him, watching the pull of his breath grow more and more ragged. I give him a long hard stare as I remove my bra and slip off my panties.

He stares at me, the expression on his face growing more and more wild as the seconds tick past. Naked, I glide toward him, practically floating on air.

He won't initiate. Hawke is a man who takes. He's brutal when he fucks. But that's because he's a confident man who's used to taking what he wants. With me, he's cautious. Expressing his love shifted the balance of our relationship, putting power in my hands. He's on unsure footing after everything that happened. We need to shift the balance of power back to him. I know one sure way to make that happen.

I approach until I'm arm's length from him. His entire body shakes as he takes me in. His gaze sweeps my body while I close the distance, but now he focuses on my eyes. In that golden glow, I know I'm everything to him. I bite my lower lip and listen to the hitching of his breath.

"I'm yours. Whatever you want. However you need it. Take it. You don't have to worry about being gentle, or going slow. Forget everything and take me like you need to. I'm yours to use as you need."

"Quinn…" Raspy and raw, his voice shakes. "Fuck, but that's... You don't have to…"

I kneel before him and look up as he stares down at me. I know exactly what's going through his head. There's nothing subtle about me kneeling before him. I'm not offering to give him a blowjob. I'm sending a message and surrendering control. I jumped into the deep end. Now, it's time to see if he'll take the leap and join me.

"Your wish is my command." A smile ghosts across my face while an agonized moan rumbles out of his chest.

"Goddamn, but you're fucking gorgeous." His attention shifts to the door. "Any chance anyone will walk in on us?"

"No."

"You sure about this?" He reaches for his belt, unbuckling it before I can answer.

"Very."

"It's been two months, luv. I probably won't last long." His husky voice grows deeper, hoarser, harsher. "And I won't be gentle."

"I like it when you're rough." I can't help it, but I smirk and bat my lashes, teasing him.

"Girls with smart mouths need to be very careful, or they'll find themselves over my knee."

"I'll just have to be very careful what I say." I glance at the bulge in his pants. "Or, hope you find another use for my smart mouth so I don't get in trouble."

"Open that mouth." He unzips his fly and pulls out his cock. He fists the base while looking down at me with his smoldering gaze. "I love you."

"I know."

"We could just go to dinner." He's testing my resolve. "We could talk."

"I'd rather you feed me your dick. Food is highly overrated."

"Take me in." He presses the tip of his cock against my lips. "Swallow me whole."

He fills my mouth and shoves all the way in. Before I gag, he slides back out. His eyes close, and deep moans spill from his mouth. He rocks his hips forward and back as I suck and lick and take him in. As his desire builds, his control slips.

"Fuck, that feels good."

I'm obsessed with him, with watching him take his pleasure. This feels good. It feels more like us, and what we should be. As his cock slides in and out of my mouth, I sift through all the anger and hurt feelings over the past two months. I know he never meant to hurt me, and I truly forgive him.

He reaches down and threads his fingers in my hair. I can tell he's been holding back, still uncertain about what's happening. Most likely, he thought he'd have to beg and grovel a bit more for my forgiveness; sex would come later.

Frankly, I don't want to wade through all those messy emotions.

His grip tightens on my hair. A sharp tug steals my breath. The slow, steady rhythmic glide of his hips turns fevered and urgent. I feel the moment he comes unglued and releases his restraint. His hips jerk and buck as he comes with a low, throaty growl and several powerful thrusts. Yeah, there's nothing slow or gentle about my Hawke.

When he pulls out, he grips my chin and forces me to look up at him.

"Two months is far too long. I've missed that." He toes off his shoes and kicks them aside. "My turn." With a growl, he pushes me backward and stands over me as he tugs on his tie and strips out of his white Oxford shirt. He kicks off his pants and strips out of his underwear.

A quick scan of the office brings an evil gleam to his eyes. "I wonder what Tom will think when he finds out I've fucked you on every surface."

"I think Tom will want another office."

"I agree. And we'll work on that tomorrow. For now, I want to hear you scream. Oh, and Quinn?"

"Yes?" I lean back on my elbows and enjoy every delicious inch of his chiseled body.

"Tonight, I'm going to fuck your brains out. Tomorrow, we'll see about getting MindScapeVR going. Tomorrow night, we're going to see your brothers."

"My brothers?"

"Yeah, I need to get their permission."

"You don't really need their permission for this."

His low, rumbly laugh is like drizzling liquid chocolate all over my body. I ache for him.

"No, but I do if I'm to ask you to marry me."

"Um, what?"

He kneels on the floor, and his gaze cuts to my legs. More specifically to what's between them.

"First things first. You got to suck my dick. I'm going to feast on your pussy. Then, we'll order in. After that, I'm going to fuck you against that wall. On that sofa." He grins. "I'm going to take you from behind while I bend you over that desk. And I'm going to watch your tits bounce as you climb on top of me and go for a ride."

"Can we talk about the marriage thing?"

"Nope." He gives a sharp shake of his head. "Can't do that until after I speak with your brothers. We have some shit to sort out, seeing how I broke your heart, and they probably want to chop off my balls. I want to make sure we're all in agreement about you belonging to me."

"You didn't break my heart, just kind of squeezed it a little too hard."

He grabs my ankles and forces my legs apart. "That'll never happen again. I swear on my life. And, to make sure you vouch for me..." A look of carnal hunger fills his face as he leans down and shows me exactly why I'll vouch for him. He barely touches me before my entire body detonates.

After I recover, Hawke holds me. Our naked bodies press against each other as we stare deeply into each other's eyes. It's an intimate moment, but not because of the sex.

"I don't think you should talk to my brothers until after we're married."

"Come again?"

"They won't be as forgiving as me. You probably won't survive the encounter. I say we tell them after."

"After?" He sweeps the hair off my forehead. "Is that your way of saying yes?"

"I suppose."

"You suppose? Dammit, woman, I need a solid yes from you."

I laugh and reach between us. My fingers wrap around his dick as I give a long, firm stroke.

"Most definitely, yes."

He shifts until he's on top of me; his dick is more than recovered from my oral skills. The last waves of my orgasm still echo within me. I'm still tingly and quivering. He moves into position, placing the flare of his cock at my entrance.

"Miss Quinn Hayes…"

"Yes?"

"Will you marry me?"

"Most definitely, yes." I giggle as Hawke sinks inside of me, but soon I'm moaning as desire rushes through me.

He takes a moment to stare deep into my eyes.

"I absolutely adore you, and love you more than I ever thought possible. Among the other vows I'll soon make to you, there's this one. I'll never hurt you again. My mother will never get between us again. I hope I'm not moving too fast, but I don't want to wait. You told me to take what I want, and I want you."

I slap at his arm and laugh. "If you ever speak about your mother when you're buried balls deep inside of me again, I will send my brothers after you. Now please, your fiancée needs you to move."

"Slow and gentle? Or a little bit rough?"

"Oh, Hawke, you know I like it rough, and I absolutely love when you take control."

"Fucking music to my ears."

THIRTY-NINE

Hawke

I fulfill every promise to Quinn. After I take her on the floor, we order in, eat, and talk about Mother, her ultimatum, Cherise, and my plans for my sister. I tell her about Jack and Steve's thoughts about MindScapeVR. They want a meeting to toss around ideas as to what would be feasible and the timeframe she'll need. Her mouth drops as I explain.

"I love when I leave you speechless, but watching you gape at me gets me to thinking about a better way to utilize that luscious mouth of yours." I can't help but tease her.

"I'm sorry, but you're kind of blowing my mind right now. I have this little idea to help the aging with memory loss and declines in mental functioning, and you've just gone and blown the lid on that."

"I like to think big. Speaking of big…" I glance down at my crotch.

"Big? That's… It's… Wow, it's mind-blowing." She gives a little snicker. "And I know exactly where that comment just sent your dirty mind."

"Guilty as charged, but in my defense, you're irresistible and I like to…"

"I know exactly what you like." She makes a show of licking her fingers, demonstrating she comprehends the full extent of the decadent thoughts swirling in my head.

The night becomes a blur of talking and fucking. It's like there's a sudden rush to get to know each other on a deeper, personal level, but we still give in to our carnal needs. I simply can't get enough of my girl.

After I take her against the wall and bend her over the desk, we lie on the couch holding each other, talking softly about the future—*our* future. I thread my fingers with hers, interlocking our digits.

"What kind of ring do you want on this finger?" Of the many things I don't know about Quinn are simple things like what kind of jewelry she prefers. Come to think of it, I've never seen her wear any jewelry.

"I'm a simple girl. Nothing flashy." She clutches my hand and turns it around to kiss the backs of my knuckles.

"Hmm. I like the way you suck on my knuckles."

"I bet you do. Should I move to the floor and suck something else?"

I can't help but laugh. "As much as that excites me, I need more time to recover. I'm happy to talk. There's so much I want to know about you."

"Like?" She leans forward and presses her lips to the hollow of my throat. It's a soft, gentle kiss. One which sends shockwaves rippling through my body.

"Favorite color?" I shift in my seat trying to get comfortable as blood rushes to my crotch.

"Green."

"Like your eyes. Your eyes are mesmerizing." I can't get enough of those emerald depths.

"Yours are tawny gold. They're striking and the first thing I noticed about you."

"I bet we make beautiful babies." I tap the tip of her nose.

"You want kids?"

"Does that surprise you? I guess we should talk about that. If

I'm building a life with you, I want everything that comes with it. Home. Family. Grandkids."

"Grandkids? We're skipping ahead to grandkids?"

"Well, we need to have kids first, obviously, but I want to grow old with you. As for children, I think we need more baby-making practice. I want to make sure I do it right." My dick is getting close to recovering from all the fucking.

"Good thing we have all night." Her smile is soft and serene. "Practice sounds fun."

"So…" I stare deeply into her eyes. "Does this mean we get to ditch the condoms?"

After Mother's decree about an heir, the idea of children left me unenthused, but having kids with Quinn is different. It excites me. It's been a long time since I've looked forward to anything. With Quinn by my side, the idea of a couple of kids playing on our laps sounds like heaven.

"Not that I'm in a rush, but I'm not against it." I don't want her thinking I want to saddle her with kids right as MindScapeVR is getting ready for its global debut.

In fact, I'm at peace with the idea of walking away from Sterling Enterprises. Any children we have will be the product of our love, not Mother's insane ultimatum.

I'm looking forward to my life with Quinn. I've got Euphoria to keep me occupied, and hopefully, Quinn will be on board with me taking over as CEO of MindScapeVR. It's her baby, but she needs someone with solid business acumen. I bring that to the table. Together, we are going to change the world.

"About that ring…"

"You really want to marry me?" She nibbles on her lower lip, and I suppress a groan. That's my kryptonite. I don't think she knows how fucking sexy she is to me when she does that. It shows her vulnerability, her tenderness, and her willingness to open her heart to me.

"I want to marry you right now and scream it from the rooftops. Hell yes! I hope you're not getting cold feet?"

"No." She twists in my arms until we face each other. Her hand lifts to cup my face, and she drags her hand over the stubble of my beard. "No cold feet here. Just kind of in a daze. Like I'm going to wake up and this will have all been a dream."

"I know one way to fix that."

"How?"

"Marry me tonight."

"Tonight?"

"Yes, tonight."

"I think there's a waiting period, not to mention applying for a wedding license. You don't just get married."

"You do in Vegas." I yank her against me. "Let's fly to Vegas." I pause, remembering her fear of flying.

"You're serious." She cocks her head and gives me a long, hard stare.

"Yeah, but then I remembered you're not much of a flier."

"Flying coffins." She nods with vigor. "But I survived two flights. Maybe I can survive one more?"

"Is that a yes? Because if it is, I'm not kidding. Marry me tonight, or in the morning. Hell, just marry me."

"What about your mother and sister? Or my parents and my brothers?"

"We can always have a second wedding. And if you marry me, your brothers will be less likely to kill their brother-in-law. Really, when you think about it, getting married now makes the most sense."

"The most sense?"

"Yeah, since my life is on the line. You'd literally be saving my life."

"Your life." Her hand moves from my face to my chest where she draws tiny circles. Each sweep of her finger sends shivers down my spine. "Hmm, so you're saying that your life is in my hands." A serene smile curves the corner of her lips. "You're really serious about getting married tonight?"

"Well, as soon as we can book a flight and get to Vegas. No alcohol and no cold medicines, though. I need a conscious bride."

"Hmm…" Her finger dips down to my navel, and my cock takes

notice. The hungry fucker is ready for more action. "I've got an idea."

"I'm all ears." She scoots off the couch and kneels on the floor. An evil grin fills her face as she reaches for my cock.

"What are you doing?"

"If you manage to book a flight to Vegas before I make you come, then we'll get married tonight. But, if I get you to come before booking the flight, you have to face my brothers and ask for their blessing first."

"What about your father?" Her nails stroke my cock and my hips buck. "Fuuuck, that feels so good."

"Daddy isn't the one you have to convince." She wraps her fingers around my shaft, and blood surges to my dick. My hips jerk again. There's a good chance I won't win this contest.

"Where's my phone?" I've fucked her four times already. You'd think I'd be tired; there are limits to my stamina, even when it involves Quinn's fantastic mouth. Although, my dick is taking notice and growing harder by the minute.

"Here." She hands me my phone. Before I can turn it on, she coaxes my dick to life. A surge of pleasure sweeps through me as she licks along my shaft.

I suppress a groan as I desperately search for flights to Vegas.

FORTY

Hawke

In less than twelve hours, I slide a ring over Quinn's finger. It's a simple gold band with a channel of small diamonds. We'll add to it later, if that's what she wants. Honestly, I'll give Quinn anything her heart desires. Right now, that's our first kiss as a married couple.

She's a little green, fighting nausea as she recovers from the flight. No alcohol and no cold medicines made it hard on her, but she was a trooper. She held my hand, or rather squeezed it, from takeoff all the way through landing.

We walk out of the cheesy Las Vegas wedding chapel holding hands. I carry her over the threshold of the penthouse suite, and we don't leave for two full days.

While Quinn gets dressed, I catch up on my texts and emails. Angry texts from Candace Yarbrough flood my phone, demanding to know where I am, what I'm doing, and who I'm with.

Sometime soon, I expect news of my marriage to Quinn to hit the press. For now, Quinn and I fly under the radar. The outside world ceases to exist as we devour each other until exhaustion pulls us into bed for sleep rather than sex.

There are threatening messages from Mother, a woman who's

never left a text message in her life, demanding to know what I've done with Cherise. My legal team took care of that. The day Guardian HRS took Cherise, and sequestered her, was the day the courts turned over guardianship of my sister to me. I no longer need to worry about Cherise's well-being.

I plan on keeping her whereabouts to myself until Mother and I share a final conversation. I know her health is failing as the cancer progresses. While she works to ruin me, I do what I must to protect my sister

Quinn shares her dreams with me about MindScapeVR and her hopes for its ability to help those with dementia and Alzheimer's retain their mental functioning for as long as possible. She doesn't say it, but she's hopeful the adaptive learning heuristics not only slow the degradative changes but stop them altogether.

Jack, Steve, and I have brainstormed ideas as to how MindScapeVR could be applied in multiple industries. Quinn's idea really can be a singularity event, like the invention of electricity, the car, and even the internet, the world will never be the same. I respond to their email and send it off.

"Hey, hun," I call out to her. "You feeling any better?"

"Yeah, I'm better now." She comes out of the bathroom and gives a weak smile. I'm sitting on the couch with my phone in hand, figuring out our trip back to Georgia. No way am I putting her on a plane again. "What are you doing?" She crawls into my lap, straddling my legs. I show her the phone.

"Just planning our road trip back." I show her the road trip planning app I'm using.

"Road trip?"

"Yeah, I figure we'll drive back instead of fly. I know it makes you queasy." The relief showing on her face tells me I made the right decision. "Please tell me you don't get car sick?"

"I don't."

"Then it's settled."

We're packed and on our way to Georgia in less than two hours. I have four angry brothers-in-law to placate.

There are two things I need to do before relocating to

California, where I'll begin my life with Quinn. First, there's the issue of her brothers. Then there's a difficult meeting with my mother that needs to occur.

Mother deserves to know Cherise is safe. That I'll provide for my sister and make sure she lives a long and fulfilling life. And of course, Mother is dying. She may be cold-hearted, but I'm not.

I want one last chance to fix things between us. I need to know I did everything possible to make her last days as comfortable as possible. I also want her to know I love her because everyone deserves to be loved.

Quinn taught me something about forgiveness. She certainly forgave me easily enough for the pain and heartbreak I gave her. It's one of the million things I love about my bride.

My bride.

I love those words more than life itself. I take it back. I love Quinn more than life itself. With her by my side, nothing will stand in our way. Separately, we're pretty amazing people.

Together, we're unstoppable, and we're going to change the world.

FORTY-ONE

Quinn

I LEAN ON THE KITCHEN COUNTER WHILE MOTHER ROLLS OUT THE dough for biscuits. Hawke and Daddy talk in the study. The news of our elopement goes over better than I expected, like *way* better. There are hugs instead of shouts.

Mother isn't surprised. Daddy isn't either, but he's grilling Hawke about his intentions while I've been politely excused from the conversation. It's killing me not being in there, but if there's one thing about Hawke, he can take care of himself.

"Your brothers will be here soon." Mother dusts the dough with flour. "Are you ready to face them? You're looking a little less green than earlier." She never buys anything ready-made, insisting on baking from scratch.

"Thanks. I feel better now. I think it's just nerves." I rub my hands on my jeans and glance in the direction of the study. "Have you had a chance to talk them down?" Them, meaning the brothers.

"Well, your father went to Gideon's last night and took his shotgun. Of course, Gideon wanted to come over and give your new husband a piece of his mind, but Hawke should be relatively safe. Your father seems to like him well enough, and he's incredibly handsome." Mother gives a wink while I blush.

"And what about you? Are you mad we eloped?"

"I'm still getting used to the idea, but if he makes you happy, I couldn't be happier."

Considering how our relationship crashed and burned on New Year's Eve, plus Hawke's subsequent engagement announcement, we spent a good deal of last night explaining to my parents what happened, why it happened, and how we managed to run off to Vegas to get hitched.

"He makes me very happy."

"Well then, that's all a mother can hope for. If you're happy, I'm happy."

"You just said that."

"Because it's true." She gives me a long look, sweeping me in from the top of my head to the tip of my toes. "I see it in you. You glow when you look at him, and sweetie?"

"Yes?"

"The way that man looks at you is positively sinful."

"Mother!"

"Oh come on, you're a married woman. We don't have to tiptoe around sex."

"Thank you? But we don't have to talk about it either." I'd be far more comfortable having my parents think I'm a virgin than discuss my sex life.

"No need to be shy about sex, honey, especially with a man like that. You picked a looker."

Time to switch topics.

"Um, I know you're probably upset, but we're going to have a real ceremony in six months."

She gives me an odd look as she dusts the flour off her hands. Mother goes to the sink and washes her hands. "You may want to rethink that."

"Why? Don't you want to see me walk down the aisle?"

"Of course I do, but…" Her voice trails off as she heads to the kitchen desk and rummages around inside her purse. She pulls out a small, brown paper bag.

"But what?"

"You might want to take this first, before announcing any dates about a wedding." She holds out the bag.

"What's that?"

"Honey, how long have you been feeling sick?"

"It's just nerves. My brothers are about to descend on this house with pitchforks and torches. I'm more than a little worried for Hawke's safety."

"You don't need to worry about that man, honey. It's clear in the way he looks at you that he's completely in love. Your brothers will know the instant they see the two of you together. If they don't, Hawke looks like he knows how to take care of himself. But I don't think that's why you're feeling nauseous. You might want to open that." A weird, feeling comes over me as I open the top of the crumpled bag. "Have you noticed anything else?"

"What do you mean?" I glance up, delaying opening the bag.

"Maybe an increased sensitivity of your breasts when you and Hawke…"

"Mother!" The last thing I want to talk to my mother about is Hawke and I having sex.

"Open the bag, hun."

I unroll the top and peek inside. My eyes widen in shock.

"A pregnancy test?"

"Shh." Mother makes a shushing gesture and glances over her shoulder.

"You think I'm pregnant?" I lower my voice to a whisper.

"As a woman who's been pregnant five times, I have a sense about these things. You have morning sickness, and either you've switched to wearing push up bras, or your cleavage is more pronounced for another reason." My gaze keeps bouncing between the bag and my mother. "What about your period? Are you late?"

"I've been under a good deal of stress. I haven't had a regular period since before Christmas."

"Before Christmas?" Her smile widens. "Oh honey, take the test. It takes just a couple of minutes…" She comes at me and spins me around. With a little encouragement, she pushes me toward the guest bathroom. "Go on. If you are, we need to make sure to get you on vitamins and make an appointment."

"Why are you so excited?" I spin around, confused. We're a southern family with traditional values, yet she's saying nothing about whether I may or may not be pregnant? And if I work through the timing, I may be much further along than… Well, I'm not going to think about that. "Mother, we didn't get married because I'm pregnant."

"Oh, I know, sweetie. The expression on your face is clear as day. Call it mother's intuition."

"Are you disappointed?"

"Why would I be disappointed?"

"Baby before marriage?"

"Oh, please, I'm much more progressive than that. Never thought for a moment you weren't sexually active. Although, protection is there for a reason."

"We used protection. Hawke is beyond responsible."

"Well, the only foolproof contraception is abstinence, and since we know…"

"I'm done talking about having sex with my boyfriend with my mother."

"Well, he's your husband now."

"Argh!"

"Besides, you got married, not because you got pregnant, but because the two of you are deeply in love. That's all I can ask for my daughter."

"What's that?"

"To be truly, head-over-heels in love with the man you marry. Now hurry up." She glances over her shoulder. "I want to know if I have a grandbaby on the way."

"Shouldn't I tell Hawke first?"

"Well, of course, you could, but you did deny me my only daughter's wedding." Her eyes get misty with tears. Happy tears. "Give me this."

"You're going to guilt me into telling you first, aren't you?"

"Grandmother's prerogative. Now—go." She shoves me out of her kitchen.

My hands shake while I unwrap the package and read all the directions.

And I do read them.

All the directions.

I pour over the false positive results, false negative results, basically anything about the pregnancy test that could invalidate it. I rub my breasts, noticing they are more sensitive than normal. I thought Hawke and I were just having really good sex. Not that I'm going to tell my mother that.

I can't delay any longer and pull the cap off the test. It's supposed to take three full minutes to develop, but I watch the little mark on the test strip turn from a dash to a very prominent plus sign in less than a minute.

Well fuck.

I stare and stare, until there's a knock on the door.

"Luv, are you okay? Feeling sick again?" Hawke's deep voice is a soothing caress against my suddenly jangled nerves.

Holy shit. I'm pregnant.

"Um, I'm good." I flush the toilet and wash my hands. I guess Hawke will be finding out first, after all, but when I exit the bathroom, Hawke's concerned expression takes me in. Over his shoulder, my mother practically bounces up and down. Her eyes are wide, and her expression full of the most important question of all.

"You're making me worried, luv." He takes me into his arms and pulls me to his chest.

My arms wrap around him. My hand grips the pregnancy test.

Then I laugh. I laugh hard. Filled with overwhelming happiness, and more than a touch of fear, I wave to my mother. When she closes the distance, I pull back and lift on my toes to give Hawke a chaste kiss.

"I have something to tell you."

Mother gives an excited screech as she pulls the test out of my hands. She looks at the big blue plus sign and practically faints.

Daddy comes up behind her, catching her as she stumbles and begins hyperventilating.

"Tell me what?" Hawke releases me, looking on with concern over my mother's near faint.

My father takes one look at the little white stick Mother holds and his eyes practically bug out of his head. My parents are overwhelmingly happy, which fills me with joy.

Hawke, however, remains confused. He cocks his head and jabs his thumb over his shoulder at my parents.

"What's up with them?"

"They just found out they're going to be grandparents." I beam with joy.

It takes a moment. Half a breath as my words slowly sink in. The expression on his face goes from concern, to shock, to absolute elation in the span of a heartbeat.

"I'm going to be a dad?" More confusion fills his face.

"We're going to be parents."

Hawke sweeps me off my feet and spins me in a circle as his lips crash down on mine. I don't care one bit that my parents are only a few feet away. I sink into the heat of Hawke's kiss as it turns from chaste to something much more carnal.

"If you'll excuse us, Mr. and Mrs. Hayes, but I need a moment alone with my wife." Hawke switches his hold, cradling me in his arms as he unashamedly takes me to the guest room. The moment the door closes, the front door bangs open, and the boisterous sounds of my brothers fill the house.

"My brothers are here." I'm more nervous now than before.

"Then I guess we'd better lock the door." Hawke spins around, but with me in his arms, his hands are full, and he can't lock the door.

"Hawke, we can't. My brothers…"

"Will have to wait. I need to be inside of you. We'll deal with them later."

"But—we're in my parent's house."

"And they now have irrefutable proof that I've fucked their daughter." His low growl sends shivers down my spine. "You'd better lock that door, or your brothers are going to walk in while I'm buried balls deep inside of you."

"You're incorrigible."

"And you're…" He leans his forehead against mine. "Shit, Quinn, you're everything I could've ever hoped for. You've given me so much."

My brothers' voices move to the kitchen where Mother and Daddy tell them to calm down.

"I think if we don't go out there right now, my brothers will be knocking down this door. I promise to make it up to you."

"You promise?" He puts me down with a sigh.

"I promise." I cup his cheek and lift up on tiptoe. "Anything you want. Your wish is my command."

"Oh, you're going to regret saying that, because I want some very naughty things." His low, throaty laughter makes me weak in the knees. Hawke Sterling is my kryptonite.

I take his hand in mine and open the door. With a deep breath, I take my husband, and the father of our baby, to face his four, overly protective brothers-in-law.

I'd take bets on who will come out on top, but I already know who that'll be.

Hawke Sterling is a man who takes what he wants, and he wants to spend the rest of his life with me. He's not letting anyone get in his way.

I lead my husband into the kitchen and settle in to watch what happens next. Mother wraps her arm around me as Hawke faces off against my four very irate brothers. He does it with a shit-eating grin as he holds his arms out wide.

"I'm going to be a daddy."

All four of my brothers' mouths gape. Anger turns to shock. Shock turns to joy.

"Welcome to the family." Gideon reaches out to shake Hawke's hand.

I tense, but there's no reason to worry. The shake turns into a manly hug as Gideon pulls Hawke in close and slaps him on the back. Brett and Steven shake Hawke's hand. They do the chest bump, back slap thing.

Ian shouts, "I'm going to be an uncle!"

Gideon comes to me. "You happy?"

"I couldn't be more happy than I am right now."

When I look around the kitchen all I see is love. Mother and Daddy hold each other tight. My brothers tease Hawke about becoming a father. Any hostility evaporated with the happy news of a baby on the way.

Gideon wraps his arm around me and holds me tight. I'm surrounded by love. But when Hawke comes to me, I realize I've found something far more valuable.

Hawke completes me.

He leans down and whispers in my ear. "Don't forget—anything I want." His low, lusty growl brings a flutter to my belly and a shiver shooting down my spine.

"Your wish is my command." I place my hand on his chest, splaying my fingers out wide. From the molten glow of his golden eyes, I know he's got something wicked and devious in mind.

***

If you enjoyed reading about Hawke and Quinn, you'll also enjoy reading Richard and Rowan's story.

Check it out!
Get your copy of Richard: Billionaire Boys Club!

Would you give up a year of your life? What if the price was right? What if he's a prince?

When Prince Richard's latest sexual faux pas results in another royal scandal, it's something the Crown will no longer tolerate. Fortunately, Richard stumbles across a company called Infidelity, which provides their exclusive clientele discretion and ironclad nondisclosure agreements. Powerful men take what they want, or buy it outright, and it looks like Prince Richard might have found the perfect solution to exploring his darker cravings. While paying for an intimate companion isn't his style, it makes sense. What better way to ensure his sex life will become front-page news?

Turns out companionship is cheap, but happiness?

At the end of his year-long agreement, will he be left with the tattered remains of what could have been?

Not if he has any say, but with the pressure of the Crown, privilege becomes a burden, and he may have no choice but to walk away.

GRAB YOUR COPY OF THIS STEAMY, MODERN-DAY FAIRYTALE romance. Will Prince Richard be able to keep his modern-day Cinderella? Or will he lose it all? Click now to find out!

H.R.H. Richard

ELLZ BELLZ

ELLIE'S FACEBOOK READER GROUP

If you are interested in joining the **ELLZ BELLZ**, Ellie's Facebook reader group, we'd love to have you.

Join Ellie's **ELLZ BELLZ**.
The **ELLZ BELLZ** Facebook Reader Group

Sign up for Ellie's Newsletter.
Elliemasters.com/newslettersignup

Also by Ellie Masters

The LIGHTER SIDE

Ellie Masters is the lighter side of the Jet & Ellie Masters writing duo! You will find Contemporary Romance, Military Romance, Romantic Suspense, Billionaire Romance, and Rock Star Romance in Ellie's Works.

YOU CAN FIND ELLIE'S BOOKS HERE:

ELLIEMASTERS.COM/BOOKS

Military Romance

Guardian Hostage Rescue Specialists

Rescuing Melissa

(Get a FREE copy of Rescuing Melissa

when you join Ellie's Newsletter)

Alpha Team

Rescuing Zoe

Rescuing Moira

Rescuing Eve

Rescuing Lily

Rescuing Jinx

Rescuing Maria

Bravo Team

Rescuing Angie

Rescuing Isabelle

Rescuing Carmen

Rescuing Rosalie

Rescuing Kaye

Cara's Protector

Rescuing Barbi

Military Romance

Guardian Personal Protection Specialists

Sybil's Protector

Lyra's Protector

The One I Want Series

(Small Town, Military Heroes)

By Jet & Ellie Masters

EACH BOOK IN THIS SERIES CAN BE READ AS A STANDALONE AND IS ABOUT A DIFFERENT COUPLE WITH AN HEA.

Saving Abby

Saving Ariel

Saving Brie

Saving Cate

Saving Dani

Saving Jen

Rockstar Romance

The Angel Fire Rock Romance Series

EACH BOOK IN THIS SERIES CAN BE READ AS A STANDALONE AND IS ABOUT A DIFFERENT COUPLE WITH AN HEA. IT IS RECOMMENDED THEY ARE READ IN ORDER.

Ashes to New (prequel)

Heart's Insanity (book 1)

Heart's Desire (book 2)

Heart's Collide (book 3)

Hearts Divided (book 4)

Hearts Entwined (book5)

Forest's FALL (book 6)

Hearts The Last Beat (book7)

Contemporary Romance

Firestorm

(Kristy Bromberg's Everyday Heroes World)

Billionaire Romance

Billionaire Boys Club

Hawke

Richard

Brody

Contemporary Romance

Cocky Captain

(Vi Keeland & Penelope Ward's Cocky Hero World)

Romantic Suspense

EACH BOOK IS A STANDALONE NOVEL.

The Starling

~AND~

Science Fiction

Ellie Masters writing as L.A. Warren

Vendel Rising: a Science Fiction Serialized Novel

About the Author

ELLIE MASTERS is a multi-genre and Amazon Top 100 best-selling author, writing the stories she loves to read. These are dark erotic tales. Or maybe, sweet contemporary stories. How about a romantic thriller to whet your appetite? Ellie writes it all. Want to read passionate poems and sensual secrets? She does that, too. Dip into the eclectic mind of Ellie Masters, spend time exploring the sensual realm where she breathes life into her characters and brings them from her mind to the page and into the heart of her readers every day.

Ellie Masters has been exploring the worlds of romance, dark erotica, science fiction, and fantasy by writing the stories she wants to read. When not writing, Ellie can be found outside, where her passion for all things outdoor reigns supreme: off-roading, riding ATVs, scuba diving, hiking, and breathing fresh air are top on her list.

She has lived all over the United States—east, west, north, south and central—but grew up under the Hawaiian sun. She's also been privileged to have lived overseas, experiencing other cultures and making lifelong friends. Now, Ellie is proud to call herself a Southern transplant, learning to say y'all and "bless her heart" with the best of them. She lives with her beloved husband, two children who refuse to flee the nest, and four fur-babies; three cats who rule the household, and a dog who wants nothing other than for the cats to be his best friends. The cats have a different opinion regarding this matter.

Ellie's favorite way to spend an evening is curled up on a couch, laptop in place, watching a fire, drinking a good wine, and bringing forth all the characters from her mind to the page and hopefully into the hearts of her readers.

FOR MORE INFORMATION
elliemasters.com

facebook.com/elliemastersromance
twitter.com/Ellie__Masters
instagram.com/ellie_masters
bookbub.com/authors/ellie-masters
goodreads.com/Ellie_Masters

Connect with Ellie Masters

Website:
elliemasters.com

Facebook:
elliemasters.com/Facebook
Goodreads:
elliemasters.com/Goodreads
Instagram:
elliemasters.com/Instagram

Final Thoughts

I hope you enjoyed this book as much as I enjoyed writing it. If you enjoyed reading this story, please consider leaving a review on Amazon and Goodreads, and please let other people know. A sentence is all it takes. Friend recommendations are the strongest catalyst for readers' purchase decisions! And I'd love to be able to continue bringing the characters and stories from My-Mind-to-the-Page.

Second, call or e-mail a friend and tell them about this book. If you really want them to read it, gift it to them. If you prefer digital friends, please use the "Recommend" feature of Goodreads to spread the word.

Or visit my blog https://elliemasters.com, where you can find out more about my writing process and personal life.

Come visit The EDGE: Dark Discussions where we'll have a chance to talk about my works, their creation, and maybe what the future has in store for my writing.

Facebook Reader Group: Ellz Bellz

Thank you so much for your support!

Love,

Ellie

Dedication

This book is dedicated to you, my reader. Thank you for spending a few hours of your time with me. I wouldn't be able to write without you to cheer me on. Your wonderful words, your support, and your willingness to join me on this journey is a gift beyond measure.

Whether this is the first book of mine you've read, or if you've been with me since the very beginning, thank you for believing in me as I bring these characters 'from my mind to the page and into your hearts.'

Love,
Ellie

THE END